W9-BMC-886

A Heart So Fierce and Broken

Also by Brigid Kemmerer
Letters to the Lost
More Than We Can Tell
Call It What You Want

A Curse So Dark and Lonely

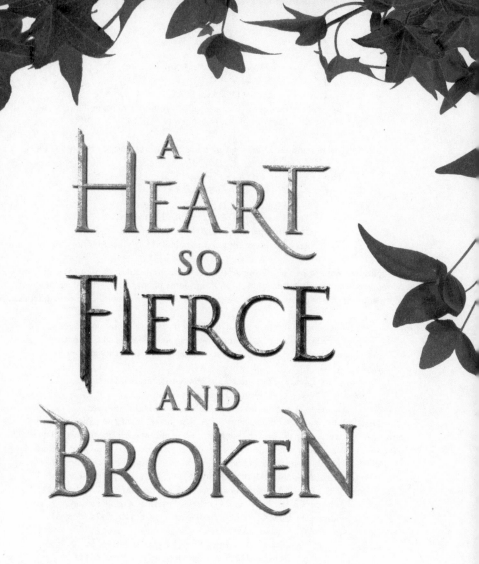

A HEART SO FIERCE AND BROKEN

BRIGID KEMMERER

BLOOMSBURY
NEW YORK   LONDON   OXFORD   NEW DELHI   SYDNEY

BLOOMSBURY YA
Bloomsbury Publishing Inc., part of Bloomsbury Publishing Plc
1385 Broadway, New York, NY 10018

BLOOMSBURY and the Diana logo are trademarks of Bloomsbury Publishing Plc

First published in the United States of America in January 2020
by Bloomsbury YA

Text copyright © 2020 by Brigid Kemmerer
Map copyright © 2020 by Kelly de Groot
Endpapers of exclusive edition copyright © Margherita Abitino

All rights reserved. No part of this publication may be reproduced or transmitted in any form
or by any means, electronic or mechanical, including photocopying, recording, or any
information storage or retrieval system, without prior permission in writing from the publisher.

Bloomsbury books may be purchased for business or promotional use.
For information on bulk purchases please contact Macmillan Corporate
and Premium Sales Department at specialmarkets@macmillan.com

Library of Congress Cataloging-in-Publication Data
Names: Kemmerer, Brigid.
Title: A heart so fierce and broken / by Brigid Kemmerer.
Description: New York : Bloomsbury, 2020. | Sequel to: A curse so dark and lonely.
Summary: The curse is finally broken, but Prince Rhen of Emberfall faces darker troubles still.
Rumors circulate that he is not the true heir and that forbidden magic has been unleashed in
Emberfall. Loyalties are tested and new love blooms in a kingdom on the brink of war.
Identifiers: LCCN 2019019168 (print) | LCCN 2019022113 (e-book)
ISBN 978-1-68119-511-7 (hardcover) • ISBN 978-1-68119-512-4 (e-book)
Subjects: CYAC: Fairy tales. | Princes—Fiction. | Magic—Fiction.
Classification: LCC PZ8.K374 He 2020 (print) | LCC PZ8.K374 (e-book) |
DDC [Fic]—dc23
LC record available at https://lccn.loc.gov/2019019168
LC e-book record available at https://lccn.loc.gov/2019022113

ISBN 978-1-5476-0566-8 (exclusive edition)

Book design by Jeanette Levy
Typeset by Westchester Publishing Services
Printed and bound in the U.S.A. by Berryville Graphics Inc., Berryville, Virginia
2 4 6 8 10 9 7 5 3 1

All papers used by Bloomsbury Publishing Plc are natural, recyclable products
made from wood grown in well-managed forests. The manufacturing processes
conform to the environmental regulations of the country of origin.

To find out more about our authors and books visit
www.bloomsbury.com and sign up for our newsletters.

This one is for you, my dear reader.

Look in the mirror.
You're a cursebreaker.
You're strong.
You're amazing.
You are changing the world by just being in it.
And I am
so
very
proud
of you.

IISHELLASA ICE FOREST

THE FROZEN RIVER

SYHL SHALLOW

CRYSTAL PALACE

WILDTHORNE VALLEY

BLIND HOLLOW

BLACKROCK PLAINS

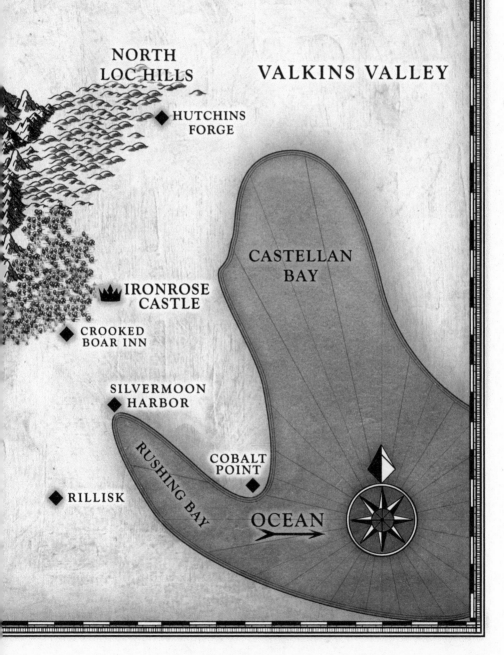

EMBERFALL

NORTH LOC HILLS

VALKINS VALLEY

◆ HUTCHINS FORGE

CASTELLAN BAY

♛ IRONROSE CASTLE

◆ CROOKED BOAR INN

◆ SILVERMOON HARBOR

RUSHING BAY

◆ COBALT POINT

◆ RILLISK

OCEAN

A Heart So Fierce and Broken

CHAPTER ONE

HARPER

I miss knowing exactly what time it is.

It's one of the few things I regret leaving behind in Washington, DC, but when darkness has fallen, dinner feels like a distant memory, and Rhen has still not returned to his chambers, I want to know what time it is. I'm no stranger to waiting in the darkness, but when I was on the streets I had my brother's cell phone, and I'd count every minute.

Now I'm Princess Harper of Disi, and Emberfall hasn't advanced to the point of having electricity.

Rhen and I have separate chambers, befitting the crown prince and the lady he's to ally his kingdom with, but he always visits before retiring to his own room.

He's never been this late. Or—I don't think he has.

The heat of the day has bled off, leaving cool air to stream through my open windows, and my fire has fallen to glowing embers. Outside, torches flicker on the guard posts that surround Ironrose, evenly spaced flares of light that keep the grounds from ever going truly dark. Such a difference from when Ironrose was cursed, when the guard posts stood cold and dark and empty, when the only people to inhabit the castle were Rhen, Grey, and me.

Now the castle is crowded with nobles and servants and guards, and we are never truly alone.

And Grey is gone. He's been gone for months.

I take the candle from my bedside, lighting it from the glowing embers on the hearth. It's a movement I make without thought anymore, the way I would have flipped a light switch back home. Zo, my personal guard and closest friend here, isn't on duty tonight, and she deserves time to sleep. Same with Freya, my lady-in-waiting. The lights in her room went dark hours ago, and I selfishly wish they hadn't. I could use a friend.

A soft knock raps at my door, and I hurry across the floor to open it.

It's not Rhen, though I wouldn't have expected him to knock. It's Jake.

When I was young, Jake was gentle and kind, the perfect older brother. Then we hit our teens, and while our mother was on her deathbed, our father drove our lives into the gutter. Jake is built like a linebacker, and to help make ends meet, he took jobs from the loan sharks who haunted our doorstep. To those outside our family, Jake quickly grew from someone lovable into someone to fear.

Being trapped in Emberfall, a country as beautiful as it is wild and dangerous, hasn't changed my brother's temperament. The day we arrived, he was out of place and unsure of himself, but he's grown into his fictional role as Prince Jacob of Disi. His dark hair has grown out a bit, and he wears a sword on his hip as if he were born carrying it. No one messed with him in DC, and few people mess with him here either.

Tonight his expression is somber.

"Hey," I say softly. "Come in."

He does, and I ease the door closed behind him.

"I'm surprised you're still up," he says.

"I'm waiting for Rhen." I pause. "I'm surprised *you're* still up."

He hesitates. "Noah and I are packing."

Noah is his boyfriend, formerly a medical resident in a busy DC emergency room, and now the castle "healer."

I raise my eyebrows. "Packing?"

My brother's expression doesn't change. "We're leaving in the morning."

This is so unexpected that I stumble back a step.

Jake's lip quirks up. "Not forever, Harp. It's not that bad."

"But—what do you mean, you're *leaving*?"

He shrugs and fidgets and moves to the window. "We've been here for months now. I know you like playing the courtly princess, but I feel like I'm living in a cage." He pauses and glances back at me. "It's only for a few weeks. A month, tops."

I blow out a breath. "A month."

A lot can happen in a month. I know that better than anyone.

"I'd have no way to check on you," I say. "What if something happens? It takes days—*weeks*—to send word sometimes. We still don't know what's happening with Syhl Shallow or Rhen's coronation or—"

He gives me a look. "You don't need to check on me, Harper."

"I can still worry about you." We were once separated after Grey snatched me off the streets of DC, and it was horrible not knowing what might have become of Jake. I don't want to feel that way again. "Have you asked Rhen? He might not think it's a good idea."

Jake's eyes turn flinty. "He's not my warden."

"I know, but—"

"He knows anyway. I already talked to him."

That draws me up short.

"I asked him not to say anything to you," Jake adds. "I wanted to tell you myself."

My mouth forms a line. "I guess you've arranged everything, then."

"No, Harp. I haven't." He pauses. "I want you to come with us."

"Jake. I can't. You know I can't."

"Yes, you can. You can get out of here just like I can." He leaves the window to stop in front of me, and when he speaks, his voice grows quiet. "He's not your warden either. You don't have to spend your nights waiting up for him."

"He's running a country," I say. "He's not out drinking with the guys."

"He's eighteen years old, and so are you." Jake pauses. "Do you want to marry him?"

The question catches my breath.

My brother is studying me. "Harp—you know that's at the end of this path if you stay here. He's set up this whole alliance with a fake country that's dependent on your marriage."

I know that. Of course I know that.

I'm quiet too long. Jake moves past me to the fireplace. "You didn't answer my question."

Marriage. "I don't—I don't know."

He throws a log onto the hearth and jabs at it with the poker.

"You shouldn't have to know. That's my point." The log begins to catch, and Jake looks at me over his shoulder. "You shouldn't be in a position where your boyfriend has to marry you to hold his country together."

I move to the couch and ease onto the cushion. "Gee, Jake, I'm so glad you came in."

He looks back at the fire, which is flickering in earnest now, making his brown hair glow with highlights of gold and red. "I know things weren't good in DC, but I don't feel like they're better here."

"We left Washington facing down a man with a gun," I say.

"I know, I know." He falls quiet, though, so I know this is not an acquiescence.

I don't know what to say to him. "I can't leave, Jake."

"You love him."

"Yes."

He sighs, then moves to sit beside me on the couch. I lean my head against his shoulder, and we stare at the fire together.

"The rumors are getting out of control," he finally says. "That he's not the rightful heir. That Karis Luran will attack again."

"Those rumors have been flying for months."

"People are beginning to talk about how forces from Disi have never arrived. That your alliance is a sham." Jake pauses, and now his eyes are sharp. "I'm not just leaving to get away from here. I want to find out what's really going on outside this castle."

"Rhen wouldn't lie to us."

Jake studies me for the longest time. "He's lying to his entire country," he finally says. "If you think he's not above lying to *us*, you need to pay attention."

I swallow. Rhen isn't like that. "You don't need to start something, Jake."

"I'm not. I'm just asking you to think." He shakes his head bitterly. "Noah said you wouldn't come. I thought you'd at least consider it."

I study him, my restless brother who did so many terrible things to keep me safe. At his core, there's kindness and compassion. I know there is. "I'm sorry."

He grits his teeth. "I wish we knew if Grey were alive or dead."

"Me too," I say, and sigh.

"Not for the same reasons you do." He looks down at me. "He's the one who trapped us here." Jake shakes his head and rubs a hand across his jaw. There's a tension in his body now. "If he ever turns up, I'm going to make him wish he never did."

It's barely a threat. Grey is likely dead—or trapped on the other side, which is equally bad. "What are you so angry about?"

Thunderclouds roll through his eyes. "I've spent months watching them use you, Harper."

"No one is *using* me—"

"Yes. They are. Grey brought you here to help break a curse you had no part of. And then when you escaped, he brought you back *again*."

"I *wanted* to come back." And I did. I don't regret the choice I made.

Until this moment, looking into Jake's eyes, I never realized that *he* regrets the choice I made. It might have saved his life, but now he's trapped here with no way to get home.

The latch at my door clicks, and I turn in surprise to find Rhen in the doorway.

The prince is still dressed in his formal clothes, a blue jacket buckled all the way to his throat and a sword in place at his hip. The firelight catches his hair and turns it gold, but his eyes are tired. He spots me and Jake by the fire and stops. The tension in the room has grown so thick that he can probably feel it.

"Forgive me," Rhen says carefully. "The hour is late. I thought you would be alone."

Jake sighs. "You *should* be alone. I'll get out." He leans forward to kiss me on the forehead. "Take care of yourself, Harper. I mean it."

That softens the edge all his other words carried. "Thanks, big brother."

Jake stops by Rhen before grabbing hold of the door handle. "I'm still leaving tomorrow," he says.

"Today, in fact," says Rhen, matching Jake's even tone. "It is well after midnight." He glances at the dark window. "Dustan will accompany you, along with a small contingent of guards. You may leave after daybreak if you wish."

That throws Jake for a moment, but he recovers quickly. "Good."

Rhen raises an eyebrow. "You thought I would go back on my word?"

"I thought you'd find other things more important."

"Indeed. I do." Rhen opens the door and holds it there. A clear dismissal.

Jake opens his mouth to argue.

Rhen can be patient when he wants to be, but I sense that now isn't one of those times. "Jake," I say. "You got what you wanted."

"Nowhere near." But it's enough to draw the fight out of my brother, and he goes through the door.

Once he's gone, Rhen crosses the room to where I'm standing. Every day seems to add new shadows beneath his eyes, a dark and guarded wariness that never seems to ease anymore.

"Are you all right?" I say as he approaches. He's always so buttoned-up after he comes out of meetings with his advisers, but today feels like a new level. He's distant. So severe that if I didn't know him, I might back away from him. "What's going on? It's late. I thought—"

His hands catch my waist, and I gasp. Then his mouth is on mine.

Rhen is so strong, so capable, that he still surprises me when he's gentle. He stalked across the room like he wanted to wage war, but he kisses me like I'm the most delicate thing in the castle. His hands are full of warmth that I can feel through my sleeping shift, soft against my waist. I put my hands against his jacket and breathe him in, letting his closeness erase some of the worry Jake stoked.

When Rhen pulls back, it's barely far enough to speak against my lips. His eyes bore into mine. "I could feel your worry on the other side of the castle," he says. He brushes a thumb across my cheek. "I can feel it now."

I blush and look down. My fingers fidget with the buckles of his jacket, as if they need straightening, but of course they don't. "I'm okay."

"Harper," he says softly. He puts a hand over mine, forcing it still.

I love the way he says my name, the way his accent lends weight to the *R*s to make it a purr. He's always so formal that my name feels like a secret just between us.

He puts a finger to my chin and lifts my gaze. "Tell me your fears."

"Jake just told me he's leaving."

"Ah." Rhen sighs. "Your brother is impatient and reckless, and the timing could be better—but it could also be worse. I would rather send him with my blessing than learn he's caused havoc somewhere in the kingdom. Dustan will not allow him to get into much trouble."

"I'm surprised you're sending your guard commander."

"I would rather not, but I have few guards I can trust on such an assignment. The Royal Guard still feels untested, but your brother is insistent he will leave whether I like it or not."

Well, that definitely sounds like Jake.

Rhen studies me. "Would you rather I send Zo?"

"No." If Jake's leaving, I can't bear the thought of losing my friend, too. "Did Jake tell you he wants me to go with him?"

That forces Rhen still. "No. And your decision?"

This is one of my favorite things about him. He's commanding and decisive and never falters—but he never takes a choice away from *me*. "I said no."

He lets out a breath, then kisses me again. "I spent so long waiting to find you that I worried fate might take you away."

I press my forehead against his neck and inhale the warmth of his scent. "I'm not going anywhere."

He holds me quietly for a moment, but I can tell his worry has not eased.

I bite at my lip, not wanting to add to his tension. "Jake said the rumors about another heir have grown."

"They have."

I press a hand against his chest, thinking about everything Jake said. "Talk to me, Rhen."

He sighs, and it sounds aggravated. "The heir exists. There are royal records with my father's seal. I wanted to accelerate the coronation, but many nobles have already made it known that they want proof that the line of succession is solid, and so I shall do my very best to provide it."

"How will you find him?"

"It may be impossible. In truth, he may not live. We have very little to go on for our search. If his mother was a magesmith, as records indicate, he should have magic like the enchantress Lilith. She once told me that the web of magic did not end with her, that she could feel another's existence. Magic has been banned from Emberfall for years, but if we spread word that someone has this power, it may not be so easy to hide."

Lilith. Just her name is enough to cause me to shudder. "What will you do if you find him?"

"If he bears magic, he will be destroyed."

I jerk back. "Rhen!"

Rhen says nothing. He doesn't need to. The look in his eyes says enough.

I take another step back. "This man is your *brother.*"

"No. He is a stranger." There's no give in his voice. "I spent a near eternity trapped by one magesmith, and it almost drove my country to ruin. I will not risk Emberfall being destroyed by another."

I'm rooted in place, filled with ice despite the fire at my side. I don't know what to say. I've seen him order a man's death before, but that was a man who'd killed one of our guards, a man who would have killed us if he'd gotten the chance.

This is different. This is calculated. Premeditated.

Rhen takes a step forward and reaches a hand to touch my face.

I flinch away, and his expression goes still. "I did not intend to upset you," he says quietly, and I know he means that. "I did not realize this would be a surprise. You saw with your own eyes the damage Lilith caused."

Yes. I did. I saw her torture Rhen time and again. He was powerless to stop her.

"I'm sure you're right," I say, even though I'm not sure at all. I draw a shaking breath and have to press a hand to my stomach.

Rhen has proven that he'll do what he needs to do to hold Emberfall together. He's proving it now.

"Do not draw away from me," he says softly, and there is a new note in his voice. Not vulnerability—never that—but something close. "Please. I cannot bear it."

He looks so tired. His body is so tense. I wonder when he last slept. I take a deep breath and chase the trembling out of my fingers, then move forward to put my arms around him.

"Tell me *your* fears," I say quietly.

"We do not even know if Lilith is dead," Rhen says. "If she were to find this heir—if they were to work together against me—"

"It's been months. She's either trapped on the other side or Grey is."

"Or he's sworn to her, as we saw, and she is biding her time."

Grey swore himself into her service to save me—just before putting his sword to Lilith's throat and disappearing to the other side. To Washington, DC.

"He wouldn't help her," I say. "Rhen. He wouldn't."

"I have to protect my people, Harper."

He leans against me, and I listen to the pattern of his breathing as it slows. I lay a hand against his cheek, and his eyes close. There was a moment, months ago, when he was the monster, and he pressed his face against my hand and settled, just like this. I could feel his fear then. I can feel it now.

"You're not a monster anymore," I whisper.

"I sent guards to Grey's mother's home in Wildthorne Valley," Rhen says carefully.

My hand goes still on his cheek. "What? When?"

"Last week," he says. "To be thorough." He pauses. "They returned today."

Grey once told me that Lilith killed his whole family, leaving only his mother alive. "What did they find?"

"His mother was gone. The townspeople said she sold off her livestock and moved away months ago. No one knew where she'd gone." Another pause. "Rumor said a wounded man stayed with her for a short while, but no one saw him."

I hold my breath for a moment. "Grey could be alive," I whisper.

"Yes." Rhen's voice is hard, but I feel the worry and uncertainty behind it. "Given what they reported, I suspect Grey is very much alive."

I look up at him. "Grey wouldn't be sworn to her, Rhen."

"If he was not, why would he not return to Ironrose?"

I try to think of an answer and fail.

"Karis Luran could attack at any time," Rhen says. "The heir could appear at any time." He pauses. "And Lilith could be waiting for the perfect moment to strike."

I lean my head against Rhen's chest and look to the window

again, gazing out at the stars spanning the sky. "Oh, Grey," I say. "Where are you?"

"Indeed," says Rhen. He sighs, and in the sound, I hear the longing and sadness and worry wrapped up in the word. He brushes a kiss against my hair. "Indeed."

CHAPTER TWO

GREY

Late afternoon always bears the weight of the sun, but I don't mind, because the stables are quiet, and I rarely have more than the other stable hand for company.

This is the last place anyone will look for me, so I welcome it.

Sweat clings to my arms, attracting bits of dirt and straw as I swing the pitchfork. The heat will get worse before it gets better, but I'm used to it. Worwick's Tourney is closed for business until dark, deserted except for me and Tycho. Later, the stables will be loud with the sounds of men calling for horses or bickering over the weapons for rent at the end of the aisle. Once the drink starts flowing and the stadium is filled with people eager for a show, the noise will be deafening.

Now, though, the stadium is empty, and the stables are wanting for a good cleaning. A far cry from the extravagant luxury of Ironrose, when I was commander of the Royal Guard of Emberfall.

Tycho has been singing under his breath as he mucks the stalls, so quietly that I can't catch the melody over the sounds of horses breathing. He's small for his age, with a wiry build that makes him look closer to twelve than fifteen, but that doesn't stop him from being quick and capable. Dark-blond hair hangs just past his chin, keeping the blue of his eyes in shadow.

Tycho likes this time of day, too, for different reasons. Men with a belly full of ale sometimes come looking for entertainment after the tourney. I've heard them offer Worwick coins for an hour of Tycho's company. I've watched Worwick consider it.

The boy knows how to make himself scarce.

I've spent the last few weeks trying to make sure he knows how to defend himself instead.

"How many do you have left?" I call to him.

"Three," he calls back. He drags a forearm across his brow. "Silver hell, it's hot."

I look out the stall window at the angle of the sun. We have a few hours left until sunset. "I'll take your three. Head for the Growling Dog. Jodi said she would have crabs from Silvermoon this week."

He steps out of his stall. "Hawk. Jodi's tavern is on the other side of the city."

Hawk. Three months, and I still haven't gotten used to the name. I shove damp hair off my forehead and smile. "Then you'd better get running. Steamed crabs cost a copper apiece."

He sighs—but a moment later, I hear his feet slap the dirt floor of the aisle. "When I win, I'm ordering a *dozen*," he calls behind him.

He won't win. Even with the head start I've given him.

He's getting closer, though.

When I first came here, I was still healing from my final battle with Lilith. Nightmares plagued my sleep for weeks, leaving me exhausted and weak. Cleaning stalls and weapons took most of my energy.

Once I healed, however, the monotony of life at the tourney began leaving me bored and twitchy. I missed the physical rigors of the Royal Guard. A few hours with a pitchfork and a rag were nothing compared to hours of drills and swordplay. I began rising before the sun, running a loop of the city in the early-morning darkness, or climbing the laddered roof supports of the stadium.

I don't know how long Tycho was following me before I caught him, but it was early enough that I was still terrified of being discovered. He was lucky I didn't have a blade on me.

Or maybe *I* was lucky. My skills with weapons would definitely draw attention. If anyone comes looking for a skilled swordsman, I don't want fingers pointing to me. Sometimes I'll spar with Tycho using the blades we keep for practice, but I'm careful to execute only basic moves, and I let him get in a lot of hits.

A wagon creaks outside, with the clopping heaviness of draft horses. A man's blustering voice calls out, "Tycho! Hawk! Come see what I've got!"

Worwick. I sigh. He could have anything, from a slab of ice to a rusted nail to a fisherman's corpse.

Considering this heat, I very much hope it's not the latter.

I step out of the stables, wiping my hands along my trousers. The wagon carries a massive crate, taller than a man, covered by a huge length of fabric that's tied down at the corners. The draft horses are slick with sweat, froth dripping from their mouths.

Worwick always drives the animals too hard. I'll have to wash them down before running across the city. Tycho might win today after all.

Worwick looks like he's found a pile of the king's silver. He practically bounces down from the seat of the wagon, and considering his heft, that's saying something. He pulls a rag from his pocket and mops his drenched brow. "You won't believe this," he says. "You simply won't believe this."

"What do you have?" I say.

"Where's Tycho?" Worwick all but cackles with glee. "I want to see his reaction."

Racing me to the tavern for steamed crabs that I'll have to buy if you drag this out too long. "I sent him into the city for an ointment for one of the horses."

"Ah. Too bad." He sighs with disappointment. "I'll just have to see yours, then."

I likely won't have much of a reaction, and he knows it. Worwick finds me stoic and unimaginative. I spent far too long serving the crown prince—in both his human and his monster form—to bat an eye at anything Worwick might have under this sheet.

He's not a bad man, just a bit crude, and too driven by what will bring him an extra coin for his pocket. As Commander Grey, I would have pitied him.

As Hawk, I simply tolerate him.

"Go ahead, then," I say.

"Help me untie the canvas."

The ropes are tight and double knotted. I'm on the second corner when I realize he's still on the ground, watching me.

Typical. The second rope gives, and I flip the sheet high.

It's a cage. I'm staring down at . . . a creature I can't identify.

It's somewhat human-shaped, with dark-gray skin, the color of a cloudy night sky. Wings bound with rope sprout from its back, and there's a length of tail that curls limply along the ground of the cage. It has clawed hands and feet, and a shock of black hair that's matted with sweat.

It's not moving.

"Goodness," says Worwick. "Do you think it died?"

"If it's not dead, it's close." I cast a dark look at him. "How long has it been covered up like that?"

"Two hours."

"In this heat?"

He puts a hand to his mouth. "Oh dear."

"It needs water." When he doesn't move, I jump off the wagon and fetch a bucket from the stable.

The creature still hasn't moved by the time I return. I climb back on the wagon and crouch beside the cage. I watch its ribs expanding slowly. At least it's breathing. I take a handful of water and extend my hand through the bars, trickling it along its face. Its nose is slightly narrower than a human's, its jaw wider. The water makes a trail along the smoke-colored skin.

"What is it?" I say to Worwick. "Where did you get it?"

"It's a scraver," he says. "They said it was captured far in the north, in the ice forests beyond Syhl Shallow. I won it in a game of cards! Fortune smiled on me today, my boy."

A scraver. I remember a childhood story about something like this, but it's been too long for me to recall much. "I thought those were a myth. Something to scare children."

"Apparently not."

I take another handful of water and let it run down over its face, then cluck to it like a horse. The scraver's eyelids flicker, but it does not move.

"Can you believe," says Worwick, "that they were charging two coppers just to look at it? Absolutely shameful."

My eyebrows go up. Sympathy isn't something I often hear from Worwick. "I agree."

"Exactly! For a scraver? People would surely pay five."

Ah. There it is.

When I take a third handful, the creature twitches. Its mouth moves, seeking the water. Claws scrape against the floor of the cage as it tries to pull nearer to me. Its movements are weak and pitiful.

"Easy now," I say softly. "I have more." I take another handful of water. I'll have to fetch a ladle.

The scraver inhales deeply, its nostrils flaring, and a low sound comes from its chest. I put my hand as close to its lips as I can manage.

Its eyes open, and they're all black. The low sound becomes a growl.

"Easy," I say again. "I won't hurt—"

It lunges for my hand. I'm quick, but it's quicker. Fangs sink into my wrist before I can get my arm out of the cage. I jerk free and stumble back, tripping over the bucket of water and all but falling off the wagon.

Worwick stares down at me, then bursts out laughing. "No, no. It was better that you were here. I don't think Tycho would have had the nerve to put a hand in there with it."

Silver hell. My wrist is bleeding something fierce. Dirt and sweat have already set it stinging.

The scraver has retreated to the opposite side of the cage. From here, I can tell the creature's unashamedly male. It's glaring at me: fangs half bared, eyes pools of dark warning.

"You're going to have to wait for water now," I say.

"What do you think we should do with it?" says Worwick.

I sigh. My wrist burns, and I'm starving. I'm going to have to fetch Tycho and be back before dark, or there will be hell to pay. "We can't leave it out here in the sun. Let's take the wagon into the stadium," I say. "We can figure out what to do with it after the tourney."

"Hawk, you're a good man." He claps me on the shoulder. "I'll be in my office if you need me."

Lucky me.

Tycho is sitting at the bar, a half-eaten platter of crabs in front of him and a smile on his face. It's early for the tavern, too, so the place isn't crowded, and Tycho has the bar to himself. He looks so pleased with himself that I'm almost glad Worwick rolled into the courtyard with a problem he expected me to solve.

I can't help but smile back. "Don't get cocky."

He grins at Jodi, the young woman behind the bar. "I think I'll have another dozen. Hawk is buying."

She smiles, her golden-brown eyes shining. "So you've said."

I snort. "You'll make yourself sick on what's in front of you. I'm not carrying you back."

"I know." He pushes the tray over. "The other half are for you."

I climb onto the stool beside him, and Jodi slides a plate and a knife onto the counter for me. My trip across the city was long and grueling and destroyed my appetite, but I take a crab from the pile anyway. Tycho is usually so reserved that I don't want to rain on his spirit.

Jodi comes to lean against the bar. Her brown hair hangs to her waist, with feathers and stones braided into some of the strands. She's tan from the sun, with freckles on her cheeks and a tiny gap between her front two teeth. Her chest all but spills out of her dress when she rests against her forearms, and she offers me a wide smile.

It's an effect not lost on me, but I spent so long forswearing any kind of relationship that I've forgotten what a flare of attraction could feel like.

No. That is not true. I remember Harper. I remember the kindness in her eyes and her endless tenacity and the feel of her hand under mine when I showed her how to throw knives in the snow.

That was forbidden then, and it's forbidden now. Thoughts of Harper will go nowhere useful, so I shove them away.

"Wine or ale?" Jodi says.

"Water." I split a crab leg with the knife and pull the meat free. "If you please."

She pouts. "You never drink."

I shrug. "Tycho already spent my coins on the food." This isn't true, but I have no head for spirits. It wasn't allowed when I was a guardsman, and the one time I shared a bottle with Rhen, it nearly put me on the floor. As Hawk, I worry what truths would spill from my lips if I dared to try.

Then again, maybe they wouldn't. When I was in the Royal Guard, I always felt that my life had been split into two acts. There was before, when I was a young farm boy, looking for a way to help keep my family alive.

Then there was after, when I was a guardsman, making my life by keeping the royal family alive. There were times when my family became a distant memory, almost people my imagination conjured instead of individuals I'd lived with and cared for.

Now it seems I've found a third act. Some days the castle and the curse feel as imaginary as my family. I don't know how much of Grey the guardsman is left.

Jodi sets a glass of water in front of me. I drain half in one swallow, wipe at my mouth with a napkin, then split another crab leg with the knife.

"You eat like a nobleman," she says, her tone musing. "I don't think I ever noticed that before."

My fingers hesitate, but I force my hand to move, to split another shell. She's not wrong, but it's not something I ever considered: I eat like a man who was trained to dine with royalty.

I try to do it more clumsily, though it probably looks forced. In a moment, I'm going to take off a finger with the knife. I offer Jodi a smile and give Tycho a good-natured shove. "It's more likely that you're used to drunkards digging for the meat with their teeth."

Tycho smiles shyly. "I'm not drunk, at least." His eyes fall on the makeshift bandage I wrapped around my arm. "What did you do to your wrist?"

I break the next crab leg in half with my hands, conscious of the fact that Jodi is watching me now. "Worwick has a new pet."

"A new *pet*?"

Before I can answer, the door at the front of the tavern swings open with enough force to bounce against the opposing wall. Half a dozen men come through, fully armed, their armor bearing the gold and red crest of Emberfall.

Not Royal Guardsmen, but soldiers in the King's Army. I freeze, then force myself to turn back to my food. Beside me, Tycho goes equally quiet, for his own reasons.

I suddenly find myself very much wishing for a sword at my hip. My fingers casually wrap around the hilt of the knife.

I am likely being foolish. I only got a cursory glance, but I don't recognize any of them. It would be very unlikely for them to recognize *me*. My hair has grown out a bit, and my face is unshaven.

With any luck, no one is looking for me anyway. I simply have no way to know.

One of the men steps up to the bar. He flips a bronze coin down onto the wood. "Food and wine for my men, if you please."

Jodi pockets the coin and offers a curtsy. "Right away, my lord."

He's no lord, but he'll eat that right up. Two of his men whistle from the table they've taken near the door.

The soldier tosses another bronze on the bar and clears his throat. "You have my thanks."

"As you have mine." She pockets this coin too, and as he turns away, Jodi winks at me.

I can barely smile back. I'm too worried about what they're doing here. We're far from the border. This is not a town that sees many soldiers.

The man pauses before moving away. He's looking at me now.

I take a sip from my glass and measure the weight of the knife between my fingers. I can lodge it in his throat without thought. My arm remembers the motion. It's lighter than my throwing knives were, so it wouldn't take as much—

"Are those steamed crabs?" he says. "We haven't seen shellfish in ages."

I clear my throat and force my fingers to let go of the knife. When I speak, my voice sounds rough. "Jodi makes the best in the city."

"We picked the right place then."

I finally look at him. I have to take the chance, because otherwise I'll look like I'm hiding something.

He's dark-haired, with ruddy skin and a large build. I don't recognize him at all. Relief slides through my chest, and I take a breath. "You won't regret it." I pause. "Traveling far?"

"Heading north, to Hutchins Forge," he says. "Official business."

"Of course." I offer him a nod, then slide off the bar stool. "Travel safely, Soldier." I drop a handful of coins beside my plate. "Tycho, we're due back."

We haven't finished what was on the tray, but he scurries off the stool and follows me to the door. We step out into the blazing sunlight.

Before the door swings closed, I hear one of the soldiers say, "For the love of silver, Captain, people know towns are rebelling because of another heir. The rumors are in every city."

I grab hold of Tycho's sleeve and hold my breath, hoping to hear more.

"What do you think the prince will do when he finds him?" says one of the others.

The captain snorts. "Take his head off, most likely. The king is dead. The crown prince will take his place. He's not going to let some outsider—"

The door swings shut, leaving us out in the sunlight.

Tycho peers up at me. "Those soldiers made you nervous."

I don't like that he saw right through me. I bump him with my shoulder. "They made you nervous, too."

He blushes and looks away.

I shouldn't have said that. I was trying to take the focus off myself, but instead, I put it squarely on him. "Race you back?" I say.

"I thought you were out of coppers."

"If you win, I'll do all your stalls tomorrow."

He grins and takes off without hesitation, without even considering the heat or the food that fills his belly. I'll probably find him vomiting shellfish halfway back.

I keep walking.

The king is dead.

The crown prince will take his place.

The crown prince *should* take his place. It creates a pull in my chest I did not expect. I once swore my life to Rhen, for this very reason. To be a part of something bigger than myself.

Now I am here, in the dusty streets of Rillisk, barely more than a stable hand. The secret half-brother to the Crown Prince of Emberfall. The missing heir who doesn't want to be found.

Part of absolutely nothing at all.

CHAPTER THREE

LIA MARA

I've been peering out the carriage window for miles. The air on this side of the mountains has a weight to it, a heavy stickiness that makes me wish I could travel in a vest and leggings instead of my royal robes. The beauty of the landscape is worth it, though. Beyond the mountains, Syhl Shallow consists of miles of flat farmland, broken only by occasional cities and only one narrow river. Emberfall has been a wealth of valleys and forests and varying terrain.

Plus a few burned-out cities, charred remains left by our own soldiers when Mother first tried to take this land.

Those always force my eyes back into the carriage. I have no interest in seeing the destruction wrought by our people.

A pattern of destruction I once thought I could change, until Mother named my younger sister as heir.

Across from me, my sister looks unaffected by the weather and the scenery. Nolla Verin is sitting in the shadows, embroidering with red and silver thread. Knowing her, it's an adornment for one of her horses.

She would not flinch from the sight of burned-out cities. Nolla Verin would not flinch from anything.

That is why my sister has been named heir, and not me.

Nolla Verin's mouth is curved with soft amusement. "Lia Mara. You do realize we will be seen as hostile," she says in Syssalah, our language.

I do not take my eyes off the lush greenery. "Mother has tried to raze this country. How could we be seen any differently?"

"I am thinking you would make an easy target, leaning out the window with your mouth hanging open."

I close my mouth and settle back into my seat, allowing the sheer curtain to fall over the window.

Nolla Verin's smile widens. "And everyone always says you are the clever one."

"Ah, yes. Though I do prefer that to being called the *sturdy* one."

She laughs softly. "Keep a list. When I am queen, I will have them all executed on your behalf."

When I am queen.

I smile and hope she does not see the hint of sadness behind it.

Not because I am jealous. We promised each other long ago that we would support whoever was chosen. And though she is two years younger than I am, even at sixteen she could not be better suited to inherit the crown from our mother. Nolla Verin was practically born with a bow and arrow in hand, not to mention a sword at her hip. Like our mother, she has no hesitation in using either. She can break the most aggressive horse in the stables, and in fact many of the Royal Houses have begun sending their colts to her for training, just to brag that their steeds were tamed by the great queen's daughter.

Nolla Verin and our mother also share the same affinity for swift, brutal judgment.

That is what makes me sad. My sister laughs at the thought of execution.

Because she is not joking.

Their resemblance does not end there. Nolla Verin and Mother share the same build, small and lithe and athletic—perfectly fit for the battlefield. The only trait I share with our mother is my red hair, though mine hangs to my waist, while Mother keeps hers shorter. Nolla Verin's hair is a shiny curtain of black. I am not small and I am not nimble, leading many at court to remark on my cleverness when they're being kind—and my "sturdiness" when they're not.

My sister has gone back to her embroidery. Her fingers fly back and forth across the fabric. If she is nervous, she shows no sign of it.

Our traveling party is not large. Sorra and Parrish are my personal guards, and they ride at the back. Tik and Dyhl, Nolla Verin's guards, ride at the center. My mother has four personal guards, and they surround her carriage at the front.

"What if the prince rejects Mother's offer?" I say.

Her eyes lift from the fabric. "He would be a fool. Our forces could destroy this pathetic country."

I glance at the window. So far, I have not found Emberfall to be *pathetic*. And Prince Rhen was able to drive our forces back through the mountain pass, so it seems that we would be wise to be cautious.

"Hmm," I say, "and do you think this destruction will lead to people being willing to work the waterways we so desperately need?"

"Our people can learn."

"I feel they could learn more quickly from people who already possess the skills."

She sighs patronizingly. "You would likely beg for instruction with nuts and honey."

I look away, out the window. I'd rather ask for help than order it with a sword in hand, but this is another reminder of why Nolla Verin has been chosen instead of me.

"We can leave a few alive, if need be," she says. "They'll be desperate to help."

"We can leave them *all* alive if Mother secures an alliance."

"And we will. Prince Rhen's monstrous creature is gone," Nolla Verin says. "Our spies have reported that his cities are beginning to question his right to rule. If he wants to keep this silly country, he will accept."

She is so practical. My lip quirks up. "What if you do not like him?"

She rolls her eyes. "As if that matters. I can bed a man without liking him."

I blush at her boldness. "Nolla Verin. Have you . . . *done* that?"

"Well. No." Her eyes flick up to meet mine, and her fingers go still on her embroidery. "Have you?"

My blush deepens. "Of course not."

Nolla Verin's eyes widen. "Then you should do it first and tell me what to expect. Are you bored now? I shall call for Parrish right this very moment. Or would you fancy Dyhl instead? You can have the carriage—"

I giggle and throw a brocade cushion at her. "You will do no such thing."

She dodges the pillow without missing a stitch. "I am just asking you to be sisterly."

"What of Prince Rhen's betrothed?"

"Princess Harper?" Nolla Verin pulls her thread tight and knots it off. "She can bed who she chooses, too."

"Do not be coy, Sister."

She sighs. "I am not worried. Their alliance means nothing. Three months have passed since the prince supposedly allied Emberfall with the mysterious Disi. No forces have arrived. Mother does not think the prince has been fully honest with his people, and I am inclined to agree."

I am too. While Nolla Verin prefers to spend her time on the training field, I prefer to spend hours each week under the tutelage of Mother's chief adviser, Clanna Sun, learning about military strategy or the intricate interweaving of the Royal Houses. Over the last few months, it seemed that Prince Rhen was assembling an army that could produce a threat—but somehow one has never materialized. I do find it curious that the prince would continue courting the Princess of Disi if their alliance has fallen apart. Emberfall is weak. He needs to tie himself to a country that can offer the support his land needs to thrive.

A country like Syhl Shallow.

The curtain flutters at the window, and in the distance, I see the charred remnants of another destroyed town. My throat tightens. Mother's soldiers were thorough.

I look back at my sister. "What makes you think the prince will even grant us an audience?"

"Mother has information he wants." Her fingers fly through the fabric. "Do you remember, months ago, when that enchantress came to the Crystal Palace?"

I do. The woman had beautiful alabaster skin framed by silken black tresses, and a gown of the deepest blue. When she first appeared, claiming to be a magesmith, Mother had laughed in her face, but the woman caused one of her guards to collapse at her feet without laying a hand on him. Mother granted an audience after that. They disappeared into the throne room for hours.

Nolla Verin and I had hung back to whisper about it. You didn't have to be a great student of history to know that anyone with magic had been driven out of the Iishellasa ice forests decades ago. They used their magic to cross the Frozen River, then asked to settle in Syhl Shallow, but my grandmother refused. They sought shelter in Emberfall—where they were granted asylum, but later, after some kind of trickery on the king, they were all executed.

Except, apparently, the enchantress.

"Of course," I say. "She was the last one."

My sister shakes her head. "Apparently another survived somehow. Mother told me last night while we were preparing for our journey."

Of course Mother told her, and not me. Because Nolla Verin is the heir.

I am not jealous. My sister will make a great queen.

I swallow. "Another survived?"

"Yes. She was seeking the other."

"Why?"

"Because he is more than a man with magic in his blood." She pierces the fabric with her needle. Scarlet thread flies through the white silk like a bleeding wound. "The other magesmith is the true heir to the throne of Emberfall."

I gasp. "Truly?"

"Yes." Her eyes flash. Nolla Verin *loves* a good bit of gossip. "But the prince has no idea who he is."

What a scandal. Magic is no more welcome in Emberfall than it was in Syhl Shallow. I wonder if Rhen's people know. I wonder how they will react.

I imagine living the rest of my life like this, learning information about warring kingdoms like a dog seeking scraps beside a butcher's block.

I swallow again. "Does Mother know who the heir is?"

"No. Before she left, the enchantress said there was only one man who knows his identity."

"Who?"

"The commander of the prince's guard." She ties off her thread and snaps it with her teeth. "A man named Grey."

By nightfall, we are miles from the last town we've passed, and my mother orders the guards to stop and make camp. If we were traveling through Syhl Shallow, large tents would be erected for our comfort, but here in Emberfall, we must be discreet.

Nolla Verin and I share a narrow tent. Sorra and Parrish, my guards, have spread blankets along the ground to make a round space resembling a nest of pillows and blankets. We haven't shared a space like this since we were very young, and I'm grateful for the chance to be close again.

My sister has already reclined among her pillows, and her eyes narrow mischievously. "These blankets are quite soft. Are you certain you would not prefer to share them with Parrish?"

My cheeks flare with heat. It was one thing to joke in the privacy of our carriage. Entirely another to say such things when the man in question stands on the other side of an opaque length of fabric. Being named heir has emboldened her—just as it's stripped away some of my own confidence.

"Hush," I whisper at her.

Her smile widens. "I am merely asking. It may make for a more interesting evening."

I glance at Parrish's shadow on the other side of the curtain, then shift closer to Nolla Verin. "I believe he fancies Sorra."

Her eyebrows go up. "You do?"

I arrange the blankets around me carefully and force my voice to be bored, because I do not want her to needle my guards. "I have long suspected."

I have done more than suspect. A year ago, during the midwinter celebration, I found Parrish and Sorra kissing in the wooded darkness beyond our palace. They broke apart hurriedly, stars in their eyes and a blush on Sorra's pale cheeks.

"Do not stop on my account," I said to them, then turned and fled back to the party before my own blush could flare.

No man has ever looked at me the way Parrish was looking at Sorra. I thought about that kiss far longer than I'd admit.

Sorra is always cool and distant, stoic and fierce like all the guards, with her brown hair bound into a tight braid that hangs trapped beneath her armor. She wears no adornments on her lean body, no kohl darkens her eyes or rouge brightens her cheeks, but anyone can see the gentle beauty in her face. Parrish is equally lean, slighter of build than many of the men, but he's quick and skilled. Many think he is quiet, but I know he's simply careful with his words. When I'm alone with my guards, he's rather funny. In fact, he can often pull a smile out of Sorra with barely more than a glance.

My sister is studying me. Her voice finally drops until it is almost inaudible. "Lia Mara. Do *you* fancy Parrish?"

"What? No! Of course not."

Her eyes scrutinize my face. "Do you fancy Sorra?"

"No." I finally meet her eyes. "I fancy . . ." My voice trails off, and I sigh.

"Who?" She giggles and shifts closer. "Oh, you *must* tell me."

"I fancy the idea of a man fancying me." My blush deepens. "I fancy the idea of a companion."

"Ugh." She rolls onto her back, disappointed. "You are a princess, Lia Mara. They all fancy you."

That is decidedly untrue. No man at court seeks a woman who would rather discuss extensive strategy or ancient mythology than display her skills on the battlefield—or in a ballroom. "I do not want a man to fancy me because I am Karis Luran's daughter. I do not want someone's attention because he believes I will bring him political favor in our mother's court."

"Well. That is all the women of our bloodline are worth to any man."

Her voice is so practical—this doesn't seem to bother her at all. Maybe she wasn't teasing about bedding the prince or asking me to experience it first so I can describe it to her. Maybe my sister looks at such a thing as just another royal obligation. Something else to practice so she can be perfect.

I flop down on the blankets beside her, staring up at the darkening panels of fabric. "This is why I am far more enamored of the men in my stories."

"Oh, I am certain those dry pages keep you quite warm at night."

"You're so vulgar." I giggle and turn my head to look at her.

She makes a lewd gesture and grins. I smack her hand away, and she laughs.

I know she will make an exceptional queen, but I want to remember my sister just like this, with a soft smile only for me, no vicious determination in her gaze.

A shout echoes through the camp, followed by more yelling, and then a girl screams. A man speaks rapidly in the common tongue of Emberfall, his accent much thicker than the one our tutor has. It takes me a moment to parse out the words.

"Please," he is saying. "We mean no harm. Please allow us passage."

Nolla Verin is already through the panels of our tent, and I am quick to follow.

Our guards have built a fire, and a few hare hang on a spit above it. No one is paying attention to the food, though. Tik and Dyhl have their crossbows trained on a middle-aged man who is on his knees, crouched over a young girl, blocking her with his body. A thick beard covers most of his face. A few brown pelts lie in a pile beside him.

My mother stands in the firelight, tall and lean and striking, her red hair hanging straight to her shoulders. "What is your business here?" she says.

"I am a trapper," he says. "I saw your fire and thought—" He breaks off with a gasp as Dyhl moves close enough to drive the point of his crossbow into the man's back. From where he stands, if Dyhl pulls the trigger, the force of the weapon will drive the arrow into both the man and the girl.

"I-I-I am unarmed," the man stammers.

"You wear a knife at your hip," says my mother. It's right there in plain sight. She doesn't suffer fools.

His hand shifts as if to go for the weapon, but Tik, standing in front of him, lifts his crossbow just a hair. The man's hand goes up as if to prove he's harmless. "The knife is dull!" he cries. The girl whimpers underneath him. "For skinning. Take it. Take everything I have."

My heart thuds in my chest. We've ridden past the remains of towns—destruction caused by our soldiers. The population here is sparse, but we are also trying to make our way to the prince's castle under some veil of secrecy. If we allow this man to leave and he spreads the word, we could be attacked before our arrival. As my sister said, we are in hostile territory.

Hostile because of our own actions, my thoughts whisper to me.

If I did not want to see the result of our attacks on Emberfall, I most certainly do not want to see slaughter before my own eyes.

At my side, Nolla Verin does not look affected. She looks curious. She is waiting to see how our mother will handle this invasion.

To my surprise, Mother turns to look at Nolla Verin. "My daughter will decide your fate, trapper."

My sister straightens. This is not the first time Mother has looked to either of us for a decision, but it is the first time real lives have hung in the balance.

The man's eyes lock on my sister. From below his arm, the girl peers out. Tears streak through the dust on her cheeks.

"Please," the man says, and his voice is rough. "We have no part in the quarrel between your people and ours."

I cannot see my sister's expression, but the man's eyes fill with sorrow at whatever he finds there, and he turns his head to speak softly to the girl cowering beneath him. A sob breaks from her chest.

I reach out and grasp my sister's hand. "Nolla Verin," I whisper. "We are here to find a path to peace."

She squeezes my fingers, then glances at me. I want there to be a flicker of indecision in her eyes. Of dismay at having to make such a choice.

There is none. She looks back at Dyhl. "Kill him."

The girl screams. The crossbow fires. The man collapses. The girl is no longer visible. The bolt must have gone right through them both.

Silence envelops the forest.

It does not last long. Nolla Verin looks to the guards. "Double the number of lookouts through the night. I do not want another *trapper* stumbling into our camp."

She turns on her heel and returns to our tent.

I cannot follow. Every guard in this clearing can probably sense my unhappiness.

Mother surely can.

I turn from the bodies as well. I cannot go back to our tent, but I can walk. Sorra and Parrish will follow, though I do not feel as though I deserve guards. Not now. I step into the heavy darkness surrounding the camp.

A bit of gold glints between the trees, barely caught by the firelight. I freeze, narrowing my eyes.

Not gold. Blond. Hair. A girl, larger than the one who was pinned beneath the man. Her hands are over her face, her shoulders shaking. A long strand of pelts hangs from one shoulder.

She is crying.

Her eyes meet mine, and she gasps. She goes still, panic washing over her face.

I give a brief shake of my head. So brief it's almost invisible. *No,* I want to say. *Stay away.*

Run.

"Lia Mara," my mother calls.

I should not care about one man and his daughter. *Daughters.* I swallow.

I should not care.

Mother will not call my name twice. I turn, awaiting a rebuke.

Parrish, my guard, is right there, almost beside me. He followed me into the trees, as he should, but one look at his eyes and I know he's seen the girl, too. His own crossbow hangs ready in his hand, and a swell of fear rises in my gut.

He gives a brief shake of his head, the movement as minute as mine was. "You should not walk into the forest," he says. "Who knows what other dangers hide among the trees."

I fight to keep from gasping in relief. He will not pursue her.

My gaze returns to the spot where the girl hid. Only darkness waits there now.

If I look back at Parrish, Mother will know something is amiss. I straighten my shoulders. "Yes, Mother."

"Come join me."

She is sitting by the fire. Near the bodies.

This will be my punishment. For being too soft. For begging mercy.

This is why Nolla Verin will be queen.

CHAPTER FOUR

GREY

Since we saw the soldiers at Jodi's tavern yesterday, I've been tense and irritable. I keep expecting their captain to appear at Worwick's and drag me back to Ironrose. Or worse, to drag me into the shadows behind the stadium, where they can separate my head from my body.

These worries are irrational. So few people know who I truly am and what I know.

The enchantress Lilith—who is dead. I cut her throat myself.

My mother—who is not my mother at all. I walked out of her house with nothing. I left her with all the silver and coppers I had, and every warning I thought to give. Hopefully she took the money and left. But if anyone went to her seeking me, she'd have no answer to give beyond the truth: I showed up and I left.

Karis Luran—who, if Lilith's threats were to be believed, would use this information to destroy Rhen, if he'd believe her at all.

My surly attitude has rubbed off on Tycho, made worse by the ongoing heat wave. Today's weather brought a thickening cloud cover that seemed to promise storms, but only delivered a cloying humidity that makes everything sticky and everyone miserable. He's raking the space between the stadium seats and the arena, making each drag of the tool an attack on the dirt. Dust floats into the air, settling on everything, including the expensive cushioned seats that I've just wiped down.

"Hey," I snap.

He whips around, cringing a little.

"Put the rake up," I say, forcing the edge out of my tone. I dip my rag in a bucket and wring it out to wipe the seats again. "It's just making a mess."

He must feel bad, because when he comes back, he brings another rag to wipe down the railing. We work quietly for a while, relishing the late-afternoon silence.

When he's quiet like this, he reminds me of my brother Cade, who was thirteen when I was sixteen. I don't know why, because they're not at all alike, really. Cade would talk my ear off about nothing, while I sometimes go hours without hearing a word from Tycho. But Cade could put his head down and work when he needed to. He helped run the farm after I was gone.

After Lilith killed them all, I did my best to banish my siblings from memory. Maybe shoving away my time as a guardsman has allowed earlier memories to fill the space between my thoughts. Maybe learning they weren't my siblings at all has done the same.

I'm not sure I like that. Especially since we've run out of chores.

"It's too hot to run," I say.

"It's too hot to do anything." Tycho takes a handful of water and splashes it over the back of his neck.

"Oh," I say. "I was going to ask if you wanted to get the practice blades."

"Wait. Really? Yes." He stands up straight, the heat forgotten. "Go ahead, then."

I dump the bucket behind the storage room, then hang our rags to dry. By the time I make my way over to the armory, Tycho has a light training sword in his hands, and he's swinging it in a practiced pattern. He's good enough now that I'd trust him with a real blade—in another time and place. As Hawk, I don't know any moves more advanced than simple blocks and thrusts.

We spar in the narrow space between the armory and the stables, where Worwick stores larger equipment. The scraver's cage is back here, too, our only audience, though its dark form is motionless. Worwick was serious about five coppers, because he tried charging it last night. He was getting it, too, until a man complained that he didn't pay to see a half-dead pile of skin and feathers.

Now it sleeps most of the day, cocooned in its wings.

Tycho is tiring, so I give him an opening. He spots it immediately and lunges. I barely have time to sidestep his blade.

He's panting from the effort, but he grins. "I almost got you."

I can't help smiling back. "Almost." I tap his blade away with my own and push sweat-dampened hair off my face.

"Play time is over, boys," a man calls, his voice booming through the space. I recognize the voice before I see the man: Kantor. One of Worwick's "champions."

Worwick has two men who fight in the tourney: Kantor and Journ. They're both middle-aged and good with a sword—they must be, to fight any challenger who walks in here—but their real value to Worwick is in giving the audience a good show. One of them is quiet and reserved when he's not in front of a crowd, a man who carries hard candies in his pockets for children who cheer from the sidelines, then goes home to a sweet wife and three boys of his own. A good man who works hard, fights fair, and earns an honest living.

The other one is Kantor.

Kantor is a man who bets against himself, so even when he loses, he wins. Worwick shouldn't allow it, but I'm pretty sure Kantor cuts him in on his winnings. He's loud and boorish and lies without consideration. He makes for a good villain in front of the crowds. Unfortunately it doesn't stop when he's outside the arena.

Tycho moves to return his sword to the rack, but Kantor picks up one of the real swords and deftly knocks it out of his hand, sending it into the dust.

"When are you going to learn to hold a sword like a man?" he says.

"Leave him alone," I say.

Tycho silently fetches his weapon, but I catch a glimpse of his scowl, even though he keeps his head down in front of Kantor.

Kantor has the brain of a child, and he's found an entertaining diversion, so it barely takes a shift of his weight for me to see he's going to smack Tycho's sword away again—and this time he's going to make it hurt.

I step forward, swing my practice blade down, and pin Kantor's sword to the wall.

His head whips around. His mouth hangs open, though he quickly snaps it closed.

"I should take off your hand for that." He scrapes his weapon free.

I could take off *his* hand before he'd get close to mine, but I shrug and look away. The best way to deal with Kantor is to not take him too seriously. "The practice blades dull the real ones. If you want to play, use your own, or take it up with Worwick."

He frowns, but I'm right and he knows it. His pride won't let him hang up the weapon, though. He moves away, twisting the sword in his hands, letting it cut patterns into the dust. He stops by the scraver's cage.

"What is Worwick going to do with this thing?" Kantor pokes at it with the tip of his sword, and the creature doesn't move.

"Don't hurt it," Tycho says.

"Hurt it? It's practically dead." Kantor steps close and jabs the weapon through the bars, his steel blade piercing flesh.

The scraver roars and spins to its feet in a whirl of wings and blood. It slams against the bars, claws reaching for Kantor, screeching so loudly that it echoes through the arena and the horses in the stable begin to stamp and fuss.

Kantor jerks back, trips over his own feet, and lands hard in the dust. Three long stripes of blood cross his forearm. Kantor swears and surges off the ground, lifting his sword as if he's going to plunge it into the creature's midsection.

Tycho dives in front of him, putting his back against the bars. "No!"

I expect the scraver to slice those claws into Tycho as well, but the creature falls back and growls.

Kantor looks like he's ready to go through Tycho anyway.

I step in front of him. "Enough."

Kantor lifts his sword a few inches. "Move, or I'll go through you both."

The training blade is still in my hand. My fingers tighten on the hilt.

I don't know what Kantor sees in my expression, but surprise lights in his eyes. He gives a rough laugh. "You want to fight me, boy? Over that thing?" He gestures with his blade. "Go ahead, then. See how long you last."

I'm tempted.

"What's going on?" calls Worwick, his voice booming across the small area. The screeching must have drawn his attention. It probably caught the attention of half the city.

In my peripheral vision, I see Worwick come around the corner, but I don't take my eyes off the man in front of me. Kantor doesn't take his off me.

"Kantor! Hawk!" Worwick sounds confused. "What . . . what are you doing?"

"Kantor was going to kill your scraver," pipes up Tycho. "Hawk stopped him."

"Ah, I was just fooling around," drawls Kantor. He lowers his sword and holds out his arm. "The damn thing got me good."

"You got it first," I say.

Behind me, the scraver growls again.

"Enough foolishness," says Worwick. "The Grand Marshal has dropped off a royal decree to be read before the tourney. Rumors are running wild in the street, so we'll have a packed house tonight."

That's enough to pull my attention away from Kantor. "A royal decree?"

"The prince is offering five hundred silvers to anyone who can produce someone with the blood of a magesmith."

I freeze. *The blood of a magesmith.* Rhen can't say it outright, because he'd lend legitimacy to the rumors, but he's looking for the heir.

He's looking for *me*.

"Five hundred silvers!" Kantor finally lowers his blade and turns away from me. "Worwick, I'd turn *you* in for five hundred silvers."

"Evidence of magic must be proven," says Worwick. His eyes light up. "Tycho. Hawk. You spend time in the city. You haven't seen evidence of magic in Rillisk, have you?"

As if we'd give him someone's name and allow him to claim the coins.

But at least this offers me some measure of safety. I've never been able to use magic on my own. Maybe Lilith was wrong. Maybe I'm not the heir to anything at all.

Don't you want to know the truth? she said to me. *About the blood that runs in your veins? About how you were the only guardsman to survive?*

I want her to be wrong.

She's not, though. I know she's not. My mother admitted it before I fled.

"No one has seen magic," says Tycho. "The magesmiths were killed off before I was born."

"Not all of them, apparently," says Worwick. "Hawk, are you ill?"

"No. I'm fine." I force my limbs to move, and I hang the blade along the wall.

"Kantor, did you cut my scraver?" Worwick *tsks*. "Hawk, stitch it up, would you?"

"Yes." I have no idea how I'll do that, but my brain won't stop spinning.

Five hundred silvers is a fortune to most. The people of Emberfall will turn on each other to claim it. Rhen must be desperate.

"Be ready for crowds, boys," says Worwick. "Tycho, be ready to
pour. I don't want lines for ale. We'll turn a pretty profit in gam-
bling alone, I'm sure."

"I'll make sure of it." Kantor laughs. He smacks the other man
on the shoulder good-naturedly. Worwick smiles and heads back
toward the front of the tourney.

I sigh and look at Tycho. "Fetch some ropes. I'll get the needle."

———————

The tourney doesn't close until well after midnight. When we
finally climb the ladder to our shared loft, Tycho doesn't bother to
light the lantern; he just falls into his bed. I expect him to tumble
into sleep just as quickly, but instead he says, "I can't imagine five
hundred silvers all together."

I don't need to imagine it, but I say, "I've been hearing about
that all night."

"Do you think it's heavy?"

"Heavy enough to make you walk crooked." This isn't true, but
it makes him laugh, and then he falls silent.

I stare at the worn wooden rafters over my bed. The loft smells
of hay and horses and holds the heat of the stable below, but I don't
mind. It's warm and safe and dry here. I have nothing to fear from
Tycho.

"It would buy my freedom from Worwick," he says quietly.

I turn my head to look at him, barely a dim shadow in the midnight darkness. "Your freedom?"

"I'm sworn to him." He pauses. "Two more years."

"Why?"

"Bad luck. Bad debts."

I've never seen Tycho gamble a single copper. "Not yours."

"My father." He takes a long breath. "I have two younger sisters, but I know what Worwick would have used them for. My brother is barely six. My family had nothing left to give. So . . ."

I look back at the rafters. "I once swore my life away to save my family—but my oath was freely given."

"Mine was too," he says.

This doesn't feel the same. But maybe it is.

"Two years isn't so very long," Tycho says. "How long did it take for you to earn your freedom?"

This conversation is dragging memories to the surface, memories that are better left buried. "An eternity."

Tycho laughs softly. "I know what you mean."

No. He has no idea.

When he speaks again, his voice is halting. "Hawk, I don't—I don't tell anyone." A note of worry threads between his words. "If people know I'm sworn to Worwick, they would . . . well, *he* might . . ." His voice trails off.

I consider how Tycho tends to vanish once the nights drag on and sober men are few. It makes me think better of Worwick that he doesn't work the boy into the ground. That he allows him to hide. "I'll keep your secret."

He says nothing to that, and after a moment, I look over. The darkness is nearly absolute, but his eyes catch a gleam of light from somewhere.

I wonder if he's regretting sharing this. "You have nothing to fear from me, Tycho."

"I know."

He says it so simply. It's a level of trust I envy.

"Who were you sworn to?" he says.

My eyes fall closed. Without warning, my thoughts conjure Ironrose Castle, the miles of marble hallways, the arching painted ceilings. I remember the training arena, the armory, the stables—so clearly that I could find my way around blindfolded, even now.

Do you regret your oath? Rhen once asked me.

I did not. I do not. Not even now.

Tycho is still waiting for an answer. I shake my head. "No one of consequence."

"I'd keep your secret too, Hawk." Tycho's voice is soft.

His intentions are good, and he may mean those words now, but he'd take my secret, turn me in, and buy his freedom.

"No secrets," I say lazily. I roll over, facing away from him. "Just nothing interesting to share."

He sighs, but I let my breathing go slow and even, so he thinks I have fallen asleep. Eventually, his own matches, accented by a tiny snore at the end of each breath.

Our conversation guarantees I won't fall asleep anytime soon.

When Rhen released me from my oath, he told me to begin a new life on the other side—in Washington, DC, Harper's home. My visits to her city were limited to one hour each season, so I am not ignorant of her world, but I could not imagine making my way in a place so very different from Emberfall. The customs, the clothing, the currency—I have seen it, but I do not know if I could mimic it.

The blood of a magesmith. If I have magic in my blood, I have no idea how to access it. I stare up at the rafters and remember how easily Lilith's magic used to transport me through the veil into Washington, DC. I close my eyes and remember the feeling of it. For an instant, the air around me seems heavier, and I hold my breath, wondering if I've done it.

My eyes flick open. The stable rafters hang above me. Tycho breathes softly across the loft.

Silver hell.

I pick at the threading along the edge of my mattress, pulling slowly until the seam begins to come apart. I do this carefully so I can pull the threads back together later. I ease my hand into the opening, digging through the straw until I feel the heavy weight of silver.

It's a bracelet—or it was, until I traded a day's worth of hard labor for a blacksmith to get it off my arm. Now I have a scar on my wrist and a crude three-quarter circlet of silver. When I was trapped in the curse with Rhen, Lilith bound it to my arm with magic to allow me to cross the veil to the other side.

I have no idea if it still works. It's the only magic I've ever been able to work, and it's not mine, it's Lilith's. The bracelet is enchanted with *her* magic.

I close my fingers around the loop of silver and close my eyes. Almost against my will, my brain imagines a wall—then just as quickly imagines me passing through it.

The scents of the barn and the loft disappear, and the air is suddenly cool. The quiet sound of movement from the horses has been replaced with a low hum, and I open my eyes. White walls, long, tubular lights overhead, though they're dim. Towers and towers of books stretch on forever, surrounding me. More books than I have ever seen, even in the royal library at Ironrose. This place is nothing like the castle, however. Aside from the books, everything about this room is smooth and sleek and almost unnaturally white.

I'm not in Rillisk. I'm not in Emberfall at all. I'm in Washington, DC. Or possibly miles away, wherever Rillisk would correlate in Harper's world.

The bracelet still works.

For a moment, I sit and inhale the cool air, such a relief after the weighted humidity in Emberfall. I have no idea where I am, but it's quiet and I'm safe. Rhen can't reach me here. Likely *no one* can reach me here. It's tempting to stay.

But where would I go? What would I do? No one on this side needs a swordsman—nor a stable hand, from what I've seen. The girls I used to kidnap for Rhen rarely had skills with weaponry or horses, and while I'm certain they had skills of their own that would be useful in this place, they are not skills I share.

Something metal rattles, followed by a squeak, and I scramble to my feet. I wish for a weapon, but the only thing clenched in my hand is the silver bracelet.

An older woman pushes some kind of cart around a corner. Her hair is long and gray and tied into a braid that hangs over one shoulder. She startles when she sees me, but her expression quickly smooths out. She gives me a kind smile. "I know the library is twenty-four hours, but students aren't allowed to sleep here."

I take a breath. "Forgive me."

Her eyes skip down my form, taking in my clothes from Rillisk, which are nothing like the clothes from this side. When she gets to my bare feet, her lips turn downward. "Do you have somewhere else to sleep?"

I wonder what she would do if I said no. I wonder where I

would go—or where she would send me. She appears kind. I wonder if I *could* find refuge here.

A man appears around the corner, younger and heavier than the woman, and he frowns when he sees me. He looks as startled as she was, but his eyes are more coolly assessing. He speaks low, under his breath, but I hear him anyway. "Homeless?" he whispers. "Should I call the cops?"

She gives a tiny nod, but then she takes a step closer to me. "Are you hungry? We can get you something to eat."

My ears are stuck on his question. *The cops.* Enforcers on this side. I've run into them before. They mean nothing good to someone like me.

I can find no refuge here. Not now. Not like this.

I close my eyes. Imagine the wall. Pass through.

Silent darkness, quick and sudden, presses against my eyelids. I'm safe. I'm back. I take a long breath and open my eyes.

Tycho is standing right in front of me.

Silver hell. The bracelet slips from my fingers and clatters to the wood floor.

He's wide-eyed and breathing like he's being chased. "You vanished." His eyes flick to my bed, six feet away now, then back to my face. "Then reappeared just there."

I say nothing. I can't deny it.

His eyes search mine in the darkness. "Is it you they're looking for?"

"You'll seal your fate with that question."

Tycho swallows. "Hawk. Is it you?"

Tension has joined us in the loft, a silent judge, trapping me in place. "Yes."

"What would they do if they found you?"

"They won't."

The words come out like a threat, and he flinches. It should summon sympathy in me, but it doesn't. I've learned how to lock away emotion and do what is necessary. Too well.

Tycho takes a deep breath, and he must steel his nerve, because he straightens and looks at me. He's braver than he thinks. "Tell me what they'd do."

"I do not know for sure, but it likely would not end well for me."

"They'd kill you?"

"Yes."

His voice has grown quiet. "Did you do something very bad?"

"The answer to that is long and complicated." I consider his expression. "But no. Not in the way you mean. I am not hunted for what I've *done*, but for who I *am*."

He studies me. I study him. I could break his neck in the space between breaths. I could drop his body from the loft so it would look like he fell from the ladder in the night. No one would question it. Tycho is a shadow. Likely no one would mourn.

I would.

The thought hits me like an arrow, piercing and true. I rub my hands over my face. I would mourn. I don't want to hurt him. He trusts me. Possibly *only* me.

His hand touches my forearm, and I jerk my hands down.

"I'll keep your secret," Tycho says, his voice as low and earnest as it was before this all unraveled.

"Even though you could buy your freedom?"

He looks startled, then hurt. "I'm not buying my freedom with your *death*."

It's my turn to flinch. I very nearly did exactly that to him. I take a steadying breath, then reach out to ruffle his hair and give him a good-natured shove. "I'm honored to have your trust, Tycho."

He blushes so deeply that I can see it in the near darkness. "Well, I'm honored to have yours, Hawk."

The tension between us has evaporated so smoothly that it's almost as if I imagined it. I remember what it was like to trust someone. I remember what it was like to have a *friend*. I didn't realize how much I missed it until it was so freely offered.

"Grey," I say softly. "Not Hawk."

His eyes widen, but he smiles. "Grey."

"It will put you in danger to keep my secret." My voice is grave. "If I'm caught and they find out you knew."

"Then don't get caught."

That makes me smile. "Go back to bed," I say. "The horses will be calling for their breakfast before sunrise."

He climbs back onto his bed, and I climb into mine, and silence falls between us again. It's easier this time. My heart no longer races along, looking to evade an unseen threat.

"Jodi said you eat like a nobleman," Tycho says. "Were you? Before?"

"No." It's such a relief to tell *someone* that I very much want to pour the whole story at his feet, just to share the burden. "I was a swordsman. In the Royal Guard."

"Oh." The weight of this knowledge forces him back into silence for a while, but then he rolls over to face me. "Wait."

I freeze, wondering if this will change things. "Yes?"

"Then you've been holding back. When we use the practice blades."

"Yes. I have."

"So you could teach me more?" he says.

He sounds so eager that I laugh. I likely could have bargained his silence for lessons in swordplay.

"Could you?" he presses. "If we practice in secret?"

"Yes," I say, smiling. "Yes, indeed."

CHAPTER FIVE

LIA MARA

Days pass. By the time we draw close to the prince's castle, I am travel-worn and weary. I still share a carriage with my sister, because the alternative is to share a carriage with my mother. Nolla Verin might not understand my despondency, but she won't lecture me about the duties of a ruler. She knows why I'm upset—likely *every-one* knows why I'm upset—but she makes no apology for what happened with the trapper and the girl.

I don't expect one. I don't *want* one. I know why she made the choice she did. I know our mother is proud of the choice she made.

I should be proud as well. I'm not. My thoughts are haunted by the memory of the girl cowering beneath her father.

And the tear-streaked cheeks of the girl hiding in the woods.

I have made no mention of her to anyone. Not even to Parrish. His manner seems unchanged, to the point where I started to believe that I imagined the whole thing. But that night I saw him exchange a quiet word with Sorra, and for a brief moment, her eyes shifted to me and then away.

I do not know what that means.

Nolla Verin pokes me with her embroidery needle, and I jump.

"I need you at your best, Sister," she says.

I keep my eyes on the veiled window of the carriage. "You don't need me at all. I can wait with the horses."

She sighs and rolls her eyes.

"Mother should have left me at home," I continue. After what I've seen, I would have preferred it. Despite the sting of our mother's choice, there's a touch of freedom to no longer worrying about becoming queen. The weather is cooler on the other side of the mountain, and I could have spent these days lounging in bed with a book. I could have gone for a ride along the lakeside instead of being faced with death and destruction.

These thoughts feel selfish suddenly. Cowardly. The girl and her father still would have died. I just wouldn't have known about it.

"Please, Lia Mara."

A new note hangs in my sister's voice, and it draws my attention. For all her cavalier comments, a bit of uncertainty hides in the depths of her eyes.

"You are nervous," I say.

She shrugs a bit and glances down at the square of fabric in her lap. Over the course of our journey, embroidered flowers and jewels of every color have filled the fabric to form a circle. "He is still our enemy." She pauses. "He already has a woman he loves."

"Nolla Verin." I study her. My sister is sharp-featured and beautiful, but it is her carefree confidence that turns heads everywhere she goes. "Are you afraid of being *rejected*?"

"Not *me*." She stabs her needle through the fabric. "I am afraid of our proposal being rejected. Mother will be forced to send our armies through the mountain pass to raze cities and take control of this land."

I stare at her, mouth nearly agape. It is the first time she has ever expressed dismay at military action. A small burst of hope flares in my chest.

She looks at me. "You are so surprised. Did you not think I would fear failing in front of Mother?"

I close my mouth. I should have known better. Nolla Verin does not concern herself with the loss of lives. She is concerned about disappointing *our mother*.

I need to remove the sour look from my face before she sees it. "I have the utmost faith in you, Sister."

Outside the carriage, the sound of bells peals out, loud and repetitive. Nolla Verin sits upright, stashing her embroidery in the compartment under her seat. I wonder if it is to be a gift for the prince. The thought does nothing to remove the bitter taste from my mouth.

"We have been spotted," she says in a rush. "Mother says the bells all mean something. They sound bright, don't they? Maybe this is a good omen."

They don't sound bright to me. They sound like a death knell. Maybe they mean the prince's archers will set our carriage on fire.

"A good omen indeed," I say, forcing a smile on my face.

The carriage jerks and shifts as the horses draw us onto new terrain. Cobblestones, from the feel of it. Nerves flutter in my belly despite myself. An hour ago, our guards hung our green-and-black banners and pennants from the carriages, adorning the horses with the trappings we'd kept hidden while traveling through Emberfall.

I want so badly to lean out the window to see the castle, but I would never hear the end of it. If Nolla Verin can sit across from me so prim and patient, I can do the same.

When the carriage rattles to a stop, we sit and wait. One of Mother's guards announces us and requests an audience with the prince. One of his guards announces that we must wait for the prince to decide whether he will invite us into the castle.

That will not go over well with Mother.

Indeed, I am not surprised when I hear her voice announcing that we will not wait, and if the so-called Crown Prince of Emberfall will not meet with us, she will happily return to Syhl Shallow to bring down a force of reckoning upon his people.

A male voice says, "Karis Luran. Surely you can grant me the time to cross the halls of Ironrose before declaring war."

This must be Prince Rhen. No one else would speak with such authority. He has a nice voice, a tone backed with iron but warm enough to invite conversation. I wonder what he looks like.

Across from me, Nolla Verin's face has gone carefully neutral. Not bored, but not interested either. She sits back along her bench to wait.

Almost immediately, the carriage door is drawn open by Sorra. She moves with fluid precision, every movement reflecting the training and unity among our guards. Sunlight fills the carriage in a burst, blinding us for a moment.

As oldest daughter, I am to step from the carriage first. At one time I thought it a position of honor, but over the last few days I have begun to wonder if Mother was always setting the stage for the main event: my sister.

Today, I don't mind. I am the first to see the castle built from cream-colored bricks, stretching high into the sky, gold and red pennants flying in the slight summer breeze. I am the first to see the wide marble steps leading up to the castle door, and the two dozen guards flanking our carriages. Each carries a sword and a dagger, gold and silver shining in the sunlight. Each breastplate sports a stamped crest of a lion and a rose over the heart.

I am the first to see the prince, tall and blond, as striking as my sister in his own way. His eyes give away nothing. He wears a dark-blue jacket that buckles across his chest, along with high boots. He, too, wears a sword at his hip, which takes me by surprise. Mother never wears a weapon. She says it would tell our people she does not trust them.

Beside the prince stands a pretty young woman with cream-colored skin and dark, curly hair, wearing a red gown that sweeps along the cobblestones as they approach our carriages. She walks with a limp, which makes me wonder if the hand placed against the prince's elbow is for support or to show they are together. Unlike the prince, her face reveals everything: wide, concerned eyes, mouth tight with worry.

Our presence here unnerves her.

She and I are alike in that.

Mother's voice rings out. "My elder daughter, Lia Mara."

The prince offers me a nod, which I return, and then I step to the side so Nolla Verin can emerge from the carriage.

Every eye is on my sister, but I've seen that show a thousand times, so I watch the prince. I want to see if his eyes flicker with interest.

Either he is too practiced or too indifferent, because there is none. He watches my sister step out of the carriage with the same attention he might give a passing curiosity.

"My younger daughter, Nolla Verin," says Mother. "Heir to the throne of Syhl Shallow."

The prince offers her a nod, too, but the princess beside him glances from Nolla Verin to me.

"Your younger daughter is heir?" she says.

Mother purses her lips. She does not like being questioned. "In Syhl Shallow, an heir is not determined by birth order." She looks at Rhen. "Would that your country's laws allowed for the same, and you would not be facing conflict, boy."

"I have no conflict," he says.

Mother laughs. "As always, you hide your secrets well, young prince, but I can see the weakness in the lies you weave for your people."

"My people are at peace. If you have come to sow discord, I insist that you leave at once."

"I have heard rumors that cities have begun to reject your right to rule." Mother glances at the princess. "Rumor also says the King of Emberfall has perished in Disi, is that correct?"

"That is correct," says Prince Rhen. "Have you traveled all this way to offer your condolences?"

"No. It was the work of assassins, I understand." Mother's voice is full of skepticism.

"Our people did our best to protect King Broderick," says the princess. Her voice does not carry the same authority as Prince Rhen's. Close, but not the same. Anyone else might not notice a difference, but I have been raised among royalty, and eighteen years at court has taught me the difference between people who are born to royalty and those who merely hope to imitate it.

"Your people." Mother looks at her, and her tone confirms that she has noticed the same thing. "Is that so, *Princess* Harper?"

"That is so." Her voice gains a backing of steel. Prince Rhen's fingers press over her hand on his elbow, almost as if to hold her back.

"And what of your coronation, boy?" says my mother. "Is there a celebration planned?"

The prince hesitates.

That is telling. I hold my breath.

"What of your ascension to the throne?" my mother continues. "What of your people, who demand the true heir?"

"There is no other heir," says Prince Rhen, his voice clipped. "No claim has been made. No man has appeared. I am the crown prince, and I stand ready to take the throne and lead my people."

"I have heard you offer a bounty for a man possessing the blood of a magesmith. Is that somehow related?"

His jaw tightens. "Magic wreaked havoc in my country for years, as you know. I will not allow harm to come to my people again."

"Then we have similar goals. I believe I can provide a measure of security for your people."

The prince's expression is dark. "Explain."

She holds out a hand, and Nolla Verin steps forward. "I have come to propose peace between our peoples. I have come to offer my daughter's hand to you."

Prince Rhen's expression doesn't change, but at his side, Princess Harper looks like she swallowed a live fish.

"You attempted to destroy my country and you failed," says Prince Rhen. "I will not now ally Emberfall with Syhl Shallow."

"You stopped my army with magic and trickery," my mother

says. "Now you have no monstrous creature waiting to do your bidding. You have people who are growing increasingly divided. You have *nothing* aside from my offer to protect your subjects."

He sets his jaw. "I *will not ally* with Syhl Shallow."

"I am offering my daughter, my *heir,* to rule side by side with you. Surely even you must know how rare an offer that is from my people. You will not even entertain a meeting with me?"

"I have no interest in what you can offer." His hand tightens on Harper's, and I wonder if she is now holding *him* back. "I have no interest in an alliance with your country. I can grant you safe passage back to the mountain pass, so you can return to rule Syhl Shallow and I will continue to rule Emberfall."

Nolla Verin steps forward, her black hair gleaming in the sunlight. The green and black stripes on her robes are shot through with silver stitching that glints with each movement. "I heard you were a just and fair ruler," she says. "Yet you will not offer your people the consideration of an alliance with my own?"

The prince looks down at her from where he stands on the marble steps. "I have seen the destruction wrought by your people, *girl.*"

The word is a barb meant to equate with my mother so rudely calling him *boy,* but my sister reacts as if he slapped her. Each word out of her mouth carries an edge. "I am to rule Syhl Shallow, and if you will not entertain an alliance, you would do well to consider respect for my position."

I wish I could catch her hand and squeeze it tightly, the way Harper seems to keep the prince's temper in check. This is not a man who will respond well to haughty threats.

Indeed, his eyes turn flinty. "Forgive me if I do not bear much respect for those who would slaughter my people."

I think of that trapper and his daughter again, and I have to swallow the lump of emotion that forms in my throat.

My sister raises her chin. "We are here to *stop* the needless slaughter of your people."

"We are at an impasse," says Prince Rhen. "For I do not trust you."

"What if we were to offer you information on Emberfall's missing heir?" says Nolla Verin.

Prince Rhen goes very still. Every ear in the courtyard seems to lean in. Even his own guards are curious.

"Where is your guard commander?" says my mother.

"Commander Dustan is traveling with Jacob, brother to Princess Harper and heir to the throne of Disi, along with his talented healer, Noah of Alexandria." He pauses, and his voice tightens. "They are visiting my cities to see if they can provide assistance to the people injured by *your* soldiers."

"No," says my mother. "Where is Commander Grey? The man who stood with you during my last visit."

"Commander Grey is dead. He died in the final battle with the enchantress."

At his side, Princess Harper flinches.

My mother doesn't miss it. "When we last met, I told you of your father's first marriage. I told you how it was consummated in Syhl Shallow. I told you that a halfling child was born. Do you remember?" She doesn't wait for an answer. "I told you of the tithe your father paid to keep this secret. If you think your people cannot see through your efforts to find a magesmith—to find your *brother*— then either you are a great fool or you think each of your subjects is."

His face has paled a shade, but his voice is strong. "My people know I will do whatever it takes to keep them safe."

Nolla Verin stares up at him. "If a magesmith lives, if a magesmith is heir to your throne, I would expect we would be well-suited to help each other."

"There is nothing you can offer me. Guards, escort them off the grounds."

A jolt goes through me. We've failed.

This will mean war. More death. More destruction.

"Wait," says Harper. Her voice is full of emotion. "Wait." She swallows. "Why did you ask about Grey?"

Mother stares up at her and smiles. "You do not think he is dead, do you, Princess?"

Prince Rhen turns his head and says something softly, but Harper clenches her eyes closed. A tear slips down her cheek. "We don't know."

"A pity," Mother says. "Come, Daughters. We will leave the prince to his choice."

"Wait," Harper calls. Her red skirts flare as she hurries down the palace steps. "What do you know about Grey?"

Our guards step forward to prevent her from getting anywhere close to Mother.

Prince Rhen's guards do the exact same thing.

They stare at each other across a barrier of protection. Mother's expression is carefully neutral, but Harper's is flushed, her eyes pleading.

"You should hope he is dead," says Mother. "For the sake of your prince. For the sake of his kingdom."

Harper's breath catches. "Why?"

"According to the enchantress, Grey is the only man who knows the true identity of the heir."

Harper goes white. Prince Rhen has reached her side, and his face is full of fury. "This is not the first time you have attempted to undermine my rule with trickery and lies. You will not get another chance. Leave. Now."

Mother turns for her carriage.

Nolla Verin climbs into ours. I follow, my heart thudding at a rapid pace. A guard slams the door.

"He is a *fool*," Nolla Verin says to me before the horses begin to pull away. Her voice is loud enough that I'm certain the prince will hear it.

I think of the damage we caused to this country already.

I think of that trapper in the woods, his daughter cowering beneath him.

This should have gone so differently. Nolla Verin implied I would have sought an alliance with nuts and honey—but I know I wouldn't have sought one with callous arrogance and disregard.

The prince is not a fool, I want to say.

But I am not the heir, so I don't.

CHAPTER SIX

GREY

Jodi's tavern is packed. The heat wave has men thirsty for ale and women looking for any excuse to get out of the sun. The heady scent of shellfish and baked vegetables mixes with the slightly sweet tang of liquor for those with a few more coins to pay. Tycho and I take a table near the back just to get away from the noise.

Days have passed, and our shared secret seems to have bonded him to my side like a brother. We've been sparring in the early-morning hours when the sky is barely pink and the tourney is deserted. After only a matter of days, his skill with a blade has improved exponentially. It's more than the swordplay, though. It's the trust. A wall has come down between us that I didn't even know was there.

Jodi brings a pitcher of water to replace the one we've emptied, along with a basket of steaming bread and a thick slab of cheese. She casually bumps my shoulder with her hip, then leans down close, so the feathers in her hair tickle my forearm. "I wish I could hide back here with you two."

She smells like strawberries. She must have been slicing them for the wine. "You're welcome to try." I nod at the packed front of the tavern. "I think they'd seek you out before long, though."

She pouts. "You'd protect me from them all, wouldn't you, Hawk?"

I pull a hunk of bread from the loaf. "You'd do better to ask Tycho. He's braver than I am."

She swats me on the back of the head and moves away.

I use the knife to slice a piece of cheese to add to the bread, then realize Tycho is staring at me. "What?"

His voice is low. "I think Jodi might fancy you."

Jodi couldn't be more obvious if she climbed into my lap and began unlacing my shirt. "I've noticed."

"You don't fancy her?"

I glance across the tavern, where Jodi is sashaying between tables. She flirts with all her customers, but she never lingers like she does with me.

We're far from other patrons, but I drop my voice anyway. "To be a guardsman, you had to forswear family."

"Forswear?"

"Pretend they don't exist." I hesitate. "Family is a liability. If a guardsman can be manipulated by a threat to those he cares for, he can be used against the Crown."

He frowns. "So . . . what? You're to care for *no one*?"

I think of my mother—or the woman I *thought* to be my mother—watching me leave with panicked eyes. I think of my nine brothers and sisters, slaughtered one by one as Lilith attempted to manipulate me into betraying Prince Rhen.

Her efforts did not work. My training was too thorough, my loyalty too steadfast. There was no one she could have used against me.

Unbidden, my thoughts conjure Harper, her fierce bravery countered only by her gentle kindness. I remember the day she convinced a cadre of Syhl Shallow soldiers that she was the princess of another nation. How after they left, spitting threats and promises of revenge, she didn't choose to run and hide. She asked me to show her how to throw knives.

When Lilith threatened to kill Harper, I yielded. I got down on my knees and offered to swear myself to her.

I refuse to allow these thoughts to hold any power over me. "I've forgotten how to care for anyone, Tycho."

He studies me for the longest moment. "I don't think that's true."

I consider how I almost tossed him from the hayloft, and I'm not sure what to say. I tear another piece of bread from the loaf.

"You can't train mercy out of someone," he says.

"You surely can."

He's frowning again. I tear another piece of bread and hold it out. "Eat. I don't want to have to run back."

Dutifully, he eats. We lapse into silence, and the space around us fills with the braying laughter and heady conversation that packs the tavern. Near the door, an older man with a heavy paunch is draining what must be his third tankard of ale. His name is Riley, and he's telling a story about a blind woman who was sold a donkey instead of a draft horse, and he couldn't convince her otherwise. He's one of the few blacksmiths in Rillisk, but he and Worwick share an old grudge, so he doesn't shoe our horses. He probably charged Worwick a fair price, which to Worwick would be too much.

Jodi passes our table again, her hand brushing against my arm. I entertain the thought of catching her fingers and drawing her back. It would be simple. Uncomplicated. I could lose myself further into the persona of Hawk, leaving Grey behind.

When she turns, I meet her eyes, and she smiles.

I offer one of my own, and she blushes.

This should feel easy. It doesn't. It feels like manipulation.

I break eye contact and look back at my bread. "Nearly done?" I say to Tycho, and my voice is rough.

He nods and pulls coppers from the pouch at his waist.

The door at the front of the tavern swings open, and a group of men enter slowly. The tavern is too loud and crowded for them to garner much attention, but light glints on steel, and I catch a flash of red.

I go still. My hand finds the knife.

But it's not a Royal Guard uniform. It's the Grand Marshal's enforcers. The leading man is older, with graying hair and a thick beard, a patch covering one eye. He's trailed by three others.

"Where is the blacksmith called Riley?" he announces, and there's enough weight in his voice that conversation dulls to a murmur. Every head in the tavern turns to look at the corner where Riley sits.

Riley shoves back his chair and stands. He's an honest man, so he looks more confused than concerned. "I am Riley."

"You are accused of using magic to better your trade. You will come with us."

Riley falls back a step. "I don't— I've never— I know no *magic*."

The guards have already begun surrounding him. The other men at the table have drawn away. All conversation has stopped.

Riley continues to backpedal. Men get out of his way as if he's diseased. One of the enforcers has a sword drawn.

"I know no magic!" he cries. "I am a blacksmith!"

The lead man gives a signal to the others, and the men move through the tables as if to cut off escape.

"Hawk," whispers Tycho. "Hawk—we have to—"

I silence him with a look, but his eyes still plead. I don't know if he wants me to intervene or surrender myself or something I can't fathom, but I can do nothing. I cannot draw attention to myself. Not now.

The one-eyed man seizes Riley's forearm. "You are to come with us."

Riley jerks back. His face is red, from shame or fury or both. "I have done nothing wrong! You can't seize peaceful citizens—"

"We have our orders." Another enforcer grabs his other arm.

Riley looks around desperately, but the other patrons have cleared a wide path. "Will no one speak for me?"

With a ruffle of skirts and defiance, Jodi sweeps past me. She's inhaling to protest.

I catch her arm and tug her back against me. We're far enough in the corner that we haven't drawn attention away from Riley, but if she keeps struggling, we will. "Jodi," I whisper against her hair. "Let them take him peacefully."

She strains against my arm, but she has the good sense to keep her voice down. "He's a good man."

"Then they'll question him and let him go. He'll lose a day of wages and earn a good story to tell over the next round of ale."

Across the table, Tycho's eyes are wide. I must sound sure, because Jodi relaxes.

Riley is struggling against the enforcers. He's strong, and he gets an arm free.

The one-eyed man drives a fist into his belly. Riley doubles over with a grunt and nearly falls to a knee. They get a grip on him again and half drag him to the doorway.

"You can't do this," he wheezes. "I heard about the tailor in Lackey's Keep. You can't accuse good people."

The enforcers ignore Riley, yanking him forward impassively. When they reach the door, one of the men releases his arm to grab the handle.

Riley whirls and grabs one of their weapons. I don't know his motive, whether he thinks he'll be able to fight his way free or defend himself or buy more time, but I'll never get the chance to ask him. One of the other enforcers puts a sword through his chest. A choked sound breaks from Riley's lips, and he goes down.

A collective gasp goes through the tavern.

Jodi slips free of my hold. "You monster!" she cries. She throws herself at the enforcer who stabbed Riley, shoving him away. "How *could* you?"

He catches her arm and gives her a little shake. The one-eyed man lifts his sword.

Without thought, I shove my way in front of her. His sword point finds my chest, a weight of steel against my shirtfront.

"Enough," I say. His one eye narrows.

Jodi is shaking against me.

I think of my last words to her. *They'll question him and let him go.*

I should have known better. I *did* know better.

Glances are exchanged throughout the tavern. People shift nervously. Chairs scrape against the wood floor. Shaking breath comes from all directions.

A man's voice speaks up uncertainly from near the front. "I always thought there was something unnatural about the way he could unlame a horse."

"His forge always seemed to run hotter than the others," another man agrees.

"Did you see that nag brought down from Hutchins Forge?" says a woman. "Riley said he had something special that would make its gait straight—and sure enough, he did."

That sword is still sitting against my chest. "She attacked an enforcer," says the one-eyed man.

"She's upset. She didn't mean any harm." I thrust a hand into my pocket and withdraw a handful of coppers. I hold it out to him. "Buy your men a drink on me."

He regards me coolly. Tension rides a knife's edge. The other patrons wait to see if another man is going to die.

I jingle the coins in my hand. "Worwick will be upset if I don't show up to open the tourney."

He grunts and withdraws his sword. "You tell her to mind her own business next time."

"Yes, sir." I turn and press the coins into Jodi's hand. Her eyes are full of tears, and her fingers tremble hard enough to make the coins rattle. "Buy them a drink," I say quietly.

"He was a good man," she whispers. "He was a good man, wasn't he, Hawk?"

I close her fingers around the coins to silence them. "You need to set the tavern to rights, Jodi. Don't give them a reason to start something else."

Maybe she hears the urgency in my voice, because she sucks back the tears and straightens her skirts. She nods quickly.

I look to Tycho, who's been watching with wide eyes. "Worwick will expect crowds after this. We need to get back."

Late-evening sun streaks through the city when we emerge

from the tavern. Tycho keeps his mouth shut and stays close to my side as we weave through the gathering crowds outside the tavern.

Gossip travels fast.

When we're in the deserted back alleys, Tycho ventures a question. "Do you think he was a magesmith?"

I give him a look.

He swallows. "They killed him, Hawk."

They'll likely receive a reward, too. "I told you what they'd do."

"But—how did they know if he was guilty?"

"That doesn't matter. This isn't about guilt. This is about scaring the people into believing a magesmith can be caught and killed easily. This is about proving there is no threat to the Crown." A bitter taste lingers in my mouth. A man died because of me.

I cannot outrun this. There is nowhere to go.

Tycho's voice jerks me out of my reverie. "Is that why so many people were suspicious?"

"It's easier to believe someone is guilty than to consider that an innocent man could be eating oysters one minute and bleeding on the floorboards the next."

That shocks him into silence. We walk quickly. I rub at the back of my neck, dragging sweat away. We've made good distance from the tavern, and gossip hasn't reached this far yet. A girl is driving sheep through the narrow alley, and Tycho and I pull into a doorway to let them pass.

His eyes are on me, but I can't meet his gaze. "Would you have done it?"

I watch the shorn backs of the sheep as they bleat their way past. "Done what?"

"Would you have killed him?" He swallows. "When you were a guardsman?"

I think back to my service to King Broderick, before the curse. I consider my near-eternity with Prince Rhen, when we were trapped in the halls of Ironrose. I would like to think he'd never give orders that would lead to this kind of action.

I know better. It would have cost him something, but Rhen would do it if he believed it was the only way to protect his people.

I look at Tycho. "I would have followed orders, Tycho. Whatever that meant."

He stares up at me. I can read nothing in his gaze.

The last sheep passes, and I step out of the doorway without waiting to see if he follows.

CHAPTER SEVEN

LIA MARA

We make camp long before nightfall.

Nolla Verin's temper is a force to be reckoned with. She snaps at the guards about building the fire hotter, and even snaps at our mother about revealing too much information before we had the alliance assured. Despite her words earlier, she has never been rejected, and I can tell the prince's words stung.

My sister sits beside me, staring into the fire, driving her needle into her embroidery again. "Did you see the way he clutched at that crippled princess? As if her people have given any sign that their alliance is valid." She snorts. "They allowed the king to be slaughtered! The prince is such a fool."

"You've said."

"He will regret this, Lia Mara."

"You've said that, too."

She turns those fierce eyes on me. "Do you believe otherwise?"

"I believe the prince cares for his people."

"I care for my people, too."

Maybe, but Prince Rhen has never invaded Syhl Shallow. He did not wantonly slaughter *our* people. I look away from her, back at the fire.

The silence between us thickens, turning to uncertainty.

"Do you believe I failed?" she whispers.

I look at her in surprise. "No. I believe you both seek different outcomes for your countries."

"We could be unified!"

I swallow. They did not approach Prince Rhen as if they truly sought *unity*.

"Will Mother attack?" I say softly. "Now that he has refused?"

Nolla Verin relaxes. She enjoys discussing strategy. "She will wait until the prince's people are well and truly divided over the nonsense regarding this heir. The seeds are already sown. We will capture his cities and finally have access to the open sea."

"What of this Commander Grey?" I say.

"Dead or alive, it does not matter." She knots her thread and pulls a dagger to cut the string. "You saw the prince's face when Mother said his name."

I did see Rhen's face. Harper's too. Both filled with a wash of panic and loss and fear.

Nolla Verin shakes her head. "Mother was right to reveal what we know. The gossip that a former guardsman—a *defector*, if he lives—carries this knowledge will spread quickly."

She is right. A magesmith? An heir? A rogue guardsman? The gossip will be too juicy to control, and Rhen's people are already divided.

Nolla Verin shrugs. "What we do know is what's most important: this prince's reign will soon come to an end, one way or another. Look. What do you think?"

It takes me a moment to realize she's drawing my attention to her embroidery. I've hardly looked at it since we left Syhl Shallow, but now I see she's added words in the center, the letters curved and winding through the stitched adornments throughout.

Two sisters. One heart.

The words should fill me with light and happiness. They don't. I can't scrub the memory of the slaughtered man and his daughter from my thoughts. That girl had a sister—a sister who fled because I refused to raise the alarm about her presence.

"You don't like it," says Nolla Verin.

"No, I do." I reach to take the fabric from her. My finger traces over the lettering. "Your talent is beyond compare."

"You look so sad. I thought this would cheer you."

"It does." I reach out and clasp her hand. "I am honored to have your love and to share your heart."

She smiles.

I can't help but return the smile. I do love her.

She leans in and kisses me on the cheek. "I thought it would be lovely for your pillowcase."

I press the embroidery to my chest. "I'll treasure it always."

She stands and stretches. "Will you be long? I am eager to sleep."

"Go ahead."

She eases into our tent, and her guards take their place.

I wish Sorra and Parrish would join me by the fire, because I could use Parrish's easy humor, but my mother has not yet retired, and they would never be casual in her presence.

An exhausted part of my brain expects her to come join me, to needle me about my sister's performance today, to jab and dig at my failings, but luckily she does not.

She does draw close, though, once, to drop a kiss onto my

forehead. A rare show of affection from her. "You think I forget you were my first daughter," she says.

"I do not think that."

"A mother knows."

I blush. Likely our entire queendom knows.

"I know you think I am cold and unforgiving, too," she says.

I say nothing. She's not wrong.

"I am not heartless," she says. "But outside of Syhl Shallow, the world is full of men who underestimate women. Men who undermine them. I cannot rule from a place of weakness. I do not have the luxury of mercy and sympathy. Nor will your sister."

I remain silent. Leaving an unarmed man alive doesn't seem like a *weakness*, but maybe that's why I haven't been named heir.

"You are not lesser than Nolla Verin," she says. "Remember that, Lia Mara. That is why your studies with Clanna Sun are so very important. Your sister has been named heir, but she will need your support."

"Thank you, Mother." I'm not sure what else to say. Her voice is high and clear, and this likely has more to do with informing Nolla Verin that she has been a disappointment than anything to do with me.

Mother leaves me there by the fire and retires to her own tent. Eventually, Sorra and Parrish join me on the log by the fire.

Parrish offers me a bit of dried beef from a sack, and I make a face.

He laughs and pops it into his mouth.

Sorra makes the same face I did. "He'll eat anything," she says.

"Gladly too." He pops another piece in his mouth.

I can barely summon the energy for a smile. "Mother is upset that things did not go better with the prince."

Sorra nods. "She does not want to wage war. The palace coffers are not endless. The Royal Houses are disappointed that she has not provided access to the seaport trade as she promised."

"I didn't know that." I sit up straighter. I knew we had come to rely on the tithe from Emberfall in years past, but I was unaware our reserves had run so thin that the Royal Houses were beginning to withdraw support.

Sorra smiles. "Perhaps you would hear more if you spent time at court instead of with your nose in a book."

I make a face equivalent to the one I made over the dried meat, and she laughs under her breath.

"War is costly," she says. "Even if the prince's alliance with Disi is false, it will cost a tidy sum to launch another invasion—and the Royal Houses are not willing to pay more when funds run low already."

"To say nothing of the lives lost," says Parrish.

His tone catches my attention, and I swivel my head to look at him.

He glances at Sorra, and his tone is subdued. "We should not slaughter people over access to trade routes."

I think of the girl he ignored in the woods. I wonder if Sorra knows, or if this is a secret he keeps. I wonder if this makes him a lesser guard, the way it makes me feel like a lesser sister.

Sorra holds his gaze. "In time, *our* people will suffer without them."

That was the whole reason Mother attacked in the first place. She would not be seeking an alliance at all if she hadn't failed. If Sorra is right, if Prince Rhen will not discuss an alliance, we are left with no other option.

Parrish nods somberly. "We will destroy this country—or wait for our own to fail."

"It seems there is no choice now," I say. "Mother made her decision. You guard the wrong sister if you think I can bring about change."

We look back at the flames. The camp falls silent around us, but my thoughts run too quickly for sleep to find me anytime soon.

Two sisters, one heart.

We do not share a heart. I know that much.

For all Mother's remarks about the enchantress and the magical beast that drove our forces out of Emberfall, Prince Rhen was correct: he *did* succeed once. I know from my studies that nothing unifies people like a common enemy. Right now, his country seems divided over whether he is the rightful heir, but if he can find this Commander Grey, if he can find the *heir,* then Prince Rhen can solidify his position. He cares about his people. His passion is evident. He could very well succeed again.

I unfold Nolla Verin's embroidery and trace my fingers over the neat stitching.

Two sisters, one heart.

If I share a heart with anyone, it is this prince. At least he seems merciful. Thoughtful, not callous.

I wonder how he would have reacted if Nolla Verin had approached him with thoughtfulness and respect instead of arrogance and disdain. If she had presumed to care for *his* people along with her own.

I wonder if I can find out.

You are not lesser than Nolla Verin. Your sister will need your support.

The prince wouldn't listen to my sister.

Perhaps he will listen to me.

"I want to speak with him," I say quietly.

Sorra looks at me in alarm, but Parrish's gaze is more steady. "Your mother will never allow it."

"I know." I pause. "We must be swift, before the others realize what we're doing."

His eyebrows shoot up. "You mean to go *now*?"

"Yes." My heart beats like a drum. "Saddle horses. Be as silent as possible."

I expect them to refuse. They have been my guards for years, but they are sworn to my mother. Sorra holds my eyes for so long that my mother would consider it insolence.

I know it's not.

"Please," I say softly.

"For peace," Parrish says at my side, and her gaze shifts to him. Her eyes soften.

He hooks a finger in the edge of her armor and pulls her forward. "For our future," he says. Then he brushes his lips against hers.

My cheeks burn, but I can't help but smile. "There will be time for that later. For now, we need to hurry."

Parrish grins and pulls back. Sorra's cheeks are equally pink. They turn toward where the horses are tethered, their movement silent.

When I follow to help, Parrish looks at me. His grin has softened into a smile. "You were wrong," he says.

"Wrong?"

"I believe we guard the *only* sister who can bring about change."

CHAPTER EIGHT

GREY

Gossip and unrest always generate crowds, but tonight the tourney is busier than I've ever seen it. When darkness fell, it brought cooler winds and a sky full of stars, but the stands are packed with so many bodies it's hotter than at midday.

"The prince is running scared," a man mutters as he waits in the snaking line for ale. Worwick must be turning a heady profit tonight. I've never seen the line stretch to the stables. "There've been no mage-smiths in Emberfall in decades."

I'm saddling horses for the mounted sparring, but when I'm working, I'm invisible. People speak freely without consideration.

When I was a guardsman, stationed along a wall, it was no different.

"Well, *something* controlled that beast that terrorized the castle," says another man. "Everyone says it was Karis Luran, but I don't know why anyone isn't questioning this new princess. Maybe *she's* the one who sent it. I don't trust this alliance with wherever she's from. They let our king die."

I tighten a girth and give the horse a pat on the neck.

"Rillisk has been governed by the Grand Marshal for years," scoffs a woman. "The royal family returns, and suddenly we're supposed to bend a knee? Not likely."

"Watch your voice," says the first man. "I heard there's royalty here tonight."

My fingers go still on the buckle of a bridle. The horse butts his face against my hand, and I murmur to quiet him.

The second man chuckles lazily. "Royalty? Just another princeling no one has ever heard of."

A breath eases out of my chest. Months ago, this would have been worrisome, but since the southern borders were opened, I've heard of minor royalty passing through Rillisk, as smaller lands seek to reopen trade routes.

"Hawk."

The rough voice makes me jump, but it's just Journ, Worwick's other fighter. I prefer his company to Kantor's, but right now he's pale and sweating, one hand braced on a post along the wall.

I frown. "Are you sick?"

"I took a kick from a horse. The roads are packed. Two carriages collided. I tried to help." He winces, a hand against his chest. "Worwick said you might have a poultice that you use on the horses."

I do, but if he can barely stand, a poultice won't let him fight. Little use in telling Worwick that, though. I call for Tycho to come finish with the horses, then look back at Journ. "Come to the armory. I'll see what I can do."

It's cooler back here, away from the crowds. The scraver lies motionless in its cage, though its night-dark eyes flick open as we enter the armory. Journ drops onto a stool. When he removes his shirt, half his chest is dark with bruising. He gasps from the effort it took to disrobe.

"Tell me the truth," he says breathlessly. "Does it look as bad as it feels?"

"It looks like your ribs are broken."

He swears under his breath. "Worwick will come undone."

"You can't fight like this."

"Have you seen the stands? It's barely full dark and there are no seats left. If I can't fight, Worwick will put a blade through me himself."

The words make me think of Riley the blacksmith. When I was a weapon for the Crown, guilt rarely pricked at me for the actions I was ordered to take.

Today, guilt is a thorn I cannot remove.

Journ shifts and winces. "Can you bind it? Perhaps my armor will offer some support."

"I can try." I pack stiff muslin against his rib cage while he swears at me, then bind it tightly. He sweats through the bandages before I'm done, but when I buckle his armor into place over it, he's able to stand more easily than he was before.

"You have my thanks, Hawk." He clumsily claps my shoulder, then wheezes.

"A child could run you through."

"I need the coins tonight." He takes a thin breath and pulls a sword from the rack. "Take a blade. Let me try."

I've never sparred with Journ or Kantor, because it's hard to hide skills from men who have them. But he's injured and we're alone, and Journ is a good man, so I take a sword from the rack.

He's able to feint and thrust and parry, but his movement is lumbering, and I'm not putting up much resistance.

Still, he offers a grim smile. "I might not win, but I can fight."

I swing my blade hard, and he's barely able to block the blow. While he's trying to recover, I twist my weapon, hook the hilt of his, and disarm him. The point of my sword sits at his neck before he can draw breath.

"You'll be disarmed in seconds," I say. "That's not much of a fight."

He's blinking at me. A hand presses to his side, but he says, "You've been practicing."

I lower my weapon. "Here and there."

He winces and eases back onto the stool, then sighs. Drums echo from the arena, followed by a loud cry from the stands. Worwick will be rallying the audience, opening the evening's events.

I need to get back to the arena. In this crowd, Tycho will be running like crazy to get the horses and riders out safely.

I'm stuck studying Journ, who's dragging a damp wrist across his forehead. He gives another heavy sigh, and it's full of pain. If it were Kantor, I'd let him go into the arena and take his chances.

"Why do you need the coins tonight?" I ask.

"We'll have another child by year's end." He shifts and grimaces, but there's no way to make broken ribs comfortable. "Another mouth to feed—as if it's not hard enough to fill the ones I have."

This does not feel like a moment to offer congratulations. "I didn't know."

He draws a breath that cuts short at the end, then winces and pushes himself to his feet. "We all have our burdens." He reaches for a sword belt from the wall.

In the stadium, a horse neighs, hooves pummel the ground, and the crowd cheers.

I bite at the inside of my lip, thinking of Riley.

I owe Journ nothing. I owe Worwick nothing.

Across the room, the scraver's cage rattles as it shifts and stretches. Its coal-black eyes find mine, and it hisses. The sound is full of censure, but that's probably all inside my head.

We all have our burdens.

I did nothing this afternoon. I can do something now.

"Remove your armor," I tell him.

He utters a rough laugh that ends on a wheeze. "If I get this off, I won't get it back on."

"I need to help Tycho," I say. "If you can't bend to get your greaves off, I'll be back in half an hour."

"What are you going on about?"

"You can't fight, Journ."

He closes his eyes. "Hawk. I *must—*"

"You misunderstand," I say. "*You* cannot fight. *I* can. Now remove your armor. I'll be back."

CHAPTER NINE

LIA MARA

I don't expect fanfare for our arrival.

I don't expect to be surrounded in the woods and taken prisoner, either.

Guards weren't stationed this far from the castle grounds when we arrived earlier, but maybe they widen their patrols after dark. Or more likely, maybe Rhen doesn't trust my mother to such an extent that he expected an attack.

"This is an outrage," I say to Prince Rhen's guards, who are binding my hands. "I have told you that we come here to discuss a means to peace with your people."

Darkness blankets the woods and hides the expressions of most of the men surrounding us, but I can see them similarly binding Sorra and Parrish as well. They say nothing.

The guard behind me jerks tight at the rope, and I suck in a breath. "There are only three of us. I am unarmed. Surely you do not think we intended to attack the castle like *this*."

"Be cautious, Lia Mara," Sorra says quietly in Syssalah.

At the sound of her voice, one of the guards pulls a blade, but another man says, "No. Leave them unharmed. We will let the prince decide."

The man who spoke steps through the darkness to stop before me. Many of the other guards and soldiers carry longbows, but he has only a sword hanging at his hip. He's slightly older, with dark hair. He's also missing an arm.

"I've seen the kind of peace your people wish to bring to Emberfall," he says. The look in his eyes is unkind, bordering on vengeful.

I glance at his missing arm again and wonder if soldiers from Syhl Shallow caused the injury. "Our armies have withdrawn," I say. "I cannot undo what has happened to you, but I can attempt to forge a new path forward."

He grunts and turns away. A hand gives me a push between my shoulder blades, and I stride forward.

We're taken into the castle. In the daylight, the cream-colored bricks made the building look warm and welcoming, but now, in the darkness of night, the castle stands tall and foreboding. The main doors creak open, leading to a massive grand entranceway lined with velvet floor coverings, and dark wooden walls hung with tapestries in every color. The ceiling stretches high overhead, an unlit chandelier strung above us. During the day it must be a spectacle of wealth and privilege that rivals my own palace home, but just now, the shadowed corners and echoing space are unnerving.

"You will wait here," says the one-armed man. He strides across the floor and up the wide staircase along the opposing wall.

We've been gone for a while now. I wonder if the other guards have begun to wonder at our disappearance. After what happened in the courtyard this afternoon, I do not know if Mother would dare to come after us.

The longer we stand here, the more I begin to wonder at my actions.

I think of the daughter of the trapper, crouched under her father.

I think of the one-armed man who led us into the castle.

I think of the anger in his voice and the fear in the eyes of the girl hiding in the woods.

There are *people* beyond these negotiations. People whose lives will be affected by an alliance or a war or a stroke of a quill against parchment. My sister has been named heir, but she failed this afternoon.

I have one chance to make this right.

When the prince appears at the top of the staircase, I expect surprise or anger or some flash of emotion on his face, but his expression is cool and guarded, just as it was earlier. His attire is more casual, which makes me think we interrupted his sleep. The princess is not with him.

He does not hurry down the stairs but instead studies me as he descends.

I do my best to stand tall and look confident, which is more of a challenge than I expected, especially with my hands bound at the small of my back.

The prince comes to a stop five feet in front of me, and I do not flinch from the scrutiny in his gaze.

Finally, he says, "When Jamison mentioned your intent to discuss peace, you are not the sister I expected."

Of course I'm not. "I have not been named heir, but I am still a daughter of the queen."

He considers this for a moment. "If you truly wish for peace, why did you not speak up during your visit? Why attempt to sneak onto the grounds of Ironrose well after dark?" He glances at my guards. "With the bare minimum of protection, no less."

I all but feel Sorra and Parrish bristle behind me.

"Do I need protection?" I say to the prince. "You did not take action against us today, though you could have."

"Your mother is no fool," he says. "If I had harmed any of you, vengeance would have been swift and assured, I have no doubt."

That is true. Mother would not have ridden all this way without contingencies. "I do not wish to speak of violence and harm."

"Ah, yes. You wish to speak of peace." His tone is amused, but his eyes narrow slightly. "Forgive me for forgetting."

"You do not believe me."

"I believe you are either very brave or very stupid for attempting to sway my opinion of Syhl Shallow in this way."

I hold his gaze. "I am not stupid, Prince Rhen."

"You still have not answered my question. Why did you not speak of this desire for *peace* earlier?"

Because I did not wish to speak against my mother or my sister.

Because I did not know how badly things would go.

Because I did not know if he would have listened.

I still don't.

"I am here now because I wish for no further bloodshed between our people."

"I wish for the same."

He speaks those words with enough gravity that I believe them. His kingdom may be falling apart around him, but he truly does care for his people—as much as I care for mine.

"In truth," he adds, "I was surprised to hear of Karis Luran seeking an alliance at all, as she seems so certain she can claim my lands on her own terms."

I hesitate, thinking of what Nolla Verin told me, or what Sorra said beside the campfire. Prince Rhen will never believe that Mother wants to spare lives.

His eyes search my face. "If you are seeking an alliance, Lia Mara, perhaps you should begin with honesty."

"Fine," I say. "My mother needs access to your seaport trade routes and would like to be able to establish commerce between our people."

He smiles, and I know he's seen right through me. "The Queen of Syhl Shallow is lacking in silver. How interesting."

"We may be lacking in silver, but we are still wealthy in weapons and warriors."

"So I've heard." He doesn't look like I've been fully convincing. "I offered to discuss trade with your mother months ago, and she refused."

"I cannot change the past. I can only offer myself to you as a symbol of good faith."

"Offer yourself?" His smile widens. "If you know of my search for the rightful heir, then surely you know of my love for Princess Harper. If you are offering yourself as an alliance through marriage, you will be sorely disappointed."

"Ours does not need to be a marriage of love," I say, lifting my chin. "I have heard how such things work in your lands."

"Truly? Enlighten me."

This is worse than Nolla Verin's teasing. I feel my face heat, and he laughs.

I want to scowl at him, but he's so composed, and I've already lost ground. "I will not be made a spectacle, Prince Rhen. I came to you to discuss peace. To see if we could find a way to save all our people the cost of another war neither of us wishes to fight. If you would like to poke fun at me, so be it. Unbind my hands and allow me to leave. My mother and my sister could not see your love for your people, but *I* do. I thought possibly you would see the same in me."

That steals the smile from his face. He studies me for the longest time, and I never drop his gaze.

Eventually, he speaks. "I *do* love my people, as you say." He pauses, then glances at one of the guards. "Unbind her."

A knife is drawn, and my hands are cut free. A sudden feeling of hope bursts in my chest.

Another servant is sent for paper and quills. "Write a letter to your mother," the prince says. "Tell her we will discuss an alliance between our people, and you will send word to Syhl Shallow once we have agreed upon terms. Choose one of your guards to deliver it safely, so your mother will know the truth of your intent. I will send one of my guards along to retrieve Karis Luran's response. If she is willing to allow you to negotiate, then so am I."

I wet my lips and take the quill. I can hardly write fast enough to convey all the words I wish to say.

Mother, please forgive my rash actions, but I saw a path to peace and I wanted to do all I could to protect the people of Syhl Shallow as well as Emberfall. The prince has agreed to allow me to negotiate for trade and safe passage through his lands. I know Nolla Verin has been blessed with your gift to rule, but I have been blessed

with your gift of intellect and insight. Please allow me the
chance to unite our people for the good of all.

Lia Mara

I sign my name with a flourish, then draw my seal.

I look to Parrish and Sorra. "Unbind them," I say to Prince Rhen. Then, as an afterthought, I add, "If you please."

He nods to one of his soldiers, and my guards are cut free.

Parrish looks uncertain. His eyes are dark and untrusting in the dimness of the room.

Sorra is more composed, coolly considering the state of the guards surrounding us.

I fold the letter and press it into Parrish's hands. "Please," I say to him. "Please tell Mother how badly I long for this to work."

His eyes find mine, and he nods. But then he says, in Syssalah, "This does not feel right, Lia Mara."

"Do we have a choice?"

"We always have a choice."

I think of the girl in the woods. "If we expect his trust, we must extend our own."

Parrish looks up at the prince, then back at my eyes. He nods and takes the folded letter.

Prince Rhen looks to one of his guards. "Ride with her guardsman. Return with Karis Luran's response."

The man nods. "Yes, my lord."

A look passes between Parrish and Sorra, and then my guard is gone, followed by Rhen's.

I take a breath. I have done what my sister could not. We will strike an accord for peace. Mother will have access to the waterways she seeks. Lives will be spared.

Think of our future, Parrish said.

Prince Rhen takes a step toward me. "Do you truly believe your mother will agree to terms of an alliance that you have negotiated?"

"Yes," I say, "I do."

He frowns. "I believe you."

The words are right, but the expression on his face is not. I frown in return. "Then why do you look displeased?"

"I believe you trust your mother." For the first time, his eyes are not cool, but instead disappointed. "Unfortunately, I do not."

At my back, Sorra says in a rush, "This was a trap, Lia Mara."

Prince Rhen glances to his guards. "Arrest them both. Lock her guard in—"

Sorra's body slams into me, and it takes me a moment to realize she's knocking me out of reach of the man who was about to seize my arm. I stumble to the ground.

"Run!" Sorra yells at me. She whirls to draw the dagger from the guardsman's belt. Without hesitation, she drives it into his midsection, and he falls. Before he's even on the ground, she's stabbed another.

I scramble toward the door. Sorra plunges the dagger into a third guardsman, and with a quick whirl, she gets her hands on a sword, too. Blood is in the air in a crimson arc. I want to scream, but I can't find my breath. Everything is happening too fast. Guardsmen are suddenly everywhere.

One pulls a sword, swings wide, and drives it straight into Sorra.

Her body goes down. There's so much blood.

I scream, long and loud, hoping Parrish is still close, that he'll hear.

No. I don't want him to see.

A man seizes my arm and jerks me to my feet. My vision feels washed in blood. I still can't breathe.

I wanted peace, and now Sorra's bleeding out on the floor.

"You will be unharmed," the prince is saying. I can barely process the words. "But your presence here will ensure that your mother leaves Emberfall alone for good."

CHAPTER TEN

GREY

The narrow tunnel to the arena muffles the sound of the crowd. I haven't worn proper armor in months, but my limbs remember the weight. Journ is broader than I am, but his breastplate fits well enough, his bracers snug against my forearms.

"Worwick likes to rile the fighters up," Journ is saying. "He'll tell them to draw blood. Sometimes it's better to give the crowd a little."

I eye his scarred arms and say nothing. We're alone here in the tunnel, but no one knows I'm taking his place. Worwick will figure it out the instant I set foot in the arena, but by then it'll be too late for him to question it.

Hopefully I'll put on a good enough show that it won't matter after that.

"He won't like it if *you* draw blood, though," Journ says. "No one wants to be made a fool. Let them think they can win for a while."

I know this, but I let him keep talking anyway. My heart sends blood pulsing through my veins.

"Four matches," Journ says. "Can you stay alive through four matches?"

"Ask me when I'm done."

He starts to chuckle, but his breath catches and he presses an arm to his abdomen. "Most of these men don't have much skill," he says. "They're all just out to have a good time and bring home bragging rights. But sometimes they'll surprise you."

I nod. Above us, the drums begin a familiar rhythm. The resulting cheer is near deafening, even from here.

I don't need to be exceptional. I just need to put on a good show. I just need to stay alive.

I take a step toward the end of the tunnel, but Journ catches the shoulder of my armor.

"Hawk." He swallows. "I will owe you for this."

How I wish Kantor had taken a hoof to the chest instead of this man. "You owe me nothing."

"I'll have a chance to repay you one day."

I smile. "Then let's hope I survive the night."

The drums beat again. Worwick's voice calls out. "From the depths of the Valkins Valley, a man nearly forged in steel, rarely defeated, my champion, Journ of Everlea!"

I step into the arena, and the crowd screams so loud that I worry they'll bring down the roof. After the quiet dimness of the tunnel, the light and sound are overwhelming. I draw my sword the way I've seen Journ do a hundred times, then lift it high.

Worwick stands high in the crowds, and my back is to him, so I have no idea whether he's noticed me. I hold my breath and wait for his next words.

"We have a special event for you all tonight," Worwick croons, his voice carrying to the crowd. "A very special event."

He hasn't noticed. Good.

"As usual, betting is closed once the second fighter enters the arena," he calls. "I believe we're in for a good match. A man of this skill doesn't often visit Worwick's Tourney. Place your bets now. I think we'll see a lot of money change hands tonight. Who feels the kiss of luck on their cheek? Is it you? Is it *you?*"

He's good at what he does, because there's always a frantic last-minute scrambling to lay money down on the match.

"Now," calls Worwick. "Our second fighter is ready to enter the ring. Champion Journ, to your—" His voice breaks off, and he clears his throat. "Ah, *Champion Journ*, to your position, please."

Silver hell. He noticed.

Well, he can do nothing about it now. I sheathe my sword and move to the center of the arena.

"Our opponent hails all the way from Silvermoon Harbor," Worwick calls. I spot the shadow of a man jogging through the opposite tunnel. My vision narrows down to the entrance. The crowd, the arena, this is all a show.

The sword at my side, the battle before me—those things are real.

My hand finds the hilt. I cannot draw until the other man does. If he's from Silvermoon Harbor, he's likely a fisherman or a dockworker. Someone dared into this challenge by friends drunk on ale.

The man's hair becomes visible: sandy blond. Then his shoulders, the leather of his armor rich and gleaming. Not borrowed tourney armor, then. Each silver buckle sparks with light.

Gold and red stripes adorn his shoulder, bound together by a crest stamped in gold, a lion entwined with a rose.

I go still. I know that crest. I know those stripes.

"From Ironrose Castle," calls Worwick, "we have the honor to host the Commander of the Royal Guard, Dustan of Silvermoon." He winks at me from the stands, like we're in on some joke. "Be sure to keep your head, Journ."

The crowd screams with approval.

I take a few steps back before I can help myself. I know he's riling the crowd. He has no idea what this means for me.

I know Dustan. I chose him myself. He was one of the first guards to swear to Rhen under my command. Does that mean the prince is here, watching this match? I want to search the crowd, but there are too many faces. Too much noise. I cannot tear my eyes from my approaching opponent.

My instincts are screaming at me to take action, but I see no path here.

Dustan has not drawn his sword. My hand has gone slick on the hilt of my own.

He slows as he approaches, and his eyes narrow slightly. As he stops in front of me, he frowns and takes his hand off the hilt. "You look anxious," he says, his tone easy. "Journ, is it?"

The words take a moment to register in my mind.

He does not recognize me.

But of course he doesn't. It's been months. We only knew each other for a matter of weeks—and then, I was clean-shaven, with shorter hair and richly adorned armor and the manner of a leader.

Today, I am little more than a stable hand dressed up like a soldier. I'm Hawk. Or right now, I suppose I'm Journ.

Dustan leans in as if to share a secret. "The Royal Guard is not so vicious as rumor would have you believe."

He believes I am nervous about the match.

"We've been on the road for weeks," he continues. "My men dared me to enter."

Then Rhen must not be with him. The prince would not leave Ironrose for weeks—and his guard commander certainly wouldn't leave him unguarded for sport.

We've been quiet too long. The crowd is growing restless. Booted feet begin a relentless stomping. Any moment now, they'll begin chanting.

"Do not withdraw," Dustan says, misreading my silence for fear. "I'll go easy."

As predicted, the crowd begins its chant. *Fight. Fight. Fight.* It spurs my heartbeat and sharpens my focus.

Dustan puts his hand on his sword hilt and meets my eyes. There's a question in his gaze.

I give him a quick nod.

He begins to draw. As the blade slides free, recognition flickers in his expression. "Journ—is there a chance we've met before?"

"No." My sword pulls free like an old friend, and I swing hard and fast before he's ready. He barely has time to block. Our blades collide, and the crash of metal sings through the arena. The crowd roars with approval.

Dustan loses ground quickly, backpedaling as he waits for an opening to retaliate. He expected me to fall back and be an easy mark. He underestimated me—a failing I'd reprimand him for if I were still his commander.

When the opening comes, Dustan strikes with a fierceness I don't expect, and I'm forced to yield ground. My body remembers the movements, this dance of swordplay. When he swings for my midsection I slap his blade down, and we break apart, circling.

"I *do* know you," he calls. His eyes are shadowed with anger. "Who are you?"

"I'm no one." His swords lifts, and I advance.

He's good. Better than I remember. When we break apart again, a strain builds in my forearms that he likely doesn't feel at all. An hour in the dusty arena with Tycho is not equal to the amount of time the Royal Guard spends training.

He must sense this, because his next attack is brutal and swift and brings me to the ground. I taste blood and dirt on my tongue. I roll before he can pin me, then drive off the ground to put a shoulder into his midsection.

I thought I could get him off his feet, but he's quick and grabs hold of my armor, using my momentum to his advantage. We crash to the ground together. He kneels on my sword arm before I can raise it.

It's a good move, but I know it. I use my free hand to snatch the dagger from his belt, and I aim for his throat. He swears and jerks back, but it frees my arm and puts him off balance. I surge forward and flip our positions.

He's quick enough to get his sword up to block mine, but I've got leverage. I bear down until he's in danger of cutting his own neck. He's breathing as hard as I am, but on his part, it's more anger than anything else. "Tell me who you are."

"That was a clever move," I say. "With the armor. Who taught you that?"

Dustan speaks through gritted teeth. He's straining hard, and a thin line of blood appears below his blade. "If you kill a guardsman, you'll lose your head."

He's not the only one who thinks so. The sounds from the crowd have turned to a confused murmur.

Worwick's voice calls out over the crowd, and he sounds a little strangled. "Journ! I will remind you this is not a death match."

Motion flickers from the opposite side of the arena. Other guardsmen have sensed that their commander may be in danger.

I put the point of his dagger right against the vulnerable spot just below his jaw. "Tell your men to stand down."

"That's him!" a voice shouts from the sidelines. Familiar, but I can't place it. "That's *him*. I knew he wasn't dead."

A spike of fear drives through my heart. Dustan is glaring at me—but slowly his expression changes. The anger flickers to puzzlement. "Commander Grey?"

I need to make a decision. The blades between us tremble from our opposing efforts.

"Don't you dare let him get away," shouts a voice.

"I am not your commander," I say to Dustan.

"But—"

I punch him in the side of the face with the hand holding his dagger. It barely buys me a second, but I sprint for my tunnel. An arrow whistles by my shoulder and lodges in the wall. Another quickly follows, striking my armor and skidding harmlessly away.

The tunnel opens into the storage yard, but I grab hold of the ladder mounted into the side wall and swing myself up, taking it two rungs at a time. I ease into the loft just as guardsmen pour into the yard. Dirt and cobwebs slide under my fingers, and I hold my breath. My heart sprints along, begging for air.

The crowd is going wild in the arena, voices echoing throughout the entire tourney. The men fan out, going in opposing directions. As soon as they're a safe distance away, I crawl, keeping low against the loft flooring.

I'm on the opposite side of the tourney from where Tycho and I sleep above the stables. If I were a lucky man, I could crawl the full distance, drop into the stables, and be galloping away before anyone knew better.

I think of the silver ring hidden in my mattress. I could escape completely.

Either way, I'm not a lucky man. The loft on this side of the stadium only runs as far as the armory. I'll need to climb back down and somehow make it through the packed crowds to find my way to the stables.

It takes less than ten minutes to crawl through the dusty shadows, and I find the armory empty. I drop from the loft silently, but the scraver startles and rattles against its bars, hissing at me.

I ignore it and pull knives from the wall to slide into my greaves, then add two more under my sword belt.

Worwick's voice carries over the crowd, loud through the door. "Yes, Commander." He sounds panicked. He also sounds very near. "I *assure you*, I will provide whatever assistance is necessary."

I pull back into the shadows near the scraver's cage. The ladder to the loft is beside the door into the tourney. I'm trapped here more effectively than I was in the arena. My heart beats in my throat.

The scraver screeches at me, fangs bared, clawed hands scrabbling against the floor of its cage. I remember how easily it sliced into Kantor's arm when provoked. Maybe it can do the same to armored guardsmen.

I draw a dagger and begin sawing at the rope holding the cage closed.

It stops growling.

My breathing is rapid and loud and these damn ropes are so thick. A key rattles in the lock on the door. Silver hell.

The scraver hisses at me. Then it whispers, "*Hurry.*"

My hands go still. I look up, wondering if I really heard that. My eyes lock with its solid black ones.

A cold breeze sweeps through the room. The scraver cuts a stripe across the back of my hand with his claws, and it growls, "Hurry!"

I don't have time to consider what this means. I swipe hard. The rope gives. The door opens.

The scraver launches forward with enough force to knock me back. Once clear of the cage, its wings unfurl and it screams with rage. Men shout and scramble as they try to escape its path— running into others who are trying to come through the door. Blood flies as its claws find bare skin.

I sprint through the melee, back to the ladder, and hoist myself up.

"Scraver!" I call, then whistle.

I don't wait to see if it follows. I just run.

When I reach the storage yard again, I don't drop gently from the loft. I land hard and roll. I come up running, sprinting into the dusty alleyway behind the tourney.

With a screech and a flapping of wings, the scraver sails out of the loft, gliding to the ground. I expect it to stop, like a chained dog who's been liberated and found a new master, but it doesn't. Its clawed hands and feet grip at the dusty ground, find traction, and it takes flight again, wings beating hard against the air. In seconds, it's high above me.

A whoosh of air announces an arrow, and I duck sideways, my

body responding before my thoughts do. I dodge the first, but not the second. Pain pierces my thigh, and my leg goes out. I stumble hard and fall, skidding several feet in the dust.

I force my legs to hold me again, and I'm on my feet, sword and dagger drawn, before the guardsmen get to me. There are only three. Dustan is one of them. His lip is swollen and bloodied from where I hit him. I don't know the other two, but they both have arrows nocked and waiting. One has three deep scratches across his face and jaw.

Spectators have filled the doorway to the storage yard. Journ, his face a mask of confusion. Worwick, his face a mask of anger. Tycho, his face a mask of anguish.

Worwick grips Tycho's arm, though, holding him back.

I don't take my eyes off Dustan, because his action is what will matter here.

"You'll go down fighting, won't you?" he says.

"Wouldn't you?"

"Maybe not this hard." He studies me as though he can't figure me out. "The prince has been seeking you for months. We've long suspected you were dead."

That would probably be easier. "I've committed no crime," I say to him. "Call off your men."

"I might have believed that before you ran." He pauses. "Why?"

He's not just asking about today. He's asking *why* about all of it.

"For the good of Emberfall," I say.

He must hear a note of truth in my voice, because he goes still. "Explain."

I tighten my grip on my sword. "No."

He turns his head. "Shoot his other leg."

"No!" screams Tycho. He jerks free of Worwick and runs. "No!"

Dustan turns. The bowman turns.

"Stop!" I yell. I imagine an arrow flying, piercing the boy's chest. I imagine his blood soaking into the dust. "Tycho, stop!"

He doesn't stop. I wait for an arrow to snap off the string.

One doesn't. Dustan steps forward and catches hold of Tycho's shirt before he can get to me. Tycho swings around and tries to punch him, but Dustan holds fast, tightening his grip until the collar pulls tight and Tycho makes a choking sound.

"Enough," I say. "He has nothing to do with this. Let him go."

Dustan tightens his grip and lifts his arm. Tycho makes a panicked keening sound.

This is why I forswore family. This moment exactly.

"Please," I say, and the word costs me something to say.

Dustan's gaze never leaves mine. "Do you yield?"

"You'll let him go?" I say, then realize this could mean an infinite number of ends for Tycho. "You'll leave him unharmed?"

"If I leave him unharmed, you'll surrender peacefully?"

"I swear it."

"Then so do I."

I drop my sword and my dagger, then raise my hands in surrender. He lets go. The boy falls to his knees, gasping for air.

Dustan takes my wrists and binds them with a stretch of leather.

From the dirt, Tycho looks up at me. I can't meet his eyes.

"Go back to Worwick," I tell him.

"No," says Dustan. "Brandyn. Take the boy. Bind him."

I freeze, struggling against the binding. "Dustan. You swore."

Dustan gives me a shove between the shoulder blades. "He won't be harmed. Walk."

Behind me, Tycho screams. I can't see around Dustan, but I don't need to. I know Tycho is afraid of soldiers.

I whirl and put my shoulder into Dustan's chest. He grabs hold of my armor and keeps me upright.

I open my mouth to swear at him. To beg of him. To censure him. I'm not sure which, but I don't get the chance to find out. A gauntleted hand strikes me in the jaw.

I go down without much of a fight at all.

CHAPTER ELEVEN

LIA MARA

Sorra's blood stains the panels of my robes. I have nothing else to wear, and I refuse to ask anything of the horrible man who's taken me prisoner, so I bear it.

The streaks and splashes have dried to an ugly brown against the cream fabric. My own tears stain the neckline. Both are a fitting reminder of what I've lost.

What Parrish has lost.

He spared that girl in the forest, and in return, I led his love to her death.

Perhaps I've been wrong about all of it. Surely Mother and Nolla Verin are correct in their ruthless view of the world. Maybe my wish for peace between our countries is the true weakness. Maybe my wish to be heir was. We should have launched an assault on Emberfall—indeed, Mother's adviser Clanna Sun was in favor of doing just that—and none of this would have happened.

Many more would have died.

The thought is unwelcome, and I shove it away.

The prince's soldiers have confined me to a lavish room that looks out on the castle courtyard. Sleep will likely never find me again, so I spend the night staring down at the cobblestones below. When dawn breaks, the sunlight touches my tears and dries my cheeks.

I watch the horizon, waiting to see any sign of my people coming to rescue me. Surely Mother will not believe my letter after the prince was so defiant to her and my sister. Surely my sister will demand that I be allowed to return home, or to negotiate at my side.

Surely.

I watch for hours, until the sun is fully in the sky. A lone rider appears at the edge of the woods, galloping at a steady pace. For the first time all night, hope blooms in my heart.

But then I see the gold and red of Emberfall's colors.

I sink back to the cool marble floor.

I am such a fool. I cannot believe I trusted him.

I believe you trust your mother. Unfortunately, I do not.

Rage burns through the sorrow in my chest. He's right: I do trust my mother. I trust that she will burn this castle to the ground when she comes to rescue me. I trust that she will ensure Rhen never sits on a throne. I trust that she will break every bone in his body and rip every hair from his head and burn every fiber of his—

The door to my room opens, and I choke on my fury.

Prince Rhen stands there, outfitted in rich leather with gold stitching, looking regal and perfect and cold.

I'm on the floor in dirty robes, nearly vibrating with heat and rage. I want to launch myself at him.

Instead, I stand, adopting an air as regal as his. "You will regret the actions you have taken. My mother will double the forces she was already planning to send into your cursed country."

"The forces she likely cannot afford?"

I set my jaw.

"I understand your fury," he says.

"You understand *nothing*."

"I understand a great deal." His eyes narrow. "I understand that you came here in the middle of the night with questionable motives. I understand your mother blackmailed my father for *years*, and she tried to do the same to me. I understand that your mother and sister care nothing for my people and only care for the waterways that will allow a new way to barter for coins." He takes a step closer to me, his eyes dark with his own fury. "I understand that thousands of my people have already been slaughtered because of it. *That* is what I understand."

"I know many things as well." My eyes hold his. "I know you have lied to your people."

"I have not."

"You *lie*." I spit the words at him. "I know you seek this heir because you fear his magic. I know you have imprisoned me because you fear my mother. Your actions reveal your weakness, Prince Rhen."

"On the contrary. My actions reveal my strength."

"Killing innocent people should *never* be seen as a strength."

His eyebrows go up. "Is that not what your people do?"

"*You* killed my guard, after I approached you to discuss a means to peace."

"My guards drew no weapon until yours did," he says. "I said you would be unharmed, as you see. She would have been as well."

"You deal in lies with your people, Prince Rhen." My voice almost breaks, and I heave a breath to steady it. "I will believe nothing you say."

He pulls a folded piece of parchment from his belt. "Would you believe your mother's hand?"

My breath catches. The rider returned with Mother's answer.

I rush forward and snatch it from his hand, half expecting him to hold fast, but he doesn't. Guards hover behind him in the doorway, but I've already seen what they did to Sorra, and I am not stupid, despite my actions over the last day. I step back and hastily unfold the letter.

There are Mother's words, and I'm so shocked to see them that it takes me a full moment to read at all.

In the common tongue of Emberfall, she has written:

I accept my daughter's proposal. I will grant one month for negotiations.

Below that, in Syssalah, she adds:

Do not disappoint me, Lia Mara.

My eyes hold those words far longer than it takes me to read them.

Do not disappoint me.

I did that the instant I rode away from camp with Sorra and Parrish. There is no alliance to forge. I am his prisoner. Nothing more.

I look back at Prince Rhen.

"Your mother believed your letter," he says.

"I wrote it in truth," I hiss at him.

"I will have some clothing brought. Alert your guards if you have any needs."

He pulls the door closed, then locks me inside.

CHAPTER TWELVE

GREY

I wake to a sky full of sun and a leg full of fire. A wagon rolls along underneath me, every bump proving that I'm lying on nothing more than wooden floorboards. I shift and try to roll, but my head isn't clear. Metal rattles against wood when I move.

I inhale sharply, then force myself up on one elbow. Shackles trap my wrists and ankles. My head swims.

"Go slow. You've been out for hours." A familiar man sits near the front of the wagon. Dark-brown skin, close-shorn hair. He's heavier than he was when I met him in Washington, DC, but I won't forget the man who saved my life once before.

"Healer," I say in surprise, my voice a rough rasp. My jaw aches when I speak. I lift a hand to rub at my eyes, and the chains drag across my bare wrists.

"Most people just call me Noah," he says.

They must have given me sleeping ether. My thoughts are having trouble falling into order. Six men on horseback follow the wagon, but sunlight gleams on weapons and armor and makes my head pound. An unfamiliar guardsman drives the wagon. I wince and rub at my eyes again.

Without warning, memory punches me in the gut. My eyes flash back to Noah. "Where is Tycho?" I say. "What did they do with him?"

"He's fine. He's asleep." He points. "Look."

I shift and force myself to sitting. A tight bandage encircles my thigh, and ankle chains rattle against the floorboards as I move. Tycho is curled into a ball behind me under the bench along the opposite side of the wagon, tucked as tightly as he can be into the corner. From what I can tell, he seems unharmed.

Another voice calls out, "Is he awake?"

It's the same voice that shouted from the side of the arena. Now, faced with Noah, I can place it. Jacob. Harper's brother. *Prince* Jacob to everyone in Emberfall. Heir to the throne of the imaginary Disi. Heir to nothing in reality.

He did not have a high opinion of me during the few days we knew each other. It was quite mutual. I consider the chains trapping me here and doubt that has improved.

"He's awake," says Noah, his tone resigned.

Jacob rides his horse alongside the wagon. His dark hair is longer, and he sits a horse far better than I remember, but he's still clearly Harper's brother. "You said I couldn't stab him while he was unconscious. Can I stab him now?"

"No."

"Come on." His eyes are full of righteous anger. "Tell me all the places I can hit so he doesn't die."

I meet Jacob's eyes. "You would stab a chained man?"

"Not usually, but for you I'd make an exception."

"You bear such venom for me. I have never done anything to you."

Noah snorts. Jacob's voice is low and dangerous. "You *trapped* us here."

Ah. I did do that.

Jake rides until his horse is almost against the wagon. "Besides, I'm not the only one with 'venom' for you. No one knows where you've been. Rhen has been looking for you for months. Harper has been worried you're dead. But no. You're here, and you're fine. Better than fine. Now all these guardsmen are wondering why you deserted. Why you *ran*. Want to explain that? You tried to kill their commander in the arena."

If I'd tried to kill him, he'd be dead, but the rest of Jacob's words are true. I have no explanation to give. I look away.

"Talk," says Jake. "Now."

When I say nothing, he pulls a dagger. My head snaps around. My leg feels like I carry the weight of a forge-hot iron bar through my thigh, but even shackled, I could leap out of the wagon and get my chains around his neck before he could put that blade in me.

I have nothing to lose, and maybe he can sense it. Something in his gaze falters.

"Jake," says Noah. His voice is resigned. "Just . . . put it away."

Jacob swears and shoves the dagger back into its sheath.

His words sit heavy in my thoughts, though. In truth, I regret trapping him here. I regret abandoning my duties with the Royal Guard. I regret what I know about my birthright and where that leaves me with Prince Rhen.

I look up at the sky. The air is full of summer scents of cut hay and ripening fruit. We've moved far beyond Rillisk if we're passing through farmland. I see little traffic on the road, so it must still be early. Worwick will be losing his mind to have me and Tycho taken away at the same time.

The wagon's creaks and rattles echo in the quiet morning air. There should be a guardsman riding ahead as lookout, but I see no one in the distance. The guardsmen and horses look weary. "Have we been traveling all night?"

"Yes. We're going back to Ironrose so you can take us home, and then Rhen can do whatever he wants with you."

Those words settle in my chest and take up a death grip on my heart. "Ironrose is two days' ride from Rillisk," I say. "Do you intend to drive your guardsmen to exhaustion to save a matter of hours?"

He sets his jaw. "Dustan said we can make it back after sundown. I'm not driving anyone to exhaustion."

"You've been riding all night and you intend to ride through the day." I glance at the guardsmen trailing the wagon. "With men who've likely been at your service since daybreak yesterday?"

Indecision flickers in his eyes, but he scowls. "You're not in charge anymore. I didn't trust you before, and finding out you've been hiding all this time doesn't make me trust you now. So sit there and shut up or I'll have one of the guardsmen gag you."

I shift to sit against the wagon railing and say nothing more.

Maybe he didn't expect me to obey, because he looks suspicious as he rides ahead to be parallel to Noah. Their voices are low and barely carry over the wind, but I can tell they are discussing whether it would be more prudent to wait.

I don't know, and I shouldn't care.

We press on.

The sun eventually begins its crawl up from the horizon. When I catch sight of Dustan, his jaw is dark with bruising, and he does not meet my eyes. None of them do. When Tycho wakes, he stays huddled by the bench, but the guards leave him alone, too. The heat of the day bears down on us, and eventually one of the guards throws cheese and bread and a water skin onto the floorboards. Tycho and I divide it between us. His movements are small and quick, like a rabbit, his eyes watchful.

We stay quiet. I listen, hoping for information, but the guards are careful and no one says anything to me.

Near nightfall, a guard tumbles from his horse.

Noah examines the man, then ducks his head and wipes sweat from his brow. "Heat exhaustion. We're going to have to camp for the night."

"No," says Jacob. He's glaring at me.

I raise my eyebrows and say nothing. He scowls.

"Jake." Noah sighs. "We're still hours away. I'm exhausted. You're exhausted. I want to go home as badly as you do, but we've been here for months so a few more days won't matter. You think Harper is going to decide whether to go home at midnight? Come on."

So we camp. A guardsman binds my chains to a tree, yanking at the shackles so hard he nearly pulls me off my feet. He's spoiling for a fight, and I remember what boredom and fatigue can do to a guardsman's temperament, so I don't give him one. Tycho is unchained, but he clings to the gathering darkness, hovering near the tree. I'm torn between wishing he would look for an opportunity to run, if one presents itself, and worrying he'd get himself killed.

Darkness falls—and with it, Jacob, Noah, and the guardsmen drift into sleep. Only Dustan remains awake, standing guard at the back of the wagon.

His own exhaustion is obvious, but it makes me think well of him that he put his men first.

Eventually sleep claims Tycho as well, curled into the dry grass at the base of the tree beside me. Silence fills the space between me and Dustan, broken only by the occasional pop from the cooking fire that no one bothered to bank.

I say nothing to him, and he says nothing to me, but his eyelids begin to flicker, and he shifts against the back of the wagon. Despite everything, I understand his position. Possibly better than anyone. "Commander," I say softly.

He's instantly alert, his eyes narrowing. "What?"

"Do you have cards?"

"I will not be tricked into releasing you."

I lift my shackled wrists. "I can hold cards. You need not release me."

He hesitates, but he must realize the risk is low, because he straightens and moves across the campground to sit across from me. He's cautious, staying just out of my reach, and he eyes me as he pulls a deck from a pouch on his belt.

Dustan shuffles quickly, dealing cards between us with practiced accuracy. I take up my hand, he takes up his, and we play in silence. He wins the first game, I, the second. By the time we begin the third, he's relaxed into the rhythm of the game. He's been keeping his eyes on his hands, on the shifting cards between us, but he gives me a rueful look when I lay down a prince card and capture one of his kings.

A crack of wood echoes from a copse of trees nearby, and we both snap our heads up. After a moment, a stag leaps from the foliage, then sprints off into the darkness.

We exchange a glance, then look back at our cards.

Dustan plays a four of swords. "That movement in the arena. With the armor. You asked who taught me." His eyes flick up to meet mine. "You did."

I play a nine of swords. "I know."

"You could have killed me."

I rub a hand across my jaw and sigh. "A man should not die over a bit of sport."

"But you might have escaped," he presses.

"Indeed, with a bounty on my head." I glance up at him. "I bear you no ill will, Dustan."

"That man Journ said you fought in his stead. Because he was injured."

I nod and wait for him to lay down a card.

He's watching me. "He said it was an act of kindness."

I shrug. An act of foolishness, more likely.

Dustan continues, "He said he would have withdrawn if he'd seen me enter the arena, rather than risk harming a member of the Royal Guard." He drops a card on the pile. "*You* could have withdrawn."

I lay down a card. "It is not in me to withdraw."

He considers that for a while as we play.

Eventually, he glances up. "Why did you leave?" When I say nothing, he continues, "I do not believe you're a deserter. A deserter would not have faced me."

I don't meet his eyes. "Perhaps it is easiest to assume I am."

"No. It's not." He pauses. "You said it was for the good of Emberfall. What does that mean?"

Those words were spoken when I believed he was going to put a sword through my chest. I already regret them. "I cannot tell you, Dustan. But I truly meant the words I said. I did not make my decision to leave lightly."

He sighs and rubs at his eyes. I know he's tired from the day, but true exhaustion sits behind it.

I carefully select a card from my hand and add it to the pile between us. A warm breeze makes the fire flicker. "How long have you been traveling with Prince Jacob?"

"Nearly two weeks." He shrugs. "We are on a tour of goodwill, in the hopes the healer's talents will endear Disi to the people of Emberfall."

I keep my tone easy, like no time at all has passed, and we're guardsmen sharing a fire and a game of cards. "I am surprised the crown prince would send you away."

His expression darkens, and he tosses a card onto the pile. "It is not for me to question the prince's orders."

It is, actually, if he is guard commander, but I do not correct him. I toss a card on the pile.

Dustan glances at Tycho. "Who's your shadow?"

"A stable boy." I choose my words carefully, because I do not want to give Dustan any more control over me than he already has. "He was sworn to Worwick."

"I thought he was going to throw himself on a sword to save you."

"He saw the Grand Marshal's enforcers execute a man in the tavern." I pause. "He was worried you would do the same to me."

Dustan's eyebrows go up. "A man was executed?"

"Yes." I pause and turn my cards over in my hands. "A man suspected of magic."

"Ah." He nods. "We've heard of such things in other towns." He glances around and his voice drops conspiratorially. "At court, some people have mentioned the healer, but no one has dared to accuse him directly."

"People are afraid."

Dustan shrugs. "Or greedy. The instant the prince gave the order, people were lining up to collect the reward. That enchanted monster terrorized us all for so long. He is desperate to make sure it doesn't happen again." He pauses and adds a card to the pile. "It's only a matter of time before people realize he's not just searching for a magesmith. He's searching for this missing heir."

I clear my throat. "How do you know that?"

Dustan pauses with his hand on a card. "We were both in the Grand Hall when Karis Luran revealed what she knew."

Back when I was a guardsman. Before I knew anything of my birthright. I'd forgotten. I run a hand across my jaw.

"That concerns you," says Dustan. His eyes search my face.

I study my cards. I've said too much. So has he. Long nights and heavy darkness never keep secrets well.

"I bear you no ill will either, Grey," he says. "In the arena—if you had not—if you had only said—" He breaks off and swears. "Silver hell. Why did you run? *Why?*"

"I would run again if I had the chance."

He straightens in surprise.

I hold up my shackled wrists. "I am your prisoner, Dustan. I owe you nothing. You owe me nothing. Allow me to keep my secrets."

For a moment he looks like he will challenge me, but either he's too tired or too unwilling. He sighs. "For the good of Emberfall?"

I nod and flip a card onto the pile. "For the good of all."

CHAPTER THIRTEEN

LIA MARA

At sunrise yesterday, my thoughts were a tangled mess of remorse and regret, made no better by the fact that my mother believed my letter.

At sunrise today, I wake with new purpose. I will find a way out of this castle. I will not be used as a pawn against my mother and my sister. I will not be used against my people.

These thoughts still poke at me. The prince is not using me against Syhl Shallow. He is using me to protect his people from my own.

Again, I shove those thoughts away.

Clothes were brought yesterday, as promised, but I had no interest in touching them. I was less interested in the dinner meal, some kind of seasoned shellfish that turned my stomach when I tasted it. Surely some kind of pointed commentary about the prince's access to a saltwater harbor, when my mother has none.

The gold and red ribbon that threads the sleeves of the clothing left on a chair seems *very* deliberate.

Regardless, I'd rather wear his colors than Sorra's blood. I strip off the stained robes and pull on soft calfskin leggings and a green chemise. These clothes are more formfitting than the robes were, and I feel very aware of the slope of my hips and the curves of my breasts. Nolla Verin would likely fawn over such clothes, while I feel self-conscious. I am glad the guards remain outside.

The room is lavishly appointed, with velvet blankets on the bed and silver-tipped furniture throughout. I'm too high up to jump from the window. Guards wait outside my door, and I have no doubt they'll replace this room with a prison cell if I give them cause. If I'm going to escape, I'll need to find another way.

I have time on my side, and little else.

Trellises line the outside castle walls, thick with blooming roses, but none are close enough to reach, and I doubt they would bear my weight anyway. No knives were delivered with the food, though I doubt I could overpower two armed guards on my own. Even the hearth is cold, lacking a flame in the summer heat. I can't set the room ablaze in the hope of escaping in the resulting melee.

I frown, studying the hearth. Similar to the rooms of the Crystal Palace in Syhl Shallow, the fireplace is stationed along the wall between two rooms in order to share a chimney. In the Crystal Palace, a metal barrier exists to afford privacy between rooms, but it can be removed for efficiency, if necessary. When Nolla Verin and I were children, we would sneak into rooms this way to spy on people we thought were so very important.

I wonder if the same thing exists here. I sit on the marble hearth and lean in, feeling along the blackened wall at the back.

It feels like brick. I sigh.

Then my fingers find an edge in the middle. I explore further. A small gap exists around the brick along the exterior of the fireplace.

More sure now, I hook my fingers around the brick edge at the center of the barrier and pull.

It doesn't move.

Of course it doesn't. It's a brick wall. I sigh *again*.

The door of my room clicks, and I dive out of the fireplace, balling my sooty hands into the robes I abandoned. I scrub at them hurriedly.

I expect Rhen to be returning to provoke me about my mother, but to my surprise, Princess Harper steps through the doorway. Even more surprising, she is no longer wearing the jewel-adorned gown from the day we first visited, but instead wears breeches and a chemise similar to mine. A female guard with waist-length dark braids stands behind her.

My expression must be filled with the rage I was saving for her beloved, because the princess frowns. "I should have asked if you were receiving visitors."

"Why?" I finish wiping at my hands and toss the robes onto a chair by the hearth. "Have you not heard? I am a prisoner."

Her expression turns abashed. "I have heard." She pauses. "I'm sorry."

She is *sorry*? This is so unexpected that I go still. My voice finds an edge. "Then you must not be aware of the injuries my people have visited on the subjects of your prince."

"I am." She presses a hand to her abdomen. "I'm still sorry."

After the prince's cold, steely gaze, it's a shock to see what looks like genuine concern in her expression. It steals some of my fury.

"You must think me a great fool," I say.

"No."

"Well, I do." I sink onto the marble ledge in front of the fireplace and give a humorless laugh. "I thought I could forge an alliance of peace, and instead, I am to be used as a pawn against my mother."

"I don't think you're a fool at all. I think it's . . ." She hesitates. "Admirable."

"If only you were my captor instead of your prince, then."

Her expression is so sorrowful. She begins to take a step toward me, but her guard murmurs, "My lady," in a tone of warning, and the princess stops.

I can tell from that tone and that response that they are close.

Unbidden, I think of Sorra moving to protect me. Emotion swells in my throat, warm and sudden. I swallow past it, and I look away, my jaw clenched.

Princess Harper's eyes swim with empathy. "I know you're angry. You don't—you don't have to talk to me."

I say nothing.

"I just want you to know that . . ." She trails off, and her eyes narrow slightly. "You have a black mark on your cheek."

Soot. I resist the urge to swipe it off. "A mark of mourning," I lie. "For my guard who was slaughtered."

Harper visibly flinches. "Again, I'm sorry—"

"You apologize a great deal for a princess." I take a step forward, and her guard moves closer to her, but Harper doesn't shift at all.

"I don't want to be your enemy," Harper says quietly.

I don't want to be hers. Despite our relative positions, I believe she has a core of kindness that I admire. In another lifetime, we could possibly be friends. I keep my eyes cold. "Your prince has guaranteed we can be nothing else."

A sigh escapes her lips. "I know."

We stand in silence, regarding each other. After the longest moment, she looks away. "If you change your mind, have one of the guards send for me." She pauses. "I know what it's like to be alone here."

I nod. I will never send for her, and I think she knows it.

She backs away, then slips through the door as quietly as she came.

I go back to the hearth and drive my fingertips into the sooty line in the brick. I pull with every ounce of my strength, bracing my feet against the opposing wall of the fireplace. Nothing moves. Sweat has begun to collect under the chemise. I swear under my breath.

I try again.

And again.

And again.

Finally, eventually, after what feels like an *eternity*, the brick wall shifts.

One inch, but it moved.

I roll the muscles of my shoulders to loosen them. I need more than an inch, but a small success makes me long for a bigger one.

Then I hear the bells ringing out in the courtyard, and my heart explodes with hope. I know it is unlikely, but I rush to the window to look for Mother.

Instead, I see guards coming through the trees, along with an unfamiliar wagon, bearing the gold and red of Rhen's colors.

I sigh and go back to the hearth.

CHAPTER FOURTEEN

GREY

When Rhen's father was king, one of the final trials to be admitted to the Royal Guard was a match between a guardsman and a prisoner from the dungeon. The prisoner was given a full set of armor and weapons. The guardsman was shackled, hand and foot. No armor, no weapons. If the prisoner won, he won his freedom. If the guardsman won, he was allowed to swear his life into service for the Crown.

We drew cards to match with our prisoners, and my opponent was a massive soldier named Vail. He'd been sentenced to death for stealing from the army's coffers, but rumors said he'd been caught violating bodies of the dead. He was scarred and vicious and practically twice my size when I was seventeen.

The matches took place before the royal family. Before that day, I'd only caught glimpses of them from afar: the king and his distant queen, Prince Rhen and his sisters.

A guardsman before me had fallen. The king looked disappointed.

Prince Rhen looked bored.

They rang a bell and led Vail into the arena.

I'd watched the earlier matches. Most of the other guards would retreat first, to wait for an opening. With Vail, I knew I'd never get one. He came after me with his sword, and I whipped my shackle chains around the weapon, holding fast. When he tried to pull free, I leapt for his throat and crushed his windpipe. He dropped like a rock.

The match was over in less than ten seconds. The bell had not even finished ringing.

The prince no longer looked bored.

"You're lucky he didn't take your hands off," the guard commander called from the sidelines. "Going for the blade barehanded like that."

"It was not luck," I called back.

I swore an oath the very next day. An oath that lasted an eternity.

An oath I have never regretted, until this very moment.

When the wagon stops in the cobblestone courtyard of Ironrose Castle, the guards all but drag me out. I want to dig my fingernails into the splintered floorboards. I want to run. I want to hide.

Dustan rode ahead, likely to spread word of my capture, because the courtyard is packed with people. My eyes take in everything, and it's almost too much to endure. Guards line the castle walls, but I recognize few of them. Rhen stands at the center, absolutely still. Harper stands at his side, clutching his hand. Her knuckles are white. I cannot lift my gaze to meet theirs. My vision has tunneled down to the stones at their feet, growing closer with each passing second.

The courtyard is more silent than I've ever known it, as if even the horses feel the weight of this moment. I have done nothing wrong, but guilt and shame curl like fire in my belly anyway.

Not like this, I think. *Not like this.*

But of course it could only be like this. I made sure of that three months ago.

My feet slide to a stop.

A fist cracks me between the shoulders, hard enough that I stumble forward and fall to my knees. Pain ricochets through my leg, and I bite back a cry.

"You are in front of the crown prince and his lady," says one of the guards. "You will kneel."

I must speak. I don't want to speak.

My voice is barely a rasp of sound. "Forgive me, my lord."

The guard punches me between the shoulder blades again, and this time I have to catch myself on my hands.

"You will address the prince as Your Highness," he barks.

"Forgive me," I say again. "Your Highness."

The waiting silence takes my words and swallows them up. Rhen has said nothing. Harper has said nothing. I very much wish I had the power to blink myself out of Emberfall, because I would accept any other fate that did not involve me in chains at the feet of the people I was once sworn to protect.

"Look at me," Rhen finally says.

If the words were spoken in anger or given like an order, I might have obeyed. But his voice is quiet, undercut with betrayal.

I cannot look at him. I feel as though I *have* betrayed him.

A hand grips my hair, and I realize one of the guardsmen is going to force my gaze up.

Rhen says, "No."

The hand at the back of my head lets go.

"Look at me," he says again, and this time it's an order.

I raise my head and look at him.

Prince Rhen is the same and different all at once. The uncertainty and self-doubt from the later stages of the curse are gone, replaced with fierce determination. This is a man who endured the enchantress's torture, season after season, to spare me. A man who gave up his life to save the people of Emberfall. This is the man who will be king.

His eyes, always keen, search mine, seeking answers.

"Are you sworn to another?" he asks me, and his voice is low and dangerous.

The question takes me by surprise—and at once I realize he thinks I have been gone because I was sworn to Lilith. "No, my— Your Highness."

"You have given your oath to no one?"

"To no one but you."

His mouth forms a line. "I released you from your oath."

"Then I ask that you allow me my freedom."

Rhen's eyes don't leave mine. He's trying to figure me out.

I could solve all this inquiry. *I am the heir. I am the man you seek.*

And the ironic, *I left to spare you all this trouble.*

Harper steps forward and drops to a knee before me. Her eyes are wide and dark and sorrowful. "Grey," she whispers. "Grey, please. You're . . . You're *alive*. All this time, we thought . . . we thought you were dead."

I wish I could erase the pain from her eyes—but it's lodged as deeply as the betrayal in Rhen's.

"A princess should not kneel before a prisoner," I say softly.

The words are an echo of so many I said when I was a guardsman, and I expect it to remind her of her place, to force her to her feet.

Instead, she puts a hand against my cheek, and that is almost my undoing. I close my eyes and turn my face away.

"Grey," she whispers. "Please. Help me understand. Why did you leave?"

"Commander," Rhen says sharply.

I snap my eyes to his—only to remember that I am no longer a guardsman.

The prince's expression has evened out, but he did not miss the movement. I can read no emotion on his face now.

That's never a good sign.

"Take him to a room," he says. "Clean him up, dress his wounds, and leave him unharmed. Have the kitchens send him a meal."

"Yes, my lord." Dustan grabs hold of my arm.

"And, Commander?"

I flinch but do not look up.

Rhen's eyes are cold. "Make sure he can't escape."

CHAPTER FIFTEEN

LIA MARA

I had no interest in the goings on in the courtyard until I heard a shout.

I had no idea what was going on until Princess Harper dropped to a knee and called the man Grey.

So this is the man everyone seeks. Not dead after all.

He's much younger than I expected, for a man who was commander of the prince's Royal Guard. Clanna Sun is Mother's chief adviser, and she was not elevated to that station until she reached her fifties. This man appears hardly older than I am, though he's rough and worn and injured, blood staining a bandage wrapped tightly around his thigh. His eyes are despondent, his posture defeated.

What did the guardsman say? *We found him in Rillisk, my lord. He was going by another name. Once I realized who he was, he attempted to flee.*

Why would he hide? Why would he run? If he knows the

identity of the heir, as the enchantress claimed, why would he not reveal it to his prince? If he once held such a lofty position, he must have proven his loyalty.

And if he *wasn't* loyal, if he keeps such a secret for nefarious reasons, I'd expect to see some defiance in his gaze. Some grim determination. Instead, he kneels at the prince's feet as if he would offer his life in service this very moment. His expression is full of deep remorse. He looks conflicted. He looks . . . *lost.*

They drag him away, into the castle, and I am left to wonder.

I go back to pulling at the brick barrier. I can now move it three inches in either direction. The track is old and rusty, but the more I work at it, the more success I have.

While I work, I think.

I have seen that look in Mother's guards, men and women who would lay down their lives if she requested it. It is curious to find it in a man who keeps such a secret. By virtue of that expression, I would expect him to be *desperate* to share the identity of the missing heir, especially if it's an individual who shares an affinity for magic.

The brick wall gives another inch. I drag a forearm across my sweaty forehead, likely leaving another line of soot.

What would Grey know that the prince wouldn't? Why flee? Who could he be protecting? It could not be a child. According to custom here in Emberfall, the heir must be older than Prince Rhen.

A friend? What kind of friend would inspire such devotion in a matter of months? Surely this Grey must know his life is forfeit if he keeps a secret from his prince. What friend could be worth that? What friend would *require* it?

A sibling? I could see myself keeping a secret to protect Nolla

Verin, even at the risk of my life. But of course that's ridiculous, because if Grey had a brother, then that man could only be—

My hands go still on the brick.

Suddenly I understand the conflict in Grey's expression. I understand why he would run. I understand why he would hide.

Grey *is* being loyal. He *is* protecting the prince. There's no defiance because he *was* willing to lay down his life in favor of Prince Rhen.

What did Mother say?

According to the enchantress, Grey is the only man who knows the true identity of the heir.

We all thought that meant the enchantress had revealed this knowledge to Grey—and I'm sure Prince Rhen did too.

We were wrong.

Grey knows because *he* is the heir.

CHAPTER SIXTEEN

GREY

By the time Rhen calls for me, the sun has long since set. I've been chained alone in an empty room for most of the day, and the cold of the marble floor has seeped into my bones, leaving a stiff ache that refuses to disappear. The guards followed orders, but only to the letter, so I'm clean and my wound is bandaged, but I haven't seen food since morning. I have no idea what they've done with Tycho.

Rhen waits in his chambers, the space a stark contrast to where I've been kept all day. A fire burns low in the hearth, stealing any hint of a chill, exactly as I remember. Vibrant wall hangings stretch between the windows, a wide chest of drawers sits along the opposite wall, and an impressive selection of liquors fills a cabinet in the corner. Food waits on a low table near the chest, sliced fruits and warm breads.

I consider how long it's been since I've eaten, and I wonder if the waiting food—clearly untouched, set just out of reach—was deliberate.

I consider Prince Rhen, waiting impassively in a velvet arm-chair, and I know it was.

The guards draw me to a stop before him, but I know better than to hesitate now. There is no carpeting here, but I kneel any-way, my injured leg clumsy and stiff, my chains rattling against the marble floor. The air flickers with uncertainty and betrayal.

Two guards stand at my back, while Dustan stands to Rhen's right, near the hearth. The prince says nothing, so I wait. We all wait. An ache settles into my leg, and I desperately want to ease it.

This is also deliberate.

I had almost forgotten he could be like this. Prince Rhen is a brilliant strategist and a consummate gentleman, but he can also be petty in the most creative of ways. The curse changed him—in truth, it changed us both—but it did not lessen his ability to be vindictive.

It did not lessen my ability to tolerate it either.

That thought alone allows me to meet his gaze. His eyes reveal nothing, but we have far too much history for his thoughts to be a mystery. He is well practiced in hiding emotion, but he's only ever this stoic when he's deeply unsettled.

That makes two of us.

When Rhen finally speaks, his eyes don't leave mine. "Unchain him," he orders. "Leave us."

Dustan hesitates. "My lord—"

"If Grey meant me harm, he would not have been living two days' away, under the guise of another name." Rhen doesn't look away. "Unchain him."

Dustan pulls a key from his belt and gives the other guardsmen an order to disperse. The shackles fall from my wrists and ankles, clattering on the marble, and I have to fight the urge to rub at my sore wrists. Dustan winds the chains between his hands and moves to return to his spot by the fire.

"No," says Rhen. "Go."

Dustan inhales to argue, but he must see Rhen's expression, because he withdraws, and the door eases closed.

The sudden silence magnifies every emotion. His eyes still haven't left mine, and I can read the uncertainty and betrayal in his gaze, as surely as he can read my own.

"So," he says. "Hawk, was it?"

He's clearly baiting me, which doesn't seem promising.

"Dustan tells me you weren't even working as a swordsman," he adds. "That you simply stood in for another man who was injured. To be honest, I'm surprised." He sits back and lifts one shoulder in an elegant shrug. "I told you I would write you a letter of recommendation."

My eyes narrow. I grit my teeth against the ache in my leg and will myself to remain still.

He must read the shadow of pain in my expression, because he says, "Do you wish to move?"

I cannot read his voice, and his eyes are still cold, so I do not know if this is a genuine offer or just a way to force me to admit weakness.

When I do not answer, he frowns. Some of the ice melts from his expression, and the edge in his voice softens. "You trusted me once," he says. "What have I done to lose it?"

Those words are spoken in earnest, and they take me by surprise. "My lord—Your Highness. You have done nothing."

"Something has clearly changed between us, Grey."

I look away.

"Silver hell," he says. "You were dragged before me in chains. Surely you know I can force answers from you if I wish it."

That sparks my anger. "Surely you know I am more of a danger to you in this moment than you are to me."

He straightens. "You wish to issue threats?"

"That was not a threat."

Tense silence hangs between us for a moment. I wait for him to call for guards, to cut me down for daring to challenge him.

I should know better. Prince Rhen is not his father, for better or for worse.

Not *our* father. The thought hits me hard and fast, and I'm not ready for it.

He must see the flicker of distress in my expression. "What did Lilith tell you?" he says. "Tell me what you know."

"I have committed no crime. I have asked for my freedom. Nothing more."

"Are you sworn to her?"

"No!"

His voice gains a pulse of anger. "Are you lying to me?"

"I have *never* lied to you. I cut her throat and abandoned her on the other side."

He snaps back, surprise plain on his face. His voice is little more than a hushed whisper. "Truly?"

I nod. "Truly."

For a moment, the weight of his relief is a weight in the room. A tension I wasn't aware of eases. Rhen takes a long breath and runs a hand across his jaw.

I study him. "I had not considered you would bear such worry."

His hands clench on the arms of his chair, and he half rises, rage plain on his face. "*How could you not?*"

The door swings open. Dustan looks in. "My lord—"

Rhen doesn't even look at him. "Out."

The door closes, and silence drops between us again.

Rhen's eyes narrow, turning calculating once more. "Fine. You were not sworn to her. You are clearly not dead. Why did you leave Ironrose?"

I shift my weight slightly, and it doesn't help. Sweat has begun to collect in the small of my back. "You released me from my oath. My service was done."

"You know guardsmen must be discharged officially. You do not just *leave*." The fire cracks, accenting his words. "Why did you run from Dustan?"

No answer seems safe to give.

"Karis Luran believes you know the identity of the rightful heir. She says Lilith claimed you alone knew."

"I have no information that you would find useful, Your Highness."

He smiles, but there is nothing pleasant about it. "That is a very careful answer, Grey."

My own anger flares. "You trusted *me* once. What have I done to lose it?"

"You left."

The words hit me like a knife in the back. I have to look away. Silence swells to fill the space between us again.

"My words are true," I finally say. "I left to protect you. To protect the line of succession. No good can come from this knowledge, Your Highness. I swear it."

He says nothing.

"Allow me to leave," I continue. "I will beg it of you if you wish."

"I cannot. You know I cannot. If you know anything—"

"Please." I put my hands on the floor, prepared to make good on my offer. "*Please*. I will leave here and speak of this to no one. You know I would never put you at risk—"

"I do *not* know that."

"You *do* know that," I say viciously. "I swore my life to you and to Emberfall, and I have proven it time and again."

His eyes bore into mine. I remember the last night we faced each other like this. We stood on the castle parapet. He was on the verge of becoming the monster.

He wanted to jump. To destroy himself before he could destroy his people.

He was afraid. More afraid than I've ever seen him.

I reached out and clasped his hand.

"I would prove it now," I say. "If you would offer me the chance."

Some emotion fractures in his eyes. He stands, and for half a moment, I think he will call for the guards to drag me out of here.

Instead, he extends a hand. "Get off your knees, Grey."

My heart pounds. I take his hand. He pulls me to my feet.

"Would you sit with me for a time?" he says. "I will call for a proper meal."

It's a request, not an order—which implies I can refuse.

I don't want to refuse. "Yes, Your Highness."

"Rhen," he says.

My eyebrows go up.

His expression turns a bit sheepish, his voice a bit rueful. "I have long thought we should have been friends, Grey. I should have remedied that ages ago."

"I could not have endured watching Lilith's torments on a friend," I say. "Likely you could not either."

"True," he says. "But I can dine with one."

I smile. "Yes, you can."

Despite the small sampling of delicacies along the sideboard, Rhen sends for dinner, and a massive platter of roasted beef and sugar-crusted vegetables is delivered almost at once. I eat like a condemned man facing his last meal: slowly, savoring each bite, making the food spend an eternity on my tongue. I had forgotten the splendor of food at court, and each morsel is better than anything Jodi could prepare on her best day. Rhen called for wine as well, and he sips from his glass as the fire snaps behind us.

He poured some for me, but I have not touched it.

"Still no head for it?" he says.

"Not yet."

That makes him smile.

The room is quiet while we eat, and at first, it is not an easy silence. I cannot forget why I was dragged here to begin with.

I know Rhen hasn't forgotten.

But familiarity begins to steal the tension between us. Too many memories of other shared meals blend together, many in this very room. Countless card games played late into the night when the curse seemed interminable and neither of us felt like sleeping. Racing through the woods on horseback or matching blades in the arena when he wanted a challenge. Mourning our losses in silence when the days grew long and the curse seemed it would never be broken.

He was always the prince and I was always his guardsman, so we were never truly friends. Like Rhen, I regret that. But we were trapped together for so long that we were . . . something.

I didn't realize I missed his companionship until now.

When he sets down his knife to speak, I tense, but he only says, "Tell me about the boy they captured with you."

"Tycho. He is no one. A stable hand at Worwick's Tourney." Tycho's treatment has been nagging at me since the moment I was dragged from the courtyard. "Is he well?"

"A little awestruck, according to Dustan, but he is well."

Tycho was awestruck over the possibility of five hundred silvers. Ironrose likely knocked him off his feet. "Not chained in a cell, then?"

Rhen shakes his head and lifts his glass of wine. "Noah spoke for him and said he should be cared for, and so he has been." He pauses. "Dustan said he tried to save you."

"He's lucky Dustan didn't slice him in two."

"He is not *no one*, though. Not if he'd risk his life." Rhen raises his eyebrows. "A friend?"

He is too savvy. I watched guardsmen lie to the king and get away with it, but Rhen could never be fooled.

"Yes," I concede. "A friend."

"He was sworn to this Worwick?"

I try to figure out where these questions will lead, and fail. "Yes. For his family's debts."

"I will have coins sent to buy his freedom."

The money means nothing to Rhen, but the effort behind it means something to me. He does nothing without purpose, and I wonder if this is a peace offering of sorts.

Then again, this could just as easily be a ploy to regain my trust so it can be used against me.

"A bag of the king's silver?" I snort, to cover my surprise. "Worwick will spin a better story out of that than a stable hand's freedom."

Rhen smiles. "Truly? Tell me."

I hesitate, then take a breath and tell him about Worwick and the tourney. I expect questions about why I chose to work in the stables instead of the arena, but Rhen does not press. I tell him about Jodi and the tavern, and Tycho and his love for swordplay. Mention of Jodi and Tycho leads to the events in the tavern, when the blacksmith was killed, and how that led to Tycho fearing for my life when I faced Dustan in the alley.

"A good friend, then," says Rhen.

"The nights were long," I say to him. "The days tedious. Often I was his only company, and he mine."

Rhen loses his smile, and I realize what I've said.

I take a drink of water and look away. "Surely he must have your sympathy."

That makes him laugh. "Indeed." He pauses. "Why did you leave?"

He is not demanding, the way he was before. This is a true question.

The breath slowly eases out of my lungs. "I believe you know why."

"Why will you not reveal the identity of the heir?"

There is no answer I can give him that would be satisfactory. No truth that would not ensure my death.

When I say nothing, he picks up his wine. The jewel-red liquid glows from the firelight. In one quick swallow, he drains the glass.

I know this look on his face. He is cunning. Thoughtful. Strategic. He'll figure it out himself if I'm not careful. The only thing working in my favor is that he expects the heir to have magic, and I've never shown any evidence of having any myself.

If I'd been able to use magic, I would have used it against Lilith long before now.

I feel the weight of Rhen's eyes on me. "This stable boy is too young," he muses.

I say nothing and slice through a glistening vegetable.

"Someone else at this tourney?" he says.

"If I was willing to give up command to keep this secret," I say, "you will not easily guess it."

"I could send guardsmen to Rillisk," he says. "I can have them all questioned."

"Would this be before or after you sent coins to free Tycho?"

He frowns. "Do not play with me."

"I have seen the fate of other men you intended to question. I have seen the way your orders have been carried out. No one at the tourney knows anything. Do not condemn them to death because you fear your throne may be taken from you."

His gaze sharpens. "You will remember your place here, Grey."

"You should remember yours, *friend*. You are the crown prince. This heir is no threat to you."

Rhen draws himself up, and I see the first flash of anger in his eyes. "Even *rumor* of this heir is a threat to me. To all of Emberfall.

Do you realize there are nobles who are questioning the very legitimacy of my rule? That there are whispers of Grand Marshals who no longer feel the need to acknowledge the Crown?"

Yes. I have heard these rumors.

"And what will you do?" I say. "What will you do with this heir, if you find him?"

"You know what I will do."

I swallow. Yes. I know what he will do. "He is no threat to you," I say again.

He slams his hand down on the table between us. "You cannot know that!"

"Yes—"

"You cannot!" The words explode out of him, but he breaks off and runs a hand across his jaw. He has to take a breath to steady himself, which is something I've never seen him do. "Lilith nearly killed Harper. She spent an eternity torturing us. If this man has magic, if he is of the same ilk as the enchantress . . . how can you protect him, Grey? How?"

I go still. All of a sudden, I understand his desperation to find the heir. This has nothing to do with his throne at all. Not really.

Rhen is afraid. Not of losing his throne, but afraid of the magic. Of what it might do to him, and to Emberfall.

I am the heir, Rhen. I am your brother. You have nothing to fear from me.

The words wait on my tongue, but they stall there. I watched the enforcers put a blade into Riley. I've heard the rumors from other towns. Once, I would have laid down my life to protect him, but this suddenly feels different. I am not under oath. I know I am no threat to him. I don't want to die to prove it.

Rhen said he lost my trust, but I don't think that's true. I trust him the same way I always did: to put the safety of his kingdom ahead of everything else. If he believes magic is a threat to Emberfall, our shared history—even our shared blood—would not keep me safe.

"To keep this a secret is akin to treason," Rhen says.

I say nothing. There is no path here. None.

His cheeks are flushed with anger. "Grey. Do not make me force answers from you."

"We spent season after season allowing Lilith to torture us both," I say. "Do you truly think you can?"

"I will do whatever is necessary to protect Emberfall."

"As will I," I say. "I keep this secret to protect you."

"You keep it to protect *yourself.*"

"That too."

He draws himself up, his eyes alight with fury. It's been a long time since I've seen Rhen so angry, and it's almost chilling to have it directed at me. Worse, I can now clearly see the fear buried beneath it. It pulls at cords in my chest. Season after season, he stood up to Lilith without fear. Often to spare me her torments.

"I swear to you," I say quietly. "You have nothing to fear from this man and his magic."

For a moment, I worry his fear is too potent. But then he sits back in his chair and sighs. The fury melts away. "I will grant you a day, Grey."

"A day?"

"Yes. I will grant you a day to consider your stance, at your liberty, provided you remain on the grounds of Ironrose."

"This is not a kindness. You believe I will reveal something to you. I will not."

"Shall I call for Dustan to begin severing limbs right now, then?"

"I'd rather you didn't."

He smiles, but it's more regretful than amused. "I've missed you, Grey."

"And I you."

"You have until sunset tomorrow." He raises his voice. "Commander!"

I'm returned to a different room, but this time, no shackles encircle my wrists. A guard remains outside, but as promised, I'm allowed some liberty. A low fire burns in the hearth, and a pitcher of water, a kettle of tea, and a selection of sweetcakes waits on a side table. Before I can touch them, a servant enters, bringing a pile of folded clothing.

"His Highness thought these would be more to your liking," he says, leaving the clothes on a chair before exiting quickly.

I pick through them. Everything is made of fine leather and expensive cloth.

I *know* Rhen doesn't think I can be lured into revealing the heir by extravagance. Maybe this part of his friendship is true.

A shadow flickers in the corner of the room.

I keep my hand on the clothing, running my fingers along a carefully stitched seam, but my attention is on the shadow now.

Maybe Rhen hopes to assassinate me. But that's ridiculous. He could have had it done right in front of him.

Another small movement, by the draperies surrounding the corner window.

I straighten and sigh and stretch as though tired, then move along the wall, extinguishing the sconces one by one, making a show of preparing for bed. When I reach the sconce by the corner, I plunge my hand into the draperies, aiming for a throat or an arm.

Instead, I find the clear features of a face. A woman cries out and flails at me through the lengths of gauzy fabric.

I jerk the drapes wide and pin her against the wall, one hand against her throat and the other gripping her arm above her head.

It's a girl I've never seen before. Red hair hangs long and straight, past the curves that accentuate her waist. Soot streaks her face and arms. Her eyes are wide, her breathing quick.

"Who are you?" I demand, my voice low.

"My name is Lia Mara," she whispers, her voice thick with the accent of Syhl Shallow. "And *you're* the rightful heir."

CHAPTER SEVENTEEN

LIA MARA

In person, Grey is much larger than he appeared in the courtyard. Considering his injured leg, I didn't expect him to be so quick or so violent, which is rather unfortunate because he's about to crush my throat. His body pins mine against the wall, but my fingers dig at his wrist.

"Please," I say, my voice strained. "I have little time."

His grip doesn't loosen. "How do you know who I am?"

"My mother." Spots begin to flare in my vision. Breath rakes across my tongue. "Please—I need to speak with you."

He studies me for the longest moment, until I'm certain I will lose consciousness. He's extinguished most of the oil lamps along the wall, so shadow cloaks us both. His eyes are deep set and dark, like charred wood in a burning hearth, so much darker than eyes native to Syhl Shallow.

His hand eases on my neck, and sweet air floods my lungs. The weight of his body still holds me against the wall. No man has ever been this close to me. Even with his hand against my throat, Grey is not being *rough*, but he's close enough for me to feel his heart beat nearly against my own. A flush colors my cheeks, and I hope it's too dark for him to see.

His fingers tap at my neck. "Now you have little to say?"

I swallow. "I did not—you are not what I expected."

"I did not expect to find a girl hiding in the draperies, so we have that in common. Who are you?"

"Lia Mara." I pause. "My mother is Karis Luran."

He inhales sharply, and his fingers flex against my throat.

"I am not your enemy!" I whisper quickly.

"A spy from Syhl Shallow is certainly not a friend."

"Prince Rhen knows I'm here." His expression turns skeptical. "Well—not *here*," I amend. "I may only have a short time before the guards discover I'm missing."

"You are his prisoner."

"No. Yes." Grey is so unyielding that I turn flustered. "I did not—I am not a spy. I came to the castle with a proposal of peace."

"Ah, a proposal of peace. So often delivered in such a way."

I make a frustrated sound and snap at him in Syssalah. "*Fell siralla!* Would you stop talking? I am trying to explain."

He raises his eyebrows, as if to say, *go on*.

I quickly explain what happened when I arrived, how Rhen refused my offer and took me prisoner. When I get to the part where he executed Sorra, my voice begins to waver.

Grey's expression does not change.

I steady myself and continue. "I saw you brought into the courtyard. I knew who you must be."

"The prince himself does not know," he says. "How do *you*?"

"I didn't—not for sure. Mother only said you knew the true identity of the heir, so at first I believed you carried some secret. But I began to question why you would not reveal it to your prince. You were the captain of his guard, were you not?"

"Commander."

"Yes. Commander. You forswear family, yes? If the heir were another man, you would surely volunteer that information."

His eyes reveal nothing. I wonder if my hypothesis worries him. If *I* figured it out, surely the prince can.

"He will kill you if he finds out," I say softly.

"As a matter of course." He says this without emotion, without one breath of doubt.

"But you must have magic if you are the son of a magesmith! Why would you allow yourself to be taken prisoner?"

He swears. "Maybe I have the blood of a magesmith, but so far it has done me little good."

I study him. "You could escape. My mother seeks you as well."

"I want nothing from Karis Luran."

His voice carries an edge like a knife, and I flinch. "She would offer her support to your claim on the throne."

"I seek no claim to the throne."

"Not even if it means peace between Syhl Shallow and Emberfall?"

"Peace between our countries cannot be achieved through trickery and treason." His hand is very warm on my throat, a reminder that he could kill me right here and all my hopes would die with me. "Based on your story, it seems you've learned that lesson yourself."

I frown. "I will not apologize for trying to save the lives of thousands of people. You and your prince may believe that the solution to all life's challenges exists at the end of a sword, but I do not." I look him dead in the eye. "If you will not accept my offer of assistance—"

"I will not."

I square my shoulders, but all it does is press my chest into his. I force my voice to remain level. "I will ask you to unhand me, so I can return to my room to await my fate."

He's staring at me like he's unsure what to make of me.

"Now," I add.

It's a bold request. He could call for guards, and they would certainly put me somewhere I can't slip through the fireplace. He could kill me himself, to keep his secret.

The weight of his scrutiny crackles in the air between us.

He frowns, but his hand slips away from my neck.

Before he can say anything, the door creaks, and he jerks back. I dash behind the curtains again.

I expect him to drag me back out, to use my trickery and escape to his advantage, but instead, he says, "Move to the corner. You'll be better hidden."

I slide along the stone wall, shifting silently until I hear a guard announce, "Harper, Princess of Disi."

Even my breathing stops. Why would the princess visit a former guardsman?

"My lady." Grey's voice, hushed with surprise. No, more than surprise. He was so impassive when he faced me that I wish I could see his face now.

A rush of skirts indicates she's moving. I allow myself a slow breath and pull deeper into the corner. All the sconces in this part of the room are dark. Surely I'm well hidden. I peek around the edge of the curtain.

What I see almost makes me give myself away entirely.

They are *embracing*. My heart gives a sudden lurch in my chest.

I've been longing for a book in my hours here, but this is almost worth the hours of boredom in that room. The princess and the guardsman. What an absolute *scandal*. Nolla Verin will faint when I tell her.

If I can ever tell her.

Grey puts his hands on Harper's arms and draws her back. "You are the Princess of Disi. You cannot—"

"I don't care! Grey, you're *alive*."

"Indeed. Until sundown tomorrow."

The princess's face goes solemn. "Rhen told me." She takes a step forward, reaching for him, but he steps away. She stops and wrings her hands. "Please, Grey. Please tell him."

"Forgive me," he says, and his voice is gentle in a way I didn't expect. "I cannot."

"I watched what Lilith did to him, Grey. I can't watch him do something like that to you. I can't. I know why he's afraid, but I told him—he can't—" Her voice breaks. "You just came back. I can't—he can't—"

"My lady."

His voice carries a tone of command, and she steadies herself. A slender hand swipes at her face. A tear glistens in the dim candle-light. "What?"

"We once spoke of my duty to bleed so he does not. I swore an oath to die so he would not. If I die bearing this secret, and it allows him to take the throne without challenge, what difference is this?"

"This is not the same, and you know it."

"It *is* the same. It is very much the same."

Her voice turns sharp. "If he does this, I don't know if I can ever forgive him."

Grey's expression is resigned, his eyes full of shadows. "A king should place his country above the woman he loves."

Harper goes still. "That's what he said, too." She scowls. "You stupid men and your stupid ideals. You were imprisoned here together for like *ever*, but you can't just talk this out and figure out a solution?"

I was right yesterday. She and I could have been friends.

"My lady." Grey finally steps forward and touches a finger to her chin, lifting her gaze. "If you love him, you will try to understand his motives. Do not underestimate his ability to rule as he sees necessary. We have spoken of mercy and weakness."

She sighs. "I know."

"Do not underestimate my ability to stay alive either."

Her eyebrows go up, her expression turning hopeful.

Grey shrugs and drops his hand. "I have been granted a day, and I did not expect that much."

She reaches out to catch his hand, clutching it between her own. "You'll figure out a way. Promise me you'll try."

"Easily done. You have my word." He pauses. "I would ask a promise of you as well."

"Anything." Princess Harper straightens. "I'll make a case for your innocence—whatever you need. Tell me the right words. I can go to his advisers—"

"My lady. You misunderstand. My request is not that you intercede." He hesitates. "I do not want you to *watch*."

She blanches and takes a step back. "Grey . . ."

His voice is firm. "I will keep my promise if you can keep this."

She swallows. "Okay. I will." She pauses. "I'm still going to try to stop him."

He smiles, though there is little humor in it. "That is why you were destined to stand at his side."

A tear slips down her cheek, but she hurriedly wipes it away. "You must be tired, but . . ." Her voice trails off, but then she looks up, her eyes hopeful again. "Maybe we could spend some time together tomorrow? He says you can do whatever you want as long as you stay on the castle grounds."

He nods. "Yes, of course."

"I've been working on swordplay. Zo has been helping me."

His smile is a little sad. "I look forward to seeing your progress."

"Good," she says. Her face nearly crumples, but she swipes at her eyes again. "Tomorrow morning?"

"As early as you wish."

The princess slips out as quietly as she came.

Grey stalks across the room, moving quickly despite his injured leg, and tosses the curtain wide.

I stare up at him. "And to think you spoke of treachery and treason."

He frowns. "What?"

"You and the princess. No wonder you ran."

To my surprise, he laughs. "Rhen would hardly allow me an inch of freedom if that were true." He sobers quickly, which makes me think there may be more that he is not saying. "Do not speak of things you do not know."

Interesting. "Did you mean what you said? That you'd rather die than tell him you're the heir?"

"Yes."

He answers so simply, so *guilelessly*. After the polished double-speak of the prince, his forthright honesty is unexpected.

He frowns. "How *did* you get in here?"

"The fireplace. I pulled the barrier wide."

His eyebrows go up. "Those barriers have not been moved in years."

"That's probably why it took me all day."

He glances at the hearth, then back at me. Again, I am self-conscious of these clothes that reveal every curve, and I wish I could pull back into deeper shadows.

"You crawled through a lit fire?" he says.

I scowl. "It was not lit on my side, and I am more nimble than I look." Outside, bells signal the change of guard. "Will you allow me to return, or do you intend to reveal my escape to your prince?"

He studies me for the longest moment, then stands back. "My room is guarded as securely as yours is. You will find no escape through here."

I kneel on the hearth and put my back against the side wall so I can ease around the flames. "You told the princess not to underestimate your ability to stay alive."

"I've made it this far."

"So have I. Don't underestimate my abilities either." I shimmy through the narrow opening, flicking a lit ember off my sweater, mindful of his eyes watching me.

"I don't suppose you would change your mind?" I say. "About working with my mother? Working toward peace?"

"Your mother is a monster," he says.

I frown and put my hand against the brick, then ease through the gap and look at him across the flames. "Given what I've learned, so is your prince."

Without another word, I put my day's work to good use, and I pull the handle to snap the barrier smoothly back into place.

CHAPTER EIGHTEEN

GREY

When Rhen spoke of liberty and hospitality, he clearly meant it. I sleep fitfully and wake long before sunrise, but despite the early hour, I'm provided with anything I request, from a shaving kit to a platter of food to a pair of boots that fit better. Out of curiosity, I request a dagger, and the servant bobs a curtsy and says, "Right away, my lord," before dashing off.

While I wait, I stand at the window and stare out at the dawn sky, quickly brightening as the sun breaks across the horizon. The castle grounds are alive with color, from the snapping gold and red pennants to the flowers that bloom everywhere. I spent so long trapped in an eternal autumn that I'd forgotten the beauty of Ironrose at midsummer.

Lia Mara has pulled the brick divider in the hearth closed, but I found myself studying it last night. The handle is hot when I put my hand against it, the barrier heavy enough that I'd have to brace against the brick wall to pull it wide. I'm impressed by her strength and ingenuity. I'm not sure I would have even considered it.

A knock sounds at my door, and I move away from the window. "Enter."

Instead of the serving girl, Dustan pushes though the door and allows it to fall closed. "Why do you need a dagger?"

"I was curious to see how far the offer of hospitality would extend."

"This far, it would seem." He doesn't seem irritated. If anything, he seems amused.

"Who is my jailor to be today, Commander?" I ask him. "Am I confined to my quarters?"

"You are free to roam as you please." He pauses, then folds his arms. "And your 'jailor' is me."

"Then I'd like to see Tycho," I say.

Dustan nods. He leads me past the other rooms on this floor to the staircase that descends to the lowest level.

I frown. "Where is he?"

"The infirmary."

I'd been worried he would say *the dungeon*, but this is worse. "He was injured?"

"No. You'll see."

The infirmary is not large, and it was mostly open space when I was in command of the Royal Guard. A dozen cots had lined the back wall of the room, and a small bench of supplies sat near the front.

In my absence these last few months, the infirmary has been transformed. The cots—now double in number—are larger, with more plush cushioning, and a white sheet hangs between each, affording patients some privacy. The bench has been replaced with two long tables full of rolled muslin and stacks of fabric, backed by corked jars of every color. The few wall sconces that once lit the space have been replaced by large overhead chandeliers, brightening the infirmary to a space where few shadows can linger.

Near the center of the room, a pale, shirtless, middle-aged man sits on a cot, cradling his arm in his lap. Sweat glistens on his brow. On a stool in front of him sits Noah, facing away from us, and beside him, on a chair, sits Tycho.

"Touch here," says Noah, gingerly pressing his fingers against the man's shoulder. The man winces but holds still as Tycho's fingers follow the same path.

"You feel that bony mass?" says Noah. "Broken clavicle. That's the beginning of new bone formation over the fracture line."

"Broken clavicle," Tycho echoes.

The man winces again. "Is that bad?"

"No," says Noah. "I'll give you a sling."

"You've made quite a place for yourself, Noah," I say.

He glances over his shoulder. "What else was I supposed to do?"

There's a chilliness to his voice, but it's overshadowed by Tycho spinning in his chair, smiling wide. "Grey!" But then his eyes settle on Dustan, and the smile melts into wary regard. "Are you well?"

"I am well," I say. "I'm glad you've found a friend."

Noah rises from the stool and moves to one of the tables, where he picks up a folded length of muslin. "Tycho's welcome anytime. He's a quick study."

Tycho glances between Noah and me, and then his eyes flick cautiously to Dustan. "Can we go home?"

As if Worwick would welcome me with open arms. Then again, he always did like a spectacle.

These thoughts are useless. I won't be going anywhere at all.

"Not yet," I say.

At my side, Dustan gives away nothing through his expression.

"I promised Princess Harper she could demonstrate her new-found skills," I say. "Shall we go see if she is receiving visitors?"

Tycho's eyes go wide. "You know the *princess*?"

Noah rips through the length of muslin. "They go way back."

I frown at his tone, but Tycho's curiosity is already taking over. "What kind of skills?"

"The kind you'll like."

———

We meet in the courtyard at midmorning, while the sun beams down to fill the air with heat and the scents of jasmine and honey-suckle from the flowering bushes surrounding the stable. My leg is beginning to ache from all the movement, but I'll probably be chained to a rack later, so I ignore the pain.

Harper grins at me and palms three knives. "Watch. Are you watching? Watch."

Her enthusiasm is almost infectious. I can't help but smile in return. "I am watching, my lady."

Zo stands at her back, her expression full of the same suspicion and disappointment I find on the face of every guardsman I knew before.

You too swore an oath to protect the Crown, I want to say. *You would understand if you knew.*

Or maybe they wouldn't.

Harper flips one knife in her hand, then lets it fly. It sails into the space between two cobblestones, driving into the dirt with enough force that the handle vibrates.

I remember the day she first asked me to show her this, how the very act of learning weaponry seemed to be an act of defiance. At first, I thought it was against Rhen, but it didn't take me long to realize she'd grown up thinking she could never learn to defend herself. The defiance was toward *herself.* Or who she'd thought she was.

She flips the other two knives, and they land in quick succession in an almost straight line. She turns to curtsy.

I smile. "I'm impressed," I say, and mean it.

"Zo and Dustan helped me a lot." She pauses. "I'm still not very good at the sword stuff, but I'm getting better."

She wears a sword on her hip today, bearing the weight of the weapon and armor as casually as Zo does beside her. "Show me."

Their blades fly and crash together in the sunlight, but she is right. The swordplay is more clumsy and less graceful than the knives she threw into the ground. Harper struggles with balance and strength in her left side, an effect of the cerebral palsy she says has challenged her since birth.

Tycho stands nearby, hanging closer to the castle wall, silent as a ghost, but his eyes are locked on the match.

Dustan moves closer to me. He's been little more than a shadow all morning, so I'm surprised when he speaks low to say, "What has happened to the boy?"

"Perhaps he watched as you put an arrow through my leg and took him prisoner."

He ignores my tone. "It's more than that."

I shrug a bit. "I don't know his history. He does not like soldiers."

"He likes the swordplay, though."

Anyone could see that. I understand why Noah made the

comment about him being a quick study. Tycho never misses an opportunity to watch and learn. "He can handle a blade. He's quick on his feet."

Harper and Zo have broken apart. Harper is breathing quickly, but smiling.

"What do you think?" she says to me.

"I think I should watch my back."

Her smile widens, and she blushes, sliding the sword back into the sheath at her hip. Her tenacity is what I have always liked best about her. How the first day she came here, she lay in wait, then pulled a dagger on me. In Rillisk, Dustan said I'd go down fighting. So would she. When we were trapped by the curse, I never dared to allow myself to think of the girls as anything more than a means to an end.

But now the curse is broken and I find myself looking down at Harper, her dark curls shining in the sunlight, her eyes wide and piercing.

Her smile fades, sadness clouding her eyes. "I really missed you, Scary Grey."

"And I you." I offer half a smile. "But I am no longer scary."

She leans in. "You'll *never* not be scary."

For a fleeting moment, I wonder what it would feel like to trace a finger along her skin.

Rhen's going to kill me anyway. Probably.

"Zo," Commander Dustan is saying. "Allow me your sword?"

That draws my attention. Zo has given him her weapon, and Dustan has turned to face Tycho. He offers the borrowed sword. "Grey says you're quick on your feet."

Tycho has become a hare in the sights of a predator, frozen in place against the wall. A twitch of movement above him catches my eye, and I glance up.

In the shadow of the window above, that Syhl Shallow girl, Lia Mara, looks down on the courtyard. Her eyes all but glitter in the dimness, but she quickly withdraws, vanishing from view.

I blink and look at Tycho. "Go ahead." I keep my voice easy, almost bored. "Dustan will give you a fair fight."

If anything will lure him away from the wall, it's the promise of a lesson in swordplay, so I'm not surprised when he steps forward and puts his hand on the hilt. He tests the weight of the weapon and swallows.

Dustan waits until he's ready, and then, just like at Worwick's, he starts easy, with a light thrust.

Tycho nearly knocks the sword right out of his hand.

I laugh and cough to cover it, but Dustan is a good sport. He backs up and regroups, eyeing Tycho more appraisingly.

"You won't get another opening like that," I call. Tycho nods tightly. This time, when their swords meet, Dustan is less easygoing.

At some point, I become aware that Rhen has entered the courtyard. He's flanked by a few guards, and he waits near the corner of the castle, where the cobblestone walkway changes color to lead to the stable. He's watching Dustan and Tycho, though I can't read his expression from here.

Harper is whispering with Zo, so I ease across the distance between me and the prince.

When I reach him, I discover his expression is troubled, and he is watching the match as a distraction, not a point of interest.

I straighten. "Something has happened."

His eyes meet mine in surprise, and it takes me a moment to

discover why: I've spoken like a guardsman sensing a threat and seeking orders.

Rhen looks away, back at the match before us. His voice is dispassionate. "He is good. You taught him?"

"Yes."

"I can tell. He does not hesitate."

Tycho would likely fall down to hear the crown prince praise his swordplay. It's a good thing Dustan is keeping him busy. "He pays attention."

Rhen's eyes are shadowed with tension. The uncertainty from the latter months of the curse is gone, but after seeing his fear in his chambers last night, I'm not sure what's replaced it is better.

From across the courtyard, Harper has noticed we're together. I can see her weighing the decision of whether to join us.

"Silvermoon Harbor has closed its borders," Rhen finally says. "They sent word this morning."

I turn and look at him. "I do not understand."

"The Grand Marshal sent notice that they would not recognize the rule of an illegitimate heir, nor an alliance with a country that has not provided promised assistance against Syhl Shallow. They have closed their border, and they are prepared to use military force."

I go still. Silvermoon Harbor is the closest major city, as well as Emberfall's sole access to the sea. Closing the border would have a massive effect on trade and travel, to say nothing of the people who rely on the city for access to food and their livelihoods.

"They have such a force?" I say quietly.

"With private armies, they could easily have such a force." He pauses. "This is not the first city to make such a statement of refusal. But Silvermoon is by far the largest—and the only city with the might to achieve it."

"How will you respond?"

I don't expect an answer, but perhaps our history earns me more information than he'd offer otherwise.

"I will take back my city," he says.

I stare at him. "By force."

"It will quite obviously have to be."

"You will march on your own people."

"Grey." His voice is weighted with intensity. "If Silvermoon's actions are allowed to stand, other cities will follow. I cannot be at war with them *all*." His expression is grim. "There are surely other cities biding their time to see how I respond. And they are likely prepared to ally with Silvermoon."

If he tries to take back the harbor by force, it could lead to civil war. It *will* lead to civil war, if his estimations are correct. All while Syhl Shallow waits in the shadows to strike against Emberfall.

We could barely hold the country together while its people were united. With cities at war against the Crown, Karis Luran could swoop in and take everything.

I glance at that window overlooking the courtyard again.

"This is bigger than another magesmith," Rhen says. "This is about more than just magic putting my country at risk. Do you understand why I must have this information from you?"

"Yes."

His eyes light with surprise. "So you will give me the name of the heir?"

My throat stalls. If I thought offering my name would put everything to rights, I would reveal myself right here.

It won't. This has already gone too far. Executing me will not satisfy his people's quest for the heir. It no longer matters. They don't want *him*.

In his heart, Rhen surely knows that, but like me, like Harper, he will not go down without a fight.

In the courtyard, Dustan and Tycho break apart. Tycho's hair is damp with sweat, and he's breathing hard, but he looks pleased with himself. He's looking to me for something, for approval, for a word, a judgment, a critique. Something.

I can't look away from Rhen.

"No," I say. "I will not."

His expression hardens. "You will. At sundown, you will."

The words are spoken with such certainty that I feel them at my core. Season after season I never truly feared Lilith, though I hated her.

For the first time, I fear what Rhen could do.

CHAPTER NINETEEN

LIA MARA

An uncomfortable quiet has fallen over the castle. Torches in the courtyard have been lit, the cobblestones freshly swept. I do not know what Prince Rhen has planned for his former guard commander, but the guards who bring me dinner are subdued and preoccupied, all but tossing the tray on the hearth before they can leave.

"What is going on?" I ask.

One of the men ignores me, which is typical, but the other glances at the window before pulling the door closed. "Wait till full dark. You'll have a good show."

Then he's gone, and I'm locked inside as before.

I return to the window, but nothing down below gives a clue as to what's planned. A crowd is beginning to form. Morbid fascination at work. Perhaps it's another measure of the ways I am not equal to my sister, but I have no stomach for torture. Mother is no stranger to using violence to get her way, but I am rarely forced to observe it. I have no desire to watch Prince Rhen carry it out either. I've seen enough of his cruelty.

I sit on the hearth and pick through the food they've brought—shellfish again. It turns my stomach. I want to dump it out the window on the crowd below.

My fire has fallen to embers, and I do nothing to restore it. On the other side of the brick barrier, the room is silent. Not empty—I can see the flicker of shadows through the tiny gap I've left.

Grey is in there. I can sense his apprehension from here. I have so many questions about him, but so few answers.

He is the rightful heir. He should not be afraid. There is much unrest in Emberfall because of his very existence. Does he not think he would find support among the people? Why does he not wish to claim the throne? Why yield to a man who allowed his people to fall into poverty and ruin?

Light shifts through the tiny gap, and I can hear the low rumble of voices next door. Three or four guards, at least. They must be worried he will try to run. The tension is so potent I can feel my own heartbeat in my throat.

But once he's gone, the guards will be too. There will be no reason to guard an empty room.

You'll have a good show.

If I can feel the foreboding in the castle, it is likely twice as strong in the people who know what's going on.

Grey will be in the courtyard with his guards. His room will be empty and unguarded. Most likely everyone will be in the courtyard or at the windows, watching. My own guards have already delivered my evening meal, and I know from experience they will not look in on me until the guard shift changes near midnight. I've proven myself to be harmless, so they pay me little mind.

I am used to being underestimated.

For once, it's going to work in my favor.

CHAPTER TWENTY

GREY

Giving me a day of liberty seemed like an unusual choice last night. A luxury afforded in friendship.

I see now that it was a calculated move to demonstrate what I have to lose.

As sunset draws near and heavy clouds roll across the sky, I begin to seek a path to escape. My thoughts spin, but each path seems futile. Dustan must notice my restless watchfulness, because four guards now trail me everywhere I go.

I don't know what Rhen will do when I refuse to yield. He cannot torture me forever.

Then again, perhaps he can. I definitely cannot endure it forever.

The thought sends an icy breath of fear down my spine. When Lilith tortured us, we knew our bodies would eventually give out and the season would begin again. Even if her cruelty had no limit, we did.

A knock sounds at my door at the very instant the sun vanishes beyond the forest. I stand frozen between the hearth and the window. Every fiber of my body wants me to run.

There is nowhere to go.

I think of that bracelet stashed inside my mattress in the loft at Worwick's. I close my eyes and imagine the other side. I imagine passing through the veil. I imagine Harper's world, the garish lights and loud machines. I wish for magic. Hope for it. Pray for it.

A knock sounds again.

My eyes open. Nothing has changed.

Dustan moves forward to take hold of the door handle. Rhen stands outside, flanked by six guards.

"Do you yield?" he says.

I wish I could run. I wish I could fly. I wish I could reverse time and undo the curse that bound us to this castle, that bound us together and gave us this shared history that's impossible to shake while so much is at risk.

"No," I say.

"Take him."

The guardsmen approach with the chains. I should run. It would be futile, but every fiber of my being is screaming at me to fight. Maybe it's Rhen's presence that keeps me still. Maybe it's my memories of being the obedient guardsman. Maybe it's the broken look in Rhen's expression that makes me wonder if he'll go through with any of this at all. He keeps waiting for me to yield. Maybe I'm waiting for him to.

Then the shackles are locked in place, and I don't have a chance to do anything.

Few people line the dim hallways as we walk. I expect to be

taken to the dungeon, but we make the turn down the staircase to the Great Hall, then head for the heavy glass doors that lead to the courtyard where I spent the morning with Harper and Tycho.

A guardsman pushes the door wide, revealing the torchlit space beyond. A small crowd has gathered.

He's not going to yield.

My feet stop, almost of their own accord. The guards begin to drag me forward. My heartbeat roars in my ears.

"Stop." Rhen's voice. The guardsmen halt.

He turns and walks right up to me.

"Grey," he says softly. "Do not make me do this."

I cannot look at him. Each breath that fights its way out of my throat is fractured and broken.

I war with the same thoughts I've had for days: If I tell him the truth, he'll kill me. He will have to kill me. I've seen what he's done to protect Emberfall—to protect his throne.

If I say nothing . . . he's going to make me wish I was dead.

When I was a guardsman, I would have laid down my life for him, so it seems like this choice should be easy, but it's not. This is not stepping in front of a blade.

There is no blade. I am no threat.

When I say nothing, he turns away.

They drag me through the doorway. My eyes rake over the gathered crowd. No Harper. No Tycho.

Good. I can endure this crowd. I can endure this torment. Tycho is safe somewhere, hopefully guarded by Harper's kindness. Hopefully being sent home with the bag of coins Rhen promised.

Despite the dozens who have gathered in the courtyard, the space is nearly silent. A horse kicks against the wall of the nearby stable. My breathing seems to echo.

I have no idea what Rhen intends, but the guards tow me right up to the castle wall, then reach high to affix my chains to a hook suspended there.

A sudden stillness overtakes me. It's a whipping hook. There are others along the wall, but none have been used since Rhen's father sat on the throne. If a member of the castle staff wronged King Broderick in some way, he'd have them flogged out here for all to see. He'd leave them hanging here, too, for hours, until insects would gather on the wounds.

My eyes are fixed on my wrists, suspended above my head. My breathing slows fractionally. I imagine it will hurt, but I can survive a flogging. This is far preferable to being dragged by a horse or having my bones broken one by one.

I close my eyes and wait for the first bite of the lash.

Instead, I hear another set of feet being dragged along the cobblestones, someone else's fractured breath, so much quicker and more panicked than mine.

My heart stops even before he speaks. "No," he says. Chains rattle, and I know he's struggling. "Please. I don't know anything."

Tycho.

My hands jerk against the chain. There's no give, and I can't see anything but bricks and darkness. "Rhen!" I yell. "Don't do this. Let him go."

A thin whistle splits the air. I barely recognize the sound before leather lays into my back.

It hurts a thousand times more than I thought it would. It's worse than a blade. Worse than an arrow. The lash seems to bury itself in my skin before dragging free. I cry out without meaning to.

Another thin whistle. I brace myself, but this lash doesn't hit me. Tycho screams.

I see stars. I plant my feet against the wall and brace against the chains.

Another whistle. Another lash lays into my back.

I can't breathe. I can't think.

Another lays into Tycho.

"Rhen!" I can't hear myself speak. I'm not even sure I *am* speaking. "Rhen, stop! He's a boy—"

Another lash. This one is lower, and I swear I feel it touch my spine.

I've stopped hearing the whistle. I just hear Tycho scream.

Then he's babbling, the words thick with tears. "Please. Stop. Please. Please. Please."

He's talking to the guards, to Rhen, to anyone. He's not talking to me.

But he knows I could stop this.

Another lash tears into my skin, bringing pain like fire. The stars in my vision multiply. I've pulled so hard against my chains that I can no longer feel my hands.

Tycho screams again. He chokes on his breath and makes a gagging sound.

He is no one to this fight. He is nothing to Rhen. He deserves none of this. My rage seems to swallow me whole, burning me up with fury. Stars fill my eyes with blinding light.

Another lash strikes me, but this time I barely feel it. I hear the crack of the whip striking Tycho, and his resounding scream.

Something inside me snaps. A crack of lightning fills the air, a blinding white that steals my vision, as if the sun fell to earth. Wind rushes through the courtyard, raking across the wounds on my back, stealing my breath. For an instant, I think I'm dead. I can't see. I can't hear.

Then it's gone. The stars in my vision shrink down to nothing. The wind is gone.

The courtyard is silent.

I wait for the next lash, but it doesn't come. Blood is trickling from the wounds on my back, hardly noticeable on top of the raging pain. All I hear is my breathing, quick and ragged.

I struggle against the chains, expecting another lash to catch me in the back, but none comes. I manage to brace my feet against the wall, then twist against my bindings to see what I can of the courtyard.

Everyone has collapsed. Each person lies in a heap. Some have collapsed on top of each other.

None move.

I search the wall for Tycho and find him twenty feet away, hanging from his chains, unconscious.

Or dead.

My breathing is ragged for an entirely new reason. I use the chains to lever myself up the wall, until I'm high enough to unhook my shackles. It takes longer than it should, and my arms keep threatening to give out. Once there, I brace against the hook and pant with exhaustion. Every breath, every movement, causes pain in a new way. I lost count of how many times they struck me, but my back feels laid open.

I unwind the chain, then drop to the ground.

A bad choice. My injured leg gives out, and I stagger, falling to my knees. My vision goes hazy and I need to shake my head and blink.

I touch a hand to my side, where the lash curved around. The wound is deep and bleeding freely.

Rhen is not far off, collapsed on the cobblestones like the others. He is breathing and uninjured. He could be sleeping.

What happened?

I can wonder later. I need to free Tycho. I need to escape.

When I make it to his spot on the wall, I discover he's breathing, too, but it's a labored wheeze, and his back is a crisscrossed mash of bleeding lines. Tears soak his cheeks. He vomited on himself at some point. I try to reach high enough to free him, but my back protests and I cry out, sagging against the wall.

I try once more and fail. My vision goes hazy again, and I shake my head to clear it.

A shout goes up from somewhere in the castle, then another.

I redouble my efforts, but I'm too weak to lift his weight enough to pull the chains free.

A shadow appears beside me, hands closing on Tycho's waist to help lift. "Here," says a soft female voice. "I'll help you."

Lia Mara. The girl from Syhl Shallow. My thoughts are so addled and my eyes are blurry and I wonder if I'm hallucinating. "How—how did you—?"

"Hurry!" she says. "The guards in the castle did not collapse."

I hurry. I grit my teeth and leap for the bar, levering myself up the way I freed myself. Sweat drips into my eyes, and my muscles tremble, threatening to give way, but with Lia Mara supporting Tycho's weight, I'm able to twist his chains and brace against the wall. I need one inch. I throw every ounce of strength into it.

His chain clears the hook. Lia Mara tries to ease him down, but Tycho all but collapses to the ground. I nearly fall right on top of him. My fingers dig into the cobblestones, but I can't move. My arms are twitching with fatigue, and my thoughts loosen and drift.

Lia Mara is on her knees in front of me, her hair glowing red in the torchlight. "You have to run."

I can't run. I can't even stand.

"Go," I say to her.

Her eyes go from me to Tycho to the castle.

"Go," I say again. My voice breaks. "You won't find peace here."

The shouts reach the courtyard, and then guardsmen and castle servants are flooding through the doors, pouring into the open space. Lia Mara slips into the shadows.

"Find Healer Noah!" a woman shouts, followed by a man yelling, "Secure the princess!"

"No!" Harper's voice calls across the courtyard, high and panicked. "Where is he? Where's Rhen?"

"Here!" shouts a guardsman.

Suddenly Harper is there, crouching over the prince. "Rhen," she says. "Rhen, can you hear me?" She picks up his hand. "He's breathing," she says. "Noah, he's breathing."

I blink and Noah is beside her. "Strong pulse," he says, a hand against Rhen's neck. "Seems like a syncopal episode."

"A . . . *what?*"

"He fainted." The healer moves to Dustan's prone body, lying just beside Rhen, then presses a hand to his neck. "They all did." He sounds confused. "Lay them all flat," he calls to the dozens of guards and servants now swarming the courtyard. "Jake! Make sure they have an open airway."

Harper looks around. "So they all just . . ."

Her eyes lock with mine.

I have no idea what I look like, but it must be as bad as it feels, because her face pales and she locks a hand on Noah's arm.

"Grey," she breathes.

I blink again, and she's on her knees in front of me.

"Oh, Grey," she whispers. Her hand finds mine. Tears glisten on her lashes. "Grey, I had no idea."

To my right, one of the fallen guardsmen is beginning to move, shaking his head vigorously.

I brace a hand against the ground. I need to run.

"They need to get to the infirmary," says Noah. He's crouched by Tycho, and his voice is tight with fury. "I think this kid is in shock."

"They're waking up!" calls a voice from across the courtyard.

I can't be taken to the infirmary.

Harper's eyes meet mine.

"Please." The word sounds like it's been ripped from my throat.

She doesn't need me to say any more. She stands up and starts giving orders. "Carry the prince to his chambers! Boil water and have warm compresses prepared. Take any unconscious guardsmen to the infirmary. Jake! I need you."

Her brother comes to her side, pushing through the crowd of people. "Harper, what—" He breaks off as he sees me and Tycho lying in the shadows beside the castle. A long breath escapes him. "Holy—"

"Jake," says Harper in a rushed whisper. "I need you to get them out of here."

His expression hardens right up. "No way. I get him out of here and we're *never* getting home."

"Look at what Rhen—look at what he—" Her voice breaks. "You think you'll be going anywhere if he gets a chance to finish the job?"

Jake's eyes shift to me, and while his expression is grim, he is not kind and merciful like his sister. He drops to the ground beside me, putting himself at eye level.

"If I help you, I want your word that you'll take me and Noah home as soon as you can."

"Yes," I grind out.

"Swear it," he says. "Swear an oath."

"I swear it." I have no idea how I'll keep this oath, but I'll swear, and willingly, if it means getting me and Tycho out of here. "I swear to you that I will return you as soon as I am able."

"Done." He stands. "Harper. What do you want me to do?"

CHAPTER TWENTY-ONE

LIA MARA

Chaos reigns in the courtyard.

From the shadows, I watch and wait.

No one notices the two men carrying Grey and the boy out of the courtyard while everyone else is carried into the castle.

No one notices the small wagon being driven from the dark side of the stables, a brown-skinned man clucking softly to the horses.

No one notices Princess Harper staring after the wagon as it disappears into the woods.

And, finally, no one notices me slipping onto the back of a silver palfrey and vanishing into the woods myself.

CHAPTER TWENTY-TWO

GREY

I wake looking into a fire, lying facedown on a pile of soft blankets. I have no recollection of sleeping, and I recognize nothing. The walls are paneled wood, and the fireplace is small. This is not a room in the palace.

I inhale sharply, and every wound on my body protests. I bite back a cry.

"The last time I stitched you up, you ignored me and went off to fight a monster." Noah's voice is low, speaking from the opposite side of the room. "I think this might slow you down a bit more."

I fight to turn my head. Noah sits curled in a wooden chair in the corner nearest the door, a steaming mug balanced between his hands. To his left is a wide pallet bed. Tycho's face is buried in blankets, but I recognize the shock of blond hair and the lightly muscled arm that's fallen to rest on the ground.

Even from here, I can see the stripes of red that decorate his back. My eyes flinch away.

My fault.

Another man lies on the opposite side of the pallet, but all I can see are his boots. It must be Jacob.

I have no idea where we are, but at present, I do not care. I lift a hand to rub at my eyes, and even that hurts in ways I do not expect. "The lash marks required stitching?"

"A few of them did. Tycho's were more superficial, but not by much. I think they went easier on him." His quiet voice is thick with disgust.

"You are angry."

"You bet I'm angry. I know things are . . . *different* here, but it doesn't matter. War and torture are two different things."

I don't disagree with him. After everything Lilith did, this feels intensely personal—and somehow more humiliating. My hand flexes on the blanket. On the topic of humiliation, my body has needs.

"Noah," I say. "I need . . ."

"What? Oh." He uncurls from the chair.

Standing takes nearly all my strength, even with Noah hooking his hands under my arms to help lift.

"We have to go outside," he says. "You can lean on me."

I don't want to, but after a few steps, my ears are ringing and my vision goes spotty, so I do. We slip down a short hallway and out a door. The air is cool and crisp, both a relief and an assault on my bare back. Sunrise is a purple promise on the horizon. The hour is early, so Noah eases the door closed behind us. A stretch of grass leads to a small barn, bright in the lingering moonlight.

In a flash, I recognize where we are. The last time I was here, it was the dead of winter, with snow blanketing everything in white.

The Crooked Boar. The inn that offered shelter to Rhen and Harper. The inn where everything changed.

I rub at my eyes again.

He leads me to a small copse of trees. "Do you want me to stand with you?" says Noah. "Or do you want privacy?"

Right now I don't care, but I appreciate that he's allowing me a moment of dignity. "I can stand," I say, though I'm not entirely sure. He moves away, though only far enough to lean against the inn and avert his eyes. When I'm finished, he's back at my side without my asking.

"You are being kind," I say to him. "I do not think I deserve it."

"When I became a doctor, I swore an oath to help people in need." He lets me lean on him again. "Whether they deserve it or not."

We approach the door, but I hesitate. Even here, in this innocuous space, the thought of going back into a closed-up room makes my pulse speed up. "I would like to sit outside," I say.

I expect Noah to refuse, but he changes course to help me to the bench beside the back wall of the inn.

Once I'm sitting, I cannot get comfortable. I settle for bracing my forearms on my knees and gritting my teeth against the ache in my back. We sit in silence for the longest time, inhaling the dawn air.

"What exactly happened?" Noah finally says. "Why did they all drop like that?"

I remember the crack and the flash and the sudden silence.

I remember the panic in my head as I realized Rhen meant to flay Tycho to get to me.

It is a level of cruelty I never expected from him.

"I do not know," I say.

"I know magic exists here," says Noah, "but I have a hard time considering that until three dozen people drop like a rock."

My shoulders tense.

"It was you, wasn't it?" he says.

I say nothing.

"If it wasn't you," he continues, "it was Tycho, but he was unconscious and you weren't. So."

I stare at my hands. Blood has dried in the creases of my fingers, mixing with dirt and grit. "If you have figured it out, the prince will not be long behind." I glance up at the grass and the stables. "We will have to move on. The innkeeper and his family are in danger by my presence."

Though in truth, I have no idea where I will go, or where I will take Tycho.

"You're the one everyone is looking for," says Noah. "The *mage-smith*." He pauses. "The heir."

He says it like he can't quite believe it, but I nod.

"Did you know? That whole time you were trapped by the curse—did you know?"

"No." My voice sharpens with anger, fed by the pain across my back. "You think I would have endured what I did if I'd known I had some shred of magic? Truly?"

He's staring back at me impassively, and I sigh. My anger is not with Noah. "I did not find out until I took Lilith to the other side. She tried to bargain her freedom with the truth. Even then, I had no idea how to wield magic." I pause. "I still have no idea how I did what I did in the courtyard."

"When Lilith told you the truth . . . why did you run? Why did you leave?"

"Karis Luran had already spread doubt, the first day she came to Ironrose. I knew my existence would threaten the line of succession." I pause. "I thought it would be easier if everyone thought I was dead."

He's quiet for a while. "Does this seem easier, Grey?"

I think of the shadows in Rhen's eyes when we spoke in his chambers, the uneasy tension in his body when he told me about Silvermoon and everything that was at risk. "I did not consider that Rhen would fear magic more than he fears losing his throne. I should have."

Noah snorts. "Fear makes people act in ways we'd never expect."

"Indeed. He proved that last night."

"Why didn't you just tell him?" he says, but then he sighs without waiting for a reply. Anger threads between his words again. "Never mind. I saw what he was willing to do to get an answer, so I can only imagine what he would have done once he had it."

"Emberfall is already in danger of civil war. An attack by Karis Luran may be imminent, especially now that Rhen holds her daughter prisoner." I stop short as a flicker of memory breaks through the haze in my mind. Lia Mara beside me, helping to support Tycho's weight as I release him from the wall. Did that happen? Did she escape? I cannot make the memory come together, and it likely does not matter anyway. I shake my head. "Rhen is trying to keep his country together."

Noah says nothing. I shift my weight, wince, and put my arms back exactly as they were.

"You should return to Ironrose," I say. "Now, while the hour is early. You will be seen as a traitor if you are found with me."

"No."

He speaks the word so simply. I turn my head to look at him, but his jaw is set, his arms tense where they rest against his knees.

"No?"

"I already told Jake that I'd rather be complicit in helping you escape than in what Rhen was doing."

"Because of your oath?"

"Because it's *wrong*." He glances at me, and his voice is fierce. "Where I come from, people like me have a history with that . . . that kind of torture. I'm not going to be a part of it. I don't care if that makes me a traitor."

I study him. "Noah—there are already whispers of you possessing some magic of your own. If you flee with me . . ."

"Magic." He snorts. "It's *medicine*. It's science. You know what's funny? On the other side, I was judged for the color of my skin. For being attracted to men. Then I come here and no one cares about those things. *Here,* they question whether a healer is noble enough to be in love with a prince. They question how I can make a rash go away or break a fever." He rolls his eyes.

A breeze sweeps between the barn and the inn, making me shiver. My heart begs for action, but I have no action to take—and I likely can't do much anyway.

"How long will these take to heal?" I say.

"Weeks." He pauses. "Maybe less. I'll see if the innkeeper's wife has some ginger and turmeric to bring down the inflammation."

I lower my voice, though the hour is early and everyone is still asleep. "Why do they think we're here?"

"They only saw me and Jake, and they know us. We said you and Tycho were injured in an assault on the road, and we needed to stop for the night."

Innocent enough, and nothing that will arouse suspicion. I'll need to find a shirt before anyone sees my back. "Tycho has . . . been through much," I say. I glance over. "Did he wake last night?"

"Yes. Several times." He pauses. "He kept asking if we got you out, too."

I keep seeing the boy's face in the loft at Worwick's. *I'll keep your secret, Hawk.*

I run a hand across my jaw. "I should never have involved him in this. In any of this."

To my surprise, Noah laughs quietly. "You probably couldn't have stopped him. That kid would follow you off a cliff."

I inhale to answer, but thundering hoofbeats stop me. I'm on my feet before my body protests the motion.

"At least two horses," I say to Noah. "Maybe more." My hand automatically reaches for a blade, but I have nothing.

As if I could fight.

"Go inside," I say. "Hide the others. I'll take a horse. They're looking for me."

"You can't ride! You can't—"

"Go!"

We're not going to be fast enough. The hoofbeats are nearly upon the property. Guardsmen will search the premises and tear through anyone who gets in their way.

A horse appears around the side of the inn, and I realize it's all over. Of course they've sent men to prevent escape through the back. My hands are in fists. I can't feel the pain in my back any longer.

"Grey?"

I freeze. It's Harper—and behind her, on another horse, is Zo. I don't know what this means. I glance between them.

Harper swings down from the horse without hesitation. "I don't have a lot of time. Rhen is meeting with his advisers. The Royal Guard will be looking for you at full light." She fumbles with a saddlebag, then carries it across the clearing to me. Her expression is dark and full of concern. "Here, I brought you some clothes . . ." Her eyes flick down my body, and her voice trails off. "Oh, Grey."

She cannot even see the worst of it, but I know there are two lash marks that wrapped around my rib cage. One parallels a scar I earned fighting Rhen in monster form, which seems fitting somehow.

She reaches out to touch my arm, her fingers warm and gentle. When she tries to turn me, I hold fast. "No."

Her eyes meet mine, and the pity there is almost worse than the humiliation of what happened. A moment of weighted tension hangs between us, broken only when Noah steps forward to take the saddlebag.

"He needs to put a shirt on," he says.

That spurs her into action. "Um. Yes. Clothes! Here." She unbuckles the bag and drags out a shirt.

Simply sitting on the bench was painful, so I can imagine what moving my arms through sleeves will feel like.

My imagination does not do it justice. Setting my body on fire would hurt less. Noah helps as best he can, but by the time the loose fabric slides down my back, I'm dizzy and sweating.

Harper's pitying glances are not helping.

I ease onto the bench, because the alternative is collapsing at her feet. When I speak, my voice is rough. "I told you what he would do. I told you I would not fault him for it."

The words feel false as I speak them. Or . . . not false. Incomplete.

I would not have faulted Rhen for doing this to *me alone*.

Harper drops onto the bench beside me. I cannot meet her gaze.

"I fault him for it," she says quietly.

"My lady," says Zo, from near the horses. "If you wish to avoid detection, we should ride out soon."

"Not yet." Harper reaches out to take my hand. "Grey."

I finally look at her. "I cannot take your pity."

She closes her fingers on mine before I can pull away. "I don't pity you." She studies me. "It was you, wasn't it?" She pauses. "You're the one with magic."

This is different from when Noah asked the same thing. Harper was trapped with us. She risked so much. The scar across her cheek is proof of that. The thought that I might have been able to fight Lilith in a different way is almost too much to bear.

"Forgive me," I say. "I did not know."

"You're Rhen's brother." Her voice is so quiet. "All that time you were trapped together, and neither of you knew."

"It would have been worse to know," I say. But as I say the words, I realize I don't know if they're true. I frown. "And clearly it does not matter, if he plans to send the Royal Guard after me."

"I . . . I wish you had told me. I wish you had told *him*." Then she frowns, as if realizing how that would have played out. "I wish . . . I wish . . ."

"I wished a lot of things," I say, "while the curse held us captive. Wishing solves nothing." I pause and glance at Zo again. "You cannot stay here. If you are found with me . . . it would force Rhen's hand, and I do not like to think of what he might do."

Harper's expression turns stony. "First, I'd like to see him try. Second, you flattened everyone in that courtyard—including him.

He's terrified of magic trapping him again." She pauses. "He's not going to come running after you without a strategy. I want to see if I can stop him before that happens."

She is so fierce. I am reminded of why everyone in Emberfall believes she has an army at her disposal.

She won't be able to stop Rhen, though. If he was willing to do what he did, he's not going to stop now.

The door at the back of the inn rattles. I expect the innkeeper or his wife, but instead, Tycho stumbles through. He's shirtless and pale, his eyes a little wild.

Jacob is right behind him, rubbing at his eyes. "See? I told you they were still here. Hey, Harp."

"Hey," she says, but her eyes are on the boy. "Tycho. Here. Sit."

It's not an order, but he bows his head and murmurs, "Yes, my lady," before easing onto the bench as gingerly as I did.

Harper gets a good look at his back and her steely eyes return to mine. Her jaw is clenched. "This is too far."

I do not challenge her. We all fall into silence. A breeze pulls a shiver out of Tycho.

I need a plan. When I first ran from Ironrose months ago, I was injured, but not badly. No one was looking for me, so I was able to find work at Worwick's.

Now everyone will be looking for me. And likely Tycho, too.

Neither of us is in any position to defend ourselves. Anyone who offers shelter will be at risk.

"We need to run," I say.

Tycho looks at me. His eyes are clouded with pain and exhaustion, but hope flares when he hears my words. "Yes."

I shake my head. "I have nowhere for us to go."

At the edge of the building, motion flickers in the early-morning mist and shadows. A cloaked body steps around the corner.

I stand. Zo draws her sword.

"Be at ease." Lia Mara draws back her hood. "I have somewhere for you to go."

CHAPTER TWENTY-THREE

LIA MARA

Less than twelve hours ago, I watched this man receive a lashing until it exposed the muscle of his back, and now he's on his feet like he's ready to face an army. He must have been fierce as a guardsman. He's fierce *now*, even pale and unsteady in the cool quiet of the courtyard. The look in his eyes makes my heart skip and flutter until I'm unsure whether I should run or stand my ground or find a weapon.

"What are you doing here?" he says, and only the whisper of strain in his voice reveals his weakness.

"The same as you, I believe."

"You *followed* us."

I raise my eyebrows. "You were half dead. It was hardly challenging."

Princess Harper puts a hand on her guard's arm. "Put up your sword," she says quietly. To me, she says, "You have somewhere they can go?"

"Of course. He would be welcome in Syhl Shallow."

"No," says Grey.

"I am offering sanctuary," I say. "In a place where Prince Rhen cannot pursue you."

"So you are suggesting I trade one sovereign's torture for another's."

"*Torture?*" I nearly laugh out loud. "You are the rightful heir to Emberfall. My mother will not harm you." Mother will probably line his pockets with silver and fill his ears with promises. Nolla Verin will take one look at his dark eyes and broad shoulders and fawn all over him.

I should be happy—*proud* even—but the thought makes my stomach twinge.

I take a step closer, and he tenses. I spread my hands. "You can barely stand. You said you have nowhere to go." I glance at Princess Harper. "Whatever you believe of my mother and my people, I truly did come here in the hopes of bringing peace to both our countries. I would offer peace now."

Harper frowns, and she looks up at him. "Grey—you aren't safe here."

"Syhl Shallow is several days' ride from here." He takes a slow breath. "And that is if we ride hard."

"Then we travel while we can," I say, "and rest when you need."

"No," says the man standing near the inn wall. I recognize him and the healer from the day they dragged Grey into the courtyard. Prince Jacob. His skin is tan from midsummer, his hair dark and curly like Harper's.

Harper swears under her breath and says, "Jake. Please."

"He's sworn to me now. If he's going anywhere, it's up to me."

My eyes snap to Grey. "You are the crown prince and you swore your life to another?"

"I didn't swear my life. And I am *not* the crown prince." Grey cuts a glance at Jacob. "I swore passage as soon as I am able. To return you to Disi, I need the bracelet gifted by the enchantress— and it was left in Rillisk when you arrested me."

Prince Jacob swears.

"I told you it wouldn't be easy," says Noah. "I told you that when we first caught him."

"Tycho and I cannot return to Rillisk without being recognized," says Grey. "Rhen has likely sent guardsmen there already."

Harper's expression is grim. "He has."

Jacob folds his arms. "Fine. Whatever. I'm still not sending him to another country where we might never see him again."

"You are all welcome to travel to Syhl Shallow," I say. "I can guarantee your safety as well."

They go silent and stare at me.

Wind cuts through the yard, pulling tendrils of hair from my cloak. "I came here seeking peace. I would like the opportunity to prove it."

No one says anything.

Finally, Tycho says, "I heard that, in Syhl Shallow, the queen executes her prisoners, then eats their remains."

Now my hands form fists. "I heard that, in Emberfall, the crown prince beats innocent boys nearly to death for political gain. Ah, forgive me, I watched that with my own eyes."

Tycho flushes and looks away.

Grey runs a hand across his jaw and sighs. "We will head northwest, toward the mountain pass."

I raise my eyebrows. "You agree?"

"Not yet. But if Rhen is searching in Rillisk—if he suspects I will find allies and friends there—it makes sense to head in the opposite direction." He levels me with his gaze. "Though he may be seeking you as well, and it's no secret which way you'll go. A princess from Syhl Shallow will find few friends in Emberfall."

"Then we're well suited to help each other."

Jacob looks to Harper. "You should come with us."

"I need to go back."

"No!" he snaps. "This is too far, Harp. You know it's too far. You wouldn't come with me before, but you can come with me *now*." He pauses. "We can finally go home."

She pales a shade, but she's steadfast. "Jake—Rhen isn't cruel. You didn't see him last night—after—after you left—" Her voice breaks.

"I don't care," says Jacob.

She sniffs back her tears and straightens her back. "*I* care." She pauses and glances at Grey. "And Rhen cares, too. Grey—he had no idea."

"He knows now," says Grey. His voice is soft. "And still he sent soldiers to Rillisk."

"Please." She glances at Jacob. "Please. What he did was horrible, but you have to understand—"

"I understand we are at risk," says Grey. "And time is not on our side."

"Come with us," says Jacob.

For a moment, Harper glances between him and Grey. Her eyes linger on Grey for a moment too long. "I'm sorry I didn't stop him," she says quietly.

"A princess should not apologize—" he begins.

"I should," she says. "And a prince should." She takes a step back. "I'll do what I can. I promise."

After Harper leaves to return to Ironrose, we take the wagon. Jacob and Noah drive the horses, while a heavy length of canvas sheeting covers the back. Grey and Tycho both lie facedown on a thin layer of straw, speaking in low voices that I cannot make out over the creaks and rattles of the wagon—nor the steady beat of my pulse. I lie faceup near the side, my hands clasped over my abdomen, watching the canvas lighten as the sun finishes rising.

My comfortable carriage ride with Nolla Verin a few short days ago feels more like a dream than a memory.

I've been wondering what my sister thought when Parrish came back with my message. I'd like to think that she is hopeful for me—or at least *worried* for me.

As we drive, I wonder about Princess Harper. Grey claimed there was nothing between them, but there is surely *something*. By helping him, she puts herself at risk. She puts her *country* at risk. Along with the missing military support promised by Disi, it creates more questions than I have answers for. I could understand if *she* hoped to ally with Grey as the rightful heir, but she would never send him away. Especially not with me. She must know my mother will seek to use Grey against Rhen, but she seemed desperate to see him safely away, no matter the potential cost.

Eventually the wagon rattles to a stop, and we emerge in the middle of a forest so densely packed with trees and foliage that the sun fights to find us.

Jacob is beginning to unhitch the horses, and Grey says, "Turn them loose. They bear the royal brand. We'll have to go on foot."

"You want to *walk* to Syhl Shallow?"

"I do not want to walk anywhere at all." Grey looks up and around, blinking at the streaks of sunlight that peek between leaves. "We can find horses in the next city." His eyes shift to Harper's brother. "I would ask for your sword."

Jacob snorts. "Well, I would tell you no."

Grey takes a step closer to him. His wounds have seeped through his shirt to create a maze of pink and red lines across his back, and he moves stiffly. "*Your* life is not at stake. Mine is."

Jacob folds his arms, and his eyes turn flinty. "You can barely stand up straight. What are you going to do with it?"

"Just give him the sword," says Noah.

"Okay, sure." Jacob gives Grey an up-and-down glance. "If you can take it, you can have it."

Grey's hand flies so quickly that I barely realize he's moved until his fist cracks into Jacob's jaw. I gasp as the other man starts to fall. Grey grabs the hilt and pulls the blade free before Jacob hits the ground.

"Done." Grey points the sword at his waist. "The belt as well."

Jacob pushes himself up on one arm and spits blood into the leaves. "I hate you."

Noah sighs and picks up a heavily laden satchel and swings it over his shoulder. His warm brown eyes look to me. "Lia Mara, is it? Let's start walking. Come on, Tycho."

He turns. Compared to the other men, I appreciate his quiet, no-nonsense demeanor. I hurry to fall in step beside him. Tycho is a shadow at our back.

"You don't know where you're going!" Jake calls from behind us.

"I know which way northwest is," Noah calls back. "I'm not stitching you up again, Grey."

"You said you took an oath. You have to stitch me up no matter what." But leaves and underbrush crunch behind us, so I know they are following.

For some reason, I expected that we would walk a short while before finding a town, but we trudge through the woods for *hours*. The terrain is rough and the going slow, so no one talks until I'm starving and Grey is limping and Tycho's breathing is labored. The boy swipes sweat from his eyes, which are red, and I wonder if tears are mixed in.

"Perhaps we should rest," I say, and Tycho shoots me a grateful look.

Grey casts a look around. "We're less than five miles from the creek. We can camp there, then set out again after midnight."

Five miles. Now *I* want to cry. I shift to walk beside Tycho. His jaw is tight, and he's forcing his legs to move.

"Five miles won't take long," I say, and I'm partly trying to convince myself. "And a creek means water."

Grey must hear the encouraging note in my voice, because he looks over and catches a glimpse of Tycho's expression. "If there were steamed crabs at the end, you'd be *running* for them," he says.

A weary grin breaks through Tycho's melancholy. "I'd beat you there."

"Can we *please* not talk about food?" says Jacob.

We all fall back into silence. Grey staggers as he steps over a fallen tree, but he catches himself with a hand against another trunk. He makes no sound, but it takes him a moment before he can press on.

I've reached a point where I can't tell if this is strength or stubbornness.

"Can you not use magic to heal yourself?" I say to him. "I have heard stories of the magesmiths—"

"I cannot use magic at all."

Tycho glances over. "You used magic to free us." He pauses, then glances at me. "And—and at Worwick's."

"At Worwick's, I had an enchanted bracelet. At Ironrose . . ." He sighs. "I have no idea what happened at Ironrose."

"Maybe we should beat the crap out of you again and see what happens," says Jacob.

Grey gives him a level look. "Try."

"Don't joke about that," Noah snaps.

"Must you men make everything about violence?" I say. "Not every problem can be solved by the edge of a sword."

"Your mother surely thinks so." Grey looks at me, and his eyes are hard. "Not every problem can be solved by the tongue in your mouth, either."

The words are not suggestive, but I flush anyway. Even wounded and limping, with sweat and blood sticking his shirt to his body, he is so unyielding. I miss the easy banter of Sorra and Parrish. Easy banter that I'll never hear again, due to my choices. Due to their misplaced loyalty. I longed to be queen, but Mother made the right choice in naming Nolla Verin.

My throat is tightening, so I shake these thoughts away before they can get the better of me. "I have offered to *help* you," I say. "I am not your enemy."

"You are an enemy to Emberfall," he says. "You are a threat to the Crown."

Now I see. This is the former guardsman speaking. I hold his gaze. "So are you."

He sets his jaw and says nothing.

We hear the rush of water long before we see it flowing between trees at a rapid clip. The waterway is wider than I expect, at least twenty feet across, with occasional shallow pools where water has collected along the banks.

Tycho all but drops to his knees in the muddy bank and thrusts his hands into the flowing water, scooping it to his lips.

"We should boil it first," says Noah, but the rest of us are already following suit.

I don't recognize my thirst until the cool water touches my lips. Even locked in my room at Ironrose Castle, I still had access to food and water. I cannot remember a time where I've gone all day without sustenance. I'm slurping from my hands like an animal, but I still can't get enough.

A hand closes on my arm. "Slow," says Grey, and for the first time his voice isn't harsh, only tired. "You'll make yourself sick."

I wonder if this is an attempt to ease the tension between us, but when I look up, he's already moving away. Jacob begins collecting branches to form a pile. I dry my hands on my breeches and follow him, gathering twigs and dried leaves for kindling. He glances at me in surprise. "Hey. Thanks."

"You are surprised I would help?"

He smiles sheepishly, and it makes him look very much like his sister. There's a hardness hidden under the expression, an edge that

Harper lacks, but no deceitfulness or guile. I wonder at the vitriol between him and Grey.

"From what I know of royalty," Jacob says, "yeah, I am."

"You are royalty, too, are you not?"

His eyes shutter and turn unreadable. "Where I come from, if we want something done, we do it ourselves."

By the time we have a fire going, dusk has thrown long shadows across the stream and brought a cool breeze to wind through the trees. Somewhere in the branches above, a bird of prey screeches a warning. The silence among us is not easy or companionable. My stomach aches for food, but we have none.

"I have silver," Jacob says to Grey. "I could walk into town."

"Is a town close? I could go, too," I offer. "We could pretend to be a married couple traveling together."

Grey's dark eyes find mine. "The farther north we travel, the more the people of Emberfall have seen invaders from Syhl Shallow. Your accent would give you away." He glances at Jacob. "And yours would paint you as an outsider."

"So what? You think they're going to send word to Rhen that one random guy showed up with a weird accent?"

"The prince has offered a bounty of five hundred silvers. If you think people are not looking for bodies to sacrifice to the Crown, you are wrong indeed."

Jacob looks like he's about to retort, but Tycho says, "The enforcers executed a man in Rillisk." His expression is tense. "They didn't even have proof."

Jacob shuts his mouth.

Grey shifts his weight, then grimaces. The pink streaks on his shirt have turned to red, but he's turned down any ministrations. "You do not want to walk into a strange city after dark. Not now."

At his side, Tycho sighs. "I'd give almost anything for a platter of Jodi's crabs right now."

Grey's smile is grim. "I'd give anything for a bow and a dozen arrows."

Jacob tips his head back and stares at the sky. "I'd give anything for a burger with everything from Chewie's."

"Oh yes." Noah laughs, the sound low and warm, indicating a shared memory.

I smile, charmed. "What is a *burger*?"

I expect them to lean in and explain, but instead their expressions close off the way Jacob's did when we were gathering firewood.

"Nothing we'll ever see again," says Jacob. "Unless Grey can get us home."

I study him and consider Mother's suspicions about Disi, and the way Harper did not carry herself with the manner of a ruler—nor does Jacob. When we were debating where to find sanctuary, no one ever mentioned Disi as a place we'd be safe. Not even Princess Harper. There was no mention of assistance from the King of Disi in managing Emberfall's political unrest—and no mention of their alliance being at risk if Rhen was not the rightful heir.

Unless Grey can get us home.

My eyes flash to Grey's. "Disi can only be reached by magic."

He stares back at me, his expression inscrutable.

Now that I've found a thread to pull, it all begins to unravel. "That is why there are no forces to lend support. They are trapped in Disi."

Grey's dark eyes give away nothing, but Jacob looks abashed. Noah looks resigned.

Tycho looks *fascinated*.

"Are there forces at all?" I say, with a glance at Grey. "An army waiting on your magic?"

He says nothing.

But that says everything.

I blow a breath out between my teeth. Overhead, the bird of prey screeches again. "Quite the story your prince has told his people."

He denies nothing. "We did it to save our people. And it worked."

Well, at least that much is true. But now I understand why Rhen's subjects have begun to rise up against him. He made promises that are failing to come true. He bought their confidence with lies, and now he will be weaker than when he began.

I look at Noah and Jacob. "And you are trapped here. You cannot return home."

They exchange a glance.

"Yes," Jacob says finally. "More or less."

My heart trips along, trying to make full sense of this revelation. "And neither of you are royalty at all, are you?"

"No," says Jacob. He offers half a shrug. "Noah is really a doctor."

"Then Princess Harper is not a princess."

"She saved the prince from a terrible fate," says Grey. "She risked her life for Emberfall, and she risked her life to protect me. She may not be a princess by birth, but she is one in spirit."

We all fall silent, but now there's a contemplative tension to it. Somewhere in the darkness, another screech echoes through the trees.

Eventually, most of the men find spots in the shadows to retire to, but despite my exhaustion, my thoughts are still churning.

Grey hasn't found sleep either. When I glance over, the firelight flickers across his cheeks, and I realize he's watching me.

I meet his eyes and hold them, then wait.

"You're clever," he says.

It's not what I expected, and the word doesn't sound like a compliment—nor an insult, really. I can't read his tone. The bird of prey calls out to the night again, and I shiver.

Grey doesn't look away. "You knew I was the heir," he says, his tone very low, very thoughtful. "And you figured out the truth of Disi. What else do you know, Princess?"

I keep my eyes on the fire and try to keep any despondency from my voice. "In truth, I am not a princess. I am the elder of two sisters, but only the named heir earns that title, and that is not me."

"Then what do you know, elder sister?"

I hesitate, but he is so forthright, so *lacking* in hesitation, that it makes me want to act the same. "I know you must have been very loyal to Prince Rhen to keep this secret." I pause. "I see how loyal Tycho is to you, and I think Prince Rhen's actions must have been quite a betrayal."

Grey snaps a twig between his fingers and tosses the pieces into the fire. When he speaks, his voice is rough. "I once told him he was never cruel. I meant it as a mark of respect." He pauses. "Now I feel as though I issued a challenge, and he accepted."

Nolla Verin can be cruel, but I cannot imagine her taking something dear to me and torturing it—even for political gain. Regardless of my feelings for Rhen, these men had a history. I do not understand what it must have cost Grey to endure the beating—nor what it must have cost Rhen to have it done.

The air has grown heavy and uncomfortable, so I tilt my head and look at him, forcing my voice to be light. "Earlier, when everyone wished for food, you wished for a dozen arrows. Why?"

The ghost of a smile peeks through his sadness. "If I had a dozen arrows, we'd eat for a week."

Ah. Of course. I should have wished for a dozen arrows as well.

He winces then, and presses a hand to his side, where his shirt clings to a weeping wound. The bird screeches again, sounding closer.

"Should I wake Noah?" I whisper.

"No." Grey pulls the shirt away from the wound, his breath shaking from the effort. He shifts, then shifts again, unable to get comfortable. Another screech echoes through the woods. "If I had an arrow," he snaps, "I'd shoot that creature."

Wings beat among the trees, followed by another long screech that's cut off abruptly.

"Well." Grey stares up at the branches. "I suppose something else took care of it."

Leaves rustle, and a black shape falls out of the sky. A large goose slaps into the ground with a *thump*.

Grey swears and jerks back. I give a *yip* of surprise.

His eyes meet mine, and his hand falls on the sword lying beside him.

Out of the darkness above, another shape descends, buoyed by a pair of wide black wings that nearly span the narrow clearing. Smoky gray feet settle into the leaves silently. It's beautiful and terrifying, and I catch my breath.

"A scraver," I whisper, torn between fear and wonder. Part of me wants to scramble back, but another part wants to crawl forward and take a closer look. I've never seen one outside the pages of a book, and stories of their inhuman feats in the ice forests did not prepare me to meet one face-to-face.

"Yes, Princess," says the creature. Its words are soft, barely more than a whisper on the air. Fangs glitter in the moonlight when it speaks. Its eyes are pure black, no white showing at all. "And as for you," it says to Grey, "do you go by Hawk? Or by Grey?"

Beside me, Grey swallows. His hand is tight on the sword.

The scraver's skin absorbs the shadows as it leans toward us, shifting into a mockery of a courtly bow, wings flaring wide. "Ah, forgive me. Shall I call you Your Highness?"

CHAPTER TWENTY-FOUR

GREY

Rhen himself could have dropped from the trees and I'd be less surprised.

The scraver appears larger than it did at Worwick's, though the cage was small and I never saw it stand upright. Or clothed, for that matter; it's found black trousers somewhere, held up by a length of leather, leaving its broad chest bare. The garment makes the scraver seem more human—yet somehow *less* human at the same time.

Those claws still look just as sharp.

Beside me, Tycho stirs and runs a hand across his face. "What— what's—" His eyes settle on the scraver, and he goes still. "Am I dreaming?"

"You're awake." Noah and Jacob are asleep a little farther away, so the noise hasn't woken them yet. I can't decide if that's a good thing.

"I thought the scravers were trapped in Iishellasa," says Lia Mara, and her voice is a curious mix of fear and wonder.

The creature's glittering black eyes shift to her. "Not all."

When he speaks, his voice is low and clear, but I can feel each word against my skin, like a breath of icy wind. It's unnatural, and unnerving, and I shift my grip on the sword. Rhen is not the only one who has a bad history with magic.

"If I meant you harm, I would not have announced myself." The scraver nudges the goose with one clawed foot. "For now, I wish to help you survive."

Beside me, Tycho shivers despite the summer warmth, and I know he feels it, too. He's the first to shake off the awe, though, and he levers himself to his knees. With a wince, he crawls forward to grab the goose by the neck. He sits on his heels by the fire and begins yanking feathers free.

"The boy has some sense," says the creature.

"The boy is starving," says Tycho.

"Where did you come from, scraver?" My hand hasn't left my sword hilt.

"You know where I came from. You yourself cut the ropes, Your Highness."

"Stop calling me *Your Highness.*"

"Then stop calling me *scraver.*" He overemphasizes the word, with a *C* pulled from his throat and an *R* that ends in a low growl. This time I shiver as if ice brushed against my skin, and I'm no less inclined to take my hand off my weapon.

Beside me, Lia Mara is still and intent. "What shall we call you?" she says.

"My name is Iisak." The way he says his name is both sibilant and not, like taking the word *ice* and dragging it to a hard stop.

"Iisak," says Lia Mara. "Thank you for the goose."

I'm not ready to see Iisak as our savior yet. "You've been follow-ing us."

"I watched them take you prisoner," he says. "I watched them drag you into that castle in chains." He pauses. "I watched them tor-ture you and the boy."

Tycho frowns and keeps his eyes on the bird, but I do not look away. "Why?"

"You freed me. I owe you a debt."

"I freed you as a distraction. You owe me nothing."

"Perhaps, but you gave me the means to escape. You told me where to go."

I cannot decide if this creature is toying with me or if he's being genuine. I glance at Tycho, who's removed the larger feathers and is now struggling with the light downy ones underneath.

Unbidden, a memory comes to me. I must have been twelve or thirteen, the summer my father—the man I *thought* to be my father—was injured. My younger brother Cade was trying, and fail-ing, to pluck a goose for us to take to the market. He was desperate to help. Half our crops hadn't been harvested, and we had little to sell. We were all so hungry and worried and uncertain of what our future would hold.

Much like right now.

I shake off the memory. "Hold it into the fire," I say to Tycho. "Singe them a bit. They'll be easier to pull free." I look back at Iisak. "Am I to believe you followed me all this way because I opened your cage door?"

"I followed you because you are so clearly a magesmith, yet you use none of the powers available to you. I followed you because you are the rightful heir to the throne of this cursed country, yet you make no claim." He pauses, his black eyes narrowing. "I followed you because you travel with a daughter of Karis Luran, and I cannot reach Iishellasa by myself."

"The ice forests?" says Lia Mara. "No one can cross the Frozen River."

Iisak flares his wings, making the fire flicker. "I can." His expression darkens as his wings fold back into place. "Though perhaps not yet. I have spent months in a cage." These words bring a bitter wind that ruffles leaves overhead.

"Perhaps not ever," says Lia Mara, "if my mother discovers your existence. The scravers have been treaty-bound to stay out of Syhl Shallow since before I was born."

"So you see why I thought we might help each other."

The day has been long and exhausting and full of too many questions. I have no idea what the right decisions are. "We are traveling slowly now," I say. "But tomorrow we will find horses and weapons and cover ground more quickly."

"You will find an arrow in your back." His eyes narrow, and that low growl rolls into his voice again. "I see much from above. The cities are full of guardsmen, searching for you both."

I go still. I knew Harper wouldn't be able to force his hand. Rhen organized guards and enforcers quicker than I expected. The thought of fleeing again right now is almost too much to bear. Even if I could manage it, I doubt Tycho could.

Tycho turns from the fire. The feathers lie in a pile at his feet. "I'd kill for a dagger. Lend me the sword?"

I begin to draw the weapon, but Iisak steps forward, plucks the carcass from Tycho's hands, and, with two swipes of his claws, drops the bird in pieces at the boy's feet.

Tycho stares at the carcass, then peers up at Iisak. "Ah . . . thank you." He gingerly shifts to lay the meat on rocks that he set in the fire.

Iisak licks the blood from his claws.

I've seen enough monstrous creatures and done enough monstrous things that I don't flinch at the sight, but I expect Lia Mara to grimace. Instead, she looks intrigued. "How did you get *out* of Iishellasa without breaking the treaty?"

The creature smiles. "I didn't."

"So you hope I will intercede for you with my mother."

"If I only cared for myself, I would attempt to sneak through Syhl Shallow alone." He pauses. "I believe your mother has something of great value to me. I am willing to risk punishment for breaking the treaty to acquire it."

"What is it?" I say.

"That is between me and the queen."

Lia Mara studies him. "If we allow you to travel with us, what do you offer?"

Tycho glances over. "Did you see what he just did to this goose? How are you going to *stop* him from traveling with us?"

Iisak smiles, but his fangs make it more frightening than reassuring. "I can see what you cannot, from the air. I can scout the cities for guards and enforcers before you attempt trade." His eyes level with mine. "Until then, I can feed your people, Your Highness."

They're not my people, but my pride takes a blow anyway. "Stop calling me that."

"I can help you find your magic."

I shiver as another unnaturally cold breeze slides across my back, making the lash marks sting. "How?"

"We are both creatures of magic. The magesmiths were once allies with my people." Iisak steps forward, and I tense, putting my hand on the sword again. Tycho wasn't wrong. I've already seen the damage Iisak can do.

The scraver stops, dropping to a crouch in the leaves in front of me. "If you knew how to use your magic, you would not fear me at all."

I swallow. His eyes are level with mine, and I wonder how I ever missed the keen intelligence there. Nonetheless, it's like meeting the gaze of a predator. Lia Mara has gone absolutely still beside me.

Iisak holds out a hand. "Your wrist, Your Highness?"

I remember what happened the day Worwick had me yank the canvas off the scraver's cage, how I tried to feed him water and he sank those fangs into my arm. There's a glint of challenge in his eyes now, and I'm distantly aware of Tycho and Lia Mara waiting with held breath.

I let go of the sword and hold out my hand.

I expect his touch to be icy, the way his words feel, but his fingers are warm as he turns my arm over to bare the underside.

He drags a razor-sharp claw along the jagged scar left by his teeth, and I fight to keep still. "You could have healed this."

"You could've not bitten me."

He ignores my tone. "Your blood is full of magic," he says. "I would wager that you call upon it without knowing. Have you ever survived an injury that would've killed another?"

"No. Never."

But then I stop. Think.

The first season, when Rhen was cursed to become a monster, he terrorized the castle and killed nearly everyone. I was injured—we all were—but I was one of few guardsmen who survived.

After the second season, I was the *only* guardsman to survive.

I've always attributed that to skill and luck.

"You could likely heal your injuries *now*," says Iisak. "The boy's as well."

"How?" says Tycho.

Iisak's eyes do not leave mine. "How do you learn to walk on two legs?"

I frown. "Balance?"

"Necessity." His claws sink into my forearm.

I swear and jerk back. Iisak holds fast, and I drag him with me. I try to swing at him with my free hand, but despite his size, he's lighter and quicker than I expect, especially when he uses my forearm as leverage and swings around to kick me in the throat.

I go down on my back, momentum shoving me through the dirt and rocks of our campsite and tearing open the wounds on my back. Pain explodes through my body. I need to think, to find the sword, to scream for help. He must have severed muscle and tendon because I can no longer move my fingers. Blood streams down my arm, but my eyes see stars and darkness.

"Focus, Your Highness." He's kneeling on my chest. One hand still grips my arm, holding it up. Three long slashes run the length of my forearm. Blood seems to be everywhere. I can taste it.

"Focus," he says again.

I squeeze my eyes shut, then open. I can't breathe. Dirt and leaves grind into my back. This pain is a living, biting thing, pulling noises from my throat. Voices are yelling, wild shouts that I can't make sense of.

Iisak leans down close, until I see nothing but his eyes.

"You've done it before," he says, his voice more of a growl than a whisper. I feel frost on my skin where his breath touches. "Do it again."

My thoughts twist and spiral loose as more stars fill my vision.

Everyone is shouting. Someone is dragging at me, but Iisak growls and holds fast, his claws buried in my arm. I can't think. I can't see. My throat is burning, my lungs screaming for oxygen, but the pain is so absolute that I can't remember how to breathe.

An eternity at Prince Rhen's side, surviving his monster, surviving Lilith, surviving as a guardsman, and I'm going to die in the leaves beside a campfire because I was *stupid*.

Suddenly everyone is silent. Soft fingers touch my face. "Grey." Lia Mara's voice. Her breath is sweet and warm on my cheek. She must be kneeling in the leaves. "You survived what Prince Rhen did to you. You can survive this."

My body feels weightless, as if it's not tethered to earth. Stars aren't just in my vision. They fill my veins and flare with every beat of my heart. Each pulse steals a bit of agony, until I feel as though I must be dead, because there was so much pain, and now there's none.

Lia Mara's voice seems to come from a great distance. "Grey . . . breathe. You need to breathe." She sounds breathless herself.

"You feel the magic now," says Iisak, and *he* sounds triumphant.

I inhale, and those stars scatter, flickering down to almost nothing. But they're there, tiny points of light throughout my body.

"Open your eyes," says Lia Mara.

I blink and find her right above me. Her eyes are wide, gold in the firelight, her hair a shining curtain that hangs down over her shoulder.

Iisak still kneels on my chest, and he draws my arm into my vision. "As you see, Your Highness."

The blood is gone. The wound is gone. All that remains is the scar that existed before.

"Necessity," says Iisak.

Behind him are Tycho, Noah, and Jacob, all wide-eyed, their expressions frozen between panic and anger and relief.

I look at the smooth skin of my arm, then at Iisak. I can't find my voice.

Then I realize my back doesn't hurt either.

"What just happened?" says Jacob. "What the hell is this thing?" His hand twitches, and I realize he's clutching the sword.

Iisak growls, and his wings flare slightly. Jacob lifts the weapon.

"No," I say, my voice a rough croak, like I've been screaming. Now that I'm aware of the stars in my bloodstream, they seem to flicker everywhere. I look up at Iisak. "Let me go."

He withdraws, moving to my side to watch the others more warily.

I sit up gingerly, expecting my body to protest each movement, but it does not. Any ache and burn from the wounds on my back are gone. So is the pain in my thigh.

I take a long breath and look at my forearm again.

Blood speckles the leaves at my feet. *My* blood.

"Jacob," I say slowly, "this is Iisak."

"Iisak," echoes Noah.

"A friend," says Lia Mara.

Iisak straightens. "I have earned a place with you then?"

I flex my knee, then touch a hand to my lower back carefully. I feel no pain.

"Yes," I say, and I can't help the wonder in my voice. "Yes, you have."

After a day with nothing but stream water, the roasted goose tastes better than anything I've ever eaten. I all but tear the meat apart with my fingers. If Jodi could see me now, she'd make no comparison to noblemen. Tycho offers a piece to Iisak, but the creature makes a face, then says, "I will bring more."

His wings beat and catch the air, and then he's lost to the darkness.

Across the fire, Noah pulls meat from a bone and glances up. "Just when I think I have a handle on this place, something drops out of the sky to turn that on its head."

I give a humorless laugh.

"Everything feels fully healed?" he says.

I nod and pick every last morsel from my own bone.

"May I see?" I go still, and he adds, "You had stitches. If the skin healed over them . . ."

I nod, and he moves around the fire to kneel behind me. I lift my shirt, and a moment later, his cool fingers touch my back.

"The stitches are gone," he says, his tone thoughtful. "This looks like six weeks of healing." He hesitates.

I crane my head around to look at him. "What?"

"I don't know how your magic works"—he says *magic* like it's profane—"but it didn't undo what he did. The lash marks left scars."

When I say nothing, Noah tugs the shirt down and shifts to face me. "I can help you feel the worst of them, if you want to."

I don't want to. I toss the stripped bones from my meal into the fire. "I have seen the back of a beaten man."

We aren't speaking loudly, but the rest of our camping party has grown quiet, and I know their attention has fallen on me. I was already a spectacle in the courtyard. I do not like the thought of being one again. Especially not for this.

Noah must sense this, because he eases away, returning to his spot beside Jacob.

Without fanfare, another dead goose flops into the dirt, scattering leaves and making the fire flutter. Iisak descends more slowly, but he keeps his distance from the fire.

Tycho moves to take the goose again, but I wave him back to his food and take the carcass myself. I need action.

My fingers begin plucking, a long-forgotten skill that returns to my hands without effort. I focus on the sparks that seem to flow under my skin. Jacob was right—Rhen has nothing to fear from me. I do not want his throne. I do not want to harm him.

But for the first time, I feel capable of offering something more than pain and torment and fear. "I can use this magic to heal Tycho?" I say to Iisak.

"Yes."

"Show me."

"You wish me to lay his arm open to the bone?"

Across the fire, Tycho goes still. I can't tell if Iisak is teasing, but his fingers flex, which makes me think he might not be. "No," I say.

"You are exhausted. Give your power time to recover," Iisak says. "Try tomorrow night, perhaps."

I *am* exhausted—but a bit energized, too. I almost want to ask him to lay my own arm open again, just to feel the rush and swell of magic.

"If we can spare another day to walking," I say, "we should continue heading northwest without trying to secure horses. If soldiers are already searching the town here, a slow pace will work to our benefit. Rhen would expect me to find horses and weapons and move quickly, especially if he suspects Lia Mara is with me and our destination is Syhl Shallow." I glance across the fire, and her gaze meets mine.

"How much do you think Princess Harper would tell him?" she asks.

"If soldiers are searching in this direction? Everything."

"No," says Jacob. "She knows I'm with you. She wouldn't let him come after me."

I jerk feathers from the goose's neck. "She may have no choice."

Jacob rolls to his knees. "Are you saying you think he'd *hurt* her?" His tone is vicious, and he doesn't wait for an answer. "I'm going back. Right now. We should have made her come with us—"

"No. I do not think he'll hurt her." A dark part of my brain whispers that I never would have expected him to do what he did to me, either. "Even if we are found, his guards will not harm *you*. He loves her. She loves him. Rhen is afraid, but we are all safer if she is within the walls of Ironrose. If she had come with us . . . I do not like to think of what Rhen might have done to come after her."

They go silent. I continue pulling feathers.

After a moment, Tycho says, "What is he afraid of?"

"Magic." I pause and wonder how much to keep secret—but surely it makes no difference now. "Rhen was cursed before. He suffered much, and Emberfall was nearly driven to ruin. He fears being cursed again." I glance up. "He fears *me*."

"He *knows* you," says Jacob. "You're not Lilith."

Noah is studying me. "It might not matter." He pauses, and his voice is grave. "Getting free of the curse—then learning someone else might be able to hurt him again, someone he once trusted . . ."

I swallow.

You trusted me once. What have I done to lose it?

You left.

Perhaps I lost before I even began.

"Harper told me a little about what you went through," says Noah. "And she was only here for a short while." He glances at Jacob. "Rhen's been tough to live with over the last few months."

Jacob snorts. "Yeah, because he's an arrogant jerk."

Noah doesn't smile. "Or because he has PTSD." Before I can ask, he says, "Post-traumatic stress disorder. It happens when you've been exposed to something terrifying. I used to see it a lot in soldiers. Or abused kids. It's like your brain can't turn off the fear."

I glance at Tycho and think of how he shied away from those soldiers in Jodi's tavern. Rhen has always been cool and composed, the pinnacle of control. But I keep remembering the shadows in his expression in the courtyard and wonder how much of that hid what he was truly feeling. For the first time I wonder if he's truly trying to protect his people—or if he's trying to protect himself.

Either way, he wants me dead. It shouldn't matter.

I look back at the goose in my lap. I hold the bird as close to the flames as I can, letting it singe the feathers dry. Once those are also stripped from the body, I stand, but Iisak is already there. He makes quick work of the poultry, and I lay the meat across the stones.

He's licking the blood from his claws again, and I try to stop myself from wondering if he did the same with mine. It's unsettling to think that he was trapped in that cage for so long, having conscious awareness of everything that was done to him. Kantor jabbed his sword into the cage that day, for nothing more than a bit of sport. It's not the same kind of humiliation as what Rhen did to me—but it's not altogether different either.

"If you have magic," I say to him, my voice low, "how were you kept in a cage for so long?"

"My magic is not the same as yours," he says. "Yours comes from within, while mine comes from the wind and the sky. I can breathe frost and borrow snow from the clouds." He holds out a hand and blows air across his palm. Frost collects on his skin—but only for a moment. It melts almost instantly, and he shakes the water into the leaves.

"But it's summer," I say, understanding. He was nearly dead when Worwick rolled him into the tourney. I thought it was because of the canvas covering, but maybe it was more.

"Yes, Your Highness. *Here*, it is summer."

Motion catches my eye, and I find Lia Mara has moved forward to turn the meat on the stones in the fire. For the daughter of a queen, she doesn't seem to flinch from anything—not even the prospect of work. Her hair is lit with a red glow, her curves in silhouette.

She must sense my gaze, because she looks up, so I quickly avert my eyes back to Iisak. "Did you know what I was, when we were at Worwick's?"

"I knew you were a magesmith the instant I tasted your blood."

The words bring a cool wind, and I shiver.

"You so fearlessly put your hand in the cage," he continues, "so I thought you knew, that your surprise was a farce for that foolish man. Our people were once great allies, as I said. I thought you would free me once night fell."

"And then I didn't."

He smiles, teeth glittering. "You did eventually."

"I freed you to free myself," I say to him.

"And I would have cut your throat if it meant the cage would open." Leaves rustle in the trees above us, and his wings snap open. He launches off the ground in search of new prey, his voice carrying back to me. "Do not fault yourself for choices you believed were right in the moment. It is not princely."

I grunt and stare after him. "I'm not a prince," I mutter under my breath. I drop my gaze to find the fire, but instead I find Lia Mara watching me.

"You *are* a prince," she says quietly.

Maybe it's the stars in my blood, or maybe it's the lack of pain in my back or my leg. Maybe it's the fact that I feel as though I finally did something *right*.

I don't know if I'll follow her into Syhl Shallow. I don't even know if I'll survive the next few days. But for the first time, the word *prince* doesn't make me flinch.

And for the first time, I don't say a word to correct her.

CHAPTER TWENTY-FIVE

LIA MARA

By the third day, Grey estimates that we've covered seventy-five miles, always staying close to the creek. Iisak reports castle guards and enforcers in the towns when we draw near. We may not have horses, but Iisak swiped an array of supplies and weapons in the dead of night. We each have a dagger now. Two bows, though only one quiver of arrows. Two more swords. An iron pot that allows us to boil water and cook more than just roasted fowl.

When we rest at night, Grey tries to use his magic to heal Tycho, but he's been unsuccessful. I can sense his frustration, but he doesn't share his worries with me—or with anyone. Tense exhaustion seems to be a companion that silently follows us through the forest, and it's the only companion I have. We travel together, but there's a clear division among our party: Noah and Jacob, Grey and Tycho. Iisak keeps to the skies, leaving me to walk alone.

By the fourth night, the summer heat has grown oppressive, and everyone is bitter and snappish. Grey and Jacob have been sniping at each other for hours, and I'm ready to pick up a bow and shoot them both. Even Tycho has left Grey's side to sit against a tree on the opposite side of tonight's campsite, where Iisak has taken roost in the darkness of the branches. A frost-coated leaf drifts down from above, and Tycho catches it, grinning. "That's a neat trick."

I can't help but smile at the wonder in his voice.

On the other side of our campsite, Jacob is arguing. "We stole weapons," he says. "I don't see why we can't steal horses."

"One weapon would not be immediately noticed," says Grey. "Five horses would be—and their tracks easily followed."

"Yeah, but on horseback, we could get away faster."

Grey's expression is cold. "On horseback, we are a larger target—"

"I'm going for a walk," I say. My sister could be challenging in her own way, but at least we never bickered. "I'll take the bow. Perhaps we can eat something other than wild goose."

"Look," says Jacob, not even paying attention to me. "I left one jerk of a prince behind. Don't be too quick to fill the role."

I scowl and sling the quiver over my shoulder, then head into the forest with the bow.

Silence immediately greets me, warm and welcome in the slowly darkening twilight. The bow is sleek and heavier than I'm used to, the polished wood like satin. I circle the camp in gradually widening arcs, moving farther away as the sun begins to disappear. I take aim at a rotted log about a hundred yards away and let an arrow fly. The arrow sinks right into the softened wood, only a few inches below where I hoped. Maybe the weight isn't as bad as I thought.

I stride through the trees to fetch the arrow. When I straighten, movement flashes in the distance. I freeze.

A deer—no, a buck. Large and brown with beautiful dapples across its hindquarters. Two hundred yards away at least, but as wide a target as I'll ever get.

I raise the bow and nock an arrow on the string.

Suddenly every hair on my neck stands up. I hold my breath.

I'm not alone. I don't know *how* I know, but I do.

I spin, ready to fire.

A hand catches the bow, gripping the arrow in place, and I gasp, staring up at Grey. The point of the arrow sits against his chest.

Fury flares like a torch in my belly. He must see the words ready to boil out of my mouth, because he shakes his head quickly and puts a finger to his lips, then points.

The buck has been joined by three deer.

Grey is so determined and self-assured that I expect him to wrestle the bow away from me, the way he claimed the sword from Jacob.

He doesn't. He lets go of the arrow so I can turn back around.

I'm painfully aware of the position of my fingers on the bow. I wait for a correction of some sort, a comment on my stance or a question of my ability, but he's silent at my back. I draw the bowstring tighter and release. The arrow flies.

The buck falls without a sound. The other deer scatter in a burst of motion.

"Nice kill," says Grey.

The word makes me shiver. "Thank you."

He walks toward the clearing where the animal fell. It's no wonder he was able to slip through the woods without detection. When he's alone, he moves like an assassin.

I sling the bow across my opposite shoulder and hurry to follow.

The buck is larger than I expected. From a distance, it was beautiful, but up close, its eyes have already gone glassy. I shudder.

Grey yanks the arrow free and wipes it in the grass, then holds it out to me. Bits of blood and other things glisten at the tip.

I swallow, then jam it into the quiver, thinking of that trapper and his daughter, the ones my sister condemned to death. "Shall we—" I have to clear my throat. "Shall we drag it?"

"We don't want to ruin the hide. I'll find a branch."

He does, then strips tiny twigs from the length. We use our dagger belts to lash the legs to the wood. I feel jittery and unsettled inside, especially when Grey hoists one end onto his shoulder and the head flops to the ground, antlers dragging.

I must be staring too long, because Grey says, "It's heavy. I can fetch Jacob."

"No—no, I should be able to manage." I get my shoulder under the branch and use my legs to lift, and the weight nearly takes my breath away. Each step is more of a stagger.

Mother would be mortified. Anything requiring brute strength would be seen as lesser—a burden relegated to a man. Being quick and lithe and agile are valued in women. Being thoughtful and decisive.

Not hauling animals through the woods. Maybe I *should* let him fetch Jacob.

The thought feels like a slap to the cheek. I was not worthy of being queen. Perhaps I *am* only good for hauling animals through the woods.

I'm not even good for that, because I'm about to drop this branch. I gasp, "Grey—one—moment—please." Without waiting, I shove the weight off my shoulder.

Grey eases his end to the ground, then turns to lean against a tree. Darkness thickens the air, and I can't make out his expression in the shadows. I wonder if he's disappointed. Or possibly exasperated. I shouldn't care, but I do.

"My apologies," I offer.

His eyebrows flicker into a frown. "No need."

The buck's head is cocked sideways on its antlers, the dead eyes staring at me judgmentally. I grimace and glance away.

Grey is studying me, but he seizes his end of the branch. "Ready?"

No, but I nod.

He takes more of the weight this time, but I barely last two minutes. The buck flops to the ground again. I'm panting.

"Can we not drag it?" I gasp.

"You think it will somehow weigh less on the ground?" He's not even a little breathless.

I scowl at him ruefully and drag a hand across my forehead.

"We need the skin," he says. He stretches his arms overhead, flexing his shoulders, the only sign that this is an effort for him as well. "The fur will give us a good story if we're confronted in the woods. Trappers and fur traders will grow more common as we head north."

The mention of trappers and fur traders makes me frown. I take hold of the branch. "I'm ready."

This time I barely make it twenty-five paces. I'll have a good bruise tomorrow. I lean against a tree and breathe.

"You have exceptional aim," says Grey. "Where did you learn to shoot that way?"

"We have competitions every year," I say, and my breathing is ragged, but I welcome the distraction. "The Royal Houses of Syhl

Shallow all send entrants. Archery, mounted games, things like that. Have you nothing similar here?"

He shakes his head. "The guardsmen would sometimes fight to entertain the nobility, but nothing so official."

"What a shame. The Queen's Challenge is quite a spectacle." I smile, remembering. "It is a time of celebration."

He doesn't smile. "It is unusual for me to think of times of celebration in Syhl Shallow."

I flinch, thinking of Tycho's comments about my mother eating her victims.

"I meant no offense," says Grey, but there's a note in his voice that makes me wonder if he truly means that. Before I can ask, he seizes his end of the branch and hoists it onto his shoulder.

I grit my teeth and follow suit. The buck feels heavier each time. I speak in broken phrases, panting in between. "My sister, Nolla Verin—is the best. She always—takes top prize. In—in the mounted games." I pause to catch my breath. "I'm good with an arrow, but she is better. Many are better. Some of the contests—are brutal. I do not like—I do not like the violence. Even still, I look—I look forward to it each year. The food, the parties. I'm told—I'm told—"

"Lia Mara. Set it down."

I drop the branch, then brace my hands on my knees. The woods are very dark now, and I can barely make out Grey's form. He's a large shape in the darkness. We're making very slow progress, and I wait for him to tell me he'll ask one of the other men to help him. After Mother's announcement, I felt incapable at home. Like someone lesser.

After failing with Rhen, and now, in a different way, failing with Grey, I feel incapable here.

But Grey says nothing more about fetching Jacob. He's quiet for the moment, and I don't mind, because I'm trying to rub knots out of my shoulder. Eventually, he says, "We're less than two hundred yards from camp. Can you make it?"

Two hundred yards might as well be two hundred miles, but I brace myself and lever the branch onto my shoulder. "I think so."

"I know so." He says it like it's something I should be proud of. I sweat and stagger and try not to fall.

"In the Royal Guard," he says conversationally, as if I'm not gasping with every step, "we were trained to be skilled at weaponry, but that was never our primary lesson. We were taught to see ourselves as different from the people. As a group. Every day came the call and response. *Who are you? We are the Royal Guard.*"

"My mother's . . . my mother's soldiers"—I draw a ragged breath—"are trained similarly."

"If one guardsman failed to follow orders, the entire unit would be punished. It bred unity—and obedience—quickly."

"I'm sure." I nearly stumble over a rock.

"After a while," he says, "a guardsman begins to recognize anyone outside the unit as a potential threat. As a *target*. It makes it easy to follow orders when you're in a constant state of evaluate-and-disregard or evaluate-and-act."

I'm barely listening to him. My focus is squarely on the placement of my feet in the dark, and the weight of the branch on my shoulders. "I need to put this down."

"We're almost there. Keep your eyes on the fire."

I blink sweat from my eyes, and I can see the glow through the trees. I force my feet forward.

"After your mother invaded," he says, "anyone from Syhl Shallow was a threat."

I brace sweat-slicked palms against the branch to try to give my shoulder a reprieve. Part of me wants him to move faster. Another part of me wants to pitch face-first into this underbrush.

"So when I say that it is odd to think of times of celebration," he continues, "it is because I had forgotten that your people may be our enemies, but they are still people."

"Yes." We will never reach that fire. "They are people. *We* are people."

"Indeed."

I clench my eyes shut. "I cannot—I cannot—"

"You're stronger than you think. Another step."

I step.

"Another."

I lose track of how many steps are left. My eyes no longer track the fire, and instead track the movement of his body in the darkness. His voice has become hypnotic. *Another. Another. Another.*

When he finally stops, it's so unexpected that I nearly walk right out from under the branch.

"Silver hell," says Tycho. "Is that a stag?"

I drop it in the dust beside the fire and quickly follow suit. My knees hit the ground, and I do not care. "Yes."

"Finally," says Jacob. "Something with some real meat on its bones."

"Lia Mara is quite the shot," says Grey.

"Quite the brute, too," says Jacob. "How much does that thing weigh?"

Quite the brute. I don't know if I should blush or frown. I yank the quiver off my back and busy myself with putting everything back with our accumulated supplies. "It was luck."

A hand catches my arm, and I turn, ready anger on my tongue.

Grey's easy expression is gone. "Strength and skill are not matters of *luck*."

"You carried most of the weight."

"I did not. That animal is easily three times your size, and we carried it over half a mile." He pauses. "Could your sister do *that*?"

I think of Nolla Verin, with her easy smile and yards of dark hair. She can put an arrow into a dark target on a cloudy night, and no one will ever get her off a horse, but like our mother, she is slight, all fluid grace.

"No," I admit. "Physical strength is not a point of pride in Syhl Shallow."

"You did not think you could do it, and then you did. That is more than just physical strength." His eyes glitter in the darkness, and his voice is low. I'm not sure how, but he's taken the sting out of the moment, turning it into something warmer. Better. Maybe Mother would frown on this, but for the first time in a while, I suddenly feel . . . capable.

A blush finally finds my cheeks, and I glance away. I think of what he said when we were walking. My people, his people—it should make no difference. I didn't expect such a revelation from him.

After days of feeling at odds with the men around me, this moment feels meaningful. I want to cling to it for a while, to share a few more words. To hear the echo of pride in his voice that I haven't heard in so long.

"Your Highness," calls Iisak. "If none of you humans have claimed the heart, may I do so?"

Grey's eyes flick skyward, and he turns away. Whatever spark existed between us burns out to nothing.

"Have no worries, Iisak," he says. "The heart is yours."

CHAPTER TWENTY-SIX

GREY

The fire dwindles, but the others are drifting into sleep, so I do nothing to bank it. On the opposite side of the burning embers, Lia Mara is awake as well, her eyes distant and fixed on nothing. She surprised me when she forced her way through the fireplace into my room at Ironrose. She surprised me again tonight. She's so quiet and unassuming that I didn't expect her to handle a bow with such assurance. I didn't expect her to put a shoulder under that branch to carry the stag.

I am not used to people surprising me.

As if she senses my scrutiny, her eyes lift from the fire to meet mine. "You should sleep," she says. "I can keep watch until Noah wakes."

Noah is always the first to sleep, but always the first to wake, well before the sun breaks across the horizon. He says that his training as a doctor allows him to sleep anywhere, at any time. He can lie down and find sleep in seconds, a talent I envy.

When I try to sleep, I lie in the darkness and watch the stars shift overhead and think of all that will be lost if Emberfall tears itself apart in a civil war. I think of Syhl Shallow and how far we have yet to travel and whether we will be any safer there than we are here.

I prefer watching the flames die as the night stretches on.

"No," I say. "Thank you."

A hint of stubbornness flickers in her eyes. "Do you think me incapable of waking you?"

"Hardly. I think I am incapable of sleep."

"Ah." She glances away, into the darkest shadows, where Jacob, Noah, and Tycho lie in the softer leaves beneath a pine tree. Iisak is somewhere overhead in the branches, or possibly out hunting.

Tycho's lash marks have scabbed over heavily, with mottled bruising to fill in the spaces between. He still moves stiffly throughout the day and looks grateful every time we make camp.

"He is healing," says Lia Mara.

"I should be able to help him." I flex my fingers and shake my head. "This magic seems useless if it only works when my life is at risk."

"Surely you did not pick up a sword and expect to be proficient on the first day."

"No, but—but that is different."

"Why?" She uncurls from where she sits, then claims a short dagger from our stash. When she returns, she sits beside me. "Here. Practice."

"Practice?"

She takes my hand, her fingers small and cool against mine. She turns my wrist over, then lifts the dagger.

My free hand snaps out to catch her wrist. "What are you doing?"

"You let Iisak tear your arm open when you practice, but you fear a little dagger?"

"I do not fear the dagger."

Her eyebrows go up. "You fear me?"

No. Yes. Not so much *her*, but who and what she represents.

When we started this journey, I was so sure she'd be demanding and domineering, much like Karis Luran. I expected her to force an oath from my lips in exchange for safety, or for her to display some trickery or guile. I keep thinking about the first night, when I thought Iisak might kill me. The way she got down on her knees in the underbrush to hold my hand and whisper my name.

I'm not sure anymore.

I release her hand. "I've seen what you can do with an arrow."

She smiles ruefully. I brace myself for the bite of the blade, but she is quick. Blood wells before I feel the pain. Those stars wait, tiny flickers of light under my skin. They scatter when I pay attention to them, like trying to gather bits of dust in a sunbeam. A drop of blood trails down my arm to vanish into the dirt below, and I give an aggravated sigh.

"Not everything can be accomplished by force," Lia Mara says.

"Clearly."

"I know you can be gentle. I saw you with Princess Harper."

A new note enters her voice, one I do not fully understand, a mixture of uncertainty and longing and disappointment. I look up, seeking her eyes, but she keeps her gaze on the stripe of blood on my skin.

"There was nothing between me and the princess," I say.

"There was *something* between you and the princess."

"Never. Truly."

"I have a dagger, Grey." She finally looks up. Her words are taunting, but there's an element of truth in her eyes. "Do not lie to me."

"I could disarm you."

"You could be honest with me."

"The princess . . ." My voice trails off in a sigh. But of course there are no secrets. Lia Mara knows of the enchantress. She knows Disi was a sham.

"To understand my relationship with Harper," I say, "you must understand what happened to Prince Rhen. He was cursed by the enchantress Lilith. He had one autumn season to find a girl and earn her love, or he would become a monstrous beast that would terrorize Emberfall."

Lia Mara's eyes are wide. "The monstrous beast that drove out our forces?"

"One and the same." I pause. "At the end of the season, if he failed, he would become human again and the season would restart. Only . . . the dead remained dead."

She studies me. "The royal family was supposedly killed in Disi."

I look back at her and wait for her to figure it out. Speaking these words still feels too much like treason.

"He did it himself," she finally says. Her voice is hardly more than a whisper. "When he was a monster."

"Yes."

She shudders. "For the first time, he truly has my sympathy." Her eyes fix on mine. "What about you?"

"I was trapped similarly. I was charged with finding girls to break the curse."

Lia Mara frowns. "How long did it take for you to 'find' Harper?"

"Time in the castle did not pass at the same rate as time in Emberfall. I have no real way of knowing. A few years passed here, but within the walls of Ironrose . . ." Now it's my turn to shudder. "It was interminable. Harper was our final chance—and she was not even the girl I chose."

"I don't understand."

"She saw me attempting to take another young woman and attacked me with an iron bar."

Lia Mara snorts with sudden laughter. "I knew I liked her."

"She wanted nothing more than to go home. She fought for it so fiercely. But when she could not, she turned her attention to Emberfall. She renewed Rhen's faith that he could save his people." I pause. "She became a princess by her words and actions, if not by blood."

"Ah," says Lia Mara, her skepticism clear. "So it is merely *admiration* between you."

"We endured much together, but fate did not put me in her path for anything more than friendship."

"Is that because you felt nothing for her, or because you were sworn to obey the prince?"

Lia Mara is too clever by far. "Does it matter?"

She meets my eyes boldly. "Yes."

"Because I was sworn to obey the prince, I could not have feelings for another," I say. "If you are seeking sordid secrets, you will find none."

"I saw the way she looked at you, behind the inn." She pauses.

"She allowed you to escape, even knowing it would put Emberfall at risk."

"She allowed me to escape because she knows I will *not* put the kingdom at risk."

"She would have come with you, if you'd asked."

"Jacob asked, and she refused."

"Jacob is not you."

I flinch and look away. "Regardless. I would not have asked."

I expect her expression to turn cynical, but maybe she hears the truth in my words, because she frowns, her eyes sad. "You were very loyal."

Yes. I was. I look away, into the fire.

She squeezes my hand. "When a man no longer deserves your loyalty, it is not a failing of yours, Grey."

I do not know what to say. *Does* Rhen deserve my loyalty?

Her fingers brush against my wrist, feather light. "Perhaps you needed a distraction."

I look down. Beneath the blood, the wound has closed.

"Do it again," I say, and my voice is a bit rough.

The dagger lifts, and she brings it down swiftly.

This time, the blade slices through the back of her hand. She gasps.

I do too. "What are you—"

"Shh." She grips my hand and slaps it over her wound. "Heal it."

I try to force the stars to jump from under my skin and into her wound, but of course they scatter and dance, impossible for me to catch.

"*Distract* yourself," she says. "Talk. Tell me something. Ask me something. Anything."

"Who is your mother's spy inside Ironrose Castle?"

"*Fell siralla!*" She smacks me on the forehead. "Stop worrying about that foolish prince!"

It's so unexpected that I laugh.

She glances away, but her eyes are rueful. "He does not deserve your worry. Prince Rhen is not your ally."

I do not want to think about Rhen. Lia Mara's blood is sticky beneath my fingers, but I do not want to see how effectively I'm failing to heal her wound, either. I keep my hand wrapped around hers. "Tell me what you just said."

A blush rises in her cheeks. "Ah . . . I do not believe there is a translation."

"Now who is the liar?"

"*Fell siralla.*" Her blush deepens. "Stupid man."

"I believe I liked it better when there was no translation."

She laughs, and the sparks of light in my blood whirl and dance in response. Every instinct in me wants to force them across the spot where our skin touches, but I tell myself to wait, to be patient. To be *gentle*.

"How do you speak Emberish so well?" I say.

"I had tutors," she says. "Mother says it is the height of ignorance and arrogance to not speak the languages of our border countries."

That's a rather frank assessment. "I'm sure our border guards were schooled, but any tutors in Ironrose were killed in the first season of the curse."

"Truly? Jacob and Noah speak it so well."

I shake my head. "They call it English. Their language is similar on their side." I pause and turn the sounds of her words over in my head.

"*Fell siralla*," I try.

She shakes her head. "Softer. *Fell siralla*." The words fall off her lips without effort.

I try again, and she giggles. "Your words are so hard-edged. Softer."

"*Fell siralla*," I say, and this time she bites her lip to hide her smile.

She takes my free hand and brings it to her mouth to whisper against my fingertips. "*Fell siralla*."

I barely hear the words. I am thinking about the softness of her lips brushing against my fingers, gentle as a butterfly. I am certain I have touched a woman's mouth at some point in my life, but just now, none come to memory.

"Say it again." My voice has gone husky.

"*Fell siralla*."

Her fingers have gone slack on my wrist. I brush a thumb across her lower lip, and her mouth parts slightly. I find myself wondering what the line of her jaw feels like. The slope of her cheek. The curve of her ear.

Soldiers could burst from the trees this very moment, and I'd fall immediately.

"You have stopped practicing your pronunciation," she chides, but her eyes are dancing.

"Stupid man," I say dutifully.

She laughs against my fingertips—but it ends on a gasp. She pulls her arm free from mine.

"You did it."

The blood is gone, along with the slice across her forearm. I take her hand and run a fingertip along the smooth skin there.

She shivers. "See? I knew you could be gentle."

I want to touch her mouth again and prove exactly that.

"Do you think you could try it on Tycho?" she says.

Tycho. For a wild, crazy moment, I can barely remember who Tycho *is*, much less what I should be trying.

Stupid man, indeed. I cough. "Yes, I should try."

"Will you wake him, do you think?"

I do not know. I have to shake my head to clear it, but Lia Mara seems to take that for an answer. I slip across the clearing to where Tycho sleeps. His upper body is bare, because he says a shirt pulls against the wounds when he sleeps. Despite the warmth in the air, his arms are tucked close against his body, and his breathing is slow and deep.

I drop to a crouch and put a hand lightly against his shoulder.

He jerks and tries to whirl. His eyes snap open, seeking danger.

I lift my hands. "Be at ease," I whisper.

His eyes are a bit wild, and not quite awake. It makes me wonder what dreams haunt his sleep. "Grey—what—"

"There is nothing to fear," I say. "I wanted to try to heal your wounds."

"Oh. Oh." He burrows back into the pine needles, pressing his face into his forearm. His breathing eases, but there's a new tension to his body, as if he's worried it will hurt. "Go ahead."

I rest my hand against his shoulder again, as lightly as I can. The bruising is extensive, the worst of the damage stretching across his lower back. Some of the wounds are an angry red, and I know Noah worries about infection. I have never flinched from violence, but my gut tightens every time I see his injuries. I am responsible for this.

When I move my hand across a shallow lash mark, his breath catches, but he doesn't say anything.

"I don't have to try," I say quietly.

"No. Do it."

A cold lick of wind rushes between the tree branches, and I know Iisak must be near. The sparks beneath my fingers feel more sure. I close my eyes and think of Tycho at Worwick's. The way he begged for lessons in swordplay. The way he stepped in front of Kantor to stop him from hurting Iisak. The way he kept my secret, even at the risk of his own life.

My hand moves, my fingers drifting across broken skin. Tycho whimpers.

My eyes snap open. His are clenched shut, his jaw tight. Nothing is healed. A tear sits on his eyelashes. "Forgive me," I say.

"Keep trying," he whispers.

"Tycho—"

He swallows. "Keep trying."

I hesitate before touching him again. It's so much more damage than a tiny slice across the back of a hand.

"He is so trusting of you, Your Highness." Iisak's growl-soft voice draws my attention, and another cold breeze flickers between the trees. His black eyes gleam at me from the darkness. "Do not waste it."

I close my eyes and put my hand against the worst of the marks. Tycho's breathing shudders, but he keeps still. I don't know if Lia Mara speaks or if I just imagine her voice. *Gently.*

Those sparks and stars flicker and wait. I turn my thoughts away from swordplay and violence. I think of Tycho grinning about winning the race to Jodi's tavern. I think of him standing in the loft, promising to keep my secret. I think of my panic easing, how he was the first person I trusted after so long.

I'll keep your secret, Hawk.

My eyes are closed, but the stars seem to fill my vision anyway, brightening the way they did in the courtyard. They're everywhere at once. I want to grab hold of them and drive them into his wounds, the way I'd put a blade in an enemy, but now I realize that Lia Mara was right. This is a different kind of skill.

My hands brush over his injuries, and I let the stars dance along beneath my fingertips. Tycho gasps again, but I don't stop. I trace every line of broken skin, every ridge of damage, every stitch placed by Noah.

"Ah," breathes Iisak, and I shiver again. "You have discovered the knack for it."

A sob breaks from Tycho's throat, and I snatch my hand away. The stars flicker and die. I open my eyes. "Forgive—"

I stop short. The bruising is gone. The wounds have left scarring, like mine did, but the skin is closed. Tycho braces his forearms against the ground, then rises to his knees. Tears have made lines in the dirt on his face, and he's breathing as hard as he does when we race across the city.

Then I can't see anything else because he launches himself forward and wraps his arms around my neck. His breath is hitching against my shoulder like he's a child. "I knew you would fix it. I knew you would."

The emotion in his voice is so potent that my own chest feels tight. My hands are shaking like I've been in a battle. This feels powerful. This feels *useful*. I feel so many things that my thoughts cannot contain them all. Regret that this happened at all. Guilt that I could not help him before. Relief that I could help him *now*.

And underneath it all, so tiny that I almost don't acknowledge it, a kernel of pride that instead of magic bringing fear and torment, the way Lilith did, or pain and death, the way my sword would, my magic brought healing and trust, and that is not a small thing at all.

CHAPTER TWENTY-SEVEN

LIA MARA

When we wake, Iisak reports that soldiers and guardsmen are preparing to move out of the closest town, and that they will be advancing ahead of our traveling party. Grey thinks this will be our best chance to find horses, especially since we have the buck's hide to trade, and it makes for a good story. We stay in our camp throughout the day, until Iisak says they've moved on, then we wrap up the hide and antlers and plan to walk into town near sunset.

Blind Hollow is a small town burrowed into the base of the mountains that border Emberfall and Syhl Shallow. When we step out of the trees and into the valley, I'm nearly breathless from the beauty of our surroundings. The miles of blue sky overhead darken to violet in the distance. Trees climb the mountainside, stretching as far as I can see to either side. The foliage is vibrant green, but the air here is a bit cooler, leaving the bare start of red speckled throughout.

Tycho's mouth is all but hanging open. It reminds me of Nolla

Verin's comments in the carriage, when I was doing the same thing.

"Get a good look now," says Grey. "You cannot stare like that when we walk into town."

"The mountains are even bigger than I imagined."

"It's not Rillisk, that's for certain." Grey starts forward, leaving us to follow.

The five of us together would draw too much attention, so Noah and Jacob wait inside the tree line. Their accents would give them away almost immediately. Iisak has disappeared, but I imagine he won't be far.

I thought Grey might tell me to remain behind as well, but I offered to be his sister, mute ever since a childhood fever. "It might garner some sympathy," I said. "For bargaining."

The corner of his mouth tilted up, just the slightest bit, but his eyes were inscrutable. "Clever," he said, and that was that.

He's been active and occupied all day, rehanging the hide to make sure it dries, walking the path into Blind Hollow to see how much traffic we'd encounter, grilling Iisak for insights into the layout of the town and where we might run into trouble.

I spent the day with the bow and arrow, hoping to find more game so we'd have more skins to trade.

At least, that was the story I gave the men. In truth, I needed a task to busy my hands and occupy my thoughts. It didn't matter. No matter what task I gave my hands, my thoughts were all too content to focus on the moment by the fire, when Grey's thumb stroked across my lip.

Even the memory is enough to make me shiver. I keep stealing secret glances at him, as if my eyes are reluctant to look at anything else. That first night I hid in his room at Ironrose, I thought he was aggressive and cold, but after spending days in his presence, I've discovered that he's not either. He's quiet and strong and sure.

I wonder what my sister will think of him. She teased me about my inexperience with men, but now I long to whisper and giggle in the privacy of our carriage.

But of course we will not have moments of whispers and giggles once I reach the Crystal Palace in Syhl Shallow. Mother will task Nolla Verin with seducing him, so she can form an alliance before lending her support to his claim on the throne.

My entire mood sours by the time we reach the town proper. Dusk hangs over the valley, bringing a cool breeze down from the mountain. Lanterns hang near doorways, flickering with candles. The cobblestone streets aren't crowded, but enough people are out that we earn a few curious glances.

I've braided my red hair into a rope and tucked it into a belted jacket I've borrowed from Jacob. Tycho carries the pelt over his shoulder, while Grey has the antlers strung together across his back. Tycho and I each have a dagger at one hip, while Grey is the only one to carry a sword. Tycho scowled at that, but Grey said it would be unusual for simple trappers to carry many weapons.

I think of that man and his daughter again. He only had one knife at his belt.

Kill them, Nolla Verin said.

Ah, Sister.

Grey glances at me, and he must take note of my expression, because he frowns. "You look troubled," he murmurs.

I inhale to speak, then remember I am to be mute. I have no idea how to explain it all, so I shake my head, then shrug.

He moves closer. "No harm will come to you."

He thinks I am nervous about the town. I probably should be, surrounded by people who've likely seen the destruction caused by my mother's soldiers, but I am not. Rhen's guards have moved on, and Blind Hollow seems quiet and peaceful.

Still, there is something charming about his reassurance. My annoyance dissipates. I look back into his earnest eyes and nod.

Tycho inhales deeply. "Do you smell the food?"

I hadn't, but as soon as he says that, I realize I *have* been smelling food. The road is bordered by small houses and shops, but ahead there appears to be a larger establishment, with a wide thatched roof and a massive chimney spilling smoke into the air. No walls close the people in, and men and women seem to be coming and going from all sides. The scent of roasted meat fills the street, with the bitter scent of mead floating over it all.

"We'll start there," says Grey. "Hopefully we can find a buyer tonight, or someone willing to allow us to trade for horses."

A sign hangs from the corner of the roof, naming the tavern the Rusty Rooster. Tables of all sizes line the floor, and most are occupied. Grey shifts past those to head for the bar in the center of the room, where he gestures for us to sit.

The barkeep is an older man, tall and thin, with a thick beard and a shiny bald head. He offers us a bright, disarming smile. "Travelers!" he says genially. "Welcome to Blind Hollow. I am Eowen. Mead?"

"Water, if you have it," says Grey. "I am Rand. This is my sister, Mora, and my cousin Brin."

Eowen provides a pitcher and three mugs, then adds a platter of dry biscuits, jam, and cheese. "You look a bit road weary." He turns that smile on me. "Rough travel, girl?"

I wonder just how *road weary* I look. I touch my fingers to my mouth and shake my head.

Grey says, "Forgive her. My sister cannot speak."

"Eh?" Eowen laughs and slaps the bar. "She'll make a man a lucky husband, then!"

I scowl.

Grey laughs. "Indeed."

I knock over my mug of water in his direction.

He's quick and jumps back before it does much damage. I offer a simpering smile.

I expect a glare, but instead, he gives me a crooked smile, his eyes twinkling. "She doesn't know her own strength, either."

Oh. *Oh.* He's *teasing* me. My heart flutters wildly. I give the barkeep an apologetic glance as he wipes down the bar.

Tycho clears his throat and reaches for a biscuit. "We have fur to trade, if anyone in town is buying."

"There's always a market for fur, especially with winter coming." Eowen sighs, losing his smile. "We lost our local trapper, too. Poor man was killed by those vicious fiends from over the mountain."

My heart trips and stumbles in my chest.

Those vicious fiends from over the mountain.

Eowen sighs. "Now we've got the Royal Guard coming through town, looking for some kind of magesmith. Supposed to be the heir to the throne, if you can believe that. One man's as good as another, I say. No one's cared about Blind Hollow in years." He pauses. "Are you from the north? You'd know."

"I'm from Wildthorne Valley," says Grey. "I do know."

Eowen's face falls further. "Now that's a town filled with sadness. I heard there was a woman whose children were slaughtered one by one. It was done in the dead of night, they said. No one knew who did it. She showed up in the town square, covered in blood."

Beside me, Grey goes very still.

"It was after her oldest son earned a place in the Royal Guard," says Eowen. "Can you believe that? To earn that monthly silver and lose all your children?"

Grey clears his throat. "A terrible burden, I'm sure."

"What happened to your trapper?" says Tycho, his voice hushed.

The barkeep shakes his head. "Fredd. Good man. One of his girls got away. She said it was a slaughter. Those animals shot him right in the back."

I'd been piecing together the words about the woman losing all her children, but now my blood turns to ice.

I wish I could speak.

I have no idea what I would say.

"Is your sister well?" says Eowen.

Grey glances at me. I have no idea what he finds on my face, but his own eyes have gone cold and dark and inscrutable. His expression reminds me of the first night I met him. It's almost frightening.

He glances back at the barkeep. "Lingering effects from the fever that stole her voice, I'm afraid."

I try for a simpering smile again, but I'm not sure I manage it. I likely look addled.

Eowen gives me a narrow look. "Ah." Something across the tavern catches his eye, and he says, "Here's Fredd's daughter. She'll know where you can get a good price for your hide. Raina! Girl, this man has a fur to sell."

It takes everything I have to avoid following his gaze. I seize Grey's arm. My nails dig into his skin, but I can't help it.

He leans in close. "What's wrong?"

A girl's voice at our back shyly says, "I can take you to the blacksmith, sir. His son does a lot of leather and fur work. He was one of Father's best customers."

Oh, I can hear the sadness in her voice. My heart stutters in my chest.

I have no idea whether she will recognize me, but I cannot turn around. I cannot.

I am sorry, I want to say. *I am sorry.*

I remember how Harper said the same words to me, and how I rejected them.

Grey straightens, and I keep my eyes on my mug. My hand still has a tight grip on his forearm. "That would be very kind," he says. "I am sorry to hear the news of your father."

He pulls at my hand. "Come now. The girl can help us."

I can't risk her recognizing me. "We have to run," I hiss at him.

He doesn't question me further. His eyes darken with understanding. "Act ill," he breathes in a rush. "Collapse."

I ease off the stool—then allow myself to fall.

"Lia Mara!" cries Tycho.

He used my name. I hiss in alarm as Grey catches me. A collective gasp goes up around us.

"Should we fetch a healer?" a woman calls.

"A fainting spell," he says. "She has them often." To my absolute shock, he swings me up into his arms. Part of me wants to protest—but another part of me wants to stay *right here*. I press my face into his neck to hide my eyes. He smells faintly of woodsmoke.

"The girl knows me," I breathe against his skin. "I was there. In the woods."

"Forgive me," he says to Eowen. "It seems we must return to our camp until my sister can recover. Perhaps I can meet this blacksmith in the morning?"

There's a moment of silence. I force myself to keep my face turned away from the girl, though I am *desperate* to see how this is being received.

"Of course," she says.

I feel Grey offer her a nod. "Come," he says to Tycho, and then we turn.

Conversation begins to return to normal around us. We're just travelers with something to sell, just a bit of a passing oddity, nothing too interesting.

My hair is caught on Grey's arm, and I twist my neck a bit. The braid spills free of my jacket collar.

"Wait." Raina's voice calls from behind us. "What did you say your sister's name was?"

"Mora," says Grey. "Forgive me, I would like to make it back to our camp before full dark."

"No, the boy just called her something else." Raina's tiny voice gains strength. "I heard you."

"She knows," I say against his neck.

"We're going to need to run," he says. "When I put your legs down—"

"Eowen!" Raina calls. Her voice is broken and full of pain, but she's yelling, "She was there! She's the one!"

My feet hit the street. Grey's hand finds mine. Tycho is right by my side.

Shouts fill the air behind us, but we sprint across the cobble-stones. I'm not fast, but my heart lends strength to my legs, and we fly through the town, cutting between houses, ducking through alleys. A cold wind rushes through the streets, and I know Iisak must be near. Night has claimed the sky, offering shadows and darkness everywhere we turn. A woman screams as we dash through her yard.

My heart pounds. "We'll lose them in the forest," Grey says, almost dragging me. "We'll loop around this house and disappear into the trees."

Iisak screeches overhead. It sounds like a warning.

We know, I think. *We're running.*

We take the corner sharply, and I shove my feet into the ground, ready for a full out sprint.

Instead, I run straight into a gold-and-red-adorned guardsman.

CHAPTER TWENTY-EIGHT

GREY

Isak was wrong. Rhen's guardsmen haven't moved on at all.

I do not think they expected to find us—and they definitely were not prepared for us to run directly into their midst. One of them spins Lia Mara around to put a knife at her throat, but he still looks genuinely surprised to find us here.

He looks equally surprised when the tip of my sword finds the pulse point of his neck.

"Let her go," I say.

Half a dozen soldiers draw their weapons, but I do not lower mine. Lia Mara's eyes are wide and panicked, her fingers digging into the buckled bracer on the soldier's arm, trying to drag his blade away from her neck. It's less convincing than my sword, but either way, he doesn't let her go.

At my side, Tycho pulls his dagger.

As always, I wish he would run.

The shouts that have followed us from the tavern grow louder, and a crowd spills around the edge of the house. The shouts become a cacophony.

"Is it the heir?" they're asking. "Right here in Blind Hollow?"

"They found him with her, just like they said. Do you think they'll kill him?"

My eyes don't leave the soldier trapping Lia Mara. "I can kill you before you kill her." I apply a bit of pressure, and blood wells at his neck. He grunts and grits his teeth, but his grip tightens. Lia Mara makes a small sound. Her eyes clench closed, but no blood appears at her neck.

"Drop your sword, Grey," says a familiar voice from the darkness. "We have you outnumbered." Dustan moves forward until lantern light finds his features. His sword is in his hand as well, but none of the men have attacked me.

My thoughts have gone cold and dark after the conversation in the tavern, after the reminder of my mother and what she endured from Lilith. When I was a guardsman, I learned to turn off emotion and do what was necessary.

I can do that now.

"Let her go," I say. "I will not ask you again."

The soldier sucks away from my blade, but he keeps Lia Mara trapped in his grip. One of her arms hangs limply, and I wonder if he's dislocated her shoulder in the struggle. She whimpers, and a tear slips down her cheek.

The crowd's noise has dulled to a hushed murmur at my back.

There are enough soldiers here to overwhelm us. Surely one has an arrow trained on my chest right this moment. But instead of arrogance in the soldiers' expressions, I find wary regard.

It's more than just worry for the soldier at the end of my sword.

It takes me a moment to realize they're afraid of what happened in the castle courtyard. Of what *I* did in the courtyard.

"He's just a recruit," says Dustan. "Don't kill him for following orders."

"Then give him new orders."

Lia Mara gasps again. Either her movement or the guardsman's has pressed the blade into her skin. Blood appears in a crimson stripe on her throat. Her useless arm dangles against the front of his body. Another tear follows the first.

"She's the one who saved me," calls a small voice. It's Raina, the girl from the tavern. "I told you, Eowen. She's the one."

"The Crown is out for blood!" yells a woman.

Dustan's eyes flick from me to the crowd of people at my back. Rhen allowed fear to dictate his actions, and now his people are turning on him. "We'll let her go," he says to me, "if you lay down your sword."

"I've heard that before," I say.

"Don't believe him," shouts a man.

"They killed a man in Kennetty last week!" shouts another.

A piece of red fruit sails out of the darkness to hit the recruit in the head. Another quickly follows. Then what looks like a fistful of manure, thrown by an older man.

"Stop this!" yells Dustan.

Lia Mara's dangling hand brushes the hilt of the recruit's dagger. It's in her hand—and then it's in his thigh. She's loose and he's screaming before I even realize what's happened.

A brick sails out of the crowd and hits the recruit in the face. He swears, and it knocks him to the ground.

Other guardsmen surge forward. I don't know if they're starting for the crowd or for us, but more fruit and bricks start flying. I grab Lia Mara's hand. Her neck is bleeding, but she's on her feet. The other soldiers have swarmed forward to meet the rising crowd.

"Grey—" she starts, but I shove her at Tycho.

"Get her out of here," I say to him. Then I step into the fray.

"Return to your homes!" the guardsmen are shouting, but they're quickly drowned out by shouting.

The people of the town have weapons ranging from axes and staffs to a few swords. I'm stunned at how quickly the crowd grows to surround us. Their targets are the Royal Guard.

Dustan and his men are trained swordsmen, though, and people from the town fall—quickly. In my years in the Royal Guard, we were never ordered to turn against the people of Emberfall. We never needed to. This is worse than when Rhen was a monster who attacked his people. At least then, he had no awareness of what he was doing.

Blood is in the air, and my blade swings and blocks and parries, but I can't stop them all at once.

Silver arcs through the air, and I raise my sword to block—just as a fist strikes the side of my head. I go down, a booted foot on my throat, staring up at two guardsmen. One raises his arm, ready to drive his sword right down into my chest. The other aims for my face.

A sword drives into the first man's side, right at the base of his armor. Above me, an inhuman screech splits the night, and the second soldier lifts from the ground, only to be slashed by claws. Both crumple around me.

I blink, and Jacob is holding out a hand to me. His other hand holds a bloody sword. "Are you hurt?"

"No." I take his hand, and he pulls me to my feet. A short distance away, Noah is on his knees, trying to help a villager with an arrow through his leg. Behind him, a guardsman lifts his sword.

Jacob must see it at the same instant. "Noah!" He tries to rush forward, but he'll never beat a sword.

I swipe the throwing blades from the guards that fell around us, and just as quickly, they're spinning free of my hands. The guard standing over Noah takes one in the neck and one in the head. He falls almost instantly.

Jacob spins, his mouth open in surprise, but I'm already swiping more blades, aiming for the guards that have rushed in to replace the others. "Cover my back," I say to him.

He does, just as another guardsman appears out of the darkness. I'm ready with a throwing blade, but Jacob surges forward with his weapon fearlessly.

Iisak screeches again, and another guard is lifted from the crowd. Blood rains from his skin, and people scream. Others cheer. The scraver's wings beat at the night sky, and the soldier's body drops, just as lifeless.

"Retreat!" Dustan yells, and the strangled panic in his voice is clear. "Retreat!"

The remaining guardsmen turn and run.

A cheer rises from the townspeople. Blood speckles many faces. Arms are upraised in victory.

Noah is still on his knees in the mud. He's trying to help one of the fallen guards now, but I can tell from here that it's a lost cause. Beside me, Jacob is breathing heavily. "What the hell just happened?" he says.

I'm scanning the faces around us, the bodies on the ground. "Did Tycho and Lia Mara make it to the woods?"

"We met them halfway. We saw the guards turning back, and we were coming to warn—"

A hand closes on my arm, and I whirl, a knife half raised, but I find myself facing a middle-aged woman with graying hair in a long, ropy braid. "The guards were after you," she says.

A man with missing teeth presses close and speaks with a hush in his voice. "The winged creature answered your call."

"They said the heir has magic!" calls another man. "Did he conjure the creature?"

"You helped drive them away," says another woman.

"What's happening here?" says Jacob.

I pull away from the townspeople and reclaim my sword from where it's fallen. "We need to get to the woods."

The cheering has stopped, but I'm gaining more attention. A murmur runs through the crowd. Torches swing close, sending a flickering light across dozens of faces. I long for the days when I was invisible because all eyes were on the royal family. I keep my eyes down and push through the crowd. Hands reach for me and people press close as I pass, brushing against my bare arms, my clenched hands, my back. Every instinct I have cries for me to draw my sword and force these people to disperse, but I cannot. They drove away the soldiers. They *helped* me.

Jacob is not as patient. He falls back a step and yanks his sword free. "Hey! If you think he might be your heir, then back off."

It earns us a circle of space in which to move, and I stride forward.

I glance at him. "My thanks."

He holds my eyes a moment too long. "No problem."

Ahead, a group of people is clustered around someone on the ground. More torches flicker in the night, along with a few lanterns. A woman is crying. Blood coats the road.

As we draw closer, I realize the crying woman is the one on the ground. Her clothes are soaked in blood, her hands clutching her swollen belly. Even in the torchlight, I can tell her skin is ashen. Behind me, Jacob swears.

A man and a girl are kneeling beside the pregnant woman. The girl has the woman's hand clasped between her own.

When the girl looks up, I realize it's Lia Mara.

She did not run. She did not hide.

"Grey," she says, her voice wavering. "Grey, you have to help her."

"I'll find Noah," says Jacob.

I drop to a knee beside the woman. Tears have formed tracks through the blood on her face. Brown eyes blink up at me. "The baby. I'm going to lose the baby." She clenches her eyes and more tears flow.

"No," says Lia Mara softly. "No, the baby will be fine."

A knife hilt protrudes from the woman's abdomen, buried just below her rib cage.

Lia Mara's eyes meet mine. I see the plea there.

Breath eases from my lungs. This is more than a slice across the wrist. This is more than half-healed whip marks.

Jacob reappears, skidding on the blood- and mud-slicked cobblestones. "Noah is helping a guy who got trampled by one of the soldiers' horses." Then he must see the knife hilt as well, because he lets out a breath and says, "Whoa."

I look at the woman. "May I touch you?"

She nods. Her eyes are wide and glassy. "Please," she whispers.

Her breathing is ragged and fast, and I suspect her lung has been nicked by the blade. "Please."

I watched my mother bear eight other children. This woman does not seem large enough to be far into her pregnancy, though I am far from an expert. I am better at taking lives than preserving them. I place my hand near the knife hilt. Throwing blades are not very long, but they're long enough to do some damage. If I pull the weapon, she could bleed to death.

Under my hand, her belly twitches and shifts. The woman gasps, and fresh tears roll down her cheeks. "It moved."

Lia Mara smiles. "See? Your baby will live." She saves the worry in her expression for me. For this baby to live, the mother needs to live.

The stars in my blood sit ready, flickering beneath my skin. I try to remember the way it felt with Lia Mara or with Tycho, how the magic leapt from my skin to theirs. I press both hands around the hilt and try to clear my mind. The woman whimpers.

"Shh," Lia Mara says. She leans down close and presses a hand to the woman's cheek. "Look at me," she croons softly. "Your baby will be fine."

"Jacob," I say, my voice low.

"Yeah."

"Pull the knife."

He does not hesitate. The blade slips free. The woman cries out. Blood pours over my hands. The stars under my skin spark and flare and swirl.

Blood continues to flow.

"It's not working," says Jacob.

I take a breath and focus. I press my fingers against the wound, but it does nothing to stop the blood. The magic refuses to make the leap to save her. She'll be dead in minutes.

"*Gently,*" whispers Lia Mara.

Gently. I think of Tycho in the loft. I think of Lia Mara whispering against my fingertips. The stars spin and sparkle and begin to crowd my vision, adding light to the world. I need them to be faster, to close this wound and save this young mother. Lia Mara compared this to swordplay, but she was wrong. This is like grabbing hold of a sunbeam and telling it where to shine.

But the sparks and stars swirl more readily now, moving where I direct. Blood no longer flows over my fingertips. A fluttering brushes against my hand. The baby moves again.

I blink, and the stars scatter. The woman's chest lifts, and she lets out a sigh. Her eyes have fallen closed.

"The bleeding stopped," says Jacob.

I move my hands and widen the tear in the woman's clothing. No wound exists anymore.

I drag a wrist across my suddenly damp forehead and let out a breath.

"She is healed!" yells a man at my back, and a cheer goes up among the crowd. "He has magic!"

"It *is* the heir!" says a woman. Her voice lifts to cry out to the crowd. "His magic healed Mina!"

Then she drops to her knees.

I suck in a breath, but a man behind her does the same. Then another. A murmur runs through the crowd, and they all begin to kneel.

"We need to leave this place," I say to Lia Mara. She nods quickly.

When I stand, I expect to have to push through the waiting people, but to my surprise, Tycho stands there. Blood is in his hair and in streaks on his cheeks, but he looks uninjured. A small boy hangs in his arms, wailing.

"The guards trampled people to flee," Tycho says. "His leg is shattered."

A woman pushes past Tycho to drop to her knees in front of me. Her clothes are mud spattered and her hair has pulled loose from a braid. She grabs for my hand, clutching at me with surprising strength. "Please, Your Highness. Please help him."

I want to flinch at the title—but flinching feels like a luxury when people are truly suffering.

I nod at the woman. "I'll try."

CHAPTER TWENTY-NINE

LIA MARA

By the time night begins to give way to dawn, exhaustion has sunk its claws into all of us. We are given the finest rooms in the finest inn that Blind Hollow has to offer. I have a small room to myself, and a platter of food has been left beside a roaring hearth. The innkeeper brings buckets of warmed water for washing, along with clean clothes and a set of combs for my hair. After days of trudging through the woods, I am glad for the simple blue dress with a laced bodice.

Once I am clean and clothed, though, sleep seems to linger a long way off. I sit before the fire and press a trembling hand to my neck. Noah applied a bandage, but it's still sore.

No man has ever put a weapon to my throat. Not even when Rhen's guards captured me.

A soft knock raps at my door, and I jump. For the first time in my life, I regret my lack of guards—my lack of weapons. I'm frozen in place.

A voice calls from the other side, soft in the early-morning silence. "It's Grey."

I release a relieved breath and move to open the door. Grey has clearly been offered similar hospitalities. He's clean-shaven for the first time since we met in Rhen's castle, and his dark hair is damp and tousled. His trudging clothes have been replaced with fresh dark trousers and a loose knit shirt. He's kept all his weapons, I see.

I cannot decide which Grey I like more: rugged, with work-roughened hands and shadowed features in the dim light of a campfire, or this Grey, keen and sharp with eyes that see everything.

He seems surprised to find me at the door. "The others are sleeping. I thought you might be as well."

I shake my head.

He touches a finger to my chin. "You were injured."

My heart flutters, and I slap a hand over the bandage on my neck. "Hardly." My voice has gone breathy, both from remembered fear and attraction, and I have to clear my throat.

If he offers to heal it, I will refuse. His exhaustion is so potent I can almost feel it myself.

His hand drops anyway. "Iisak is watching from the roof. After they doubled back once, we suspect the soldiers will return with reinforcements." He pauses. "We cannot stay here. I will not bring bloodshed upon this town again."

I raise my eyebrows. "Does this mean you will not sleep?"

"It does."

I step back and hold open my door. "Do you care to come in?"

He hesitates. "You should rest."

"So should you. We can be stubborn together." I move away

from the door to allow him the choice and stop beside the table of food. "The innkeeper has left a carafe of wine."

He shakes his head. "Wine will have me on the floor."

I smile and pick up the pitcher of water instead. This might be the most surprising thing I have discovered about him. "Truly?"

He nods and accepts the glass of water. Despite the quiet, his eyes flick to the window, to the doorway.

"You are uneasy," I say. In a way, it's reassuring that I'm not the only one.

"Dustan will not allow us to gain a lead. I would ride out now, but the others need to sleep."

"So do *you*," I say.

He shrugs and drinks half the glass in one swallow.

"You're a good leader," I say.

He makes a face, then shakes his head. His voice is rough and tired. "I am leading no one."

I drop into one of the chairs by the fire and study him, my eyes wide. "Surely you don't mean that."

"Surely I do. Noah and Jacob seek a path home to Disi. They will follow me until I can grant it. Tycho has nowhere else to go. You are returning to your homeland." He drains the rest of the glass and refills it. "I don't think Iisak truly follows anyone at all." He glances at me. "May I sit?"

"Of course."

He removes the sword belt and lays the weapon beside his chair. He braces his arms on his knees, then runs a hand through his damp hair. He looks as though he could sleep sitting upright, and sheer strength of will is keeping him awake.

I think of the way he dragged himself through the woods for

miles, while his back was a mess of bleeding welts. I think of his quiet, encouraging voice in the dark of the woods when we were carrying that massive buck. *Another step,* he kept saying. "Don't you realize that if you woke them all and insisted we ride out this instant, they'd be dressed and ready in minutes?"

A muscle twitches in his jaw, but he says nothing.

"You were commander of Rhen's guard. Surely this is not a surprise."

"That is different."

"A lot of people in this town would follow you, too," I say. "Do you have any idea what you did for them?"

"Led vicious soldiers here?"

"*Fell siralla!* You did not lead those men here. Rhen *sent* those men here. They did not have to attack the people of Blind Hollow." My voice gains an edge. "No soldier needed to plant a knife in that woman's belly. That would have been a killing blow."

"I know."

His voice is soft and full, and I expect him to say more, but he falls quiet again.

I feel as though I have learned so much about him over the past few days, but so much remains a mystery. I spent so long hoping to be named heir, to be able to provide a better life for my people, and Mother handed it to Nolla Verin. Grey seems to be the opposite. He does not want the Crown, though it seems destined to fall squarely into his lap.

"The guards were afraid of you," I say.

He nods, and his eyes flick to the mark on my neck. "They should have been afraid of *you*. I never realized you were going for his dagger."

"I am the daughter of a queen. I know how to defend myself." Despite the words, my voice nearly wavers. *Knowing how* and *needing to* are very different things. "Would you really have killed that man?"

"If he tried to harm you? Yes."

He says the word so simply, but it sets my heart pounding again. "That should bother me."

"Why?"

I swallow and look down at my hands. "Because I truly do want peace between our countries. I mocked you for using violence as a means to settle conflict."

"It is not weakness to wish for peace."

"I can wish for peace all I want, but it didn't stop that blade at my throat." My eyes feel hot. "It didn't stop them from hurting so many people."

"We saved as many as we could."

He did that, along with Noah, Grey helping the more critical while Noah patched up minor injuries. By the time the townspeople retired to their homes, I had the impression they might build him a throne right in the town square.

Grey sighs. "And there will be no quelling this gossip."

"Why would you *want* to quell this gossip?"

He looks at me, and his eyes are full of exhaustion and sorrow. "I have no desire to take Rhen's throne, Lia Mara. I have no desire to harm his guards and soldiers. This is why I fled Ironrose. I do not want to drive Emberfall apart."

"Rhen's guards attacked these people. He issued orders to find you that caused his subjects to turn on each other. The man flayed your back open. He did the same to Tycho. I do not think you are the one driving Emberfall apart."

Grey flinches. Almost imperceptibly, but I see it.

"Forgive me," I say.

His eyes lift, finally, and find mine. "Did your mother kill that trapper? The one the barkeep spoke of?"

I go still, then look away. "Her guards did. My sister gave the order."

"And what of that girl Raina?"

I swallow. "I saw her in the woods. She saw her father and sister executed." I hesitate. "I allowed her to get to safety."

His gaze feels like a weight on my skin. I have to fight to meet his eyes again. "The barkeep mentioned a mother in Wildthorne Valley who lost all her children. Your mother?"

"Yes." He pauses. "Or no, in fact. But the woman I thought was my mother." He's quiet for a moment. "The enchantress killed them all as a means to manipulate me. When we were trapped by the curse."

I long to reach out and touch him, but I am unsure how he would receive it. "Lilith sounds truly terrible."

"She was."

It's no wonder he wants nothing to do with magic. It's no wonder Rhen fears it so deeply. The sorrow hangs over this room as heavily as the exhaustion. "It was not the magic that made her terrible, Grey."

He runs a hand over his face, and for the barest moment, I see a flicker of vulnerability in his expression. He hides it well, under this veneer of the terrifying guardsman, but he's hardly older than I am. We're both trapped by duty and circumstance, both trying to do what we can to protect our people.

"What will you do when we reach the mountain pass?" I say to him.

He raises his eyebrows in question.

"Will you accompany me into Syhl Shallow?"

When I first offered this solution, my goals were squarely in order: to prove to my mother that I can be as effective as my sister, in my own way. I would bring the heir to Emberfall right up to the steps of the palace, and for once, I would be the lauded sister. But now, after spending days in the woods with this man, I am unsure what answer I am hoping for.

At Nolla Verin's side, he would be great. I have no doubt. He has a streak of vicious practicality that would match hers, I think. I like his streak of gentle vulnerability so much more. If he stands with my sister, I doubt I'll ever see it again.

Grey studies me. "After what has happened here . . . I cannot stay in Emberfall."

The words jab at my heart, and I straighten, chasing the pain away. "My mother is prepared to assist you in claiming your throne."

"She will be disappointed."

"She will be very convincing."

His gaze sharpens. "What does that mean?"

"She will offer you silver. Any lands of your choosing. Military force. Command of her entire army, if you wish it. She is very driven to claim access to the waterways of Emberfall." I pause. "She will offer you my sister—if Nolla Verin does not offer herself first."

"None of those things will sway me, Lia Mara."

I think of that moment in the woods when the night was so quiet around us and his thumb traced across my lip. *Stupid man.*

"My sister is very beautiful," I say. "You should not refuse blindly."

His eyes are dark and intent on mine. "I am not refusing blindly."

My cheeks warm, and I look away. My eyes skip across his broad shoulders, down to the corded muscles of his forearms. I caught glimpses of him in battle, when the soldiers and townspeople clashed, and for the first time, I understand why Rhen's guards had to drag him into the castle courtyard in chains.

It must have cost him something great to allow that to be done to him.

When I lift my gaze, Grey is watching me, and my blush deepens.

"Forgive me," I say.

His eyes spark with something like mischief, but a little darker, a little warmer. "If you must ask for forgiveness, then I should as well." He glances away then, a stain of pink on his cheeks. "Now you see why I have no head for wine, to be so forward without it."

The great warrior, blushing over a bit of wordplay. I smile— but my own exhaustion catches up with me, and I have to stifle a yawn.

"You should sleep," Grey says softly.

I do not want to sleep. Every day that passes will bring us closer to Mother's palace, and an end to . . . whatever is between us.

Because of that looming end, I cannot ask him to stay.

I don't know if he's misreading my silence, but he rises from the chair and deftly buckles his sword into place. "I will leave you to your rest," he says.

He's by the door when I say, "Grey?"

"My lady?"

He's never called me that, and it sends a spark through me. I know it is a simple mark of respect, but now, between us, it feels intensely personal. *My lady.*

I stop in front of him. The door is open, so I speak softly. "I have not yet thanked you for saving my life."

His voice is equally quiet. "You saved yourself."

My cheeks warm again. "Do you think the soldiers will return?"

"I do. And soon."

I shiver, thinking of that man's blade against my throat. When I swallow, I can feel the sting and the burn. I press a hand to my neck involuntarily.

Grey's eyes are heavy and dark in the shadowed doorway. "I will guard your door."

"I should not trouble you to—"

"I may not want to be king, but I know how to be a guard." He brushes a finger along my jaw. "Fear not. No one will touch you again."

Now I shiver for an entirely different reason.

I have so many things I want to say—so many things I don't know *how* to say.

Before I can figure any of it out, Grey reaches for the door handle and pulls it closed between us.

CHAPTER THIRTY

GREY

We're given breakfast at daybreak, so much food that we can hardly eat half. The finest horses the town has to offer wait to carry us wherever we want to go. Everyone we encounter is deferential. Ladies curtsy and men bow when we pass, and we leave a trail of whispers in our wake.

All of it makes me decidedly uncomfortable. I am nothing to these people. I am fleeing Emberfall, not saving it. Every time someone calls me *Your Highness*, I flinch and expect to see Rhen.

I'm tired and irritable by the time we're on horseback, and I'm not the only one. Lack of sleep has done no one any good, but if Dustan and his men plan to circle back, we need to be quick and we need to be cautious. We gallop straight west from Blind Hollow, though it will add half a day of travel to the mountain pass. The heat of the sun presses down, but we ride on, desperate to get some distance between us and the town. Iisak soars high above, until he looks less like a creature out of a fairy tale, and more like a black hawk riding an air current.

When the sun blazes directly overhead, I slow my horse to a walk, and the others follow suit. The animal's neck and flanks are damp with sweat, so I turn into the tree line to head for the creek. When I dismount and give the horse its head, its muzzle plunges into the icy water.

"We will rest for half an hour," I say. I crouch on the bank and run a handful of water over the back of my neck.

Nearby, Tycho all but falls to his knees on the muddy bank. His cheeks are red, and he splashes water over his head before drinking it. A few yards downstream, Lia Mara is doing the same. I watch the water trickle over her neck, the end of her braid trailing in the water. Her cheeks are pink, too, tendrils of hair stuck to her forehead.

"Grey."

I straighten to find Jacob beside me. His shirt is damp, his dark hair thick with sweat. His eyes are worn and irritated. "Half an hour?" he demands.

"We should hardly stop that long."

"Everyone is exhausted. We got like two hours' sleep, and we've been riding hard all morning." He pauses, his voice lowering. "Maybe the others won't say anything to you, but *I* will."

He might have saved my life last night, but I hold no illusions about it being done for my benefit. He needs me to get him home—and he's been needling me since the morning I woke chained in the wagon. I take a step, closing the distance between us. My voice is equally low. "If you can't manage the pace, stay behind."

"Don't be a dick. I'm asking you for a day to rest—"

"A day." I laugh without any humor. "Dustan would cut our throats in our sleep. Do you need a nursemaid, too, Jacob?"

He shoves me hard, right in the chest.

I shove him back, and he nearly falls. He recovers more quickly than I'm ready for, and he tackles me around the midsection. We both go down in the icy creek. The cold steals my breath—and then the water closes over my face as he pins me.

I land a punch in his side, and it grants me a few inches of freedom to suck in a breath before Jacob swings a fist that cracks me right in the jaw. I'm underwater again, his hands trapping me there. I can't get leverage. I can't breathe. The stars wait under my skin, ready to heal me, but they can't fill my lungs with air.

Without warning, his hands fist in my shirt, and he jerks me up. I cough and gasp for breath.

"A day," he says viciously.

"Half an—"

He shoves me underwater again, and this time I distantly register Lia Mara and Tycho shouting at him. My hands are tight on his wrists, my fingers digging in, but he holds fast.

The magic waits, sparks and stars under my skin. Lilith used to draw blood with barely a touch. Surely that's not so different from healing. Pulling apart instead of putting together. Golden light begins to cloud my vision, flares of sunlight on the inside of my eyelids.

Harper will probably hate me forever if I kill her brother, but right now it's a risk I'm willing to take.

I send the sparks into his wrists. He shouts and throws himself back. I drag myself out of the creek, coughing a lungful of water onto the muddy bank beside me.

Jacob is still kneeling in the water, cradling a wrist against his chest. Blood stains his shirt, but it must not be too bad. His eyes are murderous instead of panicked.

"It's not just for them, you idiot," he says, his voice full of derision. "You're exhausted, too. There's no way I should have been able to pin you."

I cough again. My throat feels ragged and raw. We've generated an audience. Lia Mara and Tycho are on the bank, their eyes worriedly going from me to Jacob. Noah is in the water, trying to pry Jacob's arm away from his chest. Iisak crouches on the bank of the creek, waiting.

I don't look at any of them.

The worst part is that Jacob is right. I *am* exhausted. He shouldn't have been able to pin me. He shouldn't have been able to land a punch at all.

I drag myself out of the water, then shove wet hair out of my face. "Fine. You can have until nightfall." Without looking back, I head to where the horses are tethered to check our supplies.

No one follows.

I'm glad. I watch the others drift back into their quiet activities. Noah and Jacob are building a fire. Tycho looks like he's trying to coax Iisak into a game of cards, and Lia Mara asks to play as well. She glances in my direction as if intending to invite me to join them, but whatever she finds in my expression convinces her otherwise, because she looks back at the cards while Tycho deals. The thought sours my darkening mood.

Last night, Lia Mara said I was leading. She's wrong. I feel as though I'm flailing. Even when I was guard commander, I had a regimented set of duties. I had a plan. A chain of command. The prince gave orders, and I followed them.

Now, I have nothing. I have myself. Syhl Shallow might be the right destination—or it may very well be the wrong one.

Despite everything that has happened, I long for Rhen's counsel. A near-eternity trapped by the curse meant that I knew what to expect from him, and he from me.

Rhen, I think. *What would you do?*

He would not ally with Syhl Shallow. I know that much.

I sigh, dropping to sit against a tree. My eyes sting from the water in the creek, so I rub at them. Exhaustion begs me to leave them closed, so I do, just for a moment. My hand falls into my lap.

"Yeah, I knew you were tired."

I startle awake, my hands scrabbling through dirt and undergrowth for a weapon before I realize it's only Jacob. The sky at his back has turned purple, the sun a sliver to our west, peeking over the mountain ranges. I'm disoriented and panicked for a moment, but his expression isn't troubled, and all is quiet. The scent of our cooking fire wakes my belly with a vengeance. I don't even remember falling asleep.

I drag a hand across my face. "How much time has passed?"

"Not enough. Here." He holds out a steel bowl. "Eat while it's hot."

I take the bowl, and it's warm, filled with shredded meat, a hunk of melting cheese, and a heel of bread that we brought from Blind Hollow. My clothes are still damp, but hunger is more pressing, so I draw my legs up to sit cross-legged, then dip the bread into the food. I should likely thank him, but I don't. My mood still feels prickly and bitter, and I need no reminding of the way Jacob held me under the water.

When he drops to sit in the leaves across from me, his own bowl in his lap, my fingers go still. I glance up. "I am better rested now," I say darkly.

He scoops up meat and cheese on the corner of his bread. "Is that your way of saying you're going to kick my ass? Shut up and eat your food."

The words are easy, lacking venom. Not repentant, but close. We're a good distance from the fire, and it puts his eyes in shadow. I sigh and lift the bread to my mouth. We eat in silence for the longest time, until the sharp edges of my thoughts soften into something less volatile.

Jacob eventually sets his bowl aside, then pulls a cork from a bottle I didn't realize he'd carried. He holds it out to me first.

I hesitate, then shake my head.

He takes a long swig, then says, "This is why I like you better than Rhen. He wouldn't have sat here."

He's right. Rhen's pride wouldn't have allowed it. I use the remnants of my bread to scrape the last bit of cheese from the bowl. "Don't worry. I'll kill you when I'm done eating."

He smiles, but it's brief and flickers out. "You gave me hell on the road from Rillisk to Ironrose, telling me I was pushing the guardsmen too hard. You were doing the same thing."

"You were rushing needlessly. I'm trying to keep us alive."

"So am I."

My hands go still again, and I look up at him.

Jacob's expression doesn't change. "You might have noticed that last night."

When he saved my life. I scowl. "You just need me alive to get you home."

He swears and takes another draw from the bottle, then gives a humorless laugh. "Wow."

I frown and say nothing.

"You don't trust anyone at all," he says, "and I think *that*, more than anything, is what's going to bring you down."

"That is not true."

"It *is* true. You didn't trust Rhen enough to tell him who you are. You don't trust Lia Mara enough to fully commit to taking sanctuary in Syhl Shallow. I just watched you run yourself into the ground because you didn't trust the town to keep you safe—and I have a feeling I'm going to watch it again and again until Dustan puts a sword through your back."

"We were putting the town at risk—"

"Whatever. They drove those guardsmen out of there. They would have done it again. We could be sleeping in a bed right now instead of sitting in the leaves." He pauses, and his eyes are like fire. "You don't trust *me* enough to listen when I say people need to rest. You don't trust me even though I jumped into a battle to *save your life*."

I'm not sure what to say.

"You keep treating me like this bumbling idiot," he snaps, "but I'm not reckless, and I'm not weak. I held my own in DC before we ever came here, and I can hold my own in Emberfall. I got your ass out of Ironrose after Rhen tore you and Tycho apart. And I didn't just save you last night. I killed one of Rhen's guardsmen. I put *my* neck on the line. I'm ready to ride into enemy territory with you. You think this is all on the off chance that you might one day be able to get us home? Are you *kidding me*?"

"Jacob—"

"I'm not done. I know you spent like four billion years trapped in that castle with no one but Rhen, and I won't even tell you what Noah thinks that must have done to your mental state, but—" He breaks off and makes a frustrated noise. "He wasn't your friend, Grey. He had an eternity to be your friend, and he *wasn't*. Even when you were dragged back to that castle, even after *everything*, he treated you like a criminal."

"Rhen is protecting his kingdom."

"You're not his guardsman anymore. You owe him *nothing*. Stop acting like you do." I flinch. He takes a swig from the bottle again and sighs. "You saved Noah's life last night, Grey. You saved *mine*. I might have made you swear an oath to me, but we've moved way past that."

I didn't realize.

I should have.

"Forgive me—" I begin.

"Oh, shut up. Here." Jacob holds out the bottle. The amber liquor swirls and glitters in the light from the distant fire.

I inhale to refuse, but I am struck by his words. *You're not a guardsman anymore.*

I seize the bottle and upend it, swallowing fire.

Jake snorts. "Okay, take it easy, tiger."

I cough and hand it back. "That tastes terrible."

"I know. It's fantastic. That Eowen guy said it was the best he had." Jacob takes a long swallow himself. "More?"

I should refuse.

I don't. This sip burns as much as the first. My thoughts feel loose and scattered already.

Jacob is watching me. "I'm surprised you and Rhen weren't lit every day of that curse."

"He was. On occasion." On the last night of the final season, Rhen and I shared a bottle of sugared spirits and toasted our failures.

He encouraged me to escape the curse, to find a new life away from Ironrose.

He was trying to protect me.

I have long thought we should have been friends, Grey. That's what he said the day I was dragged back to the castle.

He flayed my back open the next day. Out of fear of the unknown.

He had an eternity to be your friend, Jacob said.

Suddenly I want to drain this whole bottle. For that reason alone, I shove the cork back in. "We will reach Syhl Shallow in a day's time," I say, and my voice has gone husky.

"That's what Iisak said, too."

"Lia Mara claims she can assure our safety, but I would like to offer the illusion of strength all the same."

"What does that mean?"

"Perhaps you should ride at my side."

"Like a servant?"

"No." I pause. This feels like it might be a bad idea, but my ability to care is quickly vanishing. "Like a second-in-command."

He pulls the cork free and takes a swallow. "I'm not like you. I can't be like you were to Rhen."

No. He can't. He might not be reckless and weak, but he is headstrong and impulsive.

Maybe that's not a bad thing.

Jacob is studying me. "Or are you just trying to do the same thing Rhen did?"

"What do you mean?"

"Are you trying to fake it?" His expression darkens. "Are you asking me to sit on a horse and look like hired muscle?"

I hesitate.

He rolls his eyes and goes to take another drink from the bottle.

I reach out and pull it away from him. We're both a bit drunk now, and my words feel fuzzy and a little more honest than I'm ready for. "Would you be able to do it *without* faking it?"

His eyes meet mine, and I think he's going to be flippant and defiant about this, the way he is about most everything.

Instead, he says, "Yeah. I could."

"Taking orders requires trust, Jacob. You would have to trust me."

"Like . . . not try to drown you?"

I lift my eyes skyward. "Forget I asked."

"No. I can do that." He pauses. "If you can trust me when I say you're wrong." He draws back his sleeve, where more than a dozen stitches lace up the skin of his wrist. "Instead of doing this."

My eyes widen. "You have my word."

He puts out a hand. "Deal."

I clasp it. "I may regret this when I'm sober."

"Yeah, same." He tries to jerk the bottle back from me.

"Enough." I hold fast. "We are still in danger, Jacob."

"Fine." He sighs and lets go. "And, look. If we're going to be friends, you're going to have to start calling me Jake."

CHAPTER THIRTY-ONE

LIA MARA

For the first time in days, the mood among our traveling party carries little tension. I'm playing cards with Noah and Tycho and Iisak, though the scraver seems more focused on the distant conversation between Jake and Grey.

"Can you hear them?" I say softly.

He gives a short nod, then lays a card on the pile between us.

"You shouldn't eavesdrop," says Noah. He adds another card.

"I cannot help what I am," says Iisak.

"Are they going to kill each other?" says Tycho, and his voice says he's not entirely joking.

"No," says Iisak. He pauses and surveys the cards in his hand. "The young prince is wise."

I glance over at where the young men are speaking, but they've already risen and are approaching the fire. I quickly look back at my cards.

"Your Highness," says Iisak. "Join us."

"I've told you to stop calling me that," Grey says, but his voice holds no rancor. He eases to the ground beside me unsteadily, then rubs at his eyes.

Jake trails his fingers across Noah's shoulder and says, "I'm going to crash for a few hours."

"Crash?" I echo.

Jake grins. "Sleep." Noah's hand comes up to cover his for a brief moment, then lets go. Jake disappears into the darkness.

I watch him go, very conscious of Grey at my side. I've been worried about him since the fight with Jake—no. In truth, since we rode out of Blind Hollow.

"You didn't kill each other," says Tycho.

"Not yet," Grey drawls.

"Jake is a good guy," says Noah. He rearranges the cards in his hand, then adds one to the growing pile.

Grey makes a noncommittal sound. "I have asked him to ride at my side when we enter Syhl Shallow."

Noah looks up. "Really."

Grey nods. "We will need a show of strength if we can manage it."

I look across at Iisak, meeting his coal-black eyes. Now I understand what he meant about the prince being wise.

Tycho has gone still beside Noah. I can read the emotions as they cross his face, as easily as words on a page.

I would have ridden at your side.

But you do not think I am strong enough to offer a show of strength.

Tycho recovers quickly, then lays down his cards. "I believe I will *crash* too." He uncurls from the ground.

Grey is no fool. "Tycho."

Tycho stops. Waits. The firelight flickers off his eyes.

"This is not a slight," says Grey.

"I know." He slips into the shadows effortlessly.

Grey watches him go, then sighs. "Silver hell." I think he might go after Tycho, but he puts out a hand. "I'll take his cards."

We play in silence for the longest time, the fire crackling beside us.

"Tycho is young," Grey says eventually, his voice very quiet, "and small for his age—"

"Like I said, he would follow you off a cliff," says Noah.

Grey sighs again.

"Tycho would have kept riding today," I say. Even I know Jake was right. I might not agree with his means, but I could see Grey's exhaustion all morning. He still looks sleepy, his eyes heavy-lidded.

"Jake is a good choice," says Iisak, his voice bringing a cold breeze to make the fire gutter. "Karis Luran respects strength."

Grey glances at me. "What else does she respect?"

I blush and look down at my cards. "Strength and virility. She says she chose my father because he had the most kills in battle. He is quite a powerful general in the northern part of Syhl Shallow." I don't like to think about his prowess on the battlefield, to wonder if I would have been a disappointment to both a father *and* a mother. It's bad enough to be a disappointment to one.

"He does not rule at her side?"

"Oh, no. He has no place in the palace. I do not even know him. She merely chose him to father her firstborn. She chose another when she desired to have another child."

No one says anything, and I look up from my cards to discover I have everyone's attention.

"You don't marry in Syhl Shallow?" says Noah.

"Oh. Some do. But the queen can choose her . . . her mate." My cheeks turn pink. "A queen needs no king to stand at her side."

"But she was willing to marry your sister to Rhen," says Grey.

"She'll marry Nolla Verin to you, too, if you'll claim the throne."

Grey says nothing, and I don't have the courage to look at him. I remember his quiet voice in the inn last night. *I am not refusing blindly.*

My cheeks feel warm again, my blush fed by his silence. I can feel the weight of his eyes.

"In truth," I say, "I do not understand following the lineage of *kings*, when it is the woman who bears the child. And what should birth order have to do with whether someone is fit to rule?"

Grey plays a card. "Here, we believe in fate. That is why the firstborn is considered heir. Because fate delivered that child into the world first." He glances at me. "And the mother may bear the child, but she did not put it there herself."

"So *fate* chooses your heir," I say. "You leave such a thing up to chance?"

"How is that any different from leaving the choice up to one individual?" He flips a card onto the pile and misses by a few inches.

I study him more closely. "Grey—are you unwell?"

Noah chuckles. "At least Jake had the sense to go lie down."

Grey clenches his eyes shut. "I told you I had no head for spirits."

My eyebrows go way up. Now I understand the slow drawl of his words. "You're drunk?"

He rubs at his eyes. "Perhaps a bit."

Noah's still smiling. "Jake's pretty smooth." He looks at Iisak. "What about your people? Do you have a king or a queen?"

"We have one ruler," the scraver says, and the breeze that sweeps among us is so cold that it makes me shiver. "Though I have been gone so long I no longer know who holds power." His eyes shift to me. "Your mother may know."

"What will she demand of you?" I say. "For breaking the treaty."

"Likely more than I will be willing to give."

I think of my mother, and I know he is not wrong. When he asked for the right to accompany us into Syhl Shallow, he said Mother holds something of great value to him.

Iisak lays another card on the pile. Frost tips the corners, melting into the leaves below. "I will pay whatever price she demands and return home."

I can't tell if the note in his voice is longing or disappointment—or both. "What does she have?" I say quietly.

"Something quite dear to me." He pauses. "I did not want to leave the ice forests. The scravers are not great in number, and our females can only bear one child in their lifetime. When the mage-smiths were destroyed, we were left vulnerable. The treaty with Syhl Shallow gave us some protection. To break it puts all at risk."

"It must have been very dear," says Grey, "for you to risk all you did."

"I did not intend to be gone this long." Iisak smiles ruefully, baring the edges of his fangs. "I did not intend to be captured."

"I saw you fight in Blind Hollow," says Noah. "How *did* someone capture you?"

"A bit of misplaced trust and a well-timed arrow." He lifts his arm to trace a black stripe that must be a scar. The line disappears under his wing. He glances at me. "I will be very grateful for an intercession with your mother, Princess."

"Of course." My cheeks warm, and I frown. "Though you should know that my mother rarely accepts my counsel. I may not be any ally at all, Iisak."

"Protecting her child should carry weight," he says.

I give a humorless laugh. "One would think."

"I would be greatly in your debt."

"I will do all I can," I say, and mean it.

Grey looks at me. "Your mother is a fool if she does not accept your counsel. I do not know your sister, but I find it hard to believe her wisdom and compassion surpasses yours."

Like earlier, his voice is a little too intent, his words a little too honest.

"My mother does not value *compassion*," I say.

"Then she is a fool."

I laugh softly. "You said that already."

"Rhen should have listened to you. Negotiated with you. You would care for the people of Emberfall."

"Yes," I say somberly. "I would."

"He was a fool as well."

Across the fire, Noah laughs under his breath. "You should get some more sleep, Grey."

Grey hasn't looked away from me. "You escaped through the fireplace."

I smile. "Yes. I did."

His eyes are so serious. "You stopped to help Tycho."

"I remember."

He's not smiling. "You risked yourself, Lia Mara." He pauses. "You could have been discovered."

I inhale to answer, to say that I couldn't have left that boy hanging and bleeding along the wall any more than I could have let my mother kill the trapper's daughter hiding in the woods. But Grey's hand lifts to trace the spill of hair that hangs along my face, and my breath catches.

"Brave girl," he says.

No one has ever called me brave. They've called me clever. Sturdy. Studious. Kind.

Never *brave*. My heart thrums in my chest.

In the distance, the sky rumbles. Iisak's wings ruffle, and he looks up. "The air promises rain soon."

Grey's hand drops. "How soon?"

"Within the hour, I would think."

My heart won't stop racing, but Grey gathers the cards. "Wake Jake and fetch Tycho. We'll need to find shelter."

The rain pours down before we're ready, darkening everyone's mood. The mountains tower to our left, hulking and black in the midnight darkness. My heart trips and stumbles at the sight.

Home. Home is on the other side. I might be in my own bed tomorrow night, surrounded by plush blankets and stacks of books and all the warm tea I can drink.

And Grey, who will likely be thrust at my sister. Thrust into accepting his birthright.

I'll be thrust into the shadows while more important people do more important things.

The thought stings, and I shove it away.

We ride into the hills, water soaking into our clothes. The tack turns slippery, and the horses skid in the mud, but our persistence is rewarded: we find a cave. It's not very deep, but it's wide enough that we can tether the horses out of the rain and build a fire to warm ourselves. I have fresh clothes from Blind Hollow in my pack, and though they're a tiny bit damp from where water breached the leather stitching, the leggings and blouson are a far sight better than drenched skirts. I strip out of my boots, leave the men by the fire, and move to the other side of the horses to change.

Once I'm done, I spare a quick glance over to see if they're finished as well. Grey's back is to me, and he's changed into clean dark pants, but he's still shirtless. The sight steals my breath and stops my heart. More than half a dozen scars bisect the muscles across his shoulders, thick dark lines marring the perfection of his skin.

I saw it happen, and it was terrible.

Seeing the aftermath is terrible.

Grey begins to turn, as if sensing my gaze, and I busy myself with adjusting the horse's tether. When I look up again, he's fully dressed, and he's crossed half the cave to reach me.

I swallow and wonder if he noticed me staring. I'm not sure what to say. Either the rain or the time in the cooler air has sobered him, because his eyes are clearer and sharper than they were by the fire.

I clear my throat. "Forgive me," I say. "I was—I was looking to see if you were done."

"I am." He puts a hand on the neck of the horse beside me, rubbing beneath its mane. He's so gentle with animals that it always takes me by surprise. Nolla Verin will like that about him, I think.

My throat is tight again.

"We will reach Syhl Shallow tomorrow," he says softly. "I would like to ride out before sunrise. The rain should give us a cover and allow us to reach the mountain pass unseen."

I nod, because I have no idea what my voice will sound like.

"What kind of force will we encounter on your side?"

It takes me a moment to parse out the question. He did not approach me for quiet conversation; he is seeking military strategy. Any emotion between us is locked in my thoughts, not his. I clear my throat and look away.

"We . . . we have soldiers stationed at the pass." I have to clear my throat again. "They should recognize me, but they will likely hold us at the guard station until someone can come from the palace to retrieve us." My mother will not have me riding through the streets looking like a rat pulled from a gutter.

His eyes trace my face. "Thank you."

He looks like he's about to turn away, so I clear my throat. "Grey."

He waits. "My lady?"

I'm not sure what I want from him, but I don't want this moment to end. I want to sit by the fire and teach him Syssalah. I want to touch *his* lips and whisper secrets in the dark. I want to step into him, to press my face against his chest and listen to his heartbeat. I want to trace the scars on his back and tell him how he did not deserve one single mark.

My face must be on fire.

Brave girl.

I'm not brave at all. I can't do any of that.

He touches a finger to my chin. "You should sleep. Home awaits you."

I swallow. "I don't want to sleep."

"I don't either."

His hand lingers against my face, and I shiver.

"Are you cold?" he says. "Come sit with me by the fire."

I shouldn't. We are so close to Syhl Shallow, and I have one chance to prove to my mother that I have something to offer. But Grey takes my hand and pulls me forward, and it's like he's taken hold of my heart.

When we sit, we're both cross-legged, his knee brushing against mine. I'm very aware of the contact, and I long to move closer, to feel more of his warmth instead of the fire's. I put my hands in my lap and keep my eyes on the flames as Noah and Jake unroll blankets for sleeping. Tycho is already half asleep on the other side of the fire.

When Grey stands, I look up in surprise, wondering if he's changed his mind. He must read the dismay on my face, because he offers half a smile. "I'm just getting some food," he says softly.

When he returns, he has cheese and dried beef, along with a water skin.

The dried beef reminds me of Parrish and Sorra on our last night together, and I turn it over in my hands.

"You seem sad," Grey says.

I glance up. "I was thinking of my guards."

"You were close," he says.

"Yes." I swallow past a lump in my throat. "It was my fault Sorra died."

"If she died keeping you safe, I believe she would see it as a great honor."

"Would you have considered it a great honor to die for the prince?"

"When I was a guardsman? Yes."

He truly believes that. I can hear it in his voice. "And now?"

He tears a piece of meat in half. "I knew what he would do when he found out what I was. I keep wondering if I should have just told him that first day, when I was dragged back to the castle. I wonder if things would have turned out differently."

"I think you made the right decision." I have to swipe a tear off my cheek. "I should never have tried to bargain with Rhen. I don't know why I thought he would be honorable."

"He can be." Grey pauses. "He cares greatly for his people. He was raised to be a king."

"I care greatly for my people, and I was raised to be a queen." I wipe my eyes. "That doesn't mean I should be."

He reaches out to capture a drop with his thumb, his hand lingering on my face. "I do not know your sister, but she must be impressive indeed for your mother to choose her over you."

I think of Nolla Verin and wonder if she is thinking of me. "She is," I whisper. "She will make a great queen." Another tear spills, but Grey is quick to catch it. His hand is against my cheek now. My heart flutters wildly in my chest.

"You would make a great queen," he says. "I have no doubt."

I put my hand over his. My eyes fill again. "And you would make a great king."

His expression changes, and he begins to pull his hand away, but I press it to my cheek and blink the tears away.

"You swore your *life* to him," I say. "I know enough of you to see how that must weigh on you. But did you swear your life to him alone, or did you swear your life to him as the ruler of Emberfall?

Your duty was not to the man himself, Grey. Your duty was to his country. *Your* country."

He is no longer trying to pull away. His eyes are dark and intent on mine.

"You're not arrogant," I say. "You are not cruel. You say Rhen is a man of honor, but I believe *you* are." My voice breaks. "I saw it in Blind Hollow. Your people would love you. If you would give them the chance. If you would give *yourself* the chance."

His other hand comes up to cup my face. "Please—please do not cry for me."

"Ah, *fell siralla*." I clench my eyes shut. "I am not crying for you, stupid man."

"Then why are you crying?"

"I am crying for me," I say. "Because you are a prince. More than a prince. A great man who should be king."

"Lia Mara." He's so close. His breath brushes against my lips. His hands are warm and sure on my face. I want so badly for him to close that distance. I want to fall into him.

I want . . .

His lips brush mine.

I gasp and draw back. My heart is wild in my chest. I stare at him, at the firelight painting sparks in his hair, at the heady intensity in his gaze.

I want so much. He's so close, and I long to undo the last moment in time, to press my lips back against his. The night presses in around us, and it would be so easy to forget that we are anything more than two people sharing shelter from the rain. I want more than his hands against my face, against my neck. I want more than I've ever wanted before.

I put my hands on his wrists and pull them away.

Because of everything I want, I cannot have him.

"I am crying because you are a prince," I say softly. "And I . . ." I let out a breath. "I am not a princess."

CHAPTER THIRTY-TWO

GREY

The next morning, as the clouds lighten at our back, we ride through the mountain pass toward Syhl Shallow.

I slept little through the night, worried that Dustan and his men would wait to ambush us before we could reach the pass, but a dense fog has rolled in with the chilled morning air, granting us a reprieve.

We stay quiet despite the misty cover. Iisak flies high overhead, invisible through the clouds. For now, Lia Mara rides at my side, but her gaze is trained ahead. Her back is straight and her gaze is clear, but her mood seems as heavy as the weather around us.

Mine matches.

I feel the way I did during that moment in Ironrose Castle, when my heart was begging me to dig in my heels and resist. Once I cross the border into Syhl Shallow, there will be no turning back. Seeking assistance—even sanctuary—from Karis Luran is as treasonous an act as I could conceive, short of driving a blade straight into Rhen myself.

I wonder what Dustan will report to him about what transpired in Blind Hollow, how the people turned against the guards and supported me. How we fought alongside Rhen's subjects and drove the guards and soldiers out of the town.

If I aim to fool myself, I am failing. Crossing the border will not be my first act of treason.

Considering the secret I kept, it is likely not even my second.

A horn sounds through the valley, loud and repetitive.

Lia Mara gasps and lifts her head. A large shape looms ahead of us. Green and black pennants hung high above snap in the wind. For the first time this morning, her eyes brighten.

I've heard their horns before, when they rode into Emberfall to lay siege. My hand itches to draw my sword.

Iisak floats down through the clouds to land at the back of our party. He told me this morning that he does not wish to approach in an offensive manner. If we have anything in common, dread for this moment seems to be it.

Right now, I wish for his claws and fangs and brutality to be at my side.

I remind myself again that I am not here to fight. Nor am I here to surrender.

My heart pounds in my chest, disagreeing.

Shapes appear in the mist ahead of us. Soldiers on horseback, clad in green and black. A dozen at least. Most carry crossbows.

They're all trained on us.

I force my hands to stay on the reins.

Lia Mara calls out to them. Her voice is joyous. Relieved. They shout back to her, and she looks at me quickly. Her voice is a rapid rush. "You must dismount. They want you to disarm."

I do not want to do either of these things. I want to turn this horse, gallop out of the pass, and ride straight for Ironrose to beg forgiveness.

No. I do not want that. Lia Mara's words from last night sit heavy in my thoughts, trapping me here.

I kick my feet free of my stirrups and swing off the horse, glancing back at Jacob and Noah, at Tycho, whose face is pale. They will follow my lead.

Run, my thoughts whisper, every moment of my training roaring at me to fight or retreat. *These are your enemies. You are outnumbered. Run.*

But they are not my enemies. Not now.

My fingers slip the loop at my sword belt, and the weapon drops to the ground. The daggers quickly follow. Behind me, I hear the others doing the same. My breathing feels shallow, but I step away from the horse and lift my hands to show I am unarmed.

Lia Mara is still talking, her voice melodic yet commanding. The Syhl Shallow soldiers move forward as a unit and stop a short distance away. The two in the center dismount, while the others keep their crossbows trained on us.

Jacob moves forward to stand at my side, his hands up similarly. His voice is very low, very quiet. "You don't look too sure about this."

"I'm not."

"Our weapons are still in reach. If you want to bail, say the word."

I glance over to see that he is serious. He is as fearless as Harper, and as brutal as I am.

"I underestimated you, Jake."

"Yup."

The two soldiers have reached us. They're both clean-shaven with black hair and cream-colored skin, though one is middle-aged, with gray threading the hair at his temples. His armor bears extra adornment, a leather cross dyed in green and black and outlined in silver, likely signifying him as an officer. He looks from me to Jake, and then behind us. Taking our measure in one glance. If Iisak startles him, he gives no sign of it. His cool gaze returns to mine.

When he speaks, his voice is very deep, very gruff, with a thicker accent than Lia Mara's. "You have escorted a daughter of the Crown safely to our border." He pauses, then extends a hand. "You have our thanks. My name is Captain Sen Domo. Welcome to Syhl Shallow, Prince Grey of Emberfall."

Prince Grey.

I say nothing to correct them.

⁂

Lia Mara was right. We're taken to the guard station and asked to wait for a dignitary from the palace. Unlike the redbrick buildings I'm accustomed to in Emberfall, this guard station is built directly into the side of the mountain, with walls of wood and steel meeting up against exposed rock. Few windows allow light, but torches burn in each room.

Everyone speaks my language, but I do not speak theirs, which feels like a disadvantage. I am certain *fell siralla* would not endear me to any of these guards.

Regardless, I keep my silence, because the tension here is thick and uncertain. Tycho hangs near me, or, to my surprise, near the scraver. Iisak has taken a place near one of the narrow windows, and the guards give him a wide berth. They watch us closely, though, more so once Lia Mara is escorted to a separate area. I remind myself that I once watched Karis Luran and her people with equal scrutiny, my own blade ever ready.

Eventually, food is brought, and we're granted a reprieve. The guards leave us alone, a heavy door falling into place.

Jake's eyes find mine. "Do you think we're locked in?"

"If not, there are guards waiting on the other side of the door."

Noah is the first to approach the food. The platter holds fruits and cheese, along with a wide slab of bread. He tears a small piece free but plays with it instead of sliding it into his mouth. "This feels like a holding cell." At my raised eyebrows, he adds, "Where they'd hold you before putting you in jail. In prison."

"Prison?" echoes Tycho.

"They won't put anyone in prison," I say, though I'm not entirely sure. Lia Mara made many assurances about her mother— but she also said her mother did not respect her. Karis Luran could toss us in a prison cell and negotiate with Rhen for my life—and Jake's too, as Harper's brother.

My eyes flick to the window. It's too narrow to fit through, though the misting rain has no trouble. The room is damp and cold and very much like a cell. Tycho pulls his arms more tightly against his body.

"You'll be all right," I say to him.

He meets my eyes, then nods.

Iisak uncurls from where he lounged against the wall. His wings are pinned in tightly, the only sign of his own tension. He selects an apple from the pile of fruit on the table and brings it back to Tycho. "Here," he says gently. "Eat, boy."

Jake watches this, then moves closer to me, keeping his voice down. "Does it bother you that they took Lia Mara?"

"She is Karis Luran's daughter. She is likely being questioned before we will be allowed to leave."

If we are allowed to leave.

The door swings open, and Captain Sen Domo enters. The stern expression has not left his face. I long for my sword. For anything.

He offers me a nod. "Your Highness. We will escort you to the palace. The queen is prepared to extend every hospitality to you."

This feels too easy. "And my people?"

His eyebrows flicker as if he's surprised by the question. "Why, yes, of course." His gaze drifts past me. "With the exception of your . . . creature. The queen will see him separately."

Tycho takes a step back. "No."

The scraver maintains his position by the wall. "Do not trouble yourself," he says. "They will not lay a hand on me." A low growl slides out with the words. "Is that not so, Captain?"

The captain's lip curls in distaste, but he says, "That is so." He looks back at me. "Your Highness? A carriage awaits."

CHAPTER THIRTY-THREE

LIA MARA

Clanna Sun, Mother's chief adviser, arrives at the guard station from the palace so quickly I think she must have galloped the entire way. She is an older woman, a former army general, with thick gray hair and a permanent limp from an old injury. Her face, however, almost always bears a tight smile, as if she's seen the worst things the world could offer, and she chooses to be in a good mood anyway. She has always treated me with dignity and respect, and I have always enjoyed our studies together.

She seems overjoyed to see me. Her face breaks into a wide smile, and she draws me into an embrace. "My dear, you have surprised everyone."

The words are a compliment and an insult woven together so neatly that I doubt Clanna Sun has realized the implication. She all but hauls me out of the guard station and into a carriage.

"But—but the others—" I protest.

"They are being well cared for. Your mother has insisted upon it." Clanna Sun gazes at me with something like bemused wonder on her face. "You have brought us the heir to Emberfall, Lia Mara. However did you do it?"

Warmth crawls up my cheeks, but I straighten my back. My heart is thrilling to see the glimpses of home outside the carriage window. "Prince Rhen tried to kill him. I offered Grey—" I catch myself. "I offered *Prince* Grey sanctuary beyond our borders, and he quickly agreed."

"As well he should." She clasps her hands beneath her chin. "Ah, yes. Lia Mara, this is cause for celebration indeed. When we heard of your little plan to attempt peace negotiations, we were all worried you'd never be heard from again."

That overshadows any praise. "Well, you did."

"Yes, yes." Her eyes glitter. "Tell me: Is Prince Grey prepared to make an assault on the throne? To claim it for himself?"

An assault on the throne. I swallow. "I believe it is a bit early to make assumptions."

She frowns but quickly covers it up. She fills the rest of the carriage ride with questions about Emberfall, about Grey, about that evil imposter sitting on the throne.

I long for the quiet escape of my room. My hair has dried into clumps, and I am desperate for fresh clothes. The warm bath in Blind Hollow seems like it happened a month ago.

When we reach the Crystal Palace, a wave of homesickness hits me so hard that I want to fling the carriage door open and sprint up the steps. The thousand windows of the front wall glimmer even in the cloudiest weather, and the two front fountains splash merrily. I can be calm and demure, befitting my station, but I cannot keep the broad smile off my face.

But then I see Nolla Verin standing at the top of the steps, her hands pressed together under her chin, and I throw the carriage door open to run.

Her ebony hair is long and unbound, reaching her waist, and her eyes are wide with relief and excitement. She looks younger than I remember, like a young maiden, not like the princess set to inherit our mother's throne.

The instant I get to the top, I wrap her up in my arms and swing her around.

"I missed you so very much," I say.

"And I you." Her slim arms are tight on my shoulders, and even when I stop swinging her, she holds tight. "After our spies reported what happened to Sorra . . . then, that you had escaped . . . I was so worried, Sister."

I draw back. "You know about Sorra?"

"Of course."

I glance up at the glass front of the palace, searching the faces of the guards stationed there. Many are familiar, but Parrish is not among them.

"Does Parrish know?" I ask quietly.

Her eyebrows knit together into a frown. "I am certain all the guardsmen know."

"I must see him. I must explain—"

"You have been gone for weeks, and you wish to see a *guardsman*? No, Sister. Do not be foolish." She pulls at my ragged clothing and makes a face. "Indeed the first person you should seek is a clothier." Her nose wrinkles. "Or perhaps a bucket of hot water."

I swat her on the arm, but she catches my hand and tows me toward the castle. Footmen draw the large crystal doors open as we advance.

"Come," she says. "You are the hero of the day, but we have much to accomplish."

"We do? I just arrived!"

"Oh yes." Her lovely eyes flash with intrigue. "Tell me everything. I wish to know all about this man I am to charm."

Hours later, I'm lacing a wide belt into place over black silk robes shot with threads of silver and green. My skin is freshly scrubbed, my hair washed and brushed until it hangs in a shiny auburn curtain down my back.

I rarely bother with any kind of cosmetics, but for the first time, I allow my attendants to trace my eyes with kohl and dab a bit of pink on my cheeks. Days of travel in the summer sunlight have brought out color in my face, and a new smattering of freckles cross the bridge of my nose.

"There." Nolla Verin claps from where she reclines on a chaise lounge. "My sister no longer looks like a gutter-sweep."

I make a face at her.

She, of course, looks lovely as always, eyes shining, a bit of glitter sparkling along her eyelids. Her robes are white with red stitching, her corseted belt bloodred. Her expression is cool and calculating, and I know she is already plotting how to "woo and charm" Grey.

The thought makes me turn back to my mirror. Even with a small amount of kohl and cream, I hardly recognize myself. I do not know why I bothered with any of it. I want to ask my attendants for wet cloths to wipe it all off.

"Mother will be here soon," says Nolla Verin. "She will want us to meet with the prince in the throne room."

Of course she will. I have learned that Grey and the others have been quietly brought to the palace and are receiving the same pampering that I have. Likely more. Mother will spare nothing to win his favor.

Nolla Verin sits up on the chaise. "Lia Mara."

Something in her voice makes me turn. "What?"

"You have said little about your time since escaping from Prince Rhen."

I look back at the mirror, then away, because I do not want to see my simple face, my eyes so filled with longing. Instead, I move to the window. The sun is beginning to break through the clouds, bringing a sheen to the city. In Emberfall, the castle was surrounded by acres of grass and forest, natural barriers between Rhen and his people. Here, our palace is built into the side of the mountain, and beyond the stables and training fields, we can look out on the Crystal City. Our people can look up and see their queen.

Nolla Verin appears at my side. Her hand slips over mine. Her voice is very quiet. "Sister."

I glance at her, surprised at the emotion in her voice. "Yes?"

"Did he . . . abuse you?"

"What? No!"

"Are you certain? Because you seem very different." Her voice heats with anger. "If he laid a hand on you in violence, I will carve every bone from his body, then fill every orifice with them—"

"Nolla Verin! Must you be so *graphic*?"

"I am making a *vow*. I will do it bare-handed."

"Well, I will thank you to stop turning my stomach." I make another face, this one nearly involuntary. "He never harmed me. Quite the opposite."

She flops back onto the chaise lounge. "Then tell me. Tell me about this Prince Grey."

Prince Grey. It is only the second time I have heard him referred to as *Prince Grey*, and both times my heart has fluttered. I think of the way he faced Captain Sen Domo, and I want to press a hand to my chest.

I keep my eyes on the window and my hands on the sill. I have no idea what to share about him.

He is gentle. He is kind.

No. Either of those would put him at a disadvantage with my vicious sister.

Both of those feel like secrets shared only with me. To everyone else, Grey is stoic and fierce.

He is honest and brave and loyal. He guarded my door when I was afraid to close my eyes. He is strong and sure, and he makes me feel strong and sure. He has dark eyes and careful hands, and I could listen to him speak all night long.

I swallow back tears. "He is very handsome?" I offer.

My sister says nothing.

I say nothing.

I wish I knew what expression was on her face, if she has figured me out, and if she has, what she is thinking. A breeze sweeps through the window to cool my cheeks.

All of a sudden, I want to lock my doors and hide in my room with my books and my pillows and my privacy. I do not want to watch whatever is going to happen between Grey and my sister.

Between *Prince Grey* and my sister.

I bite at my lip and try to breathe through the ache in my chest.

My doors sweep open, and a trumpet blares. The guard announces, "The Queen of Syhl Shallow, the highly esteemed Karis Luran."

I whirl without meaning to, as though I have been caught at something.

My mother looks exactly the same as I remember, but I know better than to sweep her up in my arms like I did with my sister. My mother will quite certainly not do that to *me,* especially not in front of a dozen advisers and attendants.

That said, her expression is warmer than I can remember in recent memory.

"My clever daughter," she says, holding out a hand.

Ah, so we are standing on ceremony. I should have guessed when the trumpet announced her. I cross the room, take her hand, and bow.

She catches my chin and lifts my head before I can complete the movement. "We have much to discuss, you and I."

"Yes, Mother."

"I was quite distressed when you rode off in the middle of the night on a fool's mission." Her hand has not left my chin. "I thought we might need to retire calling you *clever* at all. Luckily you seem to have redeemed yourself."

Perhaps I should have met with my mother before my sister. All my familiar defenses clink back into place, like forged steel. Trudging across Emberfall was difficult and exhausting, but never so much as this. I am already tired. "Thank you."

"Indeed," she says, "you should have known that man would attempt to use you against me. I am relieved you were able to escape, but I hope this little lesson did not go unlearned?"

My blood ices over, as if the Frozen River itself runs through my veins. My heart pumps twice as hard. "You . . . knew? You knew he had imprisoned me?"

"For certain, dear daughter. For certain." She lets go of my chin. "I would like for you to join us in the throne room as I discuss the terms with our new young ally."

He may not ally with you. He does not want any of this.

But, like the words I could not say to my sister, these are words I cannot say to my mother.

I close my mouth, steel my spine, and follow her into the hall.

CHAPTER THIRTY-FOUR

GREY

I am no stranger to finery and elegance. In Emberfall, Ironrose Castle is filled with marble and polished wood. Here, Karis Luran's palace is lined with crystal and stone, with glass everywhere. The clothes we are given are of the highest quality: brushed calfskin leggings, polished black boots with leather laces, tunics and jackets lined with silk and edged with brocade. Instead of green and black adorning the garments, which I expected, everything is trimmed in gold and red, the colors of Emberfall.

Our weapons have been returned to us, and while it's made to look like a show of trust, I know it's not. We are heavily outmanned here in the palace. We will be watched wherever we go.

I would give anything for the black uniform from my days in the Royal Guard, to have knife-lined bracers on my forearms and armor at my back. I would give anything to be invisible once again. In this fancy room with a glass wall looking out over a glass city, I feel like a beast in a cage. Noah, Jake, and Tycho all watch me. Waiting.

Waiting on *me*.

My heart is a steady thrum in my chest. I don't know how to do this.

This is different from when we were in the woods. Different from when I'd tell Tycho what horses to pull for the tourney. Different from when I was a guardsman.

As commander, I could give orders almost without thought. I know where to position guards, how to survey a crowd, how to determine who might hide a weapon or who might deserve greater scrutiny.

Lia Mara would know how to proceed. She was raised to be a queen—and it was stripped from her. As Prince Grey, I have been thrust into a role for which I am wholly unprepared.

Much like Harper, I realize. She stepped into the role of princess as if she'd been born to it. She made a good match for Rhen, relying on her wits instead of a lifetime of preparation.

Rhen always planned his moves out in advance. He was never comfortable thinking on his feet. But Harper was. She was often reckless and unconventional in her methods, but she would make a decision and act on it without hesitation.

I can do that, too. Guardsmen never have the luxury of advance notice.

I look at the others. "Karis Luran wants to use me against Prince Rhen. That is the only leverage we have here." I pause. "It is very little. Despite what happened in Blind Hollow, Rhen has been the crown prince since I was a child. His people know him. He rallied them once. Despite what is happening in Emberfall, he can rally them again. I have little doubt."

"He rallied them based on an alliance with Disi," says Jake. "And there is no alliance."

"That's going to break some major trust," says Noah. "The people already suspect something is amiss."

I glance at him. "Yes. There are no armies—and Karis Luran knows this."

"You have magic," Tycho says softly.

I flex my hand and look at my fingers. "But I have no armies. No crown. I have magic in my blood, but so far I have little talent for using it."

"I don't think saving the lives of a dozen people counts as *little talent*," says Noah.

"Karis Luran will not be impressed by the preservation of lives. She knows I was not raised as royalty. She knows I was a guardsman. She will expect me to yield and obey. She expects to use me as a pawn against Emberfall." I stop to collect my thoughts. "If I refuse to play along, she could refuse to offer sanctuary. Worse, she could hand us over to Rhen."

"Well," Noah drawls, "I don't think it's as bleak as all that." I look at him, and he runs a hand across his jaw. "Well, Rhen won't work with her. He wouldn't negotiate with Lia Mara, and he was ready to *kill* you. I don't know that he'd leap into an alliance at this point—and she wouldn't have been seeking one if she didn't need it badly. And no matter how he feels about Harper, he's definitely not going to risk his kingdom for Jake's life. We're not as powerless as you think we are."

I glance away. "Perhaps not. But I have no followers. I have no . . . no *subjects*. Parts of Emberfall may be rebelling against Prince Rhen, but some parts will *not*. He may not be able to raise a full army, but he has subjects who are sworn to him. Who will fight for him."

Tycho leaves his spot by the wall. He draws his sword.

"What are you doing?" I say.

He stops in front of me and, without hesitation, drops to one knee.

"Tycho," I say, my voice ragged. "Stop."

He lays the sword on the stone floor, then presses his hands together in front of his face. His eyes are intent and earnest. No uncertainty exists in his expression—only calm determination. "I swear fealty to you, Prince Grey of Emberfall. I swear my heart and my hands and my home, in service to you and in service to the throne. I swear my—I swear to be—" He stumbles over his words and looks aggrieved. "I forget the rest of what I'm supposed to say. But I swear to you." He swallows, and his expression is an echo of the look on his face when I said I had asked Jake to ride at my side, but he does not falter. "I know I'm just one person, but I will follow you. I will fight for you. I swear to you."

I should grab his arms, drag him off his knees, and remind him that this is treason. But as I stare down at him, emotion becomes a weight in my chest that will not lighten. This stopped being treason the moment Rhen strung up an innocent boy beside me in that courtyard. My heart has known it all along. My thoughts just needed to catch up.

Tycho is one person, but for so long, that's all Rhen had, too. I glance at Jake and Noah. I'm not alone here.

"Pick up your sword," I say to Tycho, and my voice is still rough. "Lay it across your hands. If you will swear, do it as a warrior."

Guards escort us to the throne room, led by Captain Sen Domo. Sunlight and warmth fill the space, and the windows facing the city must be fifty feet high. I have never seen such panes of glass. The back wall of the throne room is the solid rock of the mountain, deep reds and soft browns shot through with streaks of black and silver and gold. After growing up on a poor farm, Ironrose Castle left me as awestruck as Tycho when I first beheld it, but this is something different entirely. Torches have been set deep into the granite walls, flickering every few feet. A raised dais sits along the stone wall, with two thrones carved from onyx stretching high above their occupants. Guards are everywhere, but the four surrounding the dais are clad differently, their faces half-veiled in steel to make them androgynous, their weapons lighter and less obvious. The Royal Guard of Syhl Shallow.

Karis Luran sits atop the larger of the two thrones, her red hair framing a severe face of sharp cheekbones and cream-colored skin. She does not smile. To her left must be Nolla Verin, and I can see why Lia Mara spoke so highly of her sister's beauty. The girl is younger than I expected, her jet-black hair twisting in a shiny mass to pool beside her on the throne. Her skin is smooth and pale and perfect, with a pink curve of a mouth and eyes so light a brown that they appear gold.

Eyes that are not warm at all, but are instead calculating, conniving, and cold.

To her left, on a smaller chair set a slight distance apart, sits Lia Mara. After days in the woods, I'd forgotten how her red hair shines in the light, how her lips always look like they are keeping a secret that she'll share when the time is right. She looks lovely and warm and honest, and I wish with all my might that I could draw her down off the dais to stand beside me.

She will not meet my eyes.

You are a prince, and I am not a princess.

I didn't fully understand before. Now I do.

Karis Luran stares down at me. "I never thought to look down on a guardsman turned prince," she says. "Such a turn of events to benefit you."

The words sound like a compliment, but they are measured and weighed to remind me of my place. Luckily I spent years serving the royal family of Emberfall. I spent an eternity serving *Rhen*. She can try her best, but I doubt she'd come close to the nonsense I've endured.

"Yes, Your Majesty," I say evenly. "I never thought to look at you as a potential ally. How fate bewitches us all."

She smiles thinly. "You are more polite than your younger brother."

A jolt goes through me at the word *brother*, but I know better than to let it show. "Let us blame my common upbringing."

She laughs out loud at that, and this time her smile looks a bit more genuine. "I think I like you better, too." Her gaze shifts past me, to where Jake stands by my shoulder. "Is this Prince Jacob of Disi at your side?" she says. "Have you secured an alliance as well?"

I do not know if she is mocking me or trying to see if I would try to con her the way Rhen did, but either way, it does not matter. She suspects the truth—or likely *knows* the truth, if Lia Mara has spoken of our journey. "Disi was a farce to rally the people of Emberfall against your invasion."

Nolla Verin gasps out loud and whispers something to her mother.

I keep my eyes on Karis Luran. "Jake is a formidable ally in his own right."

"Indeed." She smiles. "We shall see."

That could mean anything.

"How fares the scraver we traveled with?" I say to her. "What has become of him?"

Her eyes glint with intrigue. "He has broken an accord with Syhl Shallow, Your Highness. He will be confined until I deem it appropriate to meet with him."

Again, I do not know if she is conceding something by offering me a title, or if she is mocking me—but all I can think of is Iisak, caged again.

"You seem concerned," says Karis Luran.

"He helped save my life," I say. "And that of your daughter." I pause. "I do not know of your treaty, but I believe he is due leniency."

She flicks a hand. "I will consider your words, but I do not wish to speak of that creature."

"As you say, Your Majesty." I offer her a nod.

Her gaze sharpens. Silver hell. A minor deferral, but she noticed.

Her lip curls up slightly. "I am certain you know we have sought an alliance with Prince Rhen."

"I do."

"As he is not the rightful heir, I presume we should seek this alliance with you."

"I am willing to hear your terms."

"You do realize I have far more to offer *you* than you have to offer me. I understand you arrived at my border with little more than the clothes on your back."

"Do you have *another* heir to the throne of Emberfall who is willing to hear your terms? I thought I might be the only one."

She goes very still. "Do not play with me, boy."

I hear the edge in her tone and find my own to match. "I am not Prince Rhen, and I am not King Broderick," I say. "Whatever sway you held over either does not apply to me. I may have walked into your palace with nothing, but that means I have nothing you can take from me."

"I can take your life," she snaps.

"Prince Rhen already tried," I say. "Send a message to your spy. Ask the result. I will wait."

She draws herself up, but I am more aware of Lia Mara sitting to the side, her eyes wide and fixed on me. When my eyes flick to hers, she looks away.

I turn back to Karis Luran and take a step toward the dais. "I do not seek silver, and I do not seek power. If I am to take the throne, if I am to *ally with Syhl Shallow*, it will be for the betterment of my people and the betterment of Emberfall. For no other reason. If you would like to discuss an alliance, we will face each other as equals, and we will negotiate our shared goals. But if you believe you can place a crown on my head and wield me as your puppet, you are very mistaken indeed."

Karis Luran sits back in her chair and regards me. After a moment she leans toward her younger daughter.

Nolla Verin stands, and she is more slender than her sister, with a slight frame and a narrow waist accentuated by a wide belt. Her hips sway as she approaches me. She may be quick with a bow and amazing on a horse, but she wouldn't have carried that buck ten feet.

Not just because of strength, though that's some of it. Because of temperament. Her gaze is coolly dismissive. She might have shot the stag, but she would have ordered others to carry it.

Lia Mara may not be the named heir, but she is still the daughter of the queen. Until now, I hadn't realized that in all our time in the woods, she never issued one order. She never made a single demand.

She sat in the mud to hold a dying woman's hand and begged me to save her life.

Nolla Verin extends a hand to me. "I am to be queen," she says, and even her voice is beautiful, soft and melodic. She leans into me, gazing up through her lashes. "I do not need a king to rule Syhl Shallow, just as you need no queen to rule Emberfall. But I hope that together we can prove to both our peoples that an alliance through marriage would bring peace and prosperity to all. Do you not agree?"

I take her fingers between mine and bow, as I've seen Rhen do so many times, barely brushing my lips against the back of her hand. I must be careful with this one. "We are in agreement, my lady."

When I straighten, she moves closer, until her hip brushes mine. "I believe we should have a small reception tomorrow evening, to celebrate my sister's safe return. I would like to introduce you to the Royal Houses, so you can learn all Syhl Shallow has to offer."

Her hand has not slipped free of my own. "I would be honored."

"And perhaps we can go for a ride tomorrow morning?" Her voice softens. "Privately?"

That feels like a trap. "Perhaps you can show me some of the mounted games you excel at," I say. "Your sister spoke very highly of your talents."

At that, Nolla Verin beams. "She did?" She glances at Lia Mara, and for the first time, genuine warmth fills her tone. "Thank you, dear Sister."

"Of course." Lia Mara's voice, by comparison, is wooden. "Everyone knows of your skills."

I wish she didn't have to do this.

I wish *I* didn't have to do this.

Nolla Verin looks back up at me, then gives my fingers a squeeze. "Until tomorrow, then, Prince Grey?"

"Yes, my lady. Tomorrow."

It takes every ounce of my strength to keep my eyes on her face, instead of looking past Nolla Verin to find the warm, inviting eyes of her sister.

CHAPTER THIRTY-FIVE

LIA MARA

The next morning dawns cool and clear, the last of the rain moving out, leaving wind roaring through the mountains. Sunlight glitters on the rooftops of the city, highlighting the raindrops left behind by the storm.

I'd hoped to wake to more rain, so Nolla Verin would be forced to postpone the demonstration of her riding skills, but that likely would have resulted in some indoor activity. The thought of my sister giggling over a game of dice, batting her eyelashes at Grey, is enough to make me want to burn down the castle.

All those days in the woods, I longed for the quiet comfort of my bedchamber, where I could hide with a book by the window, but today I am restless. I miss Tycho's quiet humor. I miss Noah's endless knowledge. I even miss Jake's surly sarcasm and Iisak's vicious talents.

Iisak. I do not know my mother's plans for the scraver, but I do know he was imprisoned before Grey freed him. I wonder how he is handling a return to captivity.

I have new guards waiting at my door. Conys and Bea. Both are female, both stern-faced and cold in their formality. Both chosen by my mother. The warm familiarity I shared with Sorra and Parrish is long gone. I want to find him and apologize. To share in his sorrow. To make things right. Every time I ask to see him, I am told that he has been assigned to other duties on the palace grounds.

Today, I will not ask. I will visit Iisak, and then I will do my best to find Parrish myself. I lace up a belt over my robes, loop my hair into a loose braid, and stride right past my guards without a word.

Conys and Bea fall into step behind me like silent shadows, but they do not question me. I am certain they will report my destination to my mother later, but hopefully she will be too consumed with courting Grey's consideration of an alliance to worry much about me. She always was in the past.

I deliberately take the longest route through the palace to avoid seeing Nolla Verin and Grey. Or my mother.

Instead, I turn a corner and nearly run straight into Tycho.

He falls back at once and stumbles over his words. "Lia Mara! Ah—forgive me. My lady." A blush lights his cheeks, and he attempts to bow. "Your—Your Highness?"

He's so earnest about everything he does that I can't help but smile. "Tycho. We are friends. Call me Lia Mara."

His eyes flick to my guards, then back to my face. "Things are different here."

That statement steals the smile from my face. "Not different between you and me, surely."

He grins. "As you say."

"Where were you hurrying off to?"

"Grey asked me to accompany him for his ride with Nolla Verin this morning—"

"Oh." My lips flatten into a line.

"—but your sister was quite convincing that they should be allowed to get to know each other privately."

I can imagine the scene perfectly. Nolla Verin would have rapped a riding crop across his knuckles in her effort to be *convincing*—though she probably wouldn't do it in front of Grey. "Oh, I am certain she was."

"Jake was turned away as well, but he said he was going back to bed with Noah." Another faint blush finds his cheeks.

"Well, if you find yourself without a destination, would you care to escort me to the dungeons?"

His eyebrows go up. "The . . . *dungeons?*"

"Yes. I am going to visit Iisak."

A breath escapes his lips. "Oh. We can see him? Yes. Yes, of course." Then his eyes widen. "Wait. One moment, please."

"Certainly."

He dashes down the hallway to return a few minutes later, looking rushed and flustered. He glances at my guards and stops his fidgeting, then straightens and offers his arm. That is not a custom here, but he is trying so hard, so I take his elbow as I saw ladies do in Emberfall. We walk arm in arm through the quiet torch-lit hallways.

"You look very fine," I say to him, and mean it. In the woods, he always looked a bit wild, his hair untamed and his eyes shadowed with watchful distrust. Today he is clean, his golden hair combed straight and tied into a queue. The cut of his jacket broadens his shoulders and the boots give him an inch of height, making him look less like a boy and more like a young man.

He glances shyly at me. "Thank you. So do you."

The stairs are well-lit, but Tycho hesitates before descending at my side. The dungeons are rarely occupied—and in turn, they are rarely guarded. The Stone Prison exists on the western side of Syhl Shallow to hold captives for any length of time. Only one guard waits at the bottom, a grizzly older man with a scar across one eye. He does a double take when he sees me, and stumbles to his feet, but offers little more than a nod and a curious glance. No one in this palace has ever had anything to fear from me.

"Your Highness," he says in Syssalah. "You have come to the dungeon?" He asks this as though I might be lost.

"Yes," I say. "I would like to see the scraver."

The guard grimaces and sucks a breath through his teeth. "He nearly took my arm off when I brought him breakfast. I think you'd be better served upstairs."

At my side, Tycho's hand has gone tense on my elbow, and I pat my hand over his fingers. "Iisak saved our lives on more than one occasion. I'll take my chances with my arm."

The guard nods and extends a hand toward the cells. "They put him in the last one."

I start walking, and he calls after me, "Tell that ungrateful creature that he's got the only one with a window."

When we reach the cell, I discover that the guard was right: a small window allows light down from near the ceiling. But the cell is by far the smallest, hardly eight feet square, nowhere near enough room for a man, much less a creature with a twelve-foot wingspan. Iisak's wings are folded in tight against his back, and he reclines in the shadows, his black eyes glittering in the torchlight. An iron bowl is upturned in the opposite corner, food splattered against the rock wall. I consider his diet of raw meat in the woods and wonder what they tried to feed him. It looks like porridge.

I wonder if that was on purpose, then consider the selection of this cell when so many others were available. I consider my mother.

All of this is on purpose.

I wonder what cost she will demand. I wonder if I can find out.

The scraver does not look surprised to see us. "Ungrateful, am I?" he says.

Tycho moves to the bars first. "Are you unwell?"

"I am in a cage, boy. Nothing in a cage is ever truly *well*." He bares his teeth at the guards lurking behind me, and I wonder what they would do if I attempted to press my hands against the bars as well.

Tycho dips a hand into his pocket and pulls free a handkerchief. "The servants didn't leave animal parts in my chambers," he says wryly, "but I brought you some sweet cakes and meat pies."

So *that* is what he went back to his room for.

Iisak looks startled by the offer, and he uncurls from the ground to take the wrapped food from Tycho. Those razor-sharp claws brush against the boy's fingers with surprising gentleness.

"My thanks." Iisak withdraws into the shadows again but does not unwrap the food. I wonder if he'll actually eat it.

"Do not let your kindness make you vulnerable," Iisak says. Those dark eyes shift to me. "The same advice applies to you, Princess."

"I am not worried about being vulnerable."

He smiles sadly. "Then it appears my advice is offered too late."

Tycho ignores his warnings. "Why are you in the dungeon?" he says. "Will you be harmed?"

"The queen is fond of bargains and debts. She has made it clear that my transgression will be costly. Have no worries, boy. I spent months in a cage. I can be patient."

"What will it cost?" I say.

He regards me silently in response.

I move closer to the bars, and Bea and Conys move with me, but they do not stop me. "Does she have what you seek?" I ask softly.

His eyes fall closed, and a cool thread of air swirls through the bars. "No."

No.

He could have made his way home secretly, but he took this chance.

"Are you sure?" Tycho says in a rush. "What if—"

"I am sure," says Iisak.

"What was it?" I say. "If you tell me, if I can help you—"

"You cannot help me." He sighs, and a coating of frost appears on the stone wall beside him.

"Please," I whisper. "Please let me help you."

"You cannot help me, Princess. Your mother will not yield to you. You know this as well as I do."

I blush. "I would still try."

"I know you would. That is why you need the lesson on kindness and vulnerability so very badly."

I frown.

Iisak waves a hand. "Enough of bargains and secrets. Where is our young prince?"

I don't want to think about Grey. I wish so badly that I hadn't pulled his hands away from my cheeks when we were whispering secrets in the cave.

I wish for so much, and wishing never works. I straighten my back. "Courting my sister. The *true* princess."

"*Courting?*"

"Yes."

Tycho glances at me, then glances at my guards and says nothing.

"I am not who you should be visiting, then," says Iisak.

I straighten my shoulders. "The queen would like to secure an alliance with Emberfall. I am certain Grey and Nolla Verin will get along quite well. They are due their privacy."

Iisak laughs, his fangs glinting in the light. Abruptly, his laugh shifts to a vicious growl I've never heard from him, and he pulls back farther into the shadows.

"Lia Mara." My mother speaks from behind me.

I jump and whirl and all but press my back to the bars. "Yes. Mother." Tycho looks as shocked as I do. He bows quickly and tries to pull into the shadows himself. I think he would tuck himself into the cell with the scraver if he could.

So would I. My mother's eyes are full of fire. "My plans for this creature are none of your concern."

"I thought—I thought I might be able to speak in his favor—"

"No. You may not. He has broken a treaty, and he is aware of the penalty. Return to your chambers at once."

I grab Tycho's hand and drag him with me before she can get any other ideas.

As we ascend the stairs, I hear her voice, low and brutal. "My dear, vicious creature. First we will begin with information, and then we will discuss what you can do for me . . ."

CHAPTER THIRTY-SIX

GREY

I would rather be back in the throne room facing Karis Luran, or back in the gritty arena of the tourney facing Dustan.

I would almost rather be in the courtyard of Ironrose facing Rhen.

In truth, I would rather be back in that cave on the border of Emberfall, my breath mixing with Lia Mara's. I should have kissed her. I should have bargained for her to be queen. I should have begged fate for one more night of travel, to see where this flare of attraction would lead.

Instead, I've been goaded into a horse race.

Nolla Verin sets a rapid pace into the city, cantering through the streets without regard for her surroundings. She's clearly a skilled rider, but she could do with a bit more regard for her subjects. More than one person dodges out of the way as we maneuver sharp corners and narrow alleyways.

Guards trail us, none leading, which surprises me. Perhaps they would have led, but Nolla Verin seems to be cutting her own crooked path through the city, leaving her guards to do their best to keep up. We lose some in the more crowded streets, as people are quick to yield ground to their princess, yet not as quick to avoid her Royal Guard. As a guardsman, I would have found it exhausting.

As the supposed heir to the throne of Emberfall, I also find it exhausting.

She holds the lead, but not by much. She has the advantage of knowing the city, of having a light mount that can bank and turn with little notice. She has the advantage of knowing the destination.

I'm beginning to think she wants to see if she can unseat me, but I spent more than three hundred seasons evading a monstrous beast through every forest in Emberfall. She can take any sharp turn she desires; she won't get me off this horse.

I should be enjoying this. I like horses. I like a *challenge*.

But I'm worried about Iisak. I'm worried about Lia Mara. I'd hoped to pass her as I followed Nolla Verin out of the palace, but the halls were mostly empty. I thought we might take a sedate ride through the Crystal City, during which I could ask after them both, but Nolla Verin bolted from the castle grounds and clearly expected me to give chase.

So I did.

I keep thinking of my discussion with Lia Mara, when we carried the buck through the woods, about how her people were not so different from mine. It's so directly at odds with my years of training as a guardsman, but her words weaseled their way into my thoughts and refuse to dislodge.

I want to meet Lia Mara's people.

I want to do it with her at my side.

Instead, I'm chasing her sister at a full gallop, the people and the buildings blurring into a sea of grays and reds and browns, the sun glinting off glass and silver-shot stone.

Ahead, a woman shrieks, and a small figure darts into the road ahead of us. Nolla Verin's glossy black hair streams behind her like a banner, and she shows no indication of stopping. I cannot reach her rein, but I put a heel into my horse, crowding her mount, forcing her horse to the side.

She shoots a surprised glare at me over her shoulder, but I've already looped my reins into one hand, and I sit down hard in the saddle. My horse responds immediately, hooves skidding on the pavement as I lean down to seize a fistful of fabric. I jerk the child off the ground and into my arms just before the guards gallop past.

The horse prances and fights my hold, wanting to rejoin the chase. I hold fast and look down at the child. She's about four, with shiny black hair and warm brown skin. Her expression is frozen in the space between wonder and terror.

"Be at ease," I say to her, though it's clear she does not understand the words. I make a silly face, and a tiny smile peeks through. I try another and earn a real one. "*Fell siralla,*" I whisper in a self-deprecating tone, and she giggles.

A woman appears beside me, speaking rapidly, her tone apologetic. Tears sparkle on her lashes. The little girl is already reaching for her, hands wide and clasping, and I ease her down to her mother.

Nolla Verin and the guards have doubled back to return to us, and the woman curtsies to the crown princess, clutching her daughter and speaking even more rapidly.

Nolla Verin ignores her completely. She looks at me, a curious smile on her lips. "That mother should have better control of her child."

"Her princess should have better control of her horse."

The smile vanishes. Her lips purse. In that moment, she looks very much like her mother.

I should not rile her. So much balances on what happens here. "Or perhaps your mount was traveling so fast that you did not see the girl."

A fraction of a smile returns to her face. "Perhaps. I noticed you had difficulty in keeping up with me."

"How could I not? You are clearly quite skilled."

The smile broadens and she turns away, paying the woman no heed. I am left with no choice but to follow or to emphasize her rudeness, so I nudge the horse forward and wish I had a coin to toss to the woman.

She calls after me anyway, words I cannot understand.

"What is she saying?" I say to Nolla Verin.

Her mouth tightens. "She offers her thanks."

"Ah."

She gives me a wicked glance. "Race you back to the palace?"

Eager to run over more innocents? I think. But instead, I say, "Of course, Your Highness. Do you care to take a head start?"

Her expression turns vicious, and her horse leaps forward. A taunting call floats behind her: "You will regret giving me a lead, Prince Grey."

No, I will enjoy a walk in the sunshine. I need a minute. Or an hour.

When Rhen was trying to rally his people to save Emberfall, he seemed to negotiate court politics effortlessly. One day in Syhl Shallow, and I wish I *could* find solutions to every problem at the end of a sword.

Two guards have hung back to walk with me. Their names are

Talfor and Cortney, both experienced enough in their roles that their expressions are mildly disinterested, though I can feel their eyes on me as we walk.

"We would not have trampled the girl," Cortney eventually says, and her accent is so thick that it takes me a moment to work out the words.

I nod, though I have no idea whether this is true.

"Nolla Verin is quite determined," adds Talfor. "She never yields. That is why she is so well-suited to be queen."

"An admirable quality, I am sure," I say.

"That woman did not simply offer her thanks," says Cortney.

Talfor snaps at her in Syssalah, and Cortney looks away. I know well the tone of a senior officer reprimanding one of a lower rank, so I wait before turning to Talfor. "Tell me what she said."

I do not know if they've been told to obey me, but he frowns and pulls at the collar of his uniform. That tells me enough.

"*Exactly* what she said," I add.

"She said she is grateful for such uncommon kindness." His eyes are concerned that he's said too much, because he quickly adds, "Perhaps we should ride on. If you are to have any hope of catching Nolla Verin—"

"I have little hope," I say with a shrug, making no attempt to drive my winded horse back into a gallop. "She is far too quick." We're traveling slowly now, and shopkeepers and street workers peer at us curiously. Rhen might have kept a distance from his people, but he still would have walked among them. He definitely wouldn't have run them down in the street for a bit of sport.

I wish I could drive Rhen from my thoughts.

I need to stop thinking like a guardsman and start thinking like a prince. I don't need to chase anyone through the streets.

I glance at Cortney and offer half a smile. "Do you have any coins? I'll make sure they're returned to you. I wouldn't mind a stop at whatever passes for a tavern here."

She looks shocked and shoots a glance at Talfor. The man shrugs.

Cortney's eyes meet mine, and she offers a hesitant smile. "Yes, Your Highness. I know just the place."

We eat fried slices of some root vegetable, topped with sizzling hot beef and a red sauce that's tart on my tongue. At first Talfor and Cortney speak in cautious words and measured statements, but they seem like decent guards, so I keep my manner easy. Eventually theirs matches.

"Some of us thought you'd pull your blade right in the throne room," Talfor is saying. He slices a small bit of beef on his plate. "Claim the throne right there."

"Surrounded by three dozen guards?" I say. "Did you think me a fool, too?"

Cortney chuckles. "Others have tried."

My knife goes still. "Tried to assassinate the queen?"

"Oh, yes. All the time. The queen can name an heir, but if she is killed, whoever deals the death blow is ruler by law."

Talfor laughs. "And then what, wait for the next man or woman to bury a sword in his belly? No, thank you."

I'm frozen on the first part of his statement. I wonder if Rhen knows this.

I hate that my first thought is of Rhen.

But the guards are right. If I'd pulled a sword in the throne room, I would have been dead before I touched Karis Luran. And even if I managed to strike her down, I highly doubt these men and women would have bent a knee to me.

Cortney speaks, her voice grim with dark humor. "If someone killed the queen, we'd just hold him down and let Nolla Verin kill *him*."

"The people of Syhl Shallow seem quite loyal." I slice another piece of meat and force it into my mouth.

They exchange a glance, and I realize they wonder if I am mocking them.

"In truth," I say, and mean it. "I have only been here a day, but I have not heard anyone speak ill of your queen. I have not seen disgruntled looks or hints of discontent toward your royal family."

"None would be tolerated," says Cortney. She snorts. "The Stone Prison is not full of *loyalists*."

Talfor is studying me. "You have noticed so much?"

"Once a guard, always a guard."

They exchange another glance, but this time Talfor smiles. "It seems that is no longer true, Your Highness."

Cortney leans in against the table. Her voice drops. "Is it true you can perform magic?"

Talfor snaps at her again, and I smile. "It's all right. Speak freely with me."

They exchange a glance, and then Talfor sheepishly says, "Is it true, then?"

"Yes."

"Would you show us?" says Cortney.

Someone at court will eventually demand a demonstration, and I would rather do it here, in the quiet shadows of a tavern, than in front of Karis Luran's whole court. I pull my dagger, and they straighten in alarm, but I swiftly drag it against my palm. Blood wells quickly, but I know how to find the waiting magic now. The wound closes. Effortless.

Talfor shoves back from the table. Cortney is staring with intrigue.

I swipe the blood away and take a sip from my cup, blushing a little. "As you see."

They exchange another glance. Cortney slaps her arm down on the table, then draws her own blade. "Do it to me."

I close my hand over the wound and gently ease my magic between us. I can feel when the wound is healed, but if I couldn't, her reaction would tell me. The guard's eyes go wide, and she gasps. She says something soft in Syssalah, then swipes her own blood away.

"The queen will be quite impressed," says Talfor.

"I understand she values harm over healing," I say.

He swallows. "Yes, well . . . healing is quite useful."

"I can undo healing just as easily. Would you like a demonstration?"

He draws back. "Unnecessary." He clears his throat and evaluates me with greater regard. "Your Highness."

A serving girl comes to take our plates and refill our mugs with cider. Cortney says, "Nolla Verin will be looking for us to return."

"Indeed," I say. I make no move to get up. "Do you carry playing cards, Talfor?"

He glances uncomfortably at the front of the tavern. "The queen's guests will be arriving by late afternoon."

"So is that a no?"

He gives me a rueful look. "Nolla Verin will not like this."

"Are you to be my keepers?" I say. "Will you be punished if I do not return in a timely fashion?"

Talfor looks startled again. "Our orders are to keep you out of danger." He glances at Cortney. "And to make you feel welcome."

"Well done, then."

They still look uncertain.

I lean in and drop my voice. "If there is to be an alliance between our countries, I must be seen as an equal. Nolla Verin clearly wishes to make this a competition. If I win, it is an insult to Syhl Shallow. If I lose, I am to be seen as weak. The only way to win is not to play."

Cortney clears her throat. "Once a guard indeed."

That makes me smile. "I do not wish for you to earn a reprimand on my behalf," I say. "If you would like to return to the palace, we can. But I would much rather learn about Syhl Shallow from its people than its rulers."

The guards exchange another glance, but Talfor finally sighs. He unbuckles a pouch on his belt. "Are cards the preferred diversion in Emberfall?" he says.

"They are."

He cups his palms together and shakes, resulting in the rattle and jangle of steel. His hands open and six silver cubes dance across the tabletop between us. "Welcome to Syhl Shallow, Your Highness. Here, we play with dice."

CHAPTER THIRTY-SEVEN

LIA MARA

Nolla Verin is pacing in my room, the sheer rose-colored overlay of her robes floating around her as she walks. "It has been *hours*," she says.

I keep my eyes on my book. I have ordered documentation on Iishellasa from the palace library, hoping to determine what my mother could require from Iisak, but after Grey "lost" Nolla Verin in the city, I've been hearing about nothing else for hours. "Mm-hmm."

"What could he be doing?"

I flip a page. So far all I've learned are things Iisak has already told us: that the scravers and the magesmiths were allies—and only by magic or by winged flight could anyone reach the ice forests of Iishellasa. The rocks and trees of Iishellasa were said to have special properties that left them immune to the forces of magic. The magesmiths tried to find warmer climates, but they were ultimately destroyed by the King of Emberfall.

Well, most of them were.

"Lia Mara!"

"I'm sorry, what?"

"I asked what he could be *doing*."

"I really don't know."

"Perhaps I pushed too hard. He seemed so aggravated when we raced past that child in the streets."

My eyes lift. "What happened?"

"A child ran into the road. I would not have harmed her, but he reacted as though I planned to trample her in the street—"

"Nolla Verin. What did Grey do?"

"He drove my horse to the side and plucked the child up onto his own." Her nose wrinkles. "Quite like a nursemaid, really."

My heart flutters in my chest, and I have to fix my gaze on my papers before she notices the warmth crawling into my cheeks. I turn another page. "Quite."

"No, not like a nursemaid." She makes a frustrated noise and flounces over to drop on the end of my chaise. "Dear sister, please help me."

That makes me set the documents aside. "What do you need?"

"I need to understand him. To figure out what will make him yield to whatever Mother wants from this alliance." She bites at her lip. "I cannot face a second rejection."

This feels unfair, that I should have to help my sister plot a way into Grey's heart, to manipulate him for our mother's purposes. I frown and make no effort to hide it.

"Why do you wear that look?" she whispers.

"You are asking me to help you trick him," I say. "He is a good man, Nolla Verin. I believe he would be a good king."

"I would hope so! But he will never be any kind of king if we do not unite against that wretched prince in Emberfall."

"Well, perhaps you would have had more success in turning his head if you'd made an attempt to *talk* to him instead of racing through the streets of the Crystal City."

She bites at her lip again, then sighs. "I suppose." She lies back until her head is against my knee. "He really is quite handsome. I only offered to race because he was saying so little."

I spend a moment trying to figure out the note in her voice, and when I have it, I giggle and stroke the hair back from her face. "Nolla Verin. Are you intimidated?"

She lifts her eyes to look up at me. "Would you think less of me if I said . . . a little?" She hugs her arms to her chest and sighs. "He is so very stoic. And the manner in which he declared himself to Mother . . . I do not know if I would have dared."

"Hmm." I have been trying very hard not to think of Grey, but my memory conjures him standing in the throne room, dressed in finery with the others at his back. That cool determination had been fixed in his eyes, the way it was in Blind Hollow—or the day we escaped from Prince Rhen. In front of my mother, he looked as though he would not back down from an army.

"Did you see his magic?" says Nolla Verin, her voice hushed yet full of curiosity. "When Prince Rhen tried to have him killed?"

"The prince had him flogged." I give an involuntary shudder. "It was terrible. Grey's magic caused the prince and his guards to fall unconscious. That's how we were all able to escape."

She sits up straight. "Unconscious!"

"Yes. Did our spies report otherwise?"

"Mother was told it was Rhen alone."

"No. It was everyone in the courtyard."

"How many?"

"Two dozen at least."

Her eyes are wide now. "I shall have to tell Mother. Our spies did not indicate his magic worked at such a level."

I frown, feeling as though I have put Grey at a disadvantage somehow. Then again, perhaps it is better if my sister is a bit wary. Maybe they won't try to maneuver his affections.

I have never felt so torn, so off balance. I do not want to put my country at a disadvantage either. These political games feel so unfair, when real people and true emotion sit at the center of it all.

A knock sounds at my door. "Enter," I call, almost in relief.

A servant eases through the doorway and bows to my sister, who is still sprawled on my chaise. "Your Highness. The prince has returned. The queen has indicated that he will escort you to dinner at sunset."

Nolla Verin grins, her face bright like a moonbeam.

My mouth forms a line. "You should go prepare."

⸻

My robes for dinner are pale green and shimmer in the light, and my attendants have laced a wide black belt adorned with emeralds in place over the top of them. I sneaked a slender book from my collection into a tiny bag that disappears among the folds of my robes. I wish I could read it for distraction right here at the dinner table, to avoid watching Nolla Verin using my information to manipulate Grey. But I have no desire for my mother to set my entire library on fire. So I sit, and I listen politely, and I wait for the moment when everyone will leave the tables to mingle and dance and drink, and I can vanish onto the veranda.

Candles are lit throughout the crowded hall, making every inch of silver and gold gleam. For her "small gathering," Mother has accumulated over one hundred people, mostly families from the five Royal Houses. Grey sits at the middle of the center table with Nolla Verin. His clothes are the finest Mother could provide, the colors echoing the gold and red of Emberfall. The others sit to his side: Jake and Noah and Tycho, all dressed similarly.

Nolla Verin, in white robes, leans close to Grey, brushing a hand across his forearm. His height and the breadth of his shoulders make her look like a doll beside him. A tiny, lethal, agile doll. I can't hear what she says, but he laughs.

I scowl and fix my gaze on my plate. I am at the end of the table, seated across from Lady Yasson Ru. She is at least ninety years old, and she smells like she hasn't bathed for the last five. Every word she says to me is a shout, but she is the head of the most wealthy of the Royal Houses.

Luckily, she has an attendant to distract her every time she begins speaking.

Her wrinkled face is frowning. "DOES OUR QUEEN TRULY THINK WE CAN ALLY WITH—"

"Here, my lady," says her attendant. "Have you sampled the spiced wine?" She thrusts a glass in her face.

Yasson Ru's wife, Lady Alla Ru, sits beside me, and she's already asleep.

I have no desire to look at Grey and Nolla Verin again, but my eyes are traitors, and they flick that way anyway. Her hand is on his upper arm now, and she's whispering something to him, her mouth inches from his neck. Grey is listening to her, but his eyes find mine.

I jerk my gaze away and down my own glass of spiced wine all in one gulp.

Lady Yasson Ru watches me. "YOU SHOULD BE CAUTIOUS WITH DRINKING SO QUICKLY. YOU ARE OF ROYAL—"

"My lady, more bread?" says her attendant.

I give the girl a grateful look.

I only have to survive dessert. When the plate is set before me, a pile of decadent chocolate and whipped frothy topping, I nearly pour it down my throat.

"GOODNESS," says Lady Yasson Ru. "YOU HAVE QUITE THE APPETITE."

Beside me, her wife jerks awake. "WHAT, YASSON? HAVE THEY SERVED THE FIRST COURSE?"

I ease my chair back. "If you'll excuse me."

Musicians in the corner of the room have begun to play, low drums mixed with stringed instruments combine to make my pulse step up. I slip between guards and guests and aim for the glass doors to the veranda.

No one stops me. No one cares. I am not the queen and Nolla Verin has been named heir, so I am unworthy of much attention at such a gathering. I don't want to enjoy it—but in a way, the change is nice. Right now I don't want any eyes on me.

The veranda stretches wide from the side of the castle, jutting out with a view of the dark mountains looming overhead and the moonlit city glittering to my left. Only two torches are lit out here, allowing me a perfect view of the starlit night. The air is too cool to be comfortable, but for now I will enjoy the solitude. At least, until more wine has been poured and inebriated guests begin spilling onto the veranda.

I am feeling the first effects of that spiced wine. Not enough to offer any bravery or social ease, but enough to turn my thoughts a bit free in my head.

I wonder what Nolla Verin said to make him laugh.

With a sigh, I sink into a cushioned chair. Then I pull my book free and begin to read, ever grateful for stories about other people and their adventures.

"What are you reading?"

I jump so hard I nearly fall off the chair. The book goes flying.

Grey snatches it out of the air. The ghost of a smile finds his lips. "Forgive me." He holds the book out.

I lurch to my feet and take it. I try to smooth down my robes and my hair, grateful for the warm shadows that will hide any blush on my cheeks. "I am glad you were not an assassin."

"Indeed." He casts a glance around the empty veranda. "You should have guards."

"For what purpose? No one here would have anything to gain from my death." He frowns at that, but I say, "And what of *your* guards, Your Highness?"

He smiles. "We have come to an understanding."

"What does that mean?"

"It means I do not need to beg for privacy." He pauses, and any amusement slips from his face. "I am unused to being the center of attention."

"You looked as though you were enjoying yourself at dinner." I sound snippy and jealous, and I wish I could suck the words back into my mouth.

Grey studies me, and I know he's noticed. He notices everything. "I am glad I gave that impression." He pauses. "If I am dis-
turbing you, I can return."

There does not seem to be a safe answer to that.

*No, I do not want you to return. I want you to stay here with me
in the moonlight, where I can pretend we are sitting among the trees
again, no mothers or sisters or alliances between us.*

I swallow. Grey's eyes, so dark in the night air, have not left
mine.

"Or perhaps I could join you?" he says.

I nod, because I do not trust my voice. I do not ease back into my
chair, however. Standing feels safer than sitting. Cool wind rushes
down from the mountain to slip through my robes and make me
shiver and think of Iisak, trapped in the dungeons.

Grey unbuckles his jacket and slips his arms free, then extends
it to me.

I blink at him. "What are you doing?"

"If you are cold. Is it not a custom for men to offer a lady a
jacket?"

I frown and square my shoulders. "It would be considered
impolite to acknowledge a weakness."

"How is being cold a weakness?"

Wind slips across my neck again. I am unsure how to proceed.
Wearing an article of his clothing feels very intimate, very much
like something I should not do.

I inhale and want to take the coat so very badly.

He waits, reading my silence, then adjusts his grip on the jacket,
holding it between two hands. "May I?"

I swallow, then nod, then close my eyes as he slips it around my shoulders. The leather and silk are warm from his body, the jacket heavy across my back.

"Thank you," I say.

His fingers, feather-light, brush against my chin, tilting my face up. I inhale sharply and open my eyes.

"You are far from weak, Lia Mara."

I smile slightly. "Carrying that buck nearly killed me."

"I am not talking about the buck." He pauses. "I am speaking of the moment in Blind Hollow, when you should have run for safety, but you began helping the injured. I am speaking of that moment when you offered me sanctuary, when you could have been miles away on horseback, long before dawn. I am speaking of every moment and every step of our journey here." His voice lowers. Softens. "I am speaking of that moment when Iisak tore my arm open and you took my hand."

He's so still that he might be a shadow, a whisper of imagination. If I did not have the warm weight of his jacket on my shoulders or the faint gleam of his eyes, I would not believe this was happening. I am very aware of my breathing, of his breathing. Music escapes through the doorway to invade our tiny cocoon of silence.

"Are you drunk again?" I whisper.

He laughs, and that's such a rare thing that it makes my heart skip. "Quite sober, I assure you."

I swallow. "You should be inside," I say. "You should be with Nolla Verin."

He does not move. "Why did you run from the party?"

"I did not run. I was not needed."

His eyebrows draw together. "Since the moment we arrived

here, you have hidden yourself from me. I do not understand why."

"My sister—"

"This is not about your *sister*," he growls.

"But it *is* about my sister," I insist. "Do you understand? She is the chosen heir now. The favored daughter. You ask why I would leave the party, as if I have any place there. My goals do not align with theirs. What do I have to offer?" I spread my hands wide and turn, indicating the wide expanse of air surrounding us. "I am alone on this veranda because I have nothing. Nothing! I have no throne, no crown, no country, no—"

I gasp as he catches my waist and forces me still. His hands are strong and sure against me, and his voice comes very low. "Do not *ever* say that you have nothing to offer."

I'm breathing so hard that I might cry, or laugh, or break into a million pieces that will drift away on the wind.

"Do you know," he says quietly, "when that soldier pressed a knife to your throat, I could have taken his head."

His words are so callous, so practical, belying the softness in his voice. That empty blackness glimmers in his eye, a hint at what he can become when the need arises. I shiver. "You didn't need to."

"You didn't need me to save you." He pauses. "And your words stayed my hand."

"My words?"

"You said that not every problem can be solved by the end of a sword. I have carried those words with me for days." He pauses. "Since you made me realize that I am no longer a weapon to be wielded by another."

Emotion tightens my chest, but his closeness, his warmth, have slowed my breathing. "You are not a weapon, Grey."

"I can be." His hand lifts from my waist to brush a lock of hair from my cheek. "But you are by far more dangerous."

I can hardly think with his fingers tracing a line down the side of my face. "Ah, yes, the most dangerous person at the party is always the girl sitting alone with a book."

He doesn't smile. "You underestimate yourself. Your sister seems determined to be as ruthless as possible—to impress your mother, I am sure. And while ruthlessness may have its place, I believe your brand of strength would garner greater loyalty. That is what makes you dangerous. Not because you would ride in with a blade and take control, but because you could quietly sit in this chair, in the dark, with your book"—the corner of his mouth turns up— "and you could determine the best way to achieve what needs to be done."

I flush. "No, Grey, I'm sitting here with a book because—"

He leans down and brushes his lips against mine. So light, like the touch of a butterfly's wings. Hardly a kiss, *barely* a kiss, but the motion lights a fire in my belly and robs every thought from my head, leaving us standing there, sharing breath.

His fingers are still against my cheek, his thumb beside my lip. "Forgive me," he begins. "You stopped me once before, and—"

I shake my head fiercely. "I shouldn't have."

This time, when his mouth finds mine, there's nothing light about it. His strength radiates through his hands, and his kiss is like a flame. My knees are weak and trembling, but my hands are sure and steady, finding the column of his neck, the breadth of his shoulders, the unruly hair at his nape.

Then his arms are against my back, holding me against him, and that is almost better than the addictive pull of his kisses: to be held, to feel cherished. When his mouth finally releases mine, I sigh and press my face into the hollow below his chin.

This is foolish. Risky. Terrifying. Anyone could come out onto the veranda. He should release me.

He does not. One hand is idly stroking the hair down my back, and I'm powerless with his breath in my hair and his scent buried in my head.

"*Fell siralla*," he says, and I giggle.

"*Nah*," I say. "*Fell bellama. Fell garrant. Fell vale.*"

"I hope those aren't worse than *stupid*."

I shake my head against his neck. He must feel my blush through his shirt. "Beautiful man. Brave man."

He waits, then says, "There were three."

"You notice everything!"

"What is the third?"

He never lets me back away from anything either. I love it and hate it. "You'll have to learn Syssalah to find out."

"*Fell vale*," he muses, and his terrible accent makes me giggle again. "You'll have to give me more lessons," he adds.

"Someone will."

A finger brushes my chin, and I tilt my face up. His lips find mine again. The night sky seems to close in around us, wrapping us in silence and warmth.

Then a screech splits the night.

Grey jerks his head up. "Iisak."

Another screech. Then another. Louder and more vicious than I've ever heard. I want to clamp my hands down over my ears.

I remember my mother's words to the scraver, something about tonight. Oh, what has she done?

I don't have much time to wonder, because everyone inside begins screaming.

CHAPTER THIRTY-EIGHT

GREY

People are spilling out of the doors and onto the veranda, and Lia Mara and I fight our way through them to get back into the main room. Most of the guards have a hand on their weapon, but none have drawn them. Chairs have been overturned in the rush, dishes shattered on the ground.

In the center of the room stand Karis Luran and Nolla Verin. A man's body is at their feet, his chest and abdomen torn open. Four long scratches cross his face, so badly I cannot make out his features. The scent of blood and worse things taints the air.

"No," Lia Mara whispers at my side. "No."

Iisak is off to the side, a silver band locked around his throat, attached to a glittering chain. Karis Luran holds the other end. His fangs are bared, his claws red with blood. He's drawn away from her as far as the chain will allow.

Most of the dinner guests have not run, though a few look a bit sick, their expressions a mixture of horror and fascination.

The only people who don't look fascinated are Tycho and Noah. A guard blocks them from approaching the man on the ground. Noah looks furious.

Jake appears at my side. He speaks in a low rush. "She said she had a demonstration for those who would dare defy her. Then she dragged this guy in here. We thought she was going to cut his head off or something, which was bad enough. Then one of her guards hauled Iisak in."

I had somehow forgotten why Karis Luran has such a brutal reputation among the people of Emberfall.

I had somehow forgotten what her soldiers did to our border cities.

I had forgotten because I looked to Lia Mara, instead of paying attention to who was truly in power.

I stare across the room at Iisak. His chest rises and falls rapidly, like the chain makes it hard to breathe. His eyes are cold and black and resigned.

Now he is the weapon to be wielded by another. *A steep cost*, he said. Indeed.

"Come, Your Highness," says Karis Luran. "He may already be dead."

My eyes meet hers. "I do not understand."

"We are told you can restore lives," says Nolla Verin. "Show us."

This evening was not a celebration. It was a means to a test.

I feel like such a fool to have not suspected. I take a breath and move to step forward.

Jake shifts close and blocks me with his shoulder. "Don't do it for free," he says, his voice hardly louder than breath.

I meet his eyes, reassured by the cool practicality there.

I give him a short nod, then move forward. The man's abdomen is shredded so badly that there's more blood and muscle visible than skin. Iisak's claws caught one eye, though the other is intact. One cheek is slashed so severely that I can see the teeth beneath. His breath comes very slowly.

I've never flinched at the aftermath of violence, so I do not flinch now. I look back at Karis Luran. "What payment do you offer?"

Her eyes narrow. "I offer no payment."

"Then I offer no healing. You ordered this done, not me."

Behind her, the resignation slips from Iisak's expression. His eyes are fixed on me.

"Please," Lia Mara gasps from behind me. "Please, Grey. Please save him."

The desperation in her voice tugs at my chest, and it takes everything I have to keep from dropping to a knee to press my hands to his wounds. I lock the emotion away, into the dark corner of my mind, until I feel nothing. He could die at my feet. I could pull my sword and finish the task.

No. I could not. For the first time, those thoughts fight their way loose.

I stand my ground. Karis Luran stands hers.

Finally, Nolla Verin says, "What payment do you ask?"

I consider saying, *my freedom.* Freedom from this dance, this charade, this delicate balance. In a way, I feel as chained as Iisak.

I glance at the man on the ground. His hair and beard are sandy brown, and he's built like a soldier, though he's not dressed like one. "A life for a life, I should think."

Nolla Verin meets my eyes, and she smiles. "Who would you like to kill?"

"I don't want to kill anyone. I would like the scraver's debt to be erased."

"No," says Karis Luran. Her voice is flat and level and offers no room for negotiation.

"Very well." My tone is exactly the same.

"Grey!" shouts Noah.

"Please," cries Lia Mara. My gut clenches.

"The scraver's *debt* will be erased by one year of service," says Karis Luran.

"Fine. Transfer his one year of service to me."

She regards me coolly. "You are not in a position to make demands from me. I have offered sanctuary to you and your people."

"I have made no demands. You have. And you offered sanctuary to me and my people because you hope to secure an alliance with the future King of Emberfall."

"Grey," calls Noah, "that guy's got maybe five minutes. If that."

"Is five minutes enough time for your magic to work?" says Karis Luran. "Or will you waste it negotiating?"

I don't take my eyes off her. "You are the one who requested that he be healed. Will *you* waste it negotiating?"

Her mouth turns downward slightly. "The scraver's debt must be paid. I will not turn him over to you if you will release him from his oath."

"So if I maintain his year of service, you would be willing to hand me the chain."

Her expression is so shrewd. In a way, she reminds me of Rhen. "Yes," she says. "If you can heal this man, this creature's year of service will be yours. I will indeed hand you the chain." She gives it a jerk, and Iisak growls at her but does not move. "And once we have come to terms on an alliance, you will allow me access to the scraver's"—she glances at the man on the ground—"*talents* as well?"

That seems a little too open-ended for my taste. "At my discretion."

"Three minutes," Noah calls. "He's lost a lot of blood, Grey."

Karis Luran smiles. "I truly do like you better than your brother. Yes, at your discretion. Heal Parrish for us all to see, and you will have your scraver."

Parrish. The name pulls at me, and I try to remember why. The memory won't come, and he's dying anyway. I put the thought away for later and drop to a knee in the blood. There's so much damage that I have no idea where to start. His breath makes a rattling sound.

Maybe my indecision is visible, because Noah says, "You've got to stop the bleeding. Everything else is secondary if he keeps bleeding out."

I glance at the guards blocking Noah. "Release him."

"No," says Karis Luran. "You alone. If the healer speaks again, silence him."

"Mother, please!" cries Lia Mara. "Please. Parrish followed my order."

Then I understand. I remember who Parrish is. Her guard. The one who accompanied her to Ironrose the night Rhen took her prisoner. A cold fury takes a seat in my chest.

"This man knows what he did," says Karis Luran. "If his life ends here, everyone else will know it, too."

The longer she talks, the closer this man moves toward death. I press my hands right to the worst of the damage, hoping it's the source of most of the bleeding. Blood and viscera slide beneath my fingers, and I close my eyes, looking for the sparks that have helped me before. It's easier now, like the early stages of swordplay, when it's all simple footwork and arm movements. A step here, a thrust there.

My eyes remain closed, but the flesh begins to re-form under my hands, muscle and skin pulling together. Blood no longer flows around my fingers. People nearby gasp. I hear murmurs in Syssalah.

I open my eyes and move my hands farther up, to his chest, which barely moves now. His skin has a ghastly pallor, and I've seen enough men die at the hands of a monster to know this is not a good sign. I force my magic across the bond between us, those sparks seeking the damage and healing it. These marks close, too, and Parrish's chest rises and falls rapidly. His one good eye opens, and he lets out a low groan of pain. His gaze meets mine, and he tries to throw up an arm to fight me off.

I lift my hands, which are coated in his blood. "Be at ease," I say to him. "Allow me to help you."

He does not move. His expression is full of fear, and he speaks in rapid Syssalah.

"Parrish," calls Lia Mara. Her voice breaks on a sob. But whatever she says next makes him lower his arm.

"She will kill me," Parrish says.

"She tried. Now I will try to save you." Though I'm not sure I can save his eye. It's a shredded ruin above his cheek.

He doesn't move his arm, but I press a hand to his bloody cheek. He hisses in pain and tries to jerk away, but the skin begins to knit together, and his good eye widens in surprise.

The murmurs around us grow louder.

The damaged eye re-forms, the iris and pupil swimming up

through the white. It's simultaneously the most disgusting and fascinating thing I've ever seen.

Then it's done. He's healed and I'm exhausted, and we're both sticky with blood and sweat and probably worse things.

He's staring up at me in wonder, and he's breathing as hard as I am. "This feels like a dream."

No. It feels like a nightmare. I force myself to my feet and look at Karis Luran. I hold out my blood-slick hand. "My payment."

The expression on her face is a combination of fury and irritation and approval. "Very well." She presses the taut chain into my hand. Her fingers slide through the blood on my palm.

My muscles feel primed for a different kind of battle, making my breathing shallow and my focus very narrow. I wish I could draw a sword and execute her right here. "If you'll forgive me, I should return to my rooms to change."

"Of course," she says smoothly. I cannot tell if she has lost face here or if I have. "You should not forget your jacket."

I go still. *My jacket.*

"Here." Lia Mara's voice is barely a whisper at my side. "Go. Please. Before this grows worse."

I close my bloody fingers in the crush of leather and suede, hoping to brush against hers, but she's already let go.

Nolla Verin is watching me very carefully.

I force myself to keep my eyes on my people, still blocked by the guards. The brief kiss I shared with Lia Mara seems to have happened days ago. Months ago. A lifetime ago. Now I'm covered in gore, a pure spectacle in front of strangers.

"Let my people go," I say, and somehow my voice is level. "We will return to our rooms."

Karis Luran nods, and the guards part. Tycho rushes to my side. Noah moves to Jake's.

I don't want to drag Iisak by the chain, but he hasn't moved from the shadows. I can no longer read his expression, and at this point, my nerves are too edged to care. I wrap the chain around my hand, offer a bow to Karis Luran, and start walking.

He follows willingly. I want nothing more than to drop this chain, but I'm worried someone else will pick it up.

As we leave the room, Karis Luran is speaking to her guards. "Take Parrish to the dungeon. Take his eye for good this time."

Lia Mara screams. "No! Mother—no!"

My steps freeze.

"No." Jake's hand finds my shoulder, and he gives me a good shove. "Keep walking."

I don't move. My jaw is clenched tight. I try to turn.

Jake gives me another shove. His voice sounds like I feel, quick and rushed and panicked—but he's steadfast. "He's alive. You saved his life. You gained ground today. You can't lose it now. Walk, Grey. Walk."

My feet refuse to move. We're still visible from the doorway. I have no doubt Karis Luran gave her order just now to undermine me, to send some kind of message to her daughter.

Inside the room, the man screams. I wonder if they are doing it right there.

My chest is tight, and I *know* they're doing it right there.

I try to shove past Jake. "I didn't save him for her to torture him."

Iisak hisses. "She will demand my return. She will likely have me do worse."

That makes me stop. I run a hand across my jaw. Lia Mara's screaming is etched in my brain now. So is the man's.

"It's just an eye," says Jake.

"I hate this," Noah mutters.

Me too.

Tycho takes hold of the chain. He's possibly the only person I would allow to take it from my hand, so I release it. His eyes are dark and troubled again.

"Iisak is my friend," he says. He wets his trembling lips and glances at Jake. "And it is just an eye."

This is no choice at all.

Silver hell. I set my jaw and start walking.

The screaming echoes behind us long after we reach our chambers and lock the doors.

CHAPTER THIRTY-NINE

LIA MARA

Mother strides into my room hours later. It's late enough that I should be asleep, but I knew she would be coming, so I haven't even dressed for bed. Her personal guard is with her, looking so fierce and punishing that I wonder if she's going to have me killed right here in my chambers. I leap to my feet and back away before I realize what I'm doing.

"Mother," I whisper.

Parrish's blood stains her robes, and there's a streak of it on her face, with more on her hands.

I have no doubt she's aware of every stain, and she wore them here just for me.

"Do you seek to undermine me?" she demands. "Or is this simple envy for your sister?"

"It's not—I'm not—Nolla Verin—"

"Do you have any idea what is at stake, Lia Mara?" she says. "Have you no consideration for how important this alliance is?"

"Yes." I swallow. "I do."

"Then explain to me why you would be wearing his clothing in front of every Royal House in the palace?"

"I'm sorry," I whisper. "I'm sorry."

She steps close to me. "You will make no further apologies. You will make no further mistakes. We have the heir, and the Royal Houses have pledged their funds. Tomorrow, I will seal an alliance with this man, and he will lead our people to claim his throne in Emberfall. You will remain here until then."

She turns to leave, her robes swirling in her wake.

I rush to follow her, but her guards step in front of me, and I'm drawn up short. My heart pounds in my chest. Mother has never turned her guards against me.

Once they're through the door, I cannot breathe. It latches heavily behind them.

My sister. I must speak with my sister.

I count to ten. To twenty. To one hundred. I count until my mother and her guards will be gone.

I fly to the door and throw it open. A guard swivels to block me. Instead of Bea and Conys, I find myself face-to-face with Parrish. His missing eye has been stitched closed. He's pale but steady, a staff in his hand to bar my way.

I gasp and stumble back. "Parrish—Parrish, please. I have wanted to talk to you so badly—"

His voice is cold, not revealing even a glimpse of the guard who once shared a shred of humor with me. "The queen has ordered that you will not leave this room."

This is the final blow. My mother has put him here as a reminder for me that my actions have consequences. That my actions have caused nothing but harm.

I'm staring the result right in the face. Parrish's other eye is clouded with pain and anger and regret.

"I'm sorry," I whisper.

He says nothing.

I have nothing to offer.

I reach out and close the door. I got just what I wanted: I'm alone in my room.

CHAPTER FORTY

GREY

Iisak refuses to allow me to remove the chain. I refuse to send him back to the dungeon, and I refuse to tether him in my chambers. He dragged the rattling links around the stone floor for hours until I threatened to hang him with it if he didn't stop pacing. My mood is bitter and recalcitrant, and I want nothing more than to sit in front of the fire to reevaluate every choice I've made since the moment Dustan appeared in the arena at Worwick's.

Instead, I'm staring at the fire, thinking of Lia Mara. I wish I hadn't given her my jacket. I wish I hadn't endangered her. I wish I hadn't—

"You seem unsettled, Your Highness."

I glance at Iisak. He's crouched in the darkest corner of the room, as far from the fire as possible, his eyes glittering black.

"*Stop calling me that,*" I snap.

"I believe you should get used to it."

Silver hell. I run my hands back through my hair.

"What bothers you more?" says Iisak. "The man who lost an eye or our troubled princess?"

"Can they not *both* bother me?"

"For certain."

I ordered him to stop pacing, but now he's too still. Too calm. "What if she had told you to harm *me* instead of that man? Would you so quickly have bared your claws?"

"Yes."

He answers so swiftly that it broadens my fury. I clench my teeth and wish I had asked for *anything* other than his freedom.

"I have already bared my claws to you," he says. "You healed the damage within seconds. Why would I risk her wrath and refuse her order?"

I look away from him. The fire snaps and flickers.

"I have made no secret of my desire to return home," he says. "I will spend my year sworn to you or sworn to her or whatever is required, and not one minute longer."

"I will never make you do . . . *that*."

"Do not make promises you cannot keep, Your Highness."

I glare at him again. "I told you to stop it."

"Return me to the dungeon if my presence troubles you."

"Don't tempt me."

"Is that so tempting?" His eyes narrow slightly. "Truly?"

I grit my teeth and look away again. He is baiting me, and I know it.

"I imagine there must have been an element of relief to be a guardsman," he says. "To know your actions were directed by another. To have no sense of accountability for what you were ordered to do."

He says this as if I do not feel the weight of every action I have ever taken. "You do not know anything about my time as a guardsman."

"I think it is telling that you ran from your birthright and chose an occupation near the lowest rung of Emberfall's society. Were there no privies to clean?"

"Do you wish to fight, Iisak?"

He uncurls from his position by the wall, looping the chain between his hands, each link *click-click-click*ing as it passes over his claws. "I believe the better question is, do *you* wish to fight?"

I do, actually. My heart has been calling for action since I heard Karis Luran give the order to take Parrish's eye. My muscles are tense with the need to best something.

In our final season together, the enchantress Lilith was secretly torturing Rhen each night. He would wake each morning and call for me to fight him in the arena. It was harder than any training session I ever had with the Royal Guard.

I never fully understood his need until this very moment.

I wish I could stop thinking of Rhen.

I rub at my eyes, but I sense motion in front of me and jerk my hands down. He's come close enough to touch, each movement slow and calculated. Firelight flickers off the chain, off his wings, off those night-dark eyes.

He swipes his claws at me, almost quicker than breath, but I am ready for it, and I leap back, overturning the chair. My dagger finds my hand, but the sword is out of reach.

"I don't want to fight with you," I say.

"You want to fight with *something*."

"What do you want, Iisak? Do you want me to kill you? Do you want to be put out of your misery?"

He laughs. "Do you think you could kill me?"

Without waiting for an answer, he launches himself at me again. His claws dig into my shoulder, but before I can land a hit with the dagger, he's spun away.

He's not quick enough to keep the chain out of my grasp, however. It jerks tight as he hits the limit, and I hold fast.

Despite his height, he's nowhere near as heavy as a human man, and I drag him toward me easily, his feet digging into the stone floor.

As soon as he gets close enough, I swipe with the dagger. He swipes with his claws. We both lose—or maybe we both win. He went for my hand with the chain. I went for his shoulder. We break apart, both bleeding.

He gives me no time to recover. He leaps at me again, swiping for my face, for my neck. I bat his claws away with the dagger, but my forearms take most of the damage. He must sever something vital because the weapon slips from my hand to clatter to the floor. My magic responds almost without thought, healing the damage quickly enough for me to go after him with fists and brute strength. We collide with the other chair, with the chest of drawers, with the pile of logs beside the hearth. A drapery rips down from the wall.

Iisak twists free of my hold and buries those teeth in my forearm. I punch him, and it dislodges him enough that he leaps off me, my blood staining the skin around his mouth.

I roll fast and find the sword under the chair, but Iisak is on top of me before I can draw it. His hands aim for my neck, and I'm ready for him to swipe with his claws, but instead the chain catches me in the throat and presses me down into the stone floor. It's so tight that I can't even swallow. He kneels on my sword arm.

I fight his grip with my free hand, but now he's got leverage.

I glare up at him, sure my eyes are burning with fury. I fight to grit words out. "What do you want, Iisak?"

He leans down, his face an inch from mine. Those fangs are still bared, still tinged with my blood. His breath is like a winter wind. "No. What do *you* want?"

I try to throw another punch, but he knocks my hand away, then puts his claws against my throat, right over the chain. I grip his wrist, but he tightens his fingers. I feel every single point of his claws against my skin, and I freeze. He doesn't break the skin, but if I dare to breathe, he might.

What do you want?

Those words seem to drain the fight right out of me. My chest is heaving beneath his weight, and my throat burns with emotion.

There are so many things that I *don't* want.

I don't want Lia Mara to suffer for what I've done.

I don't want the few people who've sworn to me to suffer for their allegiance.

I don't want anyone else to be harmed.

I don't want my country to fall.

I blink up at Iisak, and my vision blurs. "I don't want to be at war with Rhen."

The claws in my neck ease, and the scraver withdraws. I slide the chain away from me, then roll to sitting, rubbing at my neck. The magic in my blood rushes to heal any injury, almost without thought now.

I feel broken inside, and the sparks and flares of power can do nothing to heal that.

Iisak crouches before me, balanced on the balls of his feet. "Your brother is at war with his people. We have seen that in our travels."

I remember Rhen's steadfast determination to reclaim Silver-moon Harbor. "I know."

"Even if you were still his guardsman, the people would be resisting his rule. Have you not considered this?"

"I have." I think of everything Dustan has been forced to do since I left, and I imagine myself in his place. I don't want to think that I would have turned my blade on the people of Emberfall, but I consider the oath I once swore, and I know I would have.

I swallow again. "There are no easy choices here, Iisak."

"*Easy*," he growls. "Choices are never easy. There are good and bad options, but the most dangerous is to not make any choice at all."

I shift to sit against the hearth, seeking the warmth of the stones to combat the chill Iisak adds to the air. A part of me wishes my magic weren't so efficient. I want to feel sore and broken for a while. I sigh, then look at him. "Thank you."

He coils the chain in his hands, then nods and sits a short distance away. "I needed a battle as well."

I glance around the room, at the overturned furniture and torn draperies. "I am surprised we did not draw the guards."

"No sound escaped this room."

I blink in surprise, then smile ruefully. "Your magic?"

"It grows stronger every day." He pauses. "You did not call on yours."

"I healed myself."

He says nothing, but I can feel his icy judgment. I could have done more than heal myself.

"I would share a story with you," he finally says.

"All right."

"I would prefer this story not reach the ears of Karis Luran."

I look at him. This reminds me of the night I shared secrets with Tycho. Maybe it was our fight, or maybe it's our shared loathing of Karis Luran. Maybe he needs a confidant as badly as I once did. "I keep secrets well, Iisak."

"Our people had an *aeliix*," he says. "An heir. A prince, of sorts. He did not want to rule either." He pauses. "He resented our confinement to the ice forests. He wished to destroy our treaty with Syhl Shallow, to grant us access to the warmer skies. He claimed his birthright was a burden. Many thought he was spoiled and selfish, but much like your brother's feelings about magic, his resistance was rooted in fear. To rule is to take on the weight of all your people, to become leader instead of follower. To become parent instead of child." Iisak twists the links of the chain between his fingers. They're coated in ice that melts in the heat of the fire to drip on the floor. "Our *aeliix* fled Iishellasa through Syhl Shallow and was never heard from again."

I study him. "Is this a story about you, Iisak? Did you flee your birthright?"

"No, Your Highness."

I frown.

His eyes are so dark and resigned. His voice is very quiet, barely more than a whisper. "My son did."

I straighten. "Your . . . *son*."

"I believed Karis Luran held him captive."

In the woods, Lia Mara asked what her mother had.

Something quite dear to me, he said.

I stare at him. "So that makes you . . ."

"Their *friist*." He smiles sadly. "Their king." He glances at the

window. "Though I have been gone far longer than I ever antici-
pated. I may no longer have a crown to claim."

This is a much bigger secret than anything Tycho shared in the
loft. I suck a breath in through my teeth. "You're to be her prisoner
for a *year*, Iisak."

"I would have risked a lifetime." The fire crackles behind me,
reflecting off his eyes. "Would you not?"

When I hesitate, he smiles. "You would. Were you a father, you
would." He pauses. "When I left Iishellasa, I tried to follow his trail,
but I was captured, then traded, then sold, then gambled away."

"To Worwick," I say.

"Yes." He pauses. "And I am not *her* prisoner now." He drags
those chains across his claws again. "Your Highness, I am yours."

I swallow. "You're not my prisoner, Iisak."

"You made a bargain with Karis Luran. You cannot free me.
Too much is at stake."

There is always too much at stake. I frown again. "How do you
know she doesn't have him?"

"She would have demanded far more than a year." He uncurls
from the ground and looks out the window. "He could be long
gone—or long dead. This was the final trail I had to follow."

Now I understand why he needed a battle as well.

"I will find a way to earn your freedom," I say.

"I can survive a year on a chain," he says. "You have more pressing matters, Your Highness."

I scowl, but he's right. "Rhen rallied his people to drive Syhl
Shallow out of Emberfall. He saved his country. It is not right to
ride in and take it away from him."

"He lied to his people to keep hold of his throne." He pauses.

"To say nothing of whatever actions allowed his people to fall into desperation and poverty."

Yes. Rhen did that. I helped him do that. We had no other choice.

"From what I can see," says Iisak, "there are few paths here. If you accept your birthright and return to claim your throne, Karis Luran will lend her support in exchange for an alliance with Emberfall and access to Rhen's—to *your*—waterways."

"Yes." The fire snaps, and I draw my legs up to sit cross-legged.

"If you deny your birthright," Iisak continues, "you will have to flee this palace." His eyes are hard. "Karis Luran would not allow someone with your abilities to roam unchecked. Rhen would not either. You and your people do not speak the language here, but you could be recognized in Emberfall. This would be a challenging feat for anyone."

"So my choice is to destroy Rhen or to allow myself to be destroyed. This is no choice at all."

Iisak is quiet for a moment. "Why did you swear yourself into Prince Rhen's service?"

"I swore to protect the Crown." I hesitate. "To protect the line of succession. To protect the people of Emberfall." I hesitate again, hearing the truth in my words. "To be a part of something bigger than myself."

"And so you have."

I run a hand across my jaw. So I have.

I swore to protect the Crown, and that meant whoever was rightfully wearing it. I swore to protect King Broderick, and after his death, I swore to protect Rhen. Not just because of who he was, but because of who he represented.

Have I been fighting against myself all this time?

"Let us not forget," Iisak adds, "that you have something Rhen does not."

I roll my eyes. "Magic."

"You scoff!" His wings flare, and his eyes flash. "If you would stop fighting yourself, I believe you would find your abilities manifest very powerfully indeed. If you are the last remaining magesmith, you could be more powerful than any I have ever seen. I believe what happened to Rhen and his people is a mere fraction of what you can accomplish. Why do you think Karis Luran is so eager to undermine your talents?"

He is right. I am not sure I *like* it, but he is right. "As you say. I will draft the terms of an alliance with Karis Luran." My chest feels tight. "I will make a claim for Rhen's throne."

"Besides, I was not referring to magic alone."

"No? What else do I possess that Rhen does not?"

He smiles that terrifying smile, then tosses the length of silver chain in my lap. "You have me."

I blink at him in surprise.

"Let's battle again," he says, and he flexes his claws. "This time, use more than your bare hands."

CHAPTER FORTY-ONE

LIA MARA

Meals are brought at regular intervals, but it seems my mother was serious. I am not allowed to leave my room. My guards refuse to speak with me. I have my bed and my books and my washroom, but little else. From my window, three stories high, I can see the training yards and the stables, but after catching sight of Grey walking with Nolla Verin, I stay away from the view.

No one visits me.

I long for the companionship of my friends, but of everyone, I miss my sister the most.

I wish I could speak with her. I wish I could explain.

By the third night, I'm lying in bed, staring up at the darkness, wondering if the guards would put a sword through my body if I made an effort to rush past them.

Knowing my mother, they probably would. I should consider myself lucky that she did not do it herself.

A shadow crosses my wall, and I freeze. Movement flickers in the darkened corner, and I inhale sharply.

Before I have time to wonder if the guards would even *respond* to a shout, an icy breeze swirls through the room. "Have no fear, Princess."

Iisak. My eyes are wide, seeking any shred of light in the darkened room. As the panic bleeds away, I make out the dimness of his skin, the smoke-colored span of his wings over his shoulders. He still wears a silver collar around his neck, but the chain is gone.

I shove myself up to sitting and glance at the door. "What are you doing here?" I whisper carefully, mindful of my guards.

"Visiting a prisoner, as you once did for me."

Emotion builds in my throat, and my mouth turns downward. "You should leave before you are caught." I press my fingertips into my eyes to stop any tears from falling. "I bring nothing but trouble, Iisak."

"Perhaps, but I bring a missive from our rebellious young prince."

I thrust my hands down and blink at him. "What?"

He extends a folded piece of paper, and I nearly fall out of bed scrambling to take it. It's too late to dare light a candle—my guards would notice something was amiss. I move to the window to read in the moonlight.

Grey's handwriting is long and sloping, the words quickly formed as if he was worried he would be discovered.

Forgive me. Please forgive me. I never meant to put you at risk. If there is a way for me to negotiate for your freedom, please let me know it. Your mother plays dangerous games, and I worry that I will further endanger you or those you care for.

I keep thinking back to those brief moments on the veranda
and wondering if I should never have offered you my jacket.
My thoughts keep reminding me that you were cold, however,
and the idea of leaving you shivering is not a thought
I can bear.

Especially when my thoughts also remind me of the brief
moments after, when I hope you were not cold at all.

I want to sink back into the pillows of my bed and press this letter to my chest, but I am desperate to see what else he wrote.

I have reached an accord with your mother in an attempt to
spare more innocent lives. I tried to require your freedom
as part of our agreement, but your mother refused. If I had
the skills to magic myself into your room this very moment,
I would do it.

At your mother's insistence, I have spent a great deal of time
with your sister.

My hand tightens on the paper, and I must force myself to keep reading.

She is quite worried for you. The bold girl who raced me
through the city now speaks of nothing but concern for you.
As someone who has spent many days trying to think of
what to say to the man who is now my brother, I thought
you should know.

Yours,
Grey

Yours. But he's not mine.

A tear drips onto the paper, and I hastily swipe it away. I force my shoulders to straighten, and I look across at Iisak, hardly more than another shadow in the room.

"Is he well?" I say.

"He is trapped by circumstance, as we all are." He pauses. "But yes. He is well."

As we all are. I'm not sure if that's true. My mother does not care for the people of Emberfall. Nor does my sister. I think of that trapper and his daughter, killed without thought.

I think of the destruction we saw on our trip into Emberfall, so many days ago.

I think of Prince Rhen, and what he was willing to do to stop an heir from taking his throne.

I think of Parrish, likely standing outside my door this very moment, punished for obeying my order.

I look at Iisak, then at the window. "Can you help me get out of here?" I whisper as softly as possible, as if even giving voice to the thought will carry the words to my mother's ears.

He follows my glance, then moves to the window. "I cannot bear the weight of a human for long."

"You pulled soldiers off their horses in Blind Hollow."

"That was a matter of inches, not a three-story fall, and I was not worried about preserving their lives."

I frown, then sigh. "I can do nothing from this room, Iisak."

"If you leap from this window, the best I can offer is a slower descent toward death."

That makes me scowl. "So this is it? I'm supposed to sit here and read while Grey goes off to battle against his brother, with my *sister* at his side?"

"Would you rather be at his side?"

Warmth blooms in my cheeks before I'm ready for it. "I would rather we not war with Emberfall at all. We have already caused much damage."

"You have not caused *all* the damage to Emberfall, Princess." He pauses. "Some things even you cannot stop."

Does that mean there are things I *can* stop? Everything I've tried has ended in failure. It's likely a miracle that I was able to deliver Grey to the castle unharmed. Perhaps I should stay locked in my room while everyone else solves the world's problems.

No. The idea is abhorrent to me.

We have already caused so much harm. We cannot continue taking from Emberfall, regardless of who is in power.

Mother will not allow me to leave. Parrish will not help me. Grey's position is too precarious.

I move to my desk and remove a few sheets of paper, along with an inkwell and a quill.

"Will you deliver a message?" I say to Iisak.

"To the prince? For certain."

"No." My thoughts are swirling, thinking of what to say to Grey. But ink drips on the paper as I hastily write my message.

Two sisters, one heart. Please come to me. I need my other half.

I blow on the ink to dry it, then hold it out. "I need you to take this to my sister."

I imagined Nolla Verin reading my message and immediately coming to my door.

She does not.

I lie awake most of the night, watching as the first rays of sunlight gild my ceiling at dawn. Outside my room I hear the clatter and bustle of servants in the hall, but Nolla Verin still does not come.

By midmorning, I sit by the window hoping to catch a glimpse of my sister.

Eventually she appears, Grey at her side. My chest gives a tug at the sight of them, but today, I do not shy away from the window. Mother follows, not far behind. They meet with a cadre of soldiers on the training field, all of whom break apart into sparring groups. Grey and my sister watch over the fighters, my mother nearby. Always watching, always judging. My fingers dig into the window ledge.

Ah, Sister, I think. *Look up. Look up and see how much I need you.*

Maybe we do share a heart, because she turns from the swordplay, and her gaze lifts to find mine. I gasp as our eyes meet.

"Please," I whisper.

Even from here, I can see the sorrow in her expression, proving the weight in Grey's note.

Her lips move, forming the words very carefully: *I'm sorry.*

I fall back from the window, but not before seeing her turn back to our mother, listening to whatever she's saying, ever the dutiful heir.

That night, when the sky is inky black and the moon hangs high and full outside my window, Iisak returns with another note from Grey.

Your mother is eager to move quickly. She reveals little to me, but guards and soldiers talk, and it seems my past allows me to play both sides. I have learned much during our sparring. Your Royal Houses are similar to Rhen's Grand Marshals, and it seems she has gained their support—and funding. They are eager to access Rhen's waterways and seaports, and timing is essential now, because his kingdom is fractured and weak. We will ride into Emberfall in a few days.

I do not know how soon I will return.

I do not know if I will return.

I once spent an eternity dreading every passing minute, and now I wish for more time.

More than anything, however, I wish I could free you. I long for your strength and compassion to be at my side. All your mother and sister seem to offer is vicious brutality.

That has its place, of course, but perhaps not as much as I once thought.

Yours,

Grey

I take a long breath and blow it out. My chest aches.

I look up at Iisak. "He's going to attack Rhen."

"Yes."

I swallow and set down the letter. I knew that's what lay at the end of this road . . . but I do not like it.

I see no way out of it. All my studies, all my reading and thinking, all my cleverness and compassion, and the result is the same.

"He's wrong," I say.

"Wrong, Princess?"

"He's going to war." My voice is hollow. "He needs all the vicious brutality he can get."

CHAPTER FORTY-TWO

GREY

My hours have never been so full, my sleep never so sound. My mornings are full of lessons: in Syssalah, in court politics, in the customs and traditions of Syhl Shallow. Nolla Verin is often at my side, but she never feels like a companion, and instead feels like a spy waiting to report on my progress to her mother. I keep my guard up—and she does as well.

I share the midday meal each day with Karis Luran. Jake never leaves my side. When we dine, I am coolly distant, resentful of the way she'd so swiftly manipulated me: into proving my magic, into working against Rhen. Resentful of the way she's hidden her daughter away after such a brutal display of vengeance against that guard.

"Every time she asks for wine," Jake murmurs to me at one of our luncheons, "I expect her to cut some poor guy's wrist open over a glass."

Indeed. I do not like her. I do not trust her.

This is no secret. "You do not like me, Young Prince," she says to me on the third day.

"Do I need to?"

"No." She smiles. "To desire adoration is to make yourself vulnerable."

I definitely do not adore her. Her subjects seem to, however. Her cruelty is seen as decisive and just.

And despite my resentment, she seems to be a fair ruler. She cares for her subjects. The people of Syhl Shallow are well fed and educated. Two years of military service are required of each family—leading to a sense of unity that takes me by surprise each time I join Talfor and Cortney in the city.

Her castle coffers may be running dry without the tithe once paid by Rhen's father, but Karis Luran does what she can to support her people, and despite her brutality, they seem to love her for it. It makes me wonder how Rhen's treatment of me was received. It makes me wonder how his subjects will respond when he sends soldiers to claim back Silvermoon Harbor.

As always, I wish my thoughts carried no concern for Rhen.

My afternoons are full of drills with the guards and soldiers as we prepare to leave—and they're the only time I can relax, because I have a sword in my hand. They fight differently here, and I enjoy the challenge of learning their methods and weaponry. I don't enjoy the challenge of the dinner hour, because every evening meal includes people of importance: generals and military leaders, as well as leaders of the Royal Houses. I am not Rhen, able to influence people with hardly more than the right glance, but it seems my steady refusal to be manipulated has worked in greater favor. No one challenges me to demonstrate magic. No one challenges me at all.

No one except Iisak, who all but drags me out of my chambers after dark, insisting that we must strengthen my magic. My skills seem so small and minor compared to what I know Lilith could do.

She cursed me and Rhen, trapping us in an endless cycle of her magic. I can barely affect more than one person at a time.

On the night before we are to leave, we are on the deserted training fields in the moonlight. Iisak insists I can feed my magic into my swordplay for accuracy and damage—and once I learn *that*, I can potentially do the same for my soldiers.

It's not going well. Jake and Tycho have volunteered to help, but I need no magic to guide my sword to best them. When we break apart for the tenth time, they're exhausted. Sweat glints in the moonlight. I glance up at the palace. Sometimes I can catch a glimpse of Lia Mara, but tonight her room is dark, and no shadow fills her window.

Noah has been watching from the sidelines. "Maybe you should tie an arm behind your back," he says.

I push damp hair out of my eyes and sigh. Our time to prepare grows short. I am hurtling toward an uncertain end, but I have no idea how to stop it.

"Perhaps you need a new opponent," calls Nolla Verin.

I turn and see her striding out of the darkness, guards at her back. Instead of the robes that typically adorn her small frame, tonight she wears black leather armor trimmed with silver, her dark hair braided back with green ribbon. A sword and a dagger are already in her hands.

I raise my eyebrows. "Are you offering?"

"Yes." She lifts her blade and attacks.

I'm not completely unprepared, but I'm barely able to block before she spins and parries. I try to hook her dagger to pull it from her hand, but she ducks and whirls to regroup. I watch her movement, looking for weakness.

She gives me no time. Her next attack is brutal and swift.

My response is, too.

She breaks away again, her breathing a little quick. She smiles, and it's fierce. "If you draw blood, my mother will be displeased."

"Then you should better guard your left side." This time I attack first, putting my full strength behind it. Her sword is lighter, and she yields almost at once, but she moves quicker than thought. Her attacks seem to come from everywhere at once, and she's relentless. I remember Lia Mara praising her sister's skills—and she wasn't wrong.

In another place and time, I'd be openly admiring, but I'm tired, and this feels like more posturing. Much like the morning we raced through the city, I see no path to victory here. She's right— Karis Luran would likely have my head if I harmed her heir, alliance or not.

Her sword almost gets past my guard, and she nearly cuts a stripe across my arm.

"What was that you said about left sides?" she says.

She's right, so I smile. "Noted."

"I thought you were to be using magic to assist your swordplay. I hoped I would get a demonstration."

"So far I haven't needed assistance."

"Try to kill him," Jake calls. "That's usually what works."

Nolla Verin's eyes narrow, and she leaps forward. She's somehow even quicker. Our blades have become a blur in the moonlight. Every time she strikes, there's more strength behind it, and when she slices open my shoulder in an attempt to disarm me, I realize she really *might* be trying to kill me.

I try to hook her sword, but she's a fraction of a second too quick, and it leaves my side open. She dives in, aiming for my ribs. Those stars wait in my blood, fueled by the fight and the damage, waiting for my command. I try to send them into my weapons, hoping they'll quicken my defense and stop her.

Nolla Verin goes flying back, landing so hard in the dust of the training grounds that she skids the final distance.

Her guards are immediately in front of her, swords drawn and leveled at me.

"No!" Nolla Verin coughs. "I told him to do it."

"Told you," Jake says.

The guards slowly lower their weapons. I feel as surprised as she looks, but I sheathe my sword and walk to Nolla Verin, extending a hand. She glances at it, then springs to her feet on her own. She regards me with obvious new interest—but greater regard. "As I said. A new opponent."

"As you said."

Her breathing is faintly quick now, her cheeks pink in the moonlight. "Again?"

I hesitate.

"Yes," calls Tycho.

She draws and swings. I barely draw my sword in enough time to stop hers. Our blades clash and fly in the night air until I feel the stars waiting.

Gently, Lia Mara said in the woods.

I give those stars a subtler push.

Nolla Verin misses her next block by several inches, and she throws herself back. I take advantage and hook her sword to disarm her, but it knocks her off balance, and she goes down hard.

Her guards are there again, but Nolla Verin is grinning up at me. "That is a handy trick."

I can't help smiling back. "Magic takes too much thought. I prefer the swords alone."

"It won't take much thought with more practice," says Iisak.

This time, when I offer my hand, Nolla Verin takes it. Once she's on her feet, she looks up at me, her eyes coolly calculating. Her hand doesn't leave mine.

"Walk with me," she says.

I lose the smile, and I glance up at the dark wall of the palace. "I should retire."

"Please?"

I inhale to decline, but emotion flickers in her eyes for a brief moment. For all of Lia Mara's comments about somehow being lesser than her sister, she never once spoke ill of Nolla Verin. The girl in front of me presents a fierce demeanor to the world, but I wonder how much of that has been developed to please her mother—and what hides beneath it.

I nod and offer my arm.

Nolla Verin laughs and starts walking. "Do ladies in Emberfall truly need assistance to *walk*?"

"No. Keep your distance if you'd rather."

She huffs in surprise, and I discover I was right. So much of her aggression is a front to hide insecurity. In truth, she reminds me of Rhen a bit. They likely would have made powerful allies.

Then again, one of them probably wouldn't have survived the first week.

We walk in silence across the training fields, the shadows growing longer as we move away from the torches near the back wall of the palace. Her guards have followed at a distance, as has Jake, which surprises me.

Nolla Verin glances over her shoulder at where Tycho and Iisak remain. "Mother does not like that you've freed that creature from his tether."

"He is not my slave."

She glances up at me. "What did you threaten him with, then, to keep his obedience?"

"Nothing." I want to ask if ladies in Syhl Shallow need threats or a tether to ensure a promise is kept, but I do not wish to fight with her.

We fall into silence again. It's prickly and uncomfortable. I much preferred swinging swords. It felt like the first time she'd been open and honest with me.

Maybe because she was trying to kill me.

I consider everything I heard from Lia Mara, and everything I've gleaned on my own. Nolla Verin is quick to echo her mother's desires, and I wonder how deeply that runs. I glance at her. "Do you want this alliance?"

"Yes. It will be a boon for our people to have access to the waterways at Silvermoon Harbor, and it will benefit Emberfall to have funds to assist with rebuilding after all that was lost."

"All that was lost during the invasion by Syhl Shallow, you mean."

"All that was lost while your royal family was 'in hiding.'" She looks up at me. "Do not pin all your troubles on us."

"I am not." Though I am. A little. It's impossible not to. "That was not my question, though, Princess."

"What is your question?"

"Do *you* want this alliance?" I stop and turn to face her. "With me."

"Of course." That emotion flickers in her eyes again, but the longer I stand here speaking with her, the more I see it as uncertainty. Vulnerability. Lia Mara sang her sister's praises during our journey here, and certainly everyone I've met is quick to speak of Nolla Verin's talents on a horse, or with a bow, or with a blade. Well-earned, for certain, but maybe all her skills hide the fact that she seems so perfect for the throne because she has no backbone to defy her mother. Maybe all her skills and her parroting hide the fact that she is young, and untested, and uncertain.

After spending so much time with Lia Mara in the woods, I began to wonder why Karis Luran would choose her younger daughter to be her heir—to negotiate an alliance first with Rhen, and now with me. Lia Mara believes it is because she herself is quiet and longs for peace—that she lacks her sister's ruthlessness.

I now wonder if it is because Lia Mara would stand against her mother.

And Nolla Verin will not.

I glance back at the palace, and I can see a flutter of color at Lia Mara's window. "How long will your mother keep your sister imprisoned?"

She follows my gaze. "Lia Mara is in a royal suite in the Crystal Palace. She is hardly imprisoned."

I can hear the uncertainty in her voice. It's well hidden, but it's there. "You worry for her."

"Yes. I do."

But she will not visit her. I know as much from Iisak and the notes he brings to me. Nolla Verin will not contradict her mother's will.

Silence drops between us again, full of so many unspoken things.

Nolla Verin knows I gave Lia Mara my jacket on the terrace—but she has never mentioned it. I wonder what she suspects. What she thinks. What she worries about.

I am hardly one to complain—she likely wonders the same about me. I learned long ago how to hide every thought behind the stoic countenance of a guardsman. She likely learned the same as a princess.

Maybe I was wrong. Nolla Verin isn't like Rhen at all.

She's like me.

I think of Iisak, the night we fought. *I needed a battle, too*, he said.

I glance at her. "Are you rested, Princess?"

"Somehow I have managed it, without the assistance of your arm."

I smile. "Good."

Without warning I draw my sword, and she grins.

CHAPTER FORTY-THREE

LIA MARA

Every candle in my chambers is still lit when Iisak alights on my windowsill. I'm sure he has a note from Grey, but I have no desire to read it. I almost wish he hadn't appeared tonight. My thoughts flicker between desire and loyalty, and I doubt I'll be good company. Books and papers are spread across my chaise lounge, and a half-eaten platter of sugared fruits sits by my side.

"The hour is late," says the scraver. "I expected to find you asleep."

I don't look up at him. "Did you? Truly?"

He ignores my sarcasm. "Yes. Truly."

"I'm reading about Iishellasa. Why did the magesmiths leave while the scravers remained behind?" I peer over at him. "Why were the magesmiths not bound by a treaty?"

He ignores my questions. "You seem unsettled, Princess."

"I'm not."

He's quiet for a moment, and I wonder if he will accept my lie.

Because I am unsettled. I'll probably die locked in this room. I sometimes wonder if my mother has forgotten about me. Maybe I shouldn't have bothered escaping Rhen's castle. I certainly would have spared myself a dose of heartache.

I swallow past the thickness in my throat and look down at the papers. "About the magesmiths and the scravers. Do you know why?" I tuck an errant lock of hair behind my ear. A tear drips off my cheek to land on the documents, and I quickly swipe it away.

Iisak eases into the room, but he stops on the other side of the papers to drop to a crouch. I can feel the weight of his gaze, but I keep my eyes down.

I wait for him to pry, but he taps a finger on the papers.

"A magesmith cannot be identified by sight," he says. "And they could cross the Frozen River by virtue of magic instead of flight." He pauses. "Before the treaty was struck, we could all travel freely, but the people of Syhl Shallow were afraid of the scravers. The magesmiths tried to speak for us, but magic had already become something to fear—and we had no desire to visit harm on Syhl Shallow. Unfortunately, the desires of rulers are not always the desires of the people. Small skirmishes would occur when my people would arrive on your side of the river. A child died."

I glance up. "A scraver child?"

"A human child."

Oh. I frown.

"Your mother's mother demanded restitution. The magesmiths assisted with negotiation. We struck an agreement. The magesmiths confined themselves to Iishellasa for a time, but the ice forests can be treacherous for humans, and they grew restless and sought somewhere new to settle. By that time, your mother had come to power. Karis Luran did not want magic in Syhl Shallow, so they traveled through the mountain pass and eventually settled in Emberfall for a time."

I stare at him. "Where they were destroyed."

"Many of them. Yes." He pauses. "You see why we do not take the treaty lightly, Princess."

"But now Mother is willing to overlook Grey's magic."

"She must want access to these waterways very badly."

"Hmm." I look down again. I shuffle the papers back into a pile, then move to the wall to begin extinguishing candles. I did not intend to turn the discussion to Grey.

"You still seem unsettled," Iisak says, and an ice-cold draft swirls against my face and lifts my hair.

I blow out another candle and move to the next. I wonder if Parrish would let me pass if I set my room on fire.

Before I reach the next candle, frigid wind whips through the room, scattering papers and extinguishing all the candles at once.

I scowl at Iisak and begin scooping the papers back into a pile. "I am pleased to see that Grey and Nolla Verin are getting along so well."

"Do you think so?"

"I know what I saw."

"Ah. Shall I tell the prince you have no interest in his latest missive, then?"

My hands go still on the pile of documents. My heart is already jumping in my chest, eager to read his words—but then I think of the smile he shared with Nolla Verin, and my heart plummets with such force that I have to press a hand to my belly. "Yes," I whisper.

"Princess?"

"I'm not a princess."

He takes a step toward me, and I put up a hand. "Stop. Please stop. It is not worth it, Iisak. We must end this. What will become of it? My people are at risk if this alliance does not succeed. Are we to exchange secret notes forever?"

He regards me silently, his black eyes glittering in the near darkness.

I swipe away a tear. "This is a betrayal to my sister, Iisak. A betrayal to my *mother*. A betrayal to my country. I cannot do it. I have done enough wrong. I cannot continue."

"Wrong!" He hisses, and frost gathers on the windowpanes. "Princess, do you realize that you alone have brought this alliance to pass? If Syhl Shallow and Emberfall swear allegiance, it is because of *your* efforts to achieve peace. Grey was willing to give up his birthright to such an extent that he allowed himself to be strung up and beaten rather than acknowledge it. Yet you were able to convince him otherwise. *You*, Lia Mara. Do you realize how powerful that is?"

"Powerful! You and Grey keep insisting I have power and strength, when I have none. I am locked in this room. I am an *obstacle*."

"You are imprisoned *because* of your power. How can you not see that?"

"I am imprisoned because my mother wants Grey to be besotted with my sister. How can *you* not see that?" He inhales to say something, but I put up my hand. "No, Iisak. I am done. I cannot continue. I will watch from my window, and I will wish them well when they leave to march on Emberfall tomorrow."

He studies me in the shadowed darkness. "It is his final letter, Princess."

That forces me still. I should refuse again.

Oh, I can hardly fool myself.

Lia Mara,

I should be doing all of this for the people of Emberfall. For the people of Syhl Shallow, even. I should be undertaking all of this to achieve peace and stability. I desire those things, of course, but what drives me is that you desire these things.

I cannot bear the thought of you locked away. Your mother wields you like a weapon against me—and it is working. I tread carefully to ensure this accord proceeds toward peace, and not toward the destruction of Emberfall.

But I would abandon it all, Lia Mara. We are to leave in the morning. I was not trained as a prince. I was trained to be a weapon at the hand of another. I can do that again, for you.

Do you long for escape? Or shall I continue along this path?

Give the order and I will obey.

Yours,

Grey

My eyes close, and I press the letter to my chest. I remember his eyes in the hallway of that inn in Blind Hollow, the low rasp of his voice when we were both exhausted, but he neglected sleep to guard my door. *Fear not. No one will touch you again.*

He would give all this up to rescue me.

Because of everything I believe, I can't ask him to.

Iisak is watching me. "Shall I tell him anything?"

Emotion grips my throat again. I straighten my robes and refuse to allow any further tears to fall. "Tell him to be a great king."

———◆———

I cannot sleep. Horrific visions haunt my thoughts. My sister going off to war, sliced in two by a guard from Emberfall. Grey riding into battle, overtaken by dozens of soldiers who drive their blades into him faster than he can heal. Shadows crawl across my wall into the early morning hours as I toss and turn, tangling my bedsheets. When a faint scratching sounds at my window and a shadow fills the frame, I am equally relieved and irritated.

"Iisak—" I begin, but the figure unfolds from the window frame. No wings. Not a scraver—a man. My heart jolts and stutters, and I suck in a breath, slipping out of bed to back away.

"Be at ease, my lady."

Oh. *Oh.* "Grey," I whisper. My chest tightens, and my throat swells. I press my hands together in front of my mouth.

He moves forward to stop in front of me. His long fingers brush the tears off my cheeks. "Do not cry," he says, his voice lovely and deep.

His eyes are intent on mine, longing and uncertainty sparking there in the depths of his gaze.

Every word I said to Iisak is forgotten now that Grey is here, sharing the same air I breathe.

I glance at the window. "Iisak said he cannot bear the weight of a man. How—how did you—*how?*"

"He can bear the weight of a rope. And I can climb."

My heart refuses to stop fluttering. "It is three stories!"

His lip quirks. "Ah . . . I didn't look down."

"But—the palace guards—"

"Please." He gives me a look.

I stare up at him and want so many things. I want to kiss him again. I want to feel his fingers against my skin. I want to whisper secrets around a campfire. I want the world to narrow down to me and him and nothing else.

Everything I want goes against everything my country needs.

"You said you would obey my order," I finally say.

"I cannot be a great king if I leave my allies imprisoned."

I frown and take a step back. "You cannot rescue me. Grey— too much is at stake."

"I feel as though we both need rescuing, Lia Mara."

The torment in his expression mirrors what I feel. I press my fingers to my eyes. "You should leave."

"Do you truly want me to?"

No.

I can't say it. I don't need to say it. He doesn't move.

"We are too bound by honor and duty," he says. "It seems a cruel trick of fate to bring us together."

"I don't believe in fate," I whisper.

"Hmm. Does that make any of this feel easier?"

I swallow. "No."

"The hour is quite late," he says. "I should not have disturbed your sleep."

"I don't mind." The words are bold, and inappropriate, and all I am doing is inviting further pain and regret. I simply cannot help myself. I want to lean into him and inhale his scent.

"I would rescue you," Grey says. "If you would allow it."

My eyes snap open. I don't even remember closing them. He is so close.

"Grey . . ."

"Everyone else seeks to manipulate me," he says. He breathes a sigh. "There is no one here I can trust."

That startles me out of my swooning. "I thought you were well on your way to trusting Nolla Verin."

"Your sister seems more eager to see if she can *kill* me than anything else."

"She could not best you." I turn away, thinking of my coquettish sister. "Trust me, you have her attention."

He catches my waist, pulling me still, pulling me close. His dark eyes bore into mine. "Do I have yours?"

The room is so still and quiet, and his patience seems eternal, because he holds me there until the tension slips out of my body and I nod. "Yes," I whisper. "You do."

He leans in, his lips brushing mine with the weight of a butterfly, and my breath catches.

"Yes?" he whispers.

"Yes."

When he kisses me again, it's even slower, gentle and strong all at once, his hands holding me upright. My fingers clutch at his jacket, pulling him closer, until his body is against me, warm and solid against my sleeping shift. I feel as though I'm flying—or drowning. Warmth surges through my chest and lights a fire in me.

Finally, I pull away. Too many lives are at risk, on both sides of our border. "Grey. You can't rescue me. You can't."

He goes still. "I could have you down the rope in minutes. I know the pattern of the guards."

My heart thrills a little too much at that suggestion. "No." I draw back. "Peace with Emberfall is too important. You cannot."

"As you say." He seems to steel himself, his eyes shutting down the way they do when he must be violent.

I don't like him doing that with me. *I was trained to be a weapon at the hand of another.*

I pull him closer. "No, Grey. No." I brush my fingers over his cheeks, his eyelids, then brush my lips against his face. "Do not hide from me."

He yields to my touch, but I can feel the difference in his body now.

"You cannot rescue me," I say again, so softly that the words feel imagined. "But perhaps . . . for a while . . . you could stay."

CHAPTER FORTY-FOUR

GREY

We end up sitting beneath her window, eating leftover sugared plums and soft rolls from her dinner tray, sharing the night air and enjoying the silence. Perhaps another man would be using this time to unlace the back of her sleeping shift and cajole her into the bed, but that feels insincere. I do not like the idea of sneaking into her luxurious prison to take advantage of her. This is the first time we've ever been truly alone together, and it makes her seem more vulnerable somehow. More precious.

I don't know which of us is more committed to honor and duty, but I was ready to rappel down the castle wall with her on my back, so I think it is not me.

"What are you going to do if someone comes looking for you?" she says quietly.

"My rooms are not far. Iisak is listening for trouble. Jake and Noah are sitting awake, waiting for me to return."

"*Rooms?*" Her eyebrows go up. "Mother truly did want to make you feel welcome."

I sigh. "She wants me to feel *something*."

"You do not trust her."

I look at Lia Mara in the darkness. We are speaking of her mother, so I should deny it. But there have never been untrue words between us, and I don't want to start now. "No. I don't. Do you?"

"I trust her to do what she believes is best for Syhl Shallow."

I roll my eyes. "Exactly."

"If you had not discovered your birthright, would you have stayed with Rhen, once the curse was broken?"

"Yes, of course."

But as I say the words, I realize there is no *of course* about it. I consider those months in Rillisk, when I was just Hawk. After an endless cycle of season after season of torture at Lilith's hand, followed by the danger and destruction of the monster Rhen would become . . . there was a simplicity I craved.

I look at Lia Mara. "I was seventeen when I became a guardsman. My family was so desperate—I just wanted a way to provide for them. I don't think the king had any idea who I was." I shrug a little. "Or perhaps he knew, and he liked knowing I was close, even if he could never acknowledge me. I have no idea. No one keeps secrets like the dead."

Her eyes are warm with sympathy, but she waits.

"I had only just been assigned to guard the royal family when we were trapped by the curse. I was not an officer." I pause, remembering. "Rhen and his sisters were fickle and capricious at best, but boredom brought out the worst of their temperaments. They often lacked for entertainment, and guardsmen eager to keep their assignments were easy targets."

"You once said Rhen was never cruel."

"He had his moments, but true malice was rare." I glance at her. "Perhaps cruelty is something you must learn in order to rule."

"Do you truly believe that?"

"I see the 'loyalty' your mother has inspired in her people, and I think it must not hurt."

Lia Mara frowns. "I believe you can only push people down so far before they will rise up and rebel." She pauses. "You spoke of the curse feeling like an eternity. Even if Rhen was not cruel, I think it must have been a relief to escape that duty."

"Yes. It was." The words are almost a relief to say. Despite everything we endured together, there was an element of relief to finding myself in charge of my own future.

I could have told Rhen what I knew. Right then, right when I learned it from Lilith. I didn't.

We settle into silence again. The window is full of moonlight. My fight on the field with Nolla Verin feels like a lifetime ago. I want to wish for another path but wishing solves nothing. The minutes tick by, bringing us ever closer to the moment when I must leave.

Lia Mara eventually looks at me. Her fingers drift over mine. "I'm glad you came, Grey."

I close my fingers around hers, and she pulls me toward her again. She kisses me gently, her lips drawing at mine. Her fingers tangle in the hair at the nape of my neck, and the kiss becomes anything *but* gentle.

"I should have climbed up here days ago," I say.

"Ahh. *Fell siralla.*" She rolls her eyes and kisses me again.

"*Nah,*" I say, offering the same words she spoke on the veranda so many days ago. "*Fell bellama. Fell garrant.*"

She blinks, then laughs in surprise. "You've been practicing!"

"*Fell vale,*" I say. I kiss her, whispering against her lips. "Gentle man."

She blushes hotly, then presses her face against my chest. I hold her there and breathe.

The lock at her door clicks.

Silver hell. I all but leap through the window. The rope finds my hands by little more than a whispered prayer to fate. My feet fight to grip the wall as the rope swings wildly. My breath is a wild rush in my ears, the palace wall cold as ice in the night air.

Or maybe that's Iisak, soaring through the air to land against a ledge fifteen feet above me. His black eyes peer down at me. "Problems, Your Highness?"

I stare daggers at him and shake my head vigorously.

My breathing needs to steady. I have no idea where the guards are in their patrolling, so I cannot remain against the palace wall too long—but I also don't want to leave Lia Mara in danger. I will my frantic heartbeat to slow, then ease up a few feet to listen.

Karis Luran's voice. ". . . are progressing nicely. You see now why I have kept you confined to your room."

"Yes, Mother." Lia Mara's voice seems so small.

"I admit, I was worried he would attempt to turn his magic against us, but I have witnessed his attempts on the training fields. Perhaps his half-blood will work in our favor. He is not the threat the magesmiths once were."

I can't even scowl. She's not wrong. And I don't trust her. Why should she trust me?

My forearms strain against the rope.

"We have received word that Rhen's forces are divided between cities, and we have no time to waste. The Royal Houses would like to have a gathering to offer their blessings to our generals." Karis Luran pauses. "After your display at the last fete, I would like to demonstrate to the Royal Houses that there is no conflict between you and your sister. I would like to demonstrate that Grey is devoted to this alliance, and to Nolla Verin. You will not attend. You will keep your distance."

"Yes, Mother."

"You will not disappoint me again." The threat in her voice is clear. I remember Cortney saying, *The Stone Prison is not full of loyalists.*

Silence.

I have to shift my weight, but I don't want to risk it. I stare up at Iisak. He leans down a bit, until I'm not sure how he's maintaining his balance.

My forearms are screaming. It's surely been too long. The guards patrolling the grounds will spot me soon.

Suddenly Lia Mara's face appears above me. Anguish fills her eyes. A tear slips free and strikes my cheek.

I pull myself up a few feet until I can brace on the window ledge.

"You must go," she whispers.

"Lia Mara—"

"Please," she whispers. Another tear slips free.

I reach out to brush it from her cheek. She takes a step back, out of reach.

"Go," she whispers.

"Please. Wait." I swallow. "We have so little time—"

She swipes tears from her face and straightens. "Please. I told you I do not matter."

Above me, Iisak says, "Your Highness. The guards are beginning to turn back this way."

"I can rescue you," I say. The words come from my lips without hesitation. "This instant."

"I don't need rescuing." She chokes on her breath. "Please, Grey. We knew what was at the end of this road."

I wish for more time. There is none.

My life is full of wishes that never come true.

"This is your choice?" I say.

She straightens and wipes the tears off her face. When she speaks, her voice is unwavering and strong. "This is my choice. For my people. For yours. You said you would obey my order, and I gave it. Leave me. Be a good king."

There is no path here. I feel as though the curse never ended. The players simply changed.

Her expression is unyielding. She gave an order, and I said I would obey.

"As you say." I set my jaw, loop the rope around my boot, and rappel down the wall.

CHAPTER FORTY-FIVE

GREY

Karis Luran arrives at my door at sunrise with a full contingent of guards. Nolla Verin is at her side, her eyes narrow and guarded. "Prince Grey. We have brought new armor befitting your station, for you and your men."

A servant shifts forward and bows to me, then others move forward to flank him, holding out armor so freshly minted that I can smell the leather and oil. The black leather of the breastplate is lined with green, the colors of Syhl Shallow, but the crest emblazoned in the center is the gold and red seal of Emberfall: a lion and rose entwined, with a gold crown embossed above it, signifying royalty.

I trace my finger over the crest. The same insignia once appeared on my Royal Guard uniform—without the crown.

"Our colors together will let your people know you stand for unity," says Karis Luran.

I meet her eyes. "Will your armor bear the colors of Emberfall as well?"

Her lip curls ever so slightly. "No. It seemed foolish to go to the expense of outfitting the entire army."

So I will look to be allying with her—while she risks nothing.

I have nothing with which to bargain, though. "You have my thanks."

She smiles, and she looks like a viper. There is no love lost between me and this woman. I would cut her down right here in the hallway if Lia Mara begged for release.

"The Royal Houses will gather on the training fields," she says. "They would like to offer a blessing for our journey. I would like for you to demonstrate your magic, to show our advantage over Rhen's people." She pauses. "And you will keep that *creature* on a chain."

Behind me, Iisak hisses.

I don't even turn around. "No."

"You swore that you would maintain his year of service. You said you would require him to do my bidding. This is my will, and you will do it."

My heart is pulsing in my chest, because I sense a trap. Nolla Verin is too still.

"I will perform a feat of magic," I say woodenly. "I will not put any of my people on a *chain*."

Anger flashes in her eyes. "Then I will—"

"I will wear a chain," says Iisak, but frost curls along the stone walls of my chambers. "If it will make you feel safe, Your Majesty."

Karis Luran doesn't look at him. Her eyes don't leave mine. "You will maintain order among your people or I will maintain it myself."

"Your terms have been agreed to."

I wait for her to spring a trap, to demand more, but she turns away without another word, her guards trailing in her wake. Servants stack the offered armor inside the door, then bow and move away as well.

Only Nolla Verin remains behind. She reaches out to touch the armor her mother delivered. She traces her hand over the crest, as I did. She looks up at me. "Does it cause you pain, to know what you must do to your brother?"

I go still. "Yes," I say, and my voice is suddenly rough. "Every moment of this causes me pain."

She looks up at me in surprise, but then it fractures and shifts into dismay. I have never seen such emotion on Nolla Verin's face.

As suddenly as it appeared, the emotion vanishes, locked away, leaving only the dutiful daughter.

"I will see you on the battlefield, Prince Grey."

I offer her a bow, and she turns away.

Once she's down the hallway, Jake moves close. "What the hell just happened?"

I watch her go, sadness all but trailing her form. "Indeed."

The training fields are packed with at least twelve hundred soldiers standing at attention, their lines perfect and unbroken. Green and black pennants snap in the wind, and every inch of armor and weaponry gleams in the sunlight. The members of the Royal Houses watch from beneath tents erected along the castle walls, each sitting on a jeweled chair, waiting for the show to begin. My new armor fits well, snug and secure against my frame. Buckling it into place seemed to carry weight, like so many other moments on this journey. When

I used to don armor in the Royal Guard, it meant something. This means something, too.

Jake walks at my side, and I am glad for his steady presence. Once I wouldn't have been able to imagine it. Now I wonder how I stayed at odds with him for so very long. He was wasted on Rhen, truly. Noah and Tycho follow, Tycho holding Iisak's chain. When we walked out of the castle, Iisak said, "Does the queen think I couldn't pry this tether away from the boy?"

Tycho smiled and said, "Does the queen think you'd need to?"

It's all a show for her people. I knew it before we set foot on this battlefield. Karis Luran does not want to appear weak in front of her Royal Houses. Even my show of magic is to be temperate, nothing that would seem to overpower her.

Karis Luran and Nolla Verin wait on a dais at the front of the troops, standing with Clanna Sun and the queen's generals. My time as a guardsman sometimes feels like a distant memory, but I am no stranger to pageantry. I walk right up to the dais and bow to her.

"Your Majesty," I say. "I stand ready to ride with you into Emberfall."

There is more I am to say, but I freeze. Her gaze coolly holds mine.

"Say it," Jake hisses from behind me.

My lips are frozen. *To claim my throne.*

Motion flickers in one of the windows of the palace, and I know Lia Mara is looking down, watching this. *Be a good king.*

Would Rhen be a good king? I thought so once, but now, I don't know.

Will I?

"Grey," says Jake. He nudges me in the shoulder.

"I am ready to claim my throne," I say, "and to ally the people of Emberfall with the people of Syhl Shallow."

Karis Luran smiles. At her side, Nolla Verin is stony-faced.

"Good," says the queen. "We are eager to see you on the throne, our ally and friend, and to secure new trade routes for both our countries." She pauses for dramatic effect. "We once believed magic to be a danger to our people, but you have demonstrated that you will usher in a new era."

I nod. "I am prepared to offer your Houses a demonstration, as a show of good faith of how I can benefit Syhl Shallow."

"Very good," she says. I wait for her to indicate one of the tents, where a son apparently has a broken arm I am to heal.

But Karis Luran steps forward. "A show of loyalty," she adds. "To prove your willingness to ally with my people."

I hesitate.

"You know," she says, "I have no tolerance for those who would stand against me. You saw what I did to my guard who dared to defy me."

"Yes, Your Highness," I say, and my voice is cautious. I am not the only one who suspects a trap. Jake has moved closer, but we are surrounded by thousands of soldiers. I certainly can't fight them all. If Karis Luran means to attack me, I'm dead. I might have been able to knock Rhen and his guards back a few feet, but I have no idea if my power would cover a crowd of this size—nor if I could protect all of my people.

Behind me, Iisak growls low, and ice forms around my boots on the ground. A warning.

I know, I think.

I just don't know what to do.

"You will prove your loyalty to this alliance," she says. "You will prove that you will be loyal to Nolla Verin and to me."

"This is going to be bad," mutters Jake.

"How?" I say. "How would you like for me to prove this?"

"When you were admitted to your Royal Guard, were you put to a test?"

"Yes, of course."

"My guardsmen are put to a test as well. They must prove willing to do whatever their queen orders."

"You are not my queen," I say boldly.

Her smile widens. "Ah, yes, but you are not yet king, and your power is dependent upon mine. If you wish to claim your throne, if you and your people wish to survive your time in Syhl Shallow, you will prove your willingness to do what is right."

"Offer your challenge," I say. "I have said I will provide a display of magic."

"You saved a traitor," she says. "You spared the life of my guard Parrish."

"You asked him to," says Jake.

"Indeed," she says. "Now I will ask you to use your magic to execute a traitor. I will ask you to prove your loyalty, Prince Grey."

"No," says Noah, his voice a low rush behind me. "No. You can't."

I was trained to be a weapon at the hand of another. A cool certainty overtakes me. Magic always seems to elude me. Being a prince has never felt natural. But my people are at risk. My life is at risk. With violence and bloodshed, I am comfortable.

Tycho once looked into my eyes and said, "You can't train mercy out of someone."

You can. I know you can. I'm living proof.

"Bring your traitor," I say. "I will do what you ask."

Her smile widens, and she looks to her daughter. "Nolla Verin. Fetch your sister."

CHAPTER FORTY-SIX

LIA MARA

*N*olla Verin. *Fetch your sister.*

I wait in the window. I'm not sure what I wait for.

For Nolla Verin to refuse. That's what I'm waiting for. Grey's expression has gone cold and still. The troops wait. The Royal Houses wait. The air of anticipation is almost palpable.

I keep hoping for peace. I keep longing for empathy.

I keep expecting people to act as I would.

I forgot that my mother rules through fear and violence.

I forgot that I am worthless to her.

Nolla Verin looks stunned, but she has never had the will to refuse our mother. She nods and steps off the dais.

My heart stumbles and falls in my chest.

No. Sister.

Two sisters, one heart.

Please, Nolla Verin.

She disappears into the palace. She will be at my door in minutes. She has never failed our mother. Never.

My eyes search the room, as if weapons would magically appear on the wall.

I am such a fool. Grey offered escape, and I refused.

I throw open the door, and Parrish is there, barring the way. His ruined eye is still red, mottled bruising surrounding the stitching that holds the lids closed. I have begged for release before, and he has always refused. He never listens to my apologies, so I don't know why he would now.

"Parrish, please," I whisper.

He reaches out as if to slam the door in my face.

I throw out a hand to stop him, putting my weight into it. "Please," I say. "Please. Parrish, she will make Grey kill me."

He stares back at me, his remaining eye unreadable.

"I'm sorry," I say. "I'm so sorry for Sorra. I'm sorry. I would take her place. I would undo it if I could."

"You wanted peace," he growls, and I've never heard his voice like this. "You're getting it."

"No. Not like this. He doesn't want to kill for someone else. You don't understand. Please. Please, Parrish."

"I loved her!" he roars. "You beg me for your life. I *loved* her."

"I know." My voice breaks. "I know. I saw it every time you were together. *Please*. Nolla Verin is coming—"

"Enough." He moves to force the door closed, but I wedge myself into the opening.

He draws his dagger and puts it against my throat.

I freeze.

"I was given orders to use deadly force if you attempted to leave."

I swallow, and the blade jumps against my skin.

"Parrish," I rasp.

He says nothing. I watch emotion flash through his remaining eye, but that blade does not move.

I close my eyes. "You wanted peace, too, Parrish. You wanted peace, and Sorra wanted it for you." I have to swallow again. His blade is so sharp. "She loved you. I didn't know what—" I gasp. "I didn't know what Rhen would do."

He says nothing. Nolla Verin must be mere moments away.

"Grey saved your life," I say. "He has no part in what I did. I would take it back if I could. I would bring us back to that moment in the woods and I would say my mother was *right*."

"No," says Parrish. "You would not."

But the knife doesn't leave my neck.

He's not wrong.

"Parrish," I say. "You can run, too. You know what she will do with you if she secures this alliance. You know she seeks vengeance."

"There is nothing more she can take from me."

"She can assign you to serve in Emberfall. She can force you to work in tandem with the men who killed Sorra. She can have you serve in the very room where she died."

"Enough."

This time his voice is very quiet. My breathing is almost shaking. The weight of his dagger hasn't left my throat.

"We loved you, too," he says.

I clench my eyes shut. A tear slips free. "I know. And I loved you both as well."

The dagger slips free. "Go."

My eyes snap open. "Parrish," I whisper.

"Are you a fool?" His remaining eye blazes at me. "Go!"

"You must run. You must—"

"They are not after me, Lia Mara."

He's right. I run. I don't even have boots on, but my feet grip at the stone floor, and I round the corner.

Nolla Verin is standing there. She's in armor instead of robes, ready to ride at Grey's side to attack Emberfall. A bow is over her shoulder, a sword at her hip. Her eyes are red but determined.

I skid to a stop. My breathing is a loud rush in the hallway.

She is steady. Always steady. I cannot outrun my sister. I cannot outfight her. When she squares her shoulders and starts forward, my muscles are screaming at me to run, but I cannot.

She is my sister. My *sister*.

I raise my hands in the air. "I will not fight you, Nolla Verin."

She strides right up to me, her face so fierce. She will make such a great queen.

Then, instead of taking my hands and dragging me out of the castle, she wraps her arms around me and presses her face into my shoulder.

"I can't," she cries. "I can't."

I wrap her up in my arms and hold her. "You can," I whisper. "You can."

———————

I don't know how long we stand there. The castle is so silent. Anyone of importance is on the training fields, ready to march. Nolla Verin cries into my shoulder, and we clutch at each other for the longest time. She holds me so tightly that her weapons press into the front of my body, and I'll probably have bruises tomorrow.

If I'm alive tomorrow.

"They will come for you," I whisper eventually. My sister is here with me, and all will be well. It means nothing to vow my life for this alliance, for *peace*, if I am not willing to do as I said. I will not risk Nolla Verin along with myself. "You must take me."

"I love you," she says. She draws back and brushes the hair from my face. "I hope you know that."

"Of course I know that." I do not mention the moments wondering if she loved her quest for power more. I do not mention all our differences. Her love is potent in the air around us. When she embroidered that pillow for me, I saw her love in every stitch. "I love you, too."

She grips me so tightly. "I am sorry I did not come to you."

"Your heart was with me."

"No. My heart was uncertain." She sniffs. Her eyes search mine. "Will you tell me what happened when you were alone with Grey in the woods?"

"Nothing—truly. Nothing. We . . . we talked." My face warms. "We were friends."

"The truth, Sister." Her voice is so soft. "Please."

My heart flutters, and I press a hand to my chest. "In Emberfall, I knew I was bringing Grey home to you. I knew you would need to form an alliance with him. I knew he would find you beautiful and powerful and all the things you are."

"Something happened between you on the veranda."

I frown. "It was a mistake."

She takes my hands and clutches them between her own. "Lia Mara . . . I am not asking if you betrayed me."

I choose my words with care. "Then what are you asking me?"

"I am asking if you love him."

I shiver. "I do not know."

"You do know."

I look into her eyes. Her gaze is so piercing and clear. "I think I *could* love him." I pause. "I know what he must do. Mother is quite thorough in guaranteeing allegiance."

"I think he could love you, too." She squeezes my hands. "I hear it when he speaks of you. I see it when he looks at your window."

I turn my hands inside hers and squeeze back. "I bear you no ill wishes, Sister. I know . . . I know how things must be." My eyes threaten to well with tears, and I blink them away. "You will do what is right. He will, too. I have no doubt."

She nods—but then shakes her head. "I do not know what is right." The words are spoken in a whisper.

"Nolla Verin . . . I don't understand."

"What would you have done with the trapper in the woods?"

"What are you talking about? Why does it matter?"

"Just tell me. Please."

I push out the words. "I would have let him live."

She closes her eyes. A tear slips away from her lashes. The silence around us presses in like a weight.

I put my hands over hers. "He likely would have moved into that town and rung the alarm that we had entered Emberfall."

"Emberfall had so few forces available," she whispers. "It would not have mattered."

I agree with her.

I did not know she realized that.

"There was a sister in the woods," she says. "I saw her."

I grip her wrists. "What?"

"There was a sister. Another girl. The guards hadn't spotted her. Mother would have ordered her death as well." She lets out a breath. "I allowed her to get away."

My heart is beating so fast. My sister has never admitted any shred of empathy. "I allowed her to get away too," I say.

Her eyes stare into mine. "You did?"

"Yes. As did Parrish." And now my guard regrets every moment of it, I am certain.

"Mother always says she named me heir because I never question her," says Nolla Verin. "I do what needs to be done."

I smile sadly. "You do it well."

She shakes her head fiercely. "I do what she says because I do not have the strength to question her. You do."

"She would certainly disagree with you calling it a strength." I look up into my sister's troubled eyes and straighten my back. "I do not *matter*, Nolla Verin. You will be a great queen. He will be a great king. And our countries will finally be at peace. Do your duty, I am ready."

The field is absolutely silent when we step out of the palace. I expected Nolla Verin to bind my hands or tether me somehow, but she winds her fingers with mine and we walk onto the field together.

Mother looks pleased.

She has ordered Grey to kill me, and she looks *pleased*.

I force my eyes away from her. The soldiers standing in formation don't dare move. Her guards are ready and still. No one will question her. No one will stop this.

The grass slides under my bare feet. I wear robes with no belt, my red hair long and unbound. I am afraid to look at Grey. I am afraid that I will find doubt or sorrow or hesitation in his expression.

But I have to look at him. He must know this is the only way forward. He must know I will not fault him for doing this.

As my eyes lift, I find his men first. His *friends*. My friends. They have Iisak on a chain. Tycho looks even better in trim armor than he did in palace finery. His face is full of anguish. Noah looks disgusted. Jake looks like he wants to take on the entire army to stop this. And Grey.

Grey looks like a prince. In the combined colors of Syhl Shallow and Emberfall, he is regal and commanding. There is no hesitation. No uncertainty. The man who whispered his fears in the darkness of my bedroom is gone, leaving a prince who will be king.

I expected to find horror and misery in his gaze, but those dark eyes are cold and ready.

I would rescue you, he said so many times.

So many times I refused.

I would refuse now. But he does not offer.

Mother is speaking, but I do not hear the words. I do not need to. I hear her intent.

Cold air swirls around me, and I release Nolla Verin's hand to step forward. The sense of anticipation in the air is almost palpable. I should have seen. I should have known. My mother does not flinch. She rules by fear and power, and what better way to show her people how ruthless she can be than by killing her own daughter.

I stop in front of Grey. He says nothing. His eyes reveal nothing. I remember why I once found him frightening.

Do it, I think. *You must.*

He must kill me or she will kill him. I know it. He knows it too.

"Don't *do* this," Noah growls from behind him.

Grey does not flinch. His hands lift, settling on my shoulders, sliding upward to find my neck. My breath catches as his thumbs settle over my pulse point, and he surely must feel the steady thrumming of my heart.

I hope he will do it fast. I hope it will not hurt.

I hope. I hope. I hope.

He has not moved. His eyes are heavy and intent on mine, but there is no mercy there.

"Do it," I breathe. "You must. For our people, Grey."

"You hesitate," my mother calls. "Prince Grey, are you unwilling to prove your loyalty? Are you unwilling to do as I ask?"

"Do it," I say, my voice a low rush. His hands are cold at my throat. "Grey, you must. You cannot rescue me."

Mother takes a bow from her nearest guard, then nocks an arrow on the string. The point is leveled at me. "Shall I demonstrate true strength for you?"

"Mother, no!" says Nolla Verin.

"I would rather die at your hand than at hers!" I all but scream at him. "Do it, Grey. Please. You said you would obey any order I give. I order you! Do it!"

I hear the *swip* of an arrow. The world goes white. I suck in a breath, prepared for pain.

None comes. I blink up at Grey. We are alone, surrounded by trees, the mountains a wide stretch to my left. The sun beams down. His hands are still so secure on my neck.

"What happened?" I whisper. "What did you do?"

He looks down at me, and for the first time, his eyes reveal a hint of emotion. "I crossed over. We cannot stay."

"You . . . you crossed over?"

"If I am to be king," he says, his expression fierce and determined, "I must stop taking orders."

CHAPTER FORTY-SEVEN

GREY

I expect to return to chaos, but the training fields are oddly still silent. Lia Mara is now behind me, and my weapons are in hand. My plan is to grab my people and magic them across as well, but Karis Luran is too strategic. Too vicious. We've been gone less than a minute, but her guards have taken my people. They're on their knees, a crossbow pointed at each bowed head.

I don't know how to save them all. Lia Mara is pressed against my back, and I wonder if I saved her at their expense. She has one of my knives in each hand, but we cannot stand against an army. Cold wind swirls across the training grounds to make me shiver.

Karis Luran raises her bow. She's six feet in front of me, but I stare down at the point of that arrow and do not move. "You will not rule me by fear. You will not kill your daughter."

"Move, Prince Grey. We will finish this now. You will prove your loyalty, or I will execute your people."

"Mother. Please." Nolla Verin's voice is small and broken.

Bitter wind whips at my cheeks. Iisak's growl rolls across the training fields. I feel every spark and star in my blood waiting. I'm more sure of myself now. The magic is no longer something to fear.

"Move." Karis Luran's eyes are fixed on mine. The arrow point levels with my face. "Or I will execute you both."

"No."

"No," says Lia Mara. Her voice is fierce. She takes a step forward, her weapons raised.

"Kill them all." Karis Luran draws back the string. I hear the snap of crossbows. I have no idea whether my magic can beat an arrow, but I cast my sparks and stars wide, until my vision flares with gold.

At my side, Lia Mara's arm lifts. One of her knives goes flying. Then the other.

The arrow never strikes. Karis Luran's body jerks, and the bow clatters to the ground. She collapses in the grass. Blood is a wash of crimson along her neck.

For a moment, I think I've done it. That my magic has killed her.

But then I see the knives in her neck and upper chest. Perfect hits. Blood is pooling rapidly on the ground. A sudden hush has fallen over the training fields.

At my side, Lia Mara is breathing rapidly. "I told you," she says, her voice trembling. "I told you I could defend myself."

CHAPTER FORTY-EIGHT

LIA MARA

The scent of blood is heavy in the air. My mother's body is motionless on the ground, a dark stain spreading around her.

I drop to a knee. The dagger pierced true. Blood immediately soaks into my robes. Voices murmur in Syssalah all around me. Mother's guards have drawn swords, but no one has moved.

Nolla Verin is suddenly beside me.

I killed my mother. I can't breathe.

I can't *breathe.*

"Forgive me," I say, and a sob chokes out of my throat. My hands are sticky, and I press them to my stomach.

Someone drops to his knees beside me, and I expect Grey, but it is Noah.

He grimaces. "She was probably dead by the time she hit the ground."

"Good," says Jake behind me.

I feel as though everything is happening underwater. My movements feel too slow. I turn my head and find Noah waiting there.

"She—she killed you," I say. My voice is shaking. "I heard—I heard the crossbows."

"My magic," says Grey. He drops to a knee beside me as well. "It set the arrows off course."

I blink at him. He finds my hand and grips it in his.

My voice hitches. "Grey, what have I done?"

"You saved yourself," he says. His fingers tighten around mine. "You saved us both."

"I killed—I killed my mother."

"Breathe," he says softly.

Wings spin in the sky overhead, blotting out the sun. I blink, and Iisak stands over him, a silhouette in the sunlight. "Do more than breathe, Young Queen," he growls softly. "Stand and meet your people."

I go still.

I cannot do this.

I cannot.

I *cannot*.

"Sister."

Nolla Verin's voice draws my gaze. A tear leaks from her eyes. "I am glad it was you," she whispers.

The murmurs around us are growing louder. There are a few shouts. The soldiers have begun to shift uneasily. One of the generals is saying something about the rule of law.

"You must stand," Grey says. His tone is more urgent.

I grip his hand and pull myself to my feet. Every inch of me is trembling. The generals' arguing intensifies. Mother's personal guards look between me and Nolla Verin, and they do not put their blades away.

I should speak. I should say something. A word of command. A word of threat.

All I can do is stare at my mother's body.

Nolla Verin is the heir. Should be the heir. That is what Mother wanted.

I turn to my sister and hold out a hand.

"Can you stand?" I whisper to her. "You are the heir. You are queen. I cannot do this."

She stares up at me, then takes my hand. I pull her to her feet and take a deep breath. My sister was chosen for this. She will know what to do.

She releases my hand and takes a step back. She looks coolly out at the guards, at the soldiers, and at the generals. "My people," she calls. "Kneel to your queen."

Then she drops to her knees and presses her forehead to the ground. "Queen Lia Mara," she says.

Behind her, in a wave, every guard, every general, and every soldier does the same.

"Queen Lia Mara," they echo.

"Queen Lia Mara," says Grey, and he offers me a bow.

My chest cannot contain the emotion that I feel. My heart pounds so fast and hard that I want to set it free.

I take a deep breath and straighten my shoulders. "My people," I say, hoping the tremor in my voice is not as audible as it feels. "Rise."

CHAPTER FORTY-NINE

GREY

We do not go to war.

We do not even leave Syhl Shallow. The people want to celebrate their new queen. Unlike Emberfall, where it seems every town stands ready to take a stand against Rhen, here the people are overjoyed. Lia Mara is well known. Her people love her. They love the promise of peace she will bring to their country. Nolla Verin is always at her side, lending support when needed. The sisters are bold and triumphant in public, but they quietly grieve at night.

I feel as though I have been granted a reprieve, allowing Lia Mara space to find her footing in this new role. Her advisers insist that the Royal Houses are determined to move forward in an alliance with Emberfall, but Lia Mara meets my eyes across meeting tables and says we will wait until she can determine the best path forward for all her people.

I wonder how much of this is true concern for her armies, and how much is concern for me. I am in no rush to face Rhen, and that is no secret between us.

I would ask, but our time together is limited, and usually heavily supervised. She has gone from being "no one" to being someone of great importance. I can understand that—probably better than anyone.

Lia Mara has agreed to release Iisak from his punishment for breaking the treaty, but he has refused. He says the treaty is too important, and he will pay his penance.

He confides in me one night that he will maintain the year in Syhl Shallow because it grants him time to see if he can discover what became of his son.

"If you return to the ice forests, Lia Mara would allow you to come back," I say. "She would likely invalidate the treaty if you requested it."

"I once told you that the feelings of rulers are not always echoed in their subjects." He looks at me. "I will not risk more of my people crossing the Frozen River. The treaty keeps us safe as well."

I nod. "As you say."

A few nights later, I am sparring with Jake while Tycho and Nolla Verin trade blows nearby. He's yelling taunts at her every time she lands a hit with her sword, which is hilarious because she could likely slice him in two. Her face is shining, though, and she laughs each time. It's the lightest I've ever seen her. For the first time, there are no expectations for her to fulfill. She can just be a girl who loves her sister.

Jake takes advantage of my distraction to get inside my guard and disarm me. He looks so surprised that he almost forgets to follow it through, but then his shoulder slams into me, and I go down.

He points his sword at my throat and grins. "I've been waiting for this for *weeks*."

I smile. "Again?"

He sheathes the sword and brushes damp hair out of his eyes. "Hell no. I'm going to enjoy the win." He drops to sit on the turf beside me. We watch Tycho and Nolla Verin spar for a while, but their match has devolved into more laughter than actual swordplay.

At some point the silence between us shifts, becoming weighted.

I glance at Jake. "Something troubles you."

"When you disappeared with Lia Mara," he says slowly. "You crossed over, didn't you? Into my world."

I hesitate, then nod. "Yes."

He says nothing.

I wait, then say, "I gave you my oath, Jake." I am surprised how difficult the words are to say. For as long as I spent with Rhen, friend-ship seemed out of reach for so many reasons. With Jake, it felt effort-less. Like it was waiting there all along, and I just needed to get out of my own way.

Much like my magic.

I glance at him. "If you are ready, I will return you home."

Again, he is silent.

I wait.

Eventually, he says, "I want to stay."

I look at him in surprise, and he frowns and glances away. "When Harper went back to Rhen after what he did to you . . ." He sighs. "I think . . . I think I realized that she was never going to leave. She might be mad at him, but she loves him, you know?"

I nod. "But that does not mean you must stay."

"I know." He pauses. "But I don't have anything to go back to." He glances at me. "My life wasn't . . . it wasn't easy. Not that it's easy *here*, but . . ." His voice trails off.

Again, I wait.

Finally, Jake says, "Noah says he'll stay if I stay." He swallows. "It was different when you couldn't take us back. Now . . . now it's *my* choice."

I remember the moment Lilith told me I could take Harper home at any time. I have no idea how she built the enchantment into the bracelet I kept stashed at Worwick's . . . but I have time to learn.

"Jake—staying here will force you to make a choice, too."

He frowns. "You're going to have to face Rhen soon."

"Yes."

"It will pit me against my sister."

I think about that for a long while. I don't want to be at odds with Harper either. "If I learned anything about your sister in the time we were friends," I say, "it is that we should not underestimate her."

Days turn into weeks as the warmth of summer begins to ease into the cooler nights of autumn—my first true autumn since the curse held me captive with Rhen. I had forgotten the change in the air, the way the leaves brighten slowly at first, and then seemingly burst into reds and yellows all at once. Chimneys across the city spill smoke into the air at night and leaves begin to fall.

One particularly cold night, the palace is quiet and my friends are all occupied, so I go in search of Lia Mara. Her chambers are empty, but a guard directs me to the Great Hall—which I also find empty.

Light flickers through the doorway to the veranda, however, so I continue through.

She's in a chair reading.

"I should have looked here first," I say.

She smiles, then blushes, then eases to her feet. I do not miss that she hides the book in the folds of her robes. "I was going to ask if you'd like to dine with me, but you are always so *busy*, Prince Grey."

"You say *I* am busy? I am not running a country. I am surprised to find you doing something as unproductive as *reading*."

"Reading is not unproductive." Wind rushes down from the mountains to lift her hair and make the torches flicker. She shivers.

I shrug free of my jacket and draw it around her shoulders. The same motions I went through before, but everything is so different now.

Lia Mara looks up at me, her eyes heavy with everything that has happened between us.

I brush a lock of hair from her cheek, allowing my fingers to drift along the curve of her ear. Her lips part, and stars find her eyes, but tonight we are very much not alone. Six of her guards stand on the veranda, along with Talfor and Cortney.

I am about to allow my hand to drop, when she reaches up to hold it to her cheek.

I smile and lean in to kiss her. Softly. Chastely. Then I draw back.

Her fingers tangle in my shirt and hold me there.

"You've grown so determined," I say.

She doesn't smile. "Please don't pull away."

We have reached this point a dozen times. My heart beats a staccato rhythm in my chest, as I want nothing more than to pull her into my arms.

But things are different now. *She* is different now.

I allow my hand to drop. "What could the Queen of Syhl Shallow be reading that would make her blush?"

She lifts the book as if she'd forgotten it was there. "Ah . . . something about an alliance." Her cheeks redden further. "Between a man and a woman."

I take the book from her hands. I do not know the word on the cover, but I flip through the pages.

"I know you cannot read that," she says.

"You might be surprised." I stop on a page, recognizing a few words. "Indeed, I believe Talfor has said some of these words when he brags about his—"

She snatches the book out of my hand and raps me across the knuckles with it. "I will find you new tutors."

"Could I not learn from the queen herself?"

Her expression sobers. "Every time someone says *queen*, I feel a little jolt inside, like they're talking about my mother." She pauses. "I am sure you felt the same, when Iisak would call you *Your Highness*."

I touch her face again. I cannot help it. We have so few moments to ourselves that even this feels destined to end too quickly. My thumb traces along her jaw.

"Grey," she whispers.

Her voice is so serious that I mirror her tone. "Lia Mara?"

"What do you want to do about Rhen?"

My fingers go still against her cheek. Not, *what do you want to do about Emberfall?*

What do you want to do about Rhen?

"I do not want to go to war with him," I say. "But too many

people know the heir is real—that I live. I worry that Emberfall will tear itself apart as he tries to maintain his rule."

"He is still your brother. He is still a prince. Do you think he would yield to you?"

I look at her. "Did Rhen give you the impression he would yield to anyone?"

She frowns. Sighs. "Well, I cannot keep my Royal Houses at bay forever."

Just like that, we have returned to where we were the day I escaped Rhen's courtyard. A queen in need of an alliance. A prince without a throne.

Lia Mara looks at her fingertips resting against my chest. "The day Nolla Verin came to fetch me . . . she asked if I was in love with you."

I go still. "And what did you say?"

"I said . . . I said I *could* fall in love with you." She pauses, and her eyes flick up to find mine. "But if you do not feel the same, I do not want you to act—I do not want you to feel *obligated*—"

I grab hold of my jacket around her shoulders and pull her against me. Her mouth is warm and sweet, and her hands slip across my chest to find my shoulders. I forget the guards. I forget Emberfall and Syhl Shallow and everything between us. I lose myself in the press of her body against mine, the feel of her waist under my hands, the way her fingers press into my arms when her tongue brushes mine.

Eventually, our mouths slow, and she presses her cheek to my chest, tucking her head beneath my chin.

"Can we do this together?" she says. "Unite Emberfall and Syhl Shallow?"

It seems impossible—but so much has seemed impossible for so long.

A leaf, turned red by the changing seasons and buoyed by the wind, drifts across the veranda to settle on her chair.

"The first day of autumn was Rhen's birthday," I say to her.

"Well, instead of bringing an army," she says softly, "perhaps we should bring him a gift."

CHAPTER FIFTY

GREY

We take our time traveling through Emberfall. Instead of hiking through the woods in secrecy, we ride in style and stop at every town along the way. We spend silver and speak of hope. We eat hearty food and spin to lively music and kiss under the stars when the nights grow quiet and long.

Many people are wary of the guards from Syhl Shallow, but word has spread of what happened in Blind Hollow, and Lia Mara is charming and kind and wins their trust effortlessly.

As we travel closer to the heart of Emberfall, the rumors grow darker. We learn of larger cities, like Silvermoon Harbor, that have attempted to refuse Rhen's rule, and how he has sent soldiers to restore order, with varying success. Fear is in the air, so thick and potent I can taste it on my tongue. This close to Ironrose, there is little revelry. Instead of openly welcoming us into their midst, people take our coins and whisper their worries. Men clasp my hand furtively and say they hope I will bring unity to Emberfall—quietly pledging their allegiance.

It is humbling—and surprising.

Every time we stop, I expect to find guards and soldiers waiting to bar our progress, but none appear.

After two weeks, we reach the forest surrounding the castle. The last time I traveled through these woods, I was in chains, with Jake ready to put a knife in my back.

Today I wear the colors of Syhl Shallow and Emberfall, a queen at my side.

As we enter the forest, I hear nothing, not even the bells to announce that we are approaching.

"It is quiet," Lia Mara murmurs to me.

"Too quiet," says Jake. His voice has grown heavy. "What happened to the bells?"

"And shouldn't guards be riding out to stop us?" says Tycho.

In our traveling party, we have twenty people, so we are not a small group. We have made no secret of our destination, and even now we approach the castle openly. There should indeed be *some-one* riding out to greet us.

I frown.

"Something's wrong," says Lia Mara.

Iisak soars high above, but when I whistle, he banks and eases to the ground ahead of us.

I nod ahead. "What is happening at the castle?"

"Sixteen guards at the front, twelve at the back." He pauses. "The man you faced in the tourney is among them."

Dustan. I wonder why the guards have made no move to stop us.

I cluck to my horse and proceed. Iisak returns to the skies, but for the rest of us, our travel across the long stretch of grass to the front of the castle feels endless.

From here, I can see the line of guards. They stand at attention, just as they should, no look of alarm or worry or discontent in their expressions. Gold and red pennants snap alongside the ramparts above. I pick out Dustan right away. He is the only guardsman to meet my eyes, and his expression is cold.

He'd draw a weapon on me right now. I can tell. He's been ordered not to.

There is not something wrong. Rhen is choosing not to acknowledge our presence. This is a power play, nothing more.

Despite everything, it makes me smile. Silver hell, Rhen is *such* a cocky bastard.

I call a halt to our group, then look to Lia Mara.

"I would like to speak with him alone," I say.

Her lips part and she frowns, but she says nothing.

"He could try to kill you," says Jake.

I glance at the castle, then shake my head. "I do not think so."

Lia Mara still looks troubled. I pick up her hand and press a kiss to her palm. "If he meant me harm, he would not have allowed us to draw so close."

She keeps hold of my hand. "He harmed you once before."

"I have not forgotten."

Her eyes are dark with fear and betrayal. "I do not trust him, Grey."

"I know him better than anyone," I say. "I know what he is capable of." I put my heels against the horse's sides, and we spring forward.

"Tell Harper to come out," Jake calls from behind me. "I want to put eyes on my sister."

I ride right up to the guards. Dustan steps out of line.

"You are ordered to leave," he says, his voice low.

"I no longer take orders." I swing down from the horse and turn to face him.

To my surprise, he puts a hand on his sword. Automatically, I begin to draw mine.

"Commander." Rhen's voice drifts down from the front steps of the castle, where he stands in the shadow of a pillar.

My hand freezes. The word, his voice . . . they should not pull at strings inside me after all this time, but they still do. I cannot escape my past, no matter how much I might try.

But Dustan stops too, so I allow the sword to settle back into its sheath. I look up at Rhen. Like the swordsmen, his eyes are cold, his expression guarded.

"I would like to speak with you privately," I say.

"Why, when you campaign against me so openly?" His voice is dark and vicious.

"I am not campaigning."

"Are you not? Your journey here has been no secret."

"Nor have your actions. How many soldiers did you lose in Silvermoon?"

A muscle twitches in his jaw. "How many stripes are on your back, Grey?"

A line of ice travels up my spine, and my thoughts cool, pulling emotion out of my head, leaving only the space to do what needs to be done. "Did you not count, Rhen?"

I have never called him by his given name, and never so boldly, in front of others. It has the effect I expect: his eyes are shuttered, that muscle in his jaw tight as a bowstring. "What do you want?"

"I just told you. I would like to speak with you privately."

He makes me wait for an answer.

I had more than three hundred seasons to get used to his maneuverings, so I have no trouble waiting.

Perhaps he senses that, because he takes a step back. "We can speak in the Grand Hall."

Dustan moves to follow me up the steps, but Rhen adds, "Commander, you will wait out here."

Then we are in the castle, and the heavy wooden door falls closed, the sound echoing through the empty room. I can sense the movements of guards and servants in the halls, and I know we will never truly be alone, but right now, the castle feels colder and emptier than in all the time we were trapped by the curse.

Rhen's movements are tight and precise, and the anger in his expression is unmistakable. I watch as he circles around me, like a swordsman waiting for an opening.

"Shall we draw our swords and settle this right now?" I say darkly.

He stops, glowering. "I understand you meant to lead an army against me."

"That was before." I pause, wondering how much he knows. Wondering *how* he knows. "I did not come here to fight with you."

"I know. That is worse. I would have preferred the army."

"I have made no move against you," I say.

He gives a bark of humorless laughter. "Every move you have made has been *against* me."

He is so angry. I am angry, too, and regretful, but his has a different flavor to it, which I don't quite understand. He's so bitter, and it's a bitterness backed by pain.

I am not sure what reaction I expected, but it was not this. "In truth, I tried to spare you all of this."

"No. You tried to spare *yourself* all this. At no point did you attempt to spare me anything."

"I left," I snap. "I hid. I did not come back here willingly. *You* had me dragged back in chains." I pause. "I have not caused the discord in your kingdom."

He looks away, and I can see how much this weighs on him. He has always felt the burdens of his people so acutely.

This anger, this bitterness—it is not all about me. Pity washes through me.

"Rhen," I say quietly. I shift toward him.

He flinches and staggers back a step.

The movement is so unexpected that I freeze. Only then do I realize that the tightness of his jaw, the rigidity of his body is not fury and anger.

It's fear.

That night I knelt in his chambers, he spoke of Lilith, and I could hear the fear in his voice then, when he worried I was sworn to her. During every season, he took the brunt of her torture. The curse held us both captive, but he suffered far more than I did.

"I mean you no harm," I say.

"Do not patronize me. You have aligned yourself with a kingdom that brutalized our people. You stood with me *against* them, Grey, and now you ride in here with them. Karis Luran—"

"Karis Luran is dead."

"I know."

"How? How do you know?"

"She was not the only one with spies."

This surprises me. We had no spies when I was guard commander. We had no one at all.

I take another step forward, but this time he stands his ground. "You have also brutalized your people," I say to him. My voice is low and rough. "You are losing your country."

"I saved it once before. I will save it again."

"Deceit will not save them this time."

"And you will? With Syhl Shallow? You were a guardsman, Grey. An exceptional swordsman, but nothing more than a body to stand in front of royalty." His voice has turned vicious. "Her people will not respect you. They will not respect *her*. Karis Luran ruled by blood and fear, and their new ruler cannot expect to hold her throne with soft-spoken words."

"Do not speak of Lia Mara with disdain."

"And do you not think the Grand Marshals of my cities will look on you with equal disdain? That the man who wants to be king kneels to a woman who came to my castle in the middle of the night with naïve hopes for peace?"

"I did not kneel to her, and you would do well to consider her offer."

"I will not ally with Syhl Shallow. Not then, and not now. If that means you are my enemy, then so be it."

His voice is loud, so I make mine very soft. "I am your brother, Rhen."

He goes still.

"You once offered me your hand and called me a friend," I add.

He says nothing.

I wonder if there is any way to salvage anything with him, to move forward. Perhaps there is too much history between us.

Footsteps rustle on the steps at the back of the Grand Hall. "Grey!"

Harper crosses the room in a rush, skirts swirling with her uneven steps. She is quite possibly the only person in this castle who looks pleased to see me. I think she might stride right up to me and throw her arms around my neck the way she did that first night I was brought back to Ironrose—and then Rhen really will draw his sword.

She doesn't get a chance. Rhen catches her arm and pulls her against him. The movement isn't harsh. It's . . . distressed.

"I mean her no harm either," I say softly.

Harper doesn't pull away from Rhen. Instead, she rests her hand over his. Only then do I realize he's trembling.

"A friend would have told me," Rhen says. "A brother would have told me."

Maybe he's right. We've both made missteps here. Even when the curse began, we both made errors in judgment.

I take a step back and glance at Harper. "Your brother would like to see you before we leave."

She swallows. "Yes. Yes, of course."

Her eyes hold mine for the longest moment, and I can read the emotion there. She knows what demons haunt Rhen's thoughts, and she stands at his side. Despite everything, I am relieved to know he is not alone.

"As before," I say to her, "I could have chosen no one better, my lady."

Her lips part. Her voice is very soft. "He's trying to protect his people, Grey."

"As am I."

"You will march on my country, then," Rhen finally says.

"Our country." I hesitate. "And yes. In time."

For a heartbeat of time, his expression is bleak and dejected, but then his face smooths over and his eyes are devoid of emotion.

I pull a folded parchment from my jacket and hold it out to him. The paper is sealed with wax swirled in green and black.

He makes no move to take it. "What is this?"

"A gift, Brother."

When he still does not reach for it, Harper takes it from me. Rhen still hasn't moved. His hand has formed a fist.

"For the good of Emberfall," I say.

"Get out."

I do.

RHEN

I have been turning this parchment over in my hands for hours. I am tempted to toss it into the fireplace, because mine will not be the only eyes to read it.

"I do not recall you being so indecisive, Prince Rhen."

The voice speaks from the shadows, but I do not turn. The enchantress has been here for weeks. Taunting me. Threatening me.

I turn the parchment over in my hands again.

Harper is dining with her brother, but I would give anything for her company now.

I would give anything to reverse time to the morning Grey was brought back in chains. Before I resorted to cruelty to find the truth. Before he escaped, exposing his magic and his birthright to everyone in the courtyard.

Before Lilith appeared in my chambers with a new offer.

I glance over at the enchantress. A terrible scar runs across her neck, skin clumped and clustered where Grey's blade tried to take her life.

I tear open the parchment.

You have 60 days, Brother.
Do not make me do this.

Do not make me do this.

The same words I said to him before the guards led him into the courtyard and chained him to the wall.

My hands are shaking again.

"If only you had been this afraid the first time," she says, and her voice is a vicious whisper.

If only.

If only Grey had told me the truth.

"You could kill us both," I say to her. "Take what you want."

"If I kill you both, the armies of Syhl Shallow will take Emberfall. Your people will not follow me. I cannot affect them *all*, Your Highness." She steps closer to me, and her voice lowers. "Do you not understand that my goal has never been to rule your kingdom alone? My goal is to do it with you *by my side*."

I look away. My throat is tight. I cannot do this again. "I will let him take Emberfall. I will not fight him."

"You will if you want to keep Harper here with you." She pauses. "Do you not think she would enjoy a return to her world? It would only take me a moment."

A world where Harper was at risk every minute of every day.

A world I would have no way to reach if Lilith were to steal Harper away.

I cannot breathe.

"Grey has found a scraver," says Lilith. "He is weak now, but with help, his magic will develop quickly, and he has an army at his disposal. Right now I can best him, but in time, he will take Emberfall if we do not stand against him."

Sixty days. I wish I could tell him to make it an eternity. I wish I could warn him.

Lilith watches every move I make.

I take a deep breath. I need to formulate a plan. I clench my hands to stop their trembling. "You will not harm Harper. I want her protected at all costs."

"Of course," she says smoothly. "I hardly think Grey would allow any harm to come to her."

"I do not want her to know you are here. I do not want her to know what you are doing. Do you understand me?"

"I am very good at keeping secrets." She pauses. "Will you accept my offer? I have waited so long to claim your poor, pathetic country for my own."

Her *offer*. As if I have a choice. As if I'd sacrifice Harper to her.

I stare down at Grey's words. *Do not make me do this.*

I crumple the letter and toss it into the fire.

"Yes, Lilith," I say. "I will."

ACKNOWLEDGMENTS

Buckle up. Here we go.

A Heart So Fierce and Broken is my eleventh published novel, so it's really tempting to pull the acknowledgments from prior books and just copy and paste, especially since my kids are in the next room tormenting each other, but I am truly grateful to each and every person who supports me and my career, and I really do want to take a moment to name everyone I can.

It's also tempting to make a numbered list and just go with that, so that's what I'm going to do, especially since this is the only part of the book my editor doesn't touch.

Huge thanks go to:

1) Michael. (My husband. He's amazing. He always comes first. You would not be holding this book in your hands without his love and support backing me up.)

2) My mother. My mom is a truly special person who . . . I have no idea what I was about to say, because I just had to break up a fight between my kids. But my mother is phenomenal, and I don't know what I'd do without her. I know she'll understand why I lost track of that sentence. Thank you for everything, Mom.

3) My best friend, Bobbie Goettler. I <3 you, friend. I'm so glad we met each other on that message board so many years ago.

4) My amazing agent, Mandy Hubbard, who is brave and fearless and kind, and I don't know what I'd do without her.

5) My stellar editor, Mary Kate Castellani, who is equally brave and fearless and kind, and never gives up until my writing is the best it can be.

I can't believe I'm making a numbered list for this. But now I've started and it's only a matter of time before the boys start pummeling each other again, so onward!

6) The incredible team at Bloomsbury. Tremendous thanks go to Cindy Loh, Claire Stetzer, Anna Bernard, Lily Yengle, Courtney Griffin, Erica Barmash, Valentina Rice, Brittany Mitchell, Phoebe Dyer, Beth Eller, Ellen Holgate, Emily Moran, Emily Marples, Cal Kenny, Jeanette Levy, Donna Mark, as well as Diane Aronson and Jill Amack and the copyediting team, along with everyone else at Bloomsbury who played a role in putting this book into your hands. Please know that my gratitude is endless, and I can't tell you how much I appreciate your efforts on my behalf.

7) Many people read this manuscript, in part or in whole, and offered their input and insights. Special thanks to Bobbie Goettler, Jim Hilderbrandt, Hannah McBride, Michelle MacWhirter, Diana Peterfreund, Lee Bross, Shyla

Stokes, Steph Messa, Joy George, Bill Konigsberg, Reba Gordon, Rae Chang, Tracy Houghton, Nicole Choiniere-Kroeker, Anna Bright, and Allie Christo. This book wouldn't have gotten to this point without you all. Thank you.

8) Jodi Picoult. (Yes, really. OMG. You all should have seen my face when I got that first DM on Twitter.) Thank you for all your insight and input into this book. I still can't believe I get to call you a friend.

9) Research friends! Many thanks to Maegan Chaney-Bouis, MD, for all the medical information. I love being able to send a text about the most bizarre fantastical situations I can think of and getting a straightforward medical analysis in return. Additional thanks to Steve Horrigan of Stone Forge CrossFit for answers about rope climbing, animal carrying, military training, and hand-to-hand combat and especially for not batting an eye at my weird questions. All information given was accurate and factual; any and all errors in this book are mine.

10) Extra special thanks to book bloggers, bookstagrammers, book vloggers, and anyone who uses their voice to spread the word about books they love. You helped make this series a success, and while I can't thank each of you individually, please know that I see you and I love you and I can't thank you enough.

11) The Kemmerer boys, Jonathan, Nick, Sam, and Zach-ARY ("Spell it with the A-R-Y, Mom!!"). Thank you for

giving me the space to follow my dreams. I can't wait to see you follow your own. Then again, if you don't stop bickering, I'm going to delete this paragraph.

12) You. Yeah, you. You're a part of my dream, too. I'm so grateful that you've taken the time to read this book. It means so much to me that you've invited my characters into your heart, because I know that means you'll carry them with you forever, even if it's only in the smallest way. Thank you.